TRIAL OF THE WIZARD KING

THE WIZARD KING TRILOGY

TRIAL OF THE WIZARD KING

THE WIZARD KING TRILOGY

CHAD CORRIE

DARK HORSE BOOKS

Trial of the Wizard King: The Wizard King Trilogy Book Two

Published by
Dark Horse Books
A division of Dark Horse Comics LLC
10956 SE Main Street
Milwaukie, OR 97222

DarkHorse.com

Maps illustrated by Robert Altbauer

Library of Congress Cataloging-in-Publication Data

Names: Corrie, Chad, author.
Title: Trial of the Wizard King / Chad Corrie.
Description: First edition. | Milwaukie, OR : Dark Horse Books, 2020. | Series: The Wizard King trilogy ; book two | Summary: "The wizard king has returned. The mercenaries have scattered. Cadrith Elanis has returned to Tralodren, picking up where he left off centuries before. And while Cadrissa isn't sure how she fits into his plans, her abduction has left her with little hope of escape. Meanwhile, the other mercenaries have scattered. They did their job, received their pay, and now just want to live their lives. But events start pulling them back to each other for something grander than their own imaginations and fears can envision. But that's just the start of still more revelations and trials to come. Dark ambitions, ancient schemes, and hidden fates fill this second volume of the Wizard King Trilogy, returning readers to a world rich in history, faith, and tales of adventure-of which this story is but one of many"-- Provided by publisher.
Identifiers: LCCN 2020024118 | ISBN 9781506716282 (paperback)
Subjects: GSAFD: Fantasy fiction.
Classification: LCC PS3603.O77235 T75 2020 | DDC 813/.6--dc23
LC record available at https://lccn.loc.gov/2020024118

First edition: March 2021
Ebook ISBN 978-1-50671-633-6
Trade Paperback ISBN 978-1-50671-628-2

1 3 5 7 9 10 8 6 4 2
Printed in the United States of America

THE WIZARD KING TRILOGY

Return of the Wizard King
Trial of the Wizard King
Triumph of the Wizard King

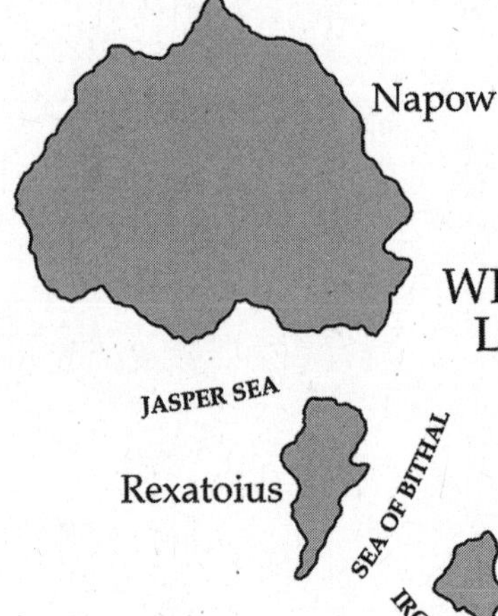
GREAT OCEAN
Napow
THE WESTERN LANDS
JASPER SEA
Rexatoius
SEA OF BITHAL
YOAN OCEAN
Breanna
IRON SEA
Irondale
Caradina
Black Isle

THE PEARL ISLANDS

N
W
E
S
0 500 1000 1500
MILES
THE BOILING SEA

2019

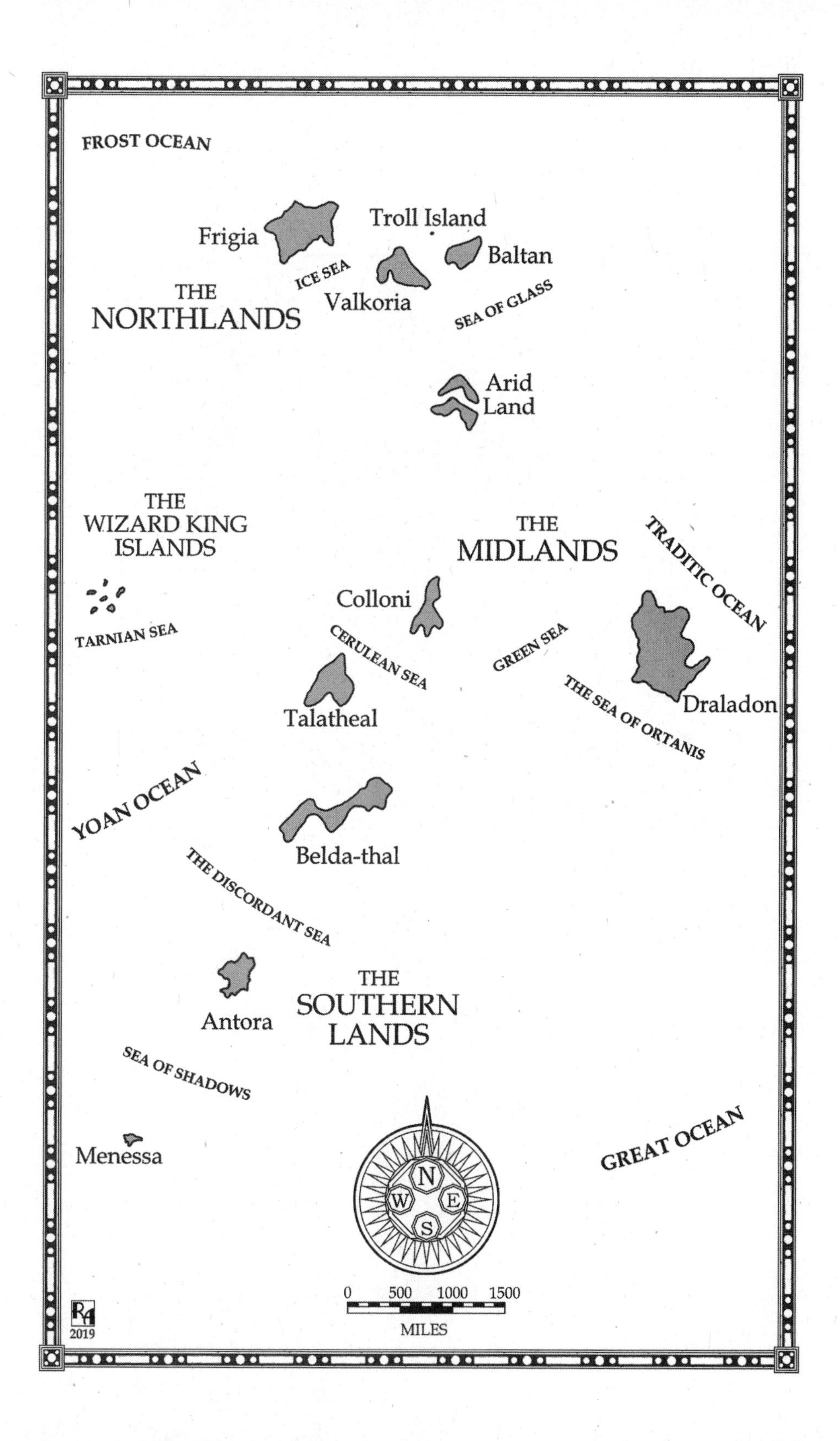
FROST OCEAN
Frigia
Troll Island
Baltan
ICE SEA
THE NORTHLANDS
Valkoria
SEA OF GLASS
Arid Land
THE WIZARD KING ISLANDS
THE MIDLANDS
TRADITIC OCEAN
Colloni
TARNIAN SEA
CERULEAN SEA
GREEN SEA
Talatheal
THE SEA OF ORTANIS
Draladon
YOAN OCEAN
Belda-thal
THE DISCORDANT SEA
THE SOUTHERN LANDS
Antora
SEA OF SHADOWS
Menessa
GREAT OCEAN
N
W
E
S
0 500 1000 1500
MILES
RA
2019

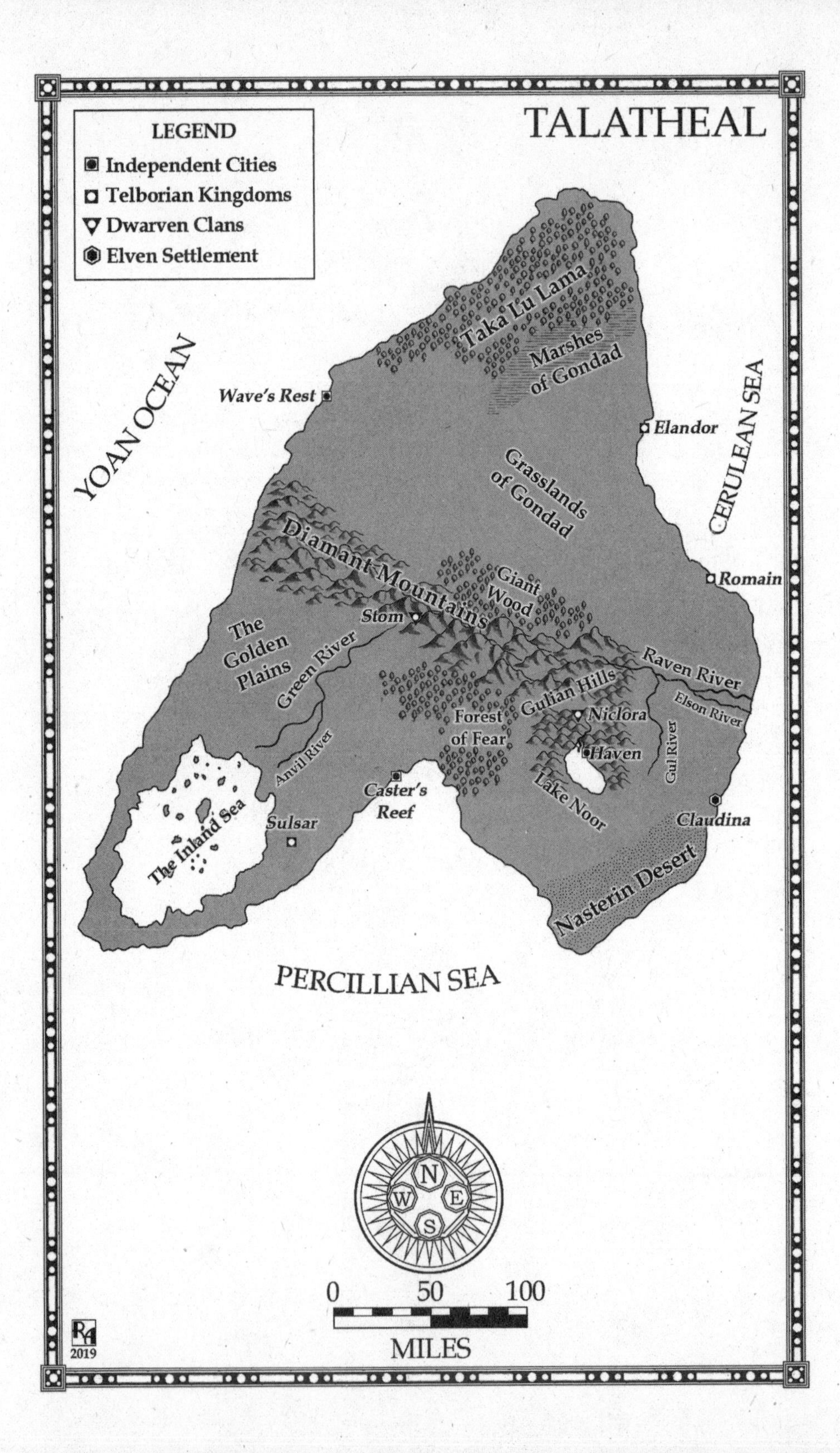
TALATHEAL
LEGEND
Independent Cities
Telborian Kingdoms
Dwarven Clans
Elven Settlement
YOAN OCEAN
CERULEAN SEA
PERCILLIAN SEA
Taka Lu Lama
Marshes of Gondad
Wave's Rest
Elandor
Grasslands of Gondad
Diamant Mountains
Giant Wood
Romain
Stom
The Golden Plains
Green River
Raven River
Gulian Hills
Elson River
Forest of Fear
Niclora
Haven
Anvil River
Gul River
Caster's Reef
Lake Noor
Claudina
Sulsar
The Inland Sea
Nasterin Desert
N
W
E
S
0
50
100
MILES
2019

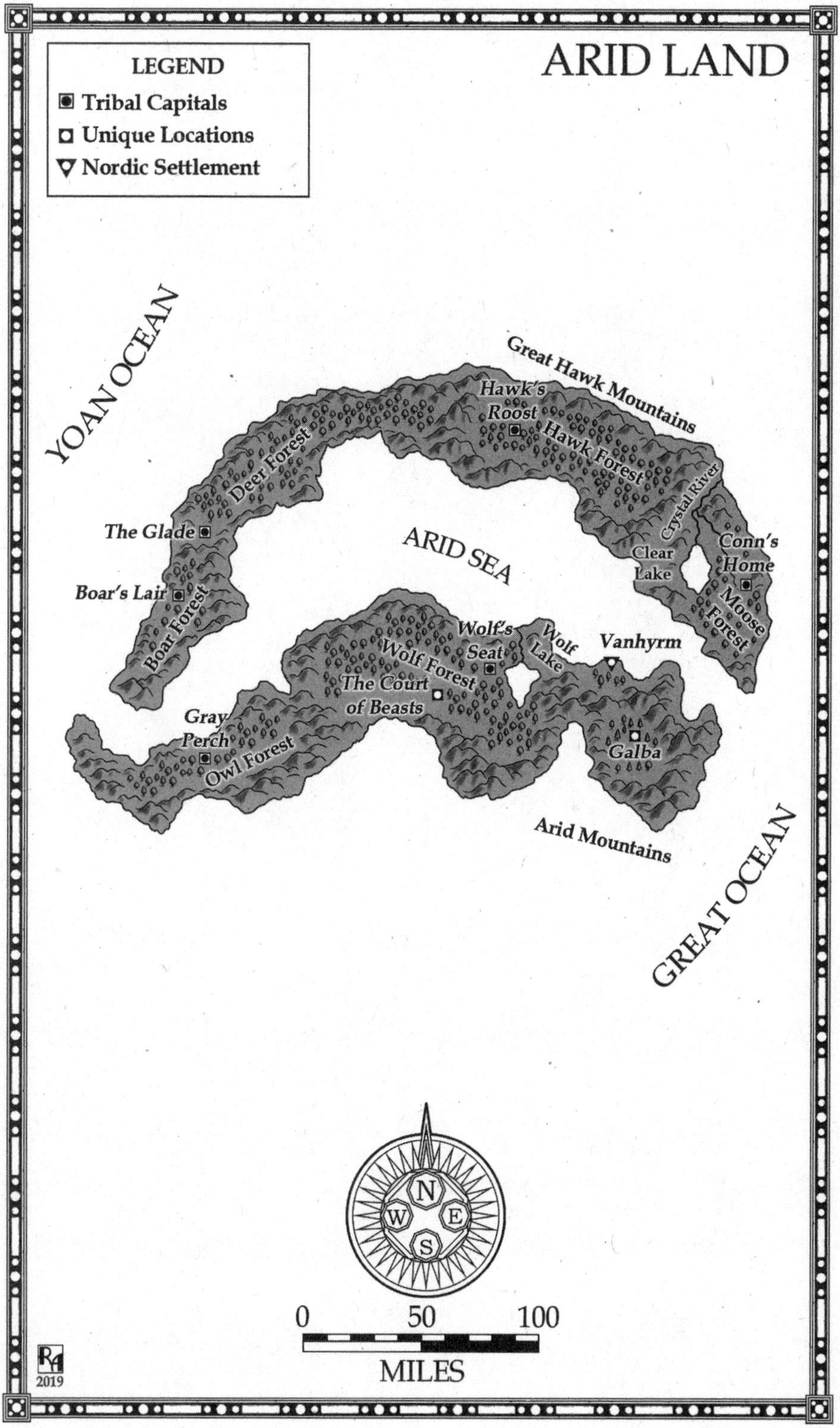

ARID LAND

LEGEND
- Tribal Capitals
- Unique Locations
- Nordic Settlement

YOAN OCEAN
Great Hawk Mountains
Hawk's Roost
Hawk Forest
Deer Forest
Crystal River
The Glade
ARID SEA
Clear Lake
Conn's Home
Boar's Lair
Boar Forest
Moose Forest
Wolf's Seat
Wolf Lake
Vanhyrm
Wolf Forest
The Court of Beasts
Gray Perch
Owl Forest
Galba
Arid Mountains
GREAT OCEAN

N
W
E
S

0 50 100
MILES

RA
2019

CHAPTER 1

Here then is the challenge we face: the two paths eventually must meet. For what is power but knowledge attained, and knowledge but an increase in power? Each is the reflection of the other. So then is there any real difference in the end what path one walks? And if so, how should one walk it knowing this truth?

—Khurai the Dark, Telborian wizard king
Reigned 60 BV–12 BV

"Wh-who are you?" Cadrissa dared to ask. She needed some answers. She'd already survived a frightening fiend, an angry wizard, and jungle-strangled ruins swarming with hobgoblins. Now she was prisoner in some ancient black tower she'd seen raised from the earth by her skeletal captor.

The lich lifted his head from the large tome he'd been paging through. The tongues of azure flame flickering in his empty sockets sent a fresh shiver down her spine. Not even his threadbare hood could dim their icy glow.

"Cadrith Elanis," he said, "the last wizard king of Tralodren." Yet again she was struck by how he could speak despite lacking a tongue and the muscles to move his jaw. And yet the jaw moved and his voice came forth.

Another burst of thunder overtook the tower and shook the shelves of the small study, though little else. Cadrissa couldn't say the same for herself. This was madness if ever there was any. Another roaring blast of thunder pounded her ears and head but she retained her focus on the lich—on Cadrith. He resumed his reading, bending back over the gruesome silver podium. It'd been created to resemble a hunched human skeleton supporting the weight of the book above it. Just one of the less-than-pleasant items she'd already encountered since they entered the tower and this terrible storm overtook them.

Had she been bolder and not afraid for her life, she might have inquired further about the book. It was clearly something important. Instead, she racked her mind for what she'd learned of the wizard kings in an attempt to make better sense of what was going on. She'd learned some of their names and the times of their rule, but there were so many more who'd made their mark on Tralodren. And given the chaos that followed their reigns, she also knew still more might have been lost to time. Could Cadrith be one of them?

His devotion to his studies left her in the awkward position of standing between him and the door to the study like a nervous pillar. She barely shifted her weight from foot to foot as she continued assessing the situation. While it might have seemed the lich was too engrossed in his reading to take notice of anything else—even a sudden dash for the door—she pushed the thought from her mind as quickly as it bobbed to the surface. Even if she could make it to the door before he could react, she was confident it'd only take just one word to place her before Asorlok's gates.

A sudden jerk of Cadrith's bony head jolted her from her thoughts. "Wait here." He said nothing more, placing the tome he'd been reading under his arm and grabbing hold of his staff.

Another rumble of thunder shook Cadrissa as Cadrith passed. She tried granting him a wide swath but her legs were unable to come completely unlocked, birthing a shaky, slow twirl instead. As he passed, she couldn't escape his icy aura. She wondered if he even felt the cold anymore, or anything else for that matter. He passed without a glance, his attention focused on the door, which was already opening as he neared.

She tried to think of something to say—some sort of protest—but nothing came. Instead, her lips were frozen half-open and her tongue clung to the roof of her mouth. And so she watched him depart with the door closing silently behind him. She was certain she heard it lock. No doubt with a spell as well. At least the light in the room remained. Her shoulders sunk with a heavy sigh. Madness.

"Wait," she repeated as she took in the various tomes and scrolls resting in the bookcase across from her. The tug to brave a look in a book or two was appealing, but there was something much more vital vying for her attention. A moment later she was marching for the door, eyes half squinting in intense study.

•●•

On the other side of the door Cadrith was making his way down the hallway, letting the magical light that followed him through the tower serve as guide. He didn't need it, of course. He'd been down these halls enough times to find the room he was seeking with his eyes closed. Though it might have been close to eight centuries since he last set foot in the tower, he'd only seen five of those years, thanks to his magic-induced sleep. But even those years had inched forward at a snail's pace.

All told, the additional amount of time worked in his favor, he supposed, at least when it came to the populace. But it wasn't them he had to contend with. Another thunderous shaking reminded him of his last encounter with Endarien. The god had tried the same tactic before and failed. He'd thought Endarien would be smart enough to try something new. Maybe he thought the tower and the spells around it had weakened over time. It didn't matter. Cadrith didn't plan on staying here long.

As he walked, he went over recent events. Everything was going as he'd planned. Sargis, his onetime demonic ally, was back in the Abyss where he belonged, and Cadrith was back in his tower with the last of his tools now safely locked up in the study. And things would be even better with Cadrissa instead of that fool Valan. After watching the other mage come unhinged when he failed to master that corrupted dranoric device, he could see how much better it—

He stopped.

He thought he saw some movement on the stairs below, some dark shape slinking about the shadows. At once his mind returned to the Abyss and the hidden enemies and trouble lurking on the peripheries, but just as quickly he brought himself back into line. He was in his tower and it was secure. None could get in but him, and nothing else was here. That was, unless . . . He spun back on his heel. No. There was no one here and there had been no one here since he'd left. Even if she'd found a way, she'd be long since dead by now. This wasn't the time for sentiment, only for continuing in his resolve.

He focused on an old door at the end of a dark hallway, deep in the tower's heart. As thick as the stone wall surrounding it, the door had grown gray over the years but still held firm. The magical energy coursing through it held it as fast and true as the day it was first set in place. He waved his skeletal hand, and it silently swung open.

As soon as he set foot inside, light burned away the darkness. Seeing the room brought everything back in rapid succession. It was here he'd spent his last days as a living man. It was also the last piece of Tralodren he'd seen before leaving for the Abyss . . . and now he'd come full circle. Just like he always knew he would.

He took in the old room in silence. After all this time, everything remained just as he'd left it. Books lined the wall to his right in giant shelves, reaching all the way to the ceiling a few feet above his head. The ancient covers resembled a cobblestone walkway rising to the top shelf. While these books seemed to have maintained their shape, Cadrith knew they'd crumble to dust with just the slightest breath. But he wasn't concerned with these anymore. They'd served their purpose and he'd learned from them all he could. His attention, instead, went to his left and an old wooden table. On top of it lay a humanoid form covered by a dusty white cloth. He didn't need to remove it to discern the body was still whole.

Shifting his attention to the wall opposite the door, Cadrith stepped forward, inspecting a circular mosaic very similar to the one in the ruins he'd used to bring himself back to Tralodren. The small azure and violet tiles had been arranged in a swirling pattern just like the one he'd found in the ruins, though this one had a selection of white and silver tiles added into the design. The portal was also only eight feet in diameter and was only half built when he'd first found it. He'd done the final work himself—each tile and spell needed to tie it together undertaken with great care. Now here he stood centuries later, gazing at it from the other side.

"You should have joined me, Kendra." He traced the jagged scar-like crack crossing the entire mosaic in a diagonal slash. Something so seemingly simple, yet it had stopped him from returning and set into motion a series of events that led to him using that foolish wizard Valan to cast the needed spell to free him from the Abyss.

In theory it shouldn't have worked as well as it did. When he happened upon the portal and the connections around it back when he was still searching for release in the Abyss, it was a far-fetched concept, as the portal wasn't meant for use between planes, just to travel between locations across Tralodren. But the longer he considered it, the further an idea manifested—and the Transducer was a great help toward that end. Steeped in chaotic magic and power, it helped tip things in his favor and allowed a slim opening for him to work his will. And when Cadrissa entered the equation, things took on an even better outcome.

She'd be much easier to control. Not to mention the other unexpected but still highly favorable boon she brought with her. He couldn't have done better if he had Kendra herself at his side. But for all her potential, Kendra hadn't had the strength to hold to the vision. She might have been powerful and skilled in magic—a wizard queen in the making—but she showed her true heart in the end . . . as had he. And now she was gone to Mortis, her body dust and memory. He refused to share the same fate.

He made his way to a small table that rested before the bookcase and set the Mirdic Tome upon it. The ancient book had been created by the titans long ago and held in it the secret to becoming a lich, among other things. Cadrith had taken it from his former master, who'd also used it to become a lich. It was part of his plan, Cadrith later learned, for surviving the coming Divine Vindication while taking his final step on the path of power. Cadrith was able to uncover these final steps and adopt them as his own. And he was now very close to their completion.

However, he wouldn't be able to do much more if he didn't take care of his time-ravaged frame. The spell he'd cast to become a lich had now finally taken its toll upon his body—what little remained. Like many self-sustaining spells, it sought out means to keep itself strong—to enforce the effect it was created to enact. For Cadrith this meant the very bones that were all he had left to inhabit were being destroyed—ironically enough—to keep them intact and him bound to them.

Such a juxtaposition was a troublesome one, but not the biggest worry. As the spell hungered for more power, it started pulling away and weakening his ability to use other spells, as he had to use his magic to counter the original spell's immediate negative effects. The result was him getting weaker all the time and Sargis eventually discovering this weakness. He'd worried this might happen. After seeing how his former master had fared in plotting the workings of his plan, he knew it wise to prepare for the worst, and so he had. A new body had been readied and safely guarded for him. He just needed to rehearse the spell for transferring his spirit into it.

The thunder and shaking hadn't ceased. And while he'd boasted Endarien wouldn't find a way inside, he didn't want to take any needless risks. Opening the Mirdic Tome, he started his studying. The tome had long ago been transcribed into a smaller book, making it more manageable for human hands even before his master's possession.

Though altered in size, it was still hefty, its brown leather spine four fingers thick. The ancient titanic text had proven to be more enduring than anything Cadrith was aware of. Long ago, he deduced the pages were created from a specially crafted leather—probably from a titan or giant. Fitting, he supposed, given the secrets they contained.

Carefully flipping through the pages, he recalled all the secrets he'd already mastered. He'd come so very far and would step even higher still. It was just a short matter of time, and all would be his. Finally he found the page and began reading.

•●•

Cadrissa stared at the door, hoping she'd discover a hint of something she'd passed over and break the spell holding it shut. She'd tried some simple spells to chip away where she could, but didn't get anything useful.

She wasn't strong enough to force it down, though that didn't stop her from ramming it a couple of times just to be sure. She had tried searching for something to pick the lock but to no avail. Not that a pick would have done any good anyway against magic, but keeping her mind searching for solutions was better than worrying when Cadrith might return . . . and what might follow.

After all she'd been through with the ruins and everything leading up to them, she didn't know how much more she could pull from her well. She had to be judicious in her spell selection. If this lich was really a wizard king, she didn't know what she was up against. She closed her eyes and focused on a final spell she hoped was strong enough to do the job. As she did so, she felt a patch of heat on her leg. The warmth came from a necklace she'd taken from the ruins in Taka Lu Lama and seemingly intensified the deeper she dipped into her well.

Unable to repress her curiosity, she retrieved the object from her pocket and made a careful study. The thin chain wasn't really that interesting, resembling just about every other one she'd seen in her young life. The golden disk-shaped pendant, however, was another story. It was about three fingers in width and probably no thicker than an average slice of cheese. It was clearly pure gold, and there definitely was some heat radiating off of it. Heat she hadn't experienced back when she first retrieved it in those dranoric ruins. The pendant was adorned with strange carvings and symbols she knew held some key to its identity and abilities. But without the proper time and resources for a greater inspection she wouldn't be making much sense of them anytime soon.

As she continued her inspection, she thought she heard whispering. It was soft and distant at first, but grew in volume, as if those who were creating it were drawing near. She couldn't make any of it out but there was definitely something being said. Not enjoying the sensation, she returned her focus on the door and the finishing of her spell.

"Calin agora naslin!" she said, belting out the words with a renewed sense of urgency.

The whole door glowed for a moment in a flash of azure light. She was surprised by the power which rose up from her well when she'd cast it, but was pleased it apparently had done the job. The door silently surrendered, sliding slightly ajar.

With the spell's completion, the whispers ceased. She took one last look around, placed the necklace back in her hidden pocket, and braved the door. The first thing she'd need to overcome was the darkness, but upon leaving the room she was pleasantly surprised when the spell that formerly lit her way renewed its efforts. So it wasn't just tied to Cadrith—anyone's movements could activate it.

She supposed having the spell set up that way was a wise precaution, for it allowed Cadrith to keep an eye out for things sneaking about, a simple means for added security. Of course, with the light also following her it would make it easier for Cadrith to track her movements as well—if he was watching for them. She had no idea where he'd gone. All the more reason she needed some speed in her task.

As she cast her eyes above, she could see another level and what looked like a ceiling. If there was a way onto the roof she could poke her head outside and scour the tower's surroundings to better identify her location. Translocation spells required knowledge of the distance between where one was and where one wanted to go. And she figured such a spell was her only way out of this mess. Providing she still had enough left in her well to pull it off.

The tower shook again. It wasn't as forceful as it had been, but was still strong enough to remind her it hadn't given up just yet. All the more reason to hurry while this window of less angry skies remained.

She took to the stairs with all her might, racing up to the top floor and then ascending another group of steps she was pleased to find ended at a wooden trapdoor. There was an old iron latch holding it shut like a crooked talon. A touch of the wooden planks revealed they were dry and warm despite being so close to the steady downpour. Neither being buried so long in the dirt nor the tower's recent raising had distressed it in any way. Clearly the door was enchanted.

She closed her eyes and concentrated on recasting the spell she'd used with the door in the study. Once again she felt the warm swell on her leg where the hidden pocket holding the necklace resided, as a wave of power, stronger than it should have been given the circumstances, poured out of her.

"Calin agora naslin." The trapdoor took on a faint azure aura that faded from sight almost as quickly as it had appeared. She reached for the latch and gave it a small tug. It slid smoothly. She slowly placed her hand under the small iron handle near the door's lip and gave a concerted push. The trapdoor flew up and back with a violent force as the rain-soaked wind slammed into her body and face.

She squinted as she pushed through the constant howl of agitated wind while ascending the final steps out onto the roof. She did her best at ignoring the slobbering slaps of rain splashing over her face and soiled golden robes along with the chaotic fingers making flailing banners of her sable hair. Craning her neck, she observed the pitch-black clouds.

She noted that they started taking the form of a colossal humanoid from the waist up. Built like the strongest of men, its bald head slowly adjusted its gaze toward the tower . . . and Cadrissa. Though it possessed just a rough shape of a face, it did have something like eyes. And these seemed fully able to take in any and all things before it. And it didn't appear to like what it saw. A sturdy arm lifted above the dark, lightning-riddled clouds before rapidly descending with a clenched fist right for her position.

Cadrissa grabbed hold of the now-slick metal handle on the trapdoor and pulled it back as she ducked down into the tower, latching it right before that great fist made its impact. The echoing thud shook everything to its core, herself included. Cadrith *had* told her it was Endarien trying to break his way into the tower.

Madness.

She dared another glance at the trapdoor. The latch still held, but she could see it quiver with each successive pounding. And each time it did, she could see sprays of water spitting onto the steps below. With the spell gone, it wouldn't be long until the trapdoor was compromised . . . and then . . .

She had to get out of there and fast. If the roof wasn't an option, there was only one other possibility. Closing her eyes, she focused her thoughts on the tower's ground floor while whispering the words that magically teleported her to it. When she opened her eyes again, she saw the solid demonic-crafted doors blocking her from her hoped-for freedom. The magical light had risen around her after her appearance, but that was now dimming as she took cautious steps forward. Above her another shaking strike reached her ears and feet.

The closer she drew to the doors the thicker the darkness became until, with just a few feet remaining, Cadrissa found herself swallowed in a thick lake of pitch. She couldn't hear the storm outside or the pounding above. All was silent. Dark and silent. Thinking Cadrith had come to deal with her at last, she didn't know what to do other than keep still, hoping for the best.

She shivered as a slight breeze twisted about her frame. The moving air felt like icy fingers dragging across her flesh, which was soaked from her previous adventure. Was this another spell meant to keep her at bay? Something to hold her until Cadrith returned? It could be a defensive option. If it was, she should have been able to at least make out some shapes by now as her eyes adjusted to the darkness.

"You will stay in the tower." An emotionless voice came from all around her. She was sure it wasn't Cadrith's. It sounded nothing like him—more an unusual mixture of male and female voices.

"Endarien?" She cupped her left hand and called forth a tongue of fire. The flame floated above the center of her palm. It was a simple spell, which after years of practice, she could cast with great ease. It was also the best spell she had for turning back at least some of the darkness.

As the simple illumination burst into existence, it almost as rapidly extinguished when she gave a startled cry, seeing a black tentacle undulating mere inches from her face. Sleek in the darkness, it was dotted with pockets of white-toothed maws chomping with a fearful energy—eager for anything they could sink those teeth into. A larger mouth capped the tip of the tentacle facing her. And while her impulse was for retreat, her legs proved traitors to the cause.

"You will stay in the tower and help Cadrith." The same voice she heard earlier issued out of all the tentacle's mouths in unison.

"Who are you?" She tried to sound braver than she felt, pushing the squeamishness down while imagining being encircled by dozens of those tentacles . . . and whatever they were connected to. At any moment they could be sliding over her body, twisting around her legs and arms and—

"Obey and you'll live." The words were spoken with such finality that she could feel an icy hand clamp itself upon her heart.

"Help him do what?" Finally her legs had come around, letting her retreat a few paces. Even though it lacked eyes, she was sure the tentacle watched her movements. "Endarien—"

"Isn't a threat." Cadrissa watched the tentacle slink back into the impenetrable darkness. "Just do what you're told."

"Who *are* you?"

"You will *stay* in the tower." The emotionless voice snarled in her ears. Cadrissa suddenly found herself ensnared by a thick coil of tentacles. Her nightmares had become flesh and were slowly squeezing all the air from her lungs. Their clammy touch wrapped her from neck to ankles as she tried seeing anything through the thick darkness. Worse still was the chattering, chomping sound of those terrible teeth, especially the ones close to her ears.

Suddenly, one of the tentacles swung out and faced Cadrissa head on, snapping the larger of the mouths at its tip just a breath away from her nose. She gave a small yip, unable to remove her wide-eyed gaze from the threat.

"Do you *understand*?" The mouth facing her growled as the tentacles' grip increased to such a painful degree that she thought she was going to pass out.

"Yes," she managed to wheeze from between clenched teeth.

The darkness began fading, the light behind it filtering through like rays of sunlight after a heavy storm. As the light increased, the study she thought she'd freed herself from came into view. And then it was all gone. The pain. The pressure. The darkness. All of it. She was back in the study with the pounding from above competing with the banging of her heart against her chest. It was then the last of her strength gave out, dropping her on the floor in a heap. And it was there she'd remain for some time, weeping.

•●•

Cadrith peered up from the Mirdic Tome and took in the cloth-draped figure behind him. He'd found the spell and was confident he was ready to enact it. Ignoring the renewed pounding of yet another of Endarien's attacks, he focused on pulling what power he could from his well. He wouldn't get a second chance.

"Gorneal orthel falish. Waquire to-rahl!" The last of his well faded from his grasp and was channeled through his staff, shooting toward the cloth-covered body in an azure shaft of light. Then, like a kitten slowly pulling apart a ball of twine, he felt the magic binding him together finally failing.

He heard the cracking of his femurs fill the room even as he felt his ribs fracture. Like dominoes, the rest of the tethers began falling away with increasing speed. His feet and legs crumbled into dusty chalk with each measured step toward the table. There was no means of comfort as his spirit untwined and traveled past his chest and arms, then neck. He felt his skull unraveling next.

His field of vision began to fade as his legs, pelvis, and chest collapsed into gray, billowing dust. As his vision failed, he imagined the twin azure tongues of flame in his sockets winking out just before his skull turned into slate-tinted sand, joining the rest of the pile and the dusty, threadbare garments. The last thing he heard was his staff clanking hollowly on the stone before darkness washed over him.

When he woke, he found himself lying on the floor. Something wasn't right. He should have awakened in his new body on the table. Sitting up, he found himself wearing a robe he hadn't seen in years. Odder still, he could feel a fading warmth again in his body. This wasn't right. The spell that made him a lich sent out constant coldness from his bones. It had to in order to keep everything well preserved, allowing him the use of his body for as long as possible.

"Cadrith?" Kendra's voice called his attention to the pregnant, blond Telborian woman rushing to his side. He'd forgotten how beautiful she'd been. "Cadrith?" Kendra took his hand.

"You're like ice." She placed her hand on his chest. He could see her fear melt into rage as she felt nothing stirring in his rib cage. Not even breath. "You didn't . . ."

"I told you," he heard himself say, "it was the only way. Now I have time to—"

Kendra's slap didn't really do anything. Pain wasn't the same thing it had once been before. He'd soon discover there wasn't so much as a sting in response to once hurtful things, just a dull awareness of their occurrence.

Kendra rose to her feet, livid. "How could you do this to us?"

"You can still join me." He heard himself repeat what he'd said all those years before. "Together we can find the throne while we wait for magic to return."

"All this time," Kendra said, watching him rise, "it was just a lie. You pretended to be so *different*—so much *better*, but in the end you're just like Raston." She crossed her arms over her protruding stomach. "No—*worse*."

This wasn't true, of course. She was just upset and wasn't thinking straight. She always did let her emotions get the better of her. If she just stopped and listened to reason—listened to what was before them. They were on the cusp of everything falling into place—so close to victory.

"Kendra . . ." Cadrith extended a hand that in time would become nothing but a skeletal shadow of its former self.

"All those months laboring to build that mosaic, saying it was for both of us. But it was really just for you. It *always* was."

His hand fell. She still wasn't seeing things clearly. He wasn't the enemy—she was, and she'd prove to be to *both* of them if she kept this up. There wasn't time to debate the finer points of what needed to be done. It was time for action.

"We can still go together."

"And *where* would that be?" Kendra huffed. "You never *did* tell me."

And for good reason. He knew how she'd react. But there was no escaping that now, was there? "The Abyss."

"The Abyss." Kendra's head dropped.

"It's away from the gods' eyes and we'd be free to—"

"I can't believe it's taken me this long to finally see you're *obsessed* with power. You'll do *anything* to get it." He saw the tears forming in Kendra's eyes. As then, he pushed any sentiment far from him. It wouldn't do any good—for either of them. "I've just been nothing but a *means* to an *end*. You don't love me—you never did."

At the time the accusation had stung him more than he thought possible, but now he knew the truth: she was right. He'd never really loved her—at least not in the truest sense of the word. He admired her, had lusted after her more than once, but loved her? Actually really cared for her the way the priests of Causilla and the bards said was right? No, he never had.

"And our child?" Kendra continued through her tears. It was pathetic really. So much confusion and fear over something so trivial. So much supposedly justified righteous wrath. Once they'd taken the throne, he would have brought their child back to life along with them. It was fear clouding her mind. And there was only fear because she hadn't decided where her place was. "You'd throw us to a pack of wolves in an instant if it could gain you anything worthwhile."

"If you just take a moment to step back—"

He was interrupted by a large booming sound: the beginning of Endarien's first attack on the tower all those centuries ago.

Kendra pressed on, undaunted. Her anger had overtaken her fear. It was fueling most of her fire. "You were right about one thing, though. It *is* time I choose my place. After all this time it's clear to me that it's *not* with you." Kendra ran from the room.

"Kendra!" Cadrith had cried out after her but knew it was too late. She had finally made her choice . . . and now was going to have to suffer through it. Another boom rattled the tower as an inky blackness spilled over the scene. A blackness that swam and swayed as it blotted out more of the light. He could imagine something alive in that mass of swarming night, something eager to clamp over him . . . But before he could dwell any further on the thought, he slipped into unconsciousness, letting his past fade away.

•●•

Just as rapidly as he passed into the darkness, Cadrith felt himself again returning to wakefulness. Before him was a sable-colored sea. Thinking he was lost somewhere in transition, it took him a moment to realize he was now in a new body. One with eyelids. Opening them brought forth a vast field of white, which he quickly understood was cloth. Flinging it away, he sat up, and found himself at the center of a swirling cloud of dust.

He felt muscles and tendons twist and moan. That was a good sign. The magic had sustained the body without any apparent trouble. Though this was temporary too. He was still a lich and in time the natural process of decay would take this body as it had his original one. But he didn't plan on having to keep this one long enough to deal with any of that.

From where he sat on the table, Cadrith saw what remained of his old form. The discarded, dusty garments reminded him of a serpent's shed skin. He supposed it was a fitting metaphor. He'd left the old behind in favor of the new. Already he felt it was no longer part of him—something weak cast aside. And then there was the deep well of magic he could feel humming with power inside him. It had been too long since he felt the strength of his true potential. Still no heartbeat, but at least he had a body strong enough to get him where he needed to go and sustain him throughout the entire process.

His attention fell to his hands. Fingernails and pale skin instead of the dry bones he was used to seeing. It would take some getting used to. Putting his hands on the skin of his face, he traced his fingers around his eyes, exploring the flesh surrounding them. Flesh that he now knew held piercing blue orbs rather than empty, flaming sockets. He smiled as his fingers ran through the short black hair that had remained all these centuries. It was amazing how quickly he'd adapted to its absence.

A small gesture brought forth a full-length mirror. The reflection marked him as a man of some thirty years with a body that still looked amazingly fresh—as if he'd just died mere moments before. In many ways he resembled the man he'd been when he'd first become a lich. As his dark smile widened, he delighted in the fact his lips now added to his charming manner. But enough of this. He needed clothing and his staff.

As soon as he'd thought of such matters, they appeared: his staff flying into his grip as a deep purple cloth fell upon his shoulders. The robe the cloth formed was embroidered on the hem with silver scrollwork and covered with ruby studs the size of a thumbnail. Black leather boots climbed from his feet to his knees. A moment later his former belt and all it held materialized about his waist. A pure-white hooded cloak gathered thickly around his neck like wave-birthed froth before flowing down to a finger's breadth from the floor. Around its hem and hood were golden stitched runes. It was a departure from his former attire in more than one way.

When he'd left for the Abyss, he'd donned an outfit and gear he assumed would have to withstand centuries while serving him well in just about any terrain. This time he knew where he was going, and what needed doing. In some ways it was a step into the past, letting him pick up and carry on where he left off. Only this time there was nothing standing in his way.

He pulled up his hood and made his way from the room with a strong stride. There was still much that had to be done, and it sounded like Endarien had finally relented in his assault.

CHAPTER 2

Knowledge is the chief thing in life.
There is nothing greater or better.
All things are tied to and flow from it.

—Ashur, Celetoric wizard king
Reigned 200 BV–100 BV

Cadrissa had stopped crying but remained slumped on the floor. Her clothing and hair had dried, and the thunder and pounding had stopped. Only a steady rain beat upon the tower's walls. Whatever had spoken to her in the darkness had ensured her Endarien wouldn't be a threat, and it seemed the god of storms and skies concurred. It was a welcome thing, she supposed, though she wasn't yet at home in the stillness. It was filled with the echoes of thoughts and memories she'd sooner shove under a mental rug rather than contend with face to face.

She'd set out to find the dranoric ruins, thinking it would be an interesting and educational adventure—but had she known where it all would lead . . . But what could she do now? No one knew where she was. Even if they did, she didn't imagine they'd be willing to come after her. Why would they? They *were* mercenaries, after all. If they still lived, they were probably in the jungles of Taka Lu Lama—far from wherever she was now—richer than when they started, and eager to move on with their lives. The only way out of this alive was to help Cadrith. But help him do what, and why?

She didn't know anything about the lich and couldn't see how they could have common ground. But if she valued her life, she had little choice but to join him. What was going on? Why was she taken? There wasn't anything random about it; of that she was sure. There had to be something he needed her for—something Cadrith, a wizard king, couldn't do on his own. But what could that possibly be? What could she offer him?

She was shaken from her thoughts by the soft clicking noise she knew was the door, and instantly leapt to her feet. A Telborian man made his way inside. She tensed, taking a step back as the door closed behind him. While trying to identify this new figure, she noticed his skull-capped staff.

"It can't be," she heard herself say in a stunned whisper.

"But it is," said the same voice she'd heard coming out of an empty skull earlier.

"But . . . how?"

Cadrith studied Cadrissa slowly. She found herself actually liking his previous, more ambiguous face better. His disapproving stare swirled the unease already sloshing about her stomach.

"What do you know about Arid Land?" The question caught her off guard.

"I-it's at the top of the Midlands," she nervously replied. "It's supposed to be a rocky wasteland."

Cadrith nodded. "Not much, I see."

"What do you want with me?" she dared ask.

Cadrith's smile sent a shudder across her frame. Yes, the fleshless skull was much better. "We're going on a journey," he said, making his way to the bookcase. "But I'll need you rested and competent enough to keep from slowing me down." She watched him pull out a dark green leather-bound book from a shelf before returning to shove the tome at her chest. "Read."

Cadrissa took hold of the book with a firm grip. Cadrith waved his hand, causing a tingling flutter to tickle her flesh. Her eyes became wider than coins as her clothing was transformed.

Her soiled golden robes changed into a white satin gown tied with a golden silk sash about her waist. The gown was cut in a plunging V from her neck to her chest. Against her back lay a hooded golden cloak of an unfamiliar lightweight fabric that glistened like starlight. Even her footwear had changed. She now wore tall black leather boots that rose to her shins, encircled with silver and ruby studs at their cuffed lips.

Though it frightened her, she also found the luxurious clothing flattering and quite beautiful. A sudden thought led her to subtly check inside a certain concealed pocket—the same pocket where, in her old outfit, she'd hidden the necklace. It was still safely in her possession. Thankfully, Cadrith had been looking elsewhere and missed her secret inspection.

"Come." Cadrith made his way to the door again, which opened for him. Cadrissa clasped the book to her side and followed the lich to another room one floor below.

"You can rest here," he said, motioning for her to enter a smaller private bedroom. The room was simple enough: a double bed with a large chest at the foot and an upright wardrobe on one side. She caught sight of her first window. It was a narrow thing and shuttered, but a welcome sight nonetheless.

"We'll be leaving once the weather's passed." Cadrith departed without a further word, the door closing and, yes, locking behind him. Cadrissa made for the bed and took a seat, resting the thick tome on her lap. The book's green cover was crafted of an unusual scaled hide. The few symbols carved in it were filled with gold. While the book was clearly old, she wasn't sure just what the symbols meant or said. Surmising Cadrith wouldn't give her a book she couldn't read, she carefully opened it and noticed the wonderfully scripted text across the title page. In an older dialect of Telboros, it read: *The True and Accurate Account of Arid Land.* Below that was a subtitle: *Home of the Syvani Elves.*

Syvani elves? She'd only been aware of the Patrious, who lived far to the west, and the Elyellium, who dominated the Midlands. The thought of a third race of elves having escaped her knowledge stirred her mind with possibilities. Forgetting about the last few hours, she ferociously began to devour the text.

•●•

Cadrith returned to the study, eager to finish his preparations. From the pouch at his waist he pulled out the objects he'd reduced in size while in the Abyss. He placed them on the floor before him and released the spell upon them. The chest and other assorted items returned to their natural size and weight, quickly filling the room. His attention, though, was on the monstrous obsidian hand that served as a pedestal for a rune-etched human skull.

The pedestal kept the scrying skull at waist height, allowing him to view it easily from where he stood. It had served him well all these years, after departing with him from this very tower centuries before. Most recently, it had helped him find his way back to Tralodren, guiding him first to Valan and then to Cadrissa. And now it would serve his purposes one last time.

Waving his hand over the skull, he whispered the words to a spell. A violet light flared up and over the time-gnawed bone. The runes etched into it burned a bright silver. Cadrith kept his attention firmly fixed on the skull's back, which was becoming translucent like a pond of glass. Waving his hand over the skull again brought forth a scene of craggy mountains lined with dark green pines.

This was Arid Land, a place said to be curtained by these same thick mountains. Though the natural wall had held back many would-be invaders for centuries, it couldn't restrain him. Another gesture brought the view further inland, to the thick pine forests that dominated the land's interior. He was getting closer. He pushed onward but began feeling resistance to his efforts. He tried shoving it aside, but the tangible force before him, like some opposing invisible barrier, stood fast. No matter how hard he tried to move the view forward, it would only advance a few inches before reverting to its previous position.

"You can't hold me back," Cadrith said, gritting his teeth and forcing more magical might behind his command. It got him a little closer, and he could see a clearing in the midst of thick forest, but the effort left a spiderweb of cracks across the skull, disrupting the silvery runes and dimming their glow. A wave of both hands over the skull brought up the image of a circle of stones erected in a post-and-lintel design.

"Galba." He bared his teeth, steeling his will and sharpening the spell.

A frenzied series of pops and snaps joined more cracks racing over the ancient bone. These rapidly widened into creeks and rivers before the whole of the skull began crumbling into fragments and dust. He watched the violet glow die from the now truly worthless device. It had served its purpose.

Satisfied, he started digging through the wooden chest near his feet, eventually pulling free another ancient tome. This he placed upon the silver podium. Flipping to the section he long ago memorized, he studied the images drawn on the vellum. Images of a throne and a stone circle that resembled the one he'd just seen.

"Almost there," he told himself, becoming lost in the collection of images, engrossed in their every detail. It had been the obsession of his former master and now it had become his. Except, where Raston had failed, he would succeed.

•●•

Cadrissa let the book fall flat into her lap. It had moved into subjects she didn't find interesting. The storm had slowed to a gentle rain, which helped in trying to forget where she was and what had happened to her. Still, reality never fled too far from her mind, no matter how much she tried crowding it out. Somewhere in the back of her thoughts she knew the time until her captor's return was dwindling. If she wanted to get any rest, now would be the time. But she just couldn't bring herself to attempt it. Sleep, while welcome, just didn't feel right in such a place. There were too many concerns—and unknowns—on the matter. Which brought her back to her thoughts . . . and reviewing what she'd read.

From what she understood, the Syvani were a very interesting—if barbaric—people who lived a sort of tribal existence in the great wilderness of Arid Land. They feared literacy and books, which struck her as strange. Oral traditions and their own memories were how they transferred their stories and histories. They feared if something were written down it would be forgotten.

An interesting theory, but lacking logic on many fronts. Chief among them: if knowledge isn't recorded and stored for later generations, then any insights died with those who held them, creating a great loss if such knowledge wasn't passed on before that person's death. It wasn't the way for a people to develop, which helped explain their perpetually rudimentary culture. After the book covered this information, topics had trailed into mundane measurements and meaningless reflections of a very fulsome sage. In short, the book proved useful as a basic overview and terrain primer, but nothing more.

She wondered why Cadrith had given it to her. Probably to keep her occupied and out of trouble. Not knowing what she was supposed to be looking for or for what purpose she was seeking it made for some challenges. She slid the book onto the bed and rose to investigate the room—or rather, her new cell.

She didn't bother with the door or the shutters. She was sure they were both magically locked. That left the wardrobe and chest—something, at least, to help pass the time. She decided on the chest first, since it was closer. She gently placed her hand on the sturdy cedar box and gave it a sharp tug. The lid slid up and open without protest. Inside, she discovered a few crumpled articles of clothing. Two pale white nightgowns of rather common make—but what rested beneath them caught her eye. She pulled out the crumpled fabric and held it before her, not sure how to react to an infant's nightgown.

Of the two adult gowns in the chest she could plainly see one was meant for a man, the other a woman, but this . . . A sudden recollection of the skull crowning Cadrith's staff exploded across her brain. She shuddered and let the garment drop back into the chest, softly closing the lid and shifting her attention to the wardrobe.

This piece was made of cedar too, and was just as sturdy. Two brass handles were on its front. Both were rather plain, worn, and cold to the touch as she grabbed hold of them. Another gentle pull parted the two doors with a small puff of air ripe with the odor of dust and old cloth.

Behind the doors she discovered a handful of robes.

A few were made for a taller man, but the rest were definitely fit for a woman of her size. None had fared as well as the clothing in the chest—she could feel the years of dust and neglect having worked into the fabric. It was like handling grave clothes. Shoving the thought aside, she focused her mental energy on figuring out what this all meant. A woman and a child—or, at least, a child's gown. Both in a tower now inhabited by a lich.

Part of her didn't want to know what it meant. Every bit of her wanted to be free of this room and this mess altogether. For a moment, she toyed with the thought of attempting another escape, but the gut-wrenching fear of what awaited her if she tried held her in her place. She was in over her head—*far* over her head. What she wouldn't give to see Dugan barreling through the door. But he wasn't coming. No one was. The more the truth sank in, the more empty she felt, and the paler the world grew around her.

Having lost any desire to explore the rest of the room, Cadrissa decided the only other option was trying to get some rest. Returning to the bed, she closed the book and placed it on the floor. She carefully lay down on top of the covers and took a deep breath. She let it out slowly as she closed her eyes, willing herself to relax and pretend she was in some safe place where resting wasn't anything she need fear. Eventually she believed her lie, and sleep overtook her.

She was awakened sometime later by the sound of the door. She rose into a sitting position just as Cadrith stepped into the room. He noted the slight disarray of the room caused by her exploration but didn't seem perturbed by it.

"Tell me about Arid Land," he said, carefully watching her with his intense blue eyes.

Cadrissa sputtered a bit before gaining some mental traction. She was still shaking the last of the sleep from her mind. "From what I've read, it's a massive forest sealed off by a wall of mountains. The Syvani who live there are said to be a form of savage elf, though the book was written by an Elyelmic sage, so I took that with a few grains of salt. He wasn't too approving of their attire or culture, but said they filled the whole land as the dominant race."

"They also follow shamans and spirits and have no talent for, nor interest in, magic," said Cadrith. "You've proven to be a quick study." Cadrissa didn't like the way he continued looking her over. "A useful trait if you're to accompany me."

"To Arid Land," she stated more than asked.

"The storm has stopped; it's time to go." Cadrith's white cloak swished behind him as he exited the room. He was gone in a heartbeat, his staff thumping in rapid rhythm with his steps.

"Come." His voice echoed down the hall, dripping with irritation.

Cadrissa jolted into action, running after him. Behind her, the room grew dark and cold as if any previous life and light in it had been mere illusion. As her own cloak fluttered out the doorway, the door closed with a whispered click, and all was still as the grave.

Cadrith headed straight for the demonic doors of the main floor, stopping once he'd come within a few feet of them. "If you do your part well, you'll be able to keep your life." The statement was matter of fact. He peered over his shoulder with a face scrubbed clean of emotion. "But if you prove you're not up to the task . . ." Cadrissa was left the honor of contemplating the array of horrible outcomes.

"I-it would help if I knew what you wanted me to do." She struggled to sound calm and assured.

"We're going to Arid Land. That's all you need to know for now." With a wave of his hand the demons released their grip, allowing the doors to open. "Now come." Cadrith exited the tower, Cadrissa following.

Outside it smelled of wet grass, a faint hint of the previous storm's heaviness still lingering in the air. Though the sky was clear again, it was far from the same bright canopy that had welcomed Cadrissa's arrival. Instead, it was now late afternoon. She'd slept longer than she realized. Cadrith stopped a few feet from the tower, causing the doors to close and lock.

Once again facing Cadrissa, he said, "You've read enough to be able to fix your mind on something, but I'm to be the anchor for the spell.

And should you try to disrupt it or attempt to flee, you'll quickly discover how foolish you were."

He closed his eyes and recited the words to a translocation spell. Cadrissa could figure that much out, but it wasn't spoken in the way she was used to. He was doing something else with it too, working it together with another spell she'd never heard before. She was so enraptured by the process that she nearly forgot to do her part until the sudden jolt of realization had her closing her eyes and focusing on Arid Land.

Arid Land.

Arid Land.

Arid Land.

Soon the concentration faded with her sense of self as she felt her body become light and airy. She didn't need to open her eyes to know they were no longer outside the tower. The smell of fresh rain was gone. In its place was a span of coldness followed by a return to some warmth as hard, rocky earth rose beneath her feet.

Opening her eyes, Cadrissa discovered they were in the midst of a majestic chain of mountains that stretched for miles in all directions. The sun had just set, spitting a vibrant pinkish glow awash over the grayish-brown stone, bringing out some of the most subtle and amazing hues. She'd never been in the mountains before and was amazed with everything. All around them were hard, jagged peaks that sank into the rising pines climbing the mountains' base. But Cadrith wasn't in any mood for enjoying such sights.

"Come." The command accompanied a strong and brisk march across the rocky terrain.

"Where are we going?" She did her best to steady her feet as she tried matching the lich's pace.

"Galba."

"How far is that?" She didn't see anything resembling civilization for as far as the fading light allowed. And there'd soon be even less to see with the coming of night. She hoped he wasn't planning on trying to descend in the dark, but wouldn't put it past him.

Cadrith was silent.

She determined it was wiser to concentrate on her footing rather than getting some answers. And she'd have had a better chance at doing so if not for the dark shape blotting out part of the horizon. She'd first caught sight of it out of the corner of her eye, giving it nothing more than a glance, but the more time passed the larger it grew, until she could make out wings. Very *large* wings.

A horrendous screech echoed across the mountains, drawing Cadrith's gaze to the now clearly visible brown bird that was growing with its descent. "What's that?" Cadrissa asked, afraid to unhook her green eyes from the sight.

"More of Endarien's wasted efforts." Cadrith planted his staff in the earth, preparing to face the creature as if it were nothing more than an annoying fly.

"It's a roc." She was able to finally put what she'd learned in her schooling and read in the tower together. In many ways, rocs were gigantic versions of hawks. She'd seen some drawings in her lifetime and had read ancient tales of firsthand encounters, but they all paled beside the real thing screeching down upon them. It was as if she'd shrunk to minute proportions and everything else had become gargantuan in comparison. Its feathers were so massive and thick they reminded her of tall trees tied together end to end.

Cadrith cast forth a black, crackling web of magical energy from his staff as the creature dove straight for them. The web wrapped itself around the roc's beak and massive head, temporarily causing it to close its golden eyes and veer off course as it sought release of its troublesome confinement.

Cadrissa ducked as the wake of its passing stirred up small pebbles, dust, and other debris, causing her eyes to run wet with tears. "We need to get out of here."

"No." Cadrith stood fast. "This will end, and end now. Endarien will learn his lesson."

There came another deafening screech, letting her know the roc had broken free of Cadrith's spell. Cadrissa managed to rub her eyes clear enough to see the roc was circling, preparing for a repeat assault. This time, Cadrith shot an azure bolt from the skull atop his staff. The roc was able to avoid the attack with a quick turn, allowing it to get right above them. A heartbeat later Cadrissa felt an iron-like vise ensnaring her body.

She heard the scream before she realized it was her own. Across from her was Cadrith. Both were wrapped tight by the roc's talons, their arms at their sides and chests squeezed, hindering any spellcasting efforts. But that wasn't the worst of it. The roc had taken to the heavens, flapping its massive wings with great gusts and lifting them higher and higher.

Cadrissa did her best to shield herself from the abusive slaps of wind pummeling her hair and face, all the while noting how tiny Arid Land was becoming beneath her. The mountains had receded into tiny mounds one might have seen children building at play. She could see the pine forests now as well, huge swaths of green seas contained behind the mountainous walls lining the two parts of Arid Land. As she rose further, the landmasses grew closer together until they almost reminded her of two spooning giants resting upon the sea.

"Where is it taking us?" she shouted.

"Nowhere," Cadrith growled. She could feel the ripples swelling from his well as the lich began enacting a spell. It was something almost primeval in nature—raw and overwhelming. Suddenly, her ears popped, and a great chill enveloped her like a thick blanket.

Craning her head, Cadrissa gaped at the sight of the silent splendor of a vast cosmic display. She'd never seen the stars as she did now: so bright and alluring, more vivid than she could ever imagine. She couldn't pull her gaze away. It was one thing to read about such things and to see them from much farther below, but never would she have dreamed she could have seen all this.

"Kralis agorlin nectro-rolis!" Cadrith's shout broke Cadrissa's musings as the lich unleashed a black burst of serpentine energy. It slithered and coiled up the roc's talon and leg, all the way to its head, where it slammed into an eye, continuing with that same force into its brain.

There came a horrid, pain-racked screech, after which the bird lurched into an awkward, motionless silence. Cadrissa knew the roc was dead, but it took a moment for the full weight of that revelation to sink in.

"Dradin . . ." she whispered at the sight of Tralodren—the actual planet—returning her stare. She was above the *planet*! She was viewing Tralodren as the gods did: a white-veined blue marble fixed within a sable ocean. How they could be so high above the world was beyond her understanding. She knew rocs could fly far, but this—suddenly she felt the roc's body shifting. The corpse had started to turn ever so slightly back toward the planet. That small turn was enough to completely spin it around so it faced Tralodren with its lone, dead eye.

"No. No. No." Cadrissa couldn't raise her voice more than a whisper before the roc began its plummeting descent with both its captives still tightly locked in its grip. The wind screamed in her ears and the tears streamed from her eyes. This was it. She was going to die.

"Do something!" she bellowed over the wind. If Cadrith heard her, she didn't know it. She tried getting a glimpse of him but couldn't make out more than the fluttering feathers flashing between them as the roc twisted against the gusts.

Tralodren loomed larger and larger. The globe spread, then flattened. Fat clouds rushed forth to greet them, and they tore through them just as quickly. Cadrissa's ears popped as she tried struggling for release. Her efforts allowed her to loosen her left arm just enough to wrench it from the coiled talon, but that was all she managed before she was frozen by what caught her gaze next. They were back over Arid Land—falling straight toward it. The jagged mountains had now turned into cruel knives, the majestic pines into lustful spears.

Regaining her sense of place, she renewed her attempts at freeing herself but was even less successful than before. All the while she kept daring terrible peeks at her certain death racing ever closer. Finally, when she knew it wouldn't make any difference, she grew still, opting to stare at the rocky expanse underneath her instead of continuing her vain attempt at escape.

The roc nearly gutted itself—and them—as it sank into the mountains like a wild sled in deep snow. Cadrissa watched the hard grayish-brown rock start to close the gap between them as it shifted into softer hills and then flat earth dotted with the beginnings of the forest.

The trees!

They were going to hit the trees!

As she scrunched her eyes and clenched her jaw, she felt the strange enveloping of another spell. She had barely registered the mere touch of its presence before the terrible sound of cracking branches and bones filled her ears. With the roc careening into the forest, Cadrissa slipped into unconsciousness.

CHAPTER 3

THE ROAD GOES EVER ONWARD, TWISTING BEYOND THE BEND;
OUR JOURNEY THUS CONTINUES UNTIL ITS FINAL END.

—Old Tralodroen rhyme

The day had been long and taxing. A ten-year-old Rowan was hunting bear with his mother. The winter months were fast approaching, and the animals would be slowing down for hibernation, making them easy prey. The meat, hide, and bones would be a welcome boon for the tribe as the months began to turn colder, making food and clothing more valuable. Rowan had shadowed his mother most of the day, learning what he could, but the biggest lesson was yet to come.

His mother turned to him. The beads in her hair and on her buckskin garb made no noise with her movements. "Time to be quiet," she whispered.

His legs were like water pumps, bobbing up and down as the body they supported impatiently waited. He watched in childlike awe as his mother moved into the cave without making a sound. He tried straining his eyes, hoping he'd find her form moving about the rocky opening, but she'd vanished like a shadow in the night. Time passed in slow, excruciating silence, and he began to imagine himself leaping into the gloomy opening in hopes of saving her from some horrific disaster. Then he heard the deep, angry roar. The bellowing grew louder and louder until at last a black furry shape charged out of the cave's mouth. Fixing his sight on the mound of growling fur loping straight for him, Rowan froze in his tracks.

"Lead him to the trap." His mother's voice echoed from the cave and snapped him from his paralysis. The huge bear easily dwarfed Rowan, who now needed to lead it to the pit dug into the forest floor some yards away.

He was quick to take flight, goading the bear on by shouting and throwing rocks at it. His mother had told him if it got enraged enough, the bear wouldn't pay much attention to its surroundings and therefore would be easier to trap. Even though Rowan was a fast runner, the bear was determined, and quickly gained on the boy. The trap had been set on the opposite side of the trees lining the rocky boundaries of the cave. As he neared the pit, he daydreamed of the hero's welcome his tribe would give him over his first kill. Though his mother had helped, he could still claim some ownership in the task. The pride swelled within him.

The bear continued gaining distance. Rowan, lost in imagination of future celebrations, tripped on a root at the trap's lip. He toppled beside the opening, fear rising. The bear took to its hind legs—raising itself to its full height—and readied for attack.

Within moments arrows filled the air, embedding themselves into the animal. The bear howled its displeasure and turned to face its assailant. Another shaft flew into one of the bear's eyes—sinking deep into its brain. The bear gave a slight whimper of protest, then convulsed into a heap beside the prostrate Rowan.

He looked from the dead bear to the source of the arrows. His eyes went wide at the sight of his mother standing not more than a few yards from him, hair blowing softly in the breeze as she lowered her bow. "Are you hurt?" Though she was tense from the recent excitement, her maternal concern still showed through.

"No," he answered, dazed.

"Thank the spirits." She lent a hand to her son and pulled him up.

As Rowan looked upon the dead bear a sense of sickness washed over him. His mother noticed. "You weren't paying attention as you ran, were you?"

"No." Rowan hung his head.

"Probably thinking of the celebration and praise you'd get after helping me lug him back to the village, right?"

He did nothing to hide his amazement. "How did you know?"

"I was your age once too." She gave his hair a tousle. "Just remember—it's easy to lose your footing if you take your focus off the path. And it's easy to lose your focus if your mind is somewhere it shouldn't be."

•●•

Rowan remained silent. Before him danced a crackling fire. Beyond it sat Nalu. Together, he and Alara had managed to find their way back to the small camp. It was a fairly easy task, since Dugan had hacked a path there through the jungle. Everything looked the same as when he last saw it. The only difference was in the nearby fallen tree. It was a bit shorter after having been chopped up for the camp's spits and watch fires.

A handful of Celetors kept watch over the camp while the rest slept under the half moon and smattering of stars moving in and out of the dark, rolling clouds. They'd arrived at dusk, just in time for a light meal, which all ate while Rowan and Alara informed Nalu and the others of what took place in the ruins. As night spread its arms over the heavens, most sought some sleep. Among those in slumber was Alara. Rowan studied the silver-haired elf sleeping no more than a few paces from him. With her pale gray skin, her peaceful face could have easily been another moon.

They'd made good time on the path but found no sign of Dugan or Vinder. The two had gone on ahead of them, jogging or running for a good distance, it seemed, as the two groups never crossed paths. They apparently didn't even stop to rest or get any supplies from the Celetors. Rowan thought that was odd, given their lack of supplies for the journey ahead, but that wasn't really his concern. They'd followed their own path now—like all the rest of them . . . including Cadrissa.

While both he and Alara were thankful to be free of the ruins, it didn't mean he could dust off his hands and move on. He'd failed in his mission. The scrolls he'd been sent to find had been taken by Gilban, and he was left to return to the keep like a shamed dog with its tail between its legs. He should have been thinking more clearly—had a plan in place *before* everyone parted ways. He knew Gilban and Alara had sought the scrolls too, but assumed they'd let him take them back to Valkoria. An idea that sounded foolish in hindsight.

"You should be sleeping too." Nalu's words caught Rowan's attention. The sandy-haired knight realized he'd been staring at Alara longer than he should. "You will need much strength for your journey."

"Thank you again for your help," he replied. Apart from the green and blue feathered necklace and the bone bracelet about his left wrist, Nalu looked just like the rest of the breechcloth-clad Celetors in the camp. "If I could repay you for the food—"

Nalu raised a hand that would have been lost to the night if not for the fire. His brown skin complemented his short, curly black hair—common among the Celetors who lived in these regions. "It is my thanks for all you did with the hobgoblins. Now we can return to our village in peace."

"I hope so," said Rowan. "But they're still in the jungle and could still pose a threat."

"Not like before," said Nalu.

"You're sure of that?" He eyed the Celetor carefully. It was nice Nalu was so optimistic, but there could still be some trouble if the hobgoblins were able to reassemble themselves in any sizable numbers.

"They will not go back to the ruins," Nalu explained. "You said they were destroyed. So now we will be in peace."

Rowan gave a nod and returned his thoughts to the fire.

"What troubles you, my friend?"

"I'm fine." He kept watching the shifting flames.

"No, you are not. There is a large log you carry across your back."

Rowan lifted his eyes while trying to keep his face as emotionless as possible. "It's just . . . life." No sooner had he given his reply than he returned to watching Alara slumber. He'd taken a greater interest in the elf since their departure. At first he'd simply sought to study her movements and actions to see what she might be seeking to do next. But as the days passed, his thoughts turned to more surface observations, such as her strange hair and skin color. In the beginning they were an oddity to him, but eventually they grew to be more familiar, and he found himself even admiring them.

This set off a frequent back-and-forth within him. On one hand was the knowledge of what he'd been told about elves, and on the other was what he saw in Alara. In many ways she was lovelier than any Nordic woman, but she wasn't a human and that was trouble. So why was he becoming more fascinated with her with each passing day? What was it that made him stop and stare for far longer than what was becoming for a knight?

"You, my friend, are troubled by more than life." Nalu's lips parted into a white crescent of a grin. "A woman has gotten hold of you."

"What woman?" he quickly snapped.

"You could have done worse," Nalu said, nodding at Alara. "She is quite lovely."

Rowan fought to hide the heat rising in his cheeks while simultaneously combating the swirling cauldron in his gut. "We're just traveling back to my boat."

"So you already have said."

"She just wants to vouch for me with my superiors."

What was wrong with him? It felt like a small war being waged inside him—clashing swords and screaming combatants seeking to claim the helm of his mind and emotions as their prize. On one side was his duty, and on the other was growing doubt and confusion. It had all started after he and Alara had left the ruins to head back to Nalu's camp. But where once it had just been a nagging sensation in his head and gut, it had now erupted into this near-constant skirmish.

"But she is quite pretty, is she not?" asked Nalu.

"She's an elf!" Rowan shook his head in an attempt to clear it. No such luck.

"Why does this trouble you?"

"*You* of all people should know," he snapped in reply. "Didn't that priest teach you anything?" He referenced the Paninian priest who'd brought the truth of Panthora to Nalu and his tribe decades before. It was one of the reasons Rowan had felt so comfortable returning to the camp. Not only were they humans, but they worshiped the same goddess—a rarity, as he'd discovered in his short travels thus far.

Nalu studied Rowan carefully before speaking again. When he did, it was with a calm and measured voice. "He did not teach us to hate elves, or any other people. In fact, much good can be gained if we continue to look to work together."

Rowan sprang from his seat, his face filled with anger. "How can you bear good feelings toward a race of cruel and greedy brigands who seek to pillage and destroy all that's good and righteous in this world? Their kind wished to eradicate all humanity from existence! You can't truly worship Panthora if you've sided with the enemy!"

Nalu remained calm throughout Rowan's diatribe. "It is not I who has bowed to the enemy, but you."

"Hold your tongue! I-I . . ." Rowan stopped himself with his hand firmly grasping the handle of his sword. He'd been ready to yank it free, slicing into Nalu with all the fury of a berserker. This same man who had been nothing but a friend to him and a help to their mission.

"What have I been saying?" He collapsed back onto the log.

"This is just what I was wondering." Nalu motioned for the other Celetors—who'd stopped to stare with a keen interest at Nalu and Rowan's recent exchange—to return to their duties. "Your knighthood must have taught you this."

Rowan was struck by the weight of Nalu's words because a part of him thought they were true. "I don't see how they could have. I was trained and taught in the glory and honor of Panthora. I would have remembered messages of hatred toward elves."

"Maybe they taught it to you in secret."

"In secret? I can't believe they'd do such a thing." He shook the suggestion from his mind. "No. There must be another explanation."

"Perhaps . . ." Nalu let the rest of his words and thoughts fall into the fire.

Rowan clasped his head in his hands. "I wish I'd just stayed at home. I should have never come on this mission."

"You do not mean that." What Nalu said resonated with some resident truth inside him. After all, if he wasn't supposed to be here, then why did Panthora guide him to the ruins—to *Gondad* even? And then there was the matter of the necklace she'd led him to as well.

"I just need to get back to Valkoria." He did his best at returning to a calmer demeanor. "Everything will fall into place once I get back to the keep."

"Then you will need your sleep," Nalu advised.

"Yeah." He remained seated for a little while longer before at last rising. He found a suitable place to lay his head enough distance from Alara while remaining just close enough to benefit from the fire's light.

As the others slumbered, Rowan tossed and turned. The more he thought about Alara, the more he heard a voice in the back of his head reminding him of the tales of how elves used other races for their own ends and how Panthora didn't support any kind sentiment toward the elven race. These thoughts conflicted with his heart, which attempted to reconcile the stark contrast between the nature Alara and Gilban had shown and what his mind said was true. It was in this turmoil that Nalu's words returned to him: *Maybe they taught it to you in secret*. Eventually, his heart and thoughts grew exhausted in their struggle and surrendered at last to sleep, much to his relief.

•●•

Dugan devoured what remained of the rabbit as the fire between him and the dwarf grew low. It wasn't eaten for pleasure so much as survival. Neither he nor Vinder had taken much in the way of anything nourishing for the last day or so . . . maybe longer. The last few days had run together into a blur he often had trouble separating into its constituent pieces. Not that it really mattered anymore. He was free, and what was in the past could now thankfully remain in the past.

"You sure you're going to be ready at dawn?" Vinder asked, watching him closely with his lone ice-blue eye. The other—his left—was covered by a black leather patch adorned with golden runes similar to those that covered his axe.

"I'll be ready," he replied, swallowing the rest of his meal.

Vinder, like Dugan, had kept his armor on. Neither wanted to be unprepared for any possible threats. While the sounds from the jungle were peaceful, one never knew what might be lurking, waiting for an opportunity. And they'd just sent a whole slew of hobgoblins running into the wilds outside the ruins they'd formerly occupied. And then there still might be some elves wandering around as well. Though he figured if any still drew breath they'd most likely be concerned with the ruins. He doubted they'd return empty handed until they made a thorough inspection of all that remained.

"Hopefully, we'll be able to find some water tomorrow." Vinder finished his own rabbit. The two had captured them just as they started to make camp around dusk. They'd run or jogged most of the way, both along the trail Dugan had hacked through the jungle and then after they emerged from it, which had helped them gain some distance.

"How far you think we got?" He attempted a survey of the area immediately around him with little success. The meager firelight didn't penetrate more than a few feet into the darkness.

"Farther than if we'd just walked the whole time." Vinder picked the last of the meat from the rabbit's bones. "And if we can keep up the pace, we should be able to get around the marshes and into the grasslands in a couple days."

Dugan nodded, his eyes fixed on the low flames. He was free from the elves and able to start a new path for his life, but his ultimate future—his final fate—was far from reassuring. He didn't like dwelling on it but pushing it out of mind wasn't going to get rid of it. He needed to deal with it, and the sooner the better.

He lifted his gaze. "How far is Haven again?"

"Longer by foot," Vinder replied. "But thankfully we're not without the means to fix that." He gave one of his bulging purses a pat. The dwarf had taken considerably more than Dugan from the cache in the ruins. In hindsight he supposed he should have been a little greedier. But he didn't really have anything to keep it in and had already taken two additional swords he thought might fetch some coin later. These he let rest beside him, keeping his gladius strapped to his waist. This, like his armor, he wanted to keep close at hand.

"As long as I get there in the end," he replied.

"You really are set on seeing it, aren't you?" Vinder ran a hand down his beard, cleaning it of any debris from his meal. Two braids, each dyed a deep crimson at the tip, easily stood out among the salt-and-pepper hair.

"You made it sound worthwhile," he returned, nonchalantly. So far their journey hadn't gotten into any real personal matters. And the longer he could maintain that status quo, the better.

"I just said it's filled with plenty of temples, priests, and wizards," said Vinder. "I didn't figure you the sort who was into all of that."

"I'm not, but it sounds like a good place to start over . . ." And it was an ideal place, if what Vinder said was true, to get some answers about other things . . .

Vinder let the matter die, clearly not one to press into affairs not his own. "Well, Elandor will be good enough for me . . . and then the mountains after that." His charcoal-gray skin helped him blend into the night. But it didn't hide the gravity that lined his features. For a long moment, neither of them spoke, each contemplating the days ahead.

"And you really think your money will still be waiting for you back in Elandor?" Dugan finally asked, eager to change the subject. He referred to something Vinder had shared earlier on one of their resting walks about how he'd entrusted his funds to a temple there before heading out to the ruins with him and the others. The concept was truly a novel one to him.

"Olthoans are honest and have a sure system in place to protect it," he replied.

"And the other temples don't?"

"Olthon is the goddess of peace and prosperity," Vinder explained. "It's part of her purpose, and her priests are known to lend money and help keep it for others."

"So *all* the temples watch other people's money?"

Vinder chuckled. "They'd certainly take it, but not all are open to the idea. You looking to find someplace safe for yours?"

"Just curious."

"Well, Haven will certainly keep you busy if you're looking."

Dugan tossed the skeletal remains of his meal into the flames. "I'll take first watch."

"Fine by me." Vinder added his rabbit bones to Dugan's before making ready for some sleep. Soon enough he rested on his side, lone eye facing away from Dugan and the fire. And in short order the dwarf started lightly snoring.

Dugan occupied himself by watching the fire slowly die. The thin flames crackled through ribs and other bones. He couldn't help imagining a blackened *human* skeleton inside a larger field of hungry fire. A body very much like his own burning for all eternity in a domain of never-ending flame . . . He quickly shook himself away from such thoughts. Sighing, he fixed his mind and eyes elsewhere, watching the rest of the jungle and thinking on what he'd have to do once he reached Haven.

•●•

Alara woke at dawn. For a moment she lay still on her back, taking in the great symphony of the jungle. It reminded her in part of her family and their farm, a place very far away from her now, and looking ever farther with each passing day. As she took a moment to soak deeper into such recollections, she tried not to dwell on the voice that asked her again if she knew what she was doing. Even though she'd made her decision, she still couldn't keep from having doubts.

She knew part of the voice was fear. She was far from home and now also Gilban, who'd been her anchor since they'd left Rexatoius. With him gone, the only way back home was the sloop docked in Elandor. Even if she dared the waves on her own, it would still be months before she caught sight of her homeland. In contrast, she supposed Gilban and Hadek were enjoying some rest after a job well done. Hadek might be a bit challenged in trying to fit into life on Rexatoius, but she was confident he'd find his way in time. In the meantime, she was stuck finding her way out of a jungle.

Faith and patience. She could hear Gilban's voice in her head. *Faith and patience.*

She could also hear the muttered voices of Nalu's tribesmen in the background, talking in their native tongue around a cook fire. With the hobgoblian threat eliminated, they'd no doubt be happy to return to their village. A rumble from her stomach caused her to sit up. If Nalu could spare some more food to help them on their way, she'd be incredibly thankful. She didn't know what they'd be able to find along the way, and without any horses and even less in the way of proper supplies, the trip back to Elandor would take even longer than before.

"You should get more rest," Nalu said as he watched Alara approach. "You have a good distance before you." He spoke in Telboros, which was a very welcome thing, considering outside of it she only knew Pacolees—her native tongue.

"Longer than you think," she said, stretching her back. "Valkoria is *quite* the trek."

"You sleep well?"

"Better than I thought I would," she confessed. Considering what she'd just been through and the present jungle setting, she'd managed to sleep without any trouble. Being close to exhaustion would do that to just about anyone. "How about you?"

"Now that my village is safe, much better." Nalu smiled.

Alara noticed Rowan's back as he sat before a cook fire with some of the other Celetors. He was still wearing his leather armor with the panther motifs worked into it. She'd never seen him take it off since they first met back in Elandor.

"That doesn't smell like parrot." She took another sniff at the new aroma dancing amid the smoke. The last time they'd been Nalu's guests he'd served them parrot, which Alara was surprised to find didn't taste as strange as she thought it would.

"No." Nalu grinned. "Serpent."

"Serpent." Alara did her best to hide her unenthusiastic expression. She was hungry enough to eat just about anything but had never thought she'd be looking at a piece of serpent on her plate. The creatures were larger, more aggressive snakes with sharp scales and a double row of teeth used to rip out their prey's throat while squeezing it to death. While surprised at their prey of choice, she wasn't about to turn it down.

"You are welcome to what you wish," Nalu said, inviting her to join the others around the fire. "You have earned it—both of you."

"Thank you." She gave a small nod.

"Come." Nalu again gestured for her to join them. "Get some strength before you leave."

Alara followed after Nalu as he led her to the others. She watched Rowan as she neared, making note of how he made no motion or even acknowledgment of her presence. She supposed he might still be upset about losing the scrolls to Gilban. He hadn't spoken much since their departure from the ruins. She hoped this wasn't going to be the way things were for the rest of the journey. If it was, they were in for a very long and uncomfortable trip.

She tried some small talk. "Sounds like we're having serpent."

Rowan lifted his head her way long enough to say, "They say it tastes like parrot."

"I guess we'll find out." She observed the large column of sizzling flesh as it spun on a spit. Cleaned and gutted, it didn't look too bad—like a large slice of fish—and, in a way, it did faintly smell like parrot, she supposed.

"I told Nalu we'd be leaving after we ate," Rowan continued, returning to watching their breakfast.

"I figured that. We need to get as much ground covered as possible. Maybe we might even run into Dugan and Vinder."

"I doubt it," he replied. "They've got a good lead on us already, and if they don't stop for much rest they'll make even better time."

"Hopefully they'll find something to eat," she said. "If they didn't stop at the camp—"

"They'll survive," said Rowan. "Just like we will. Panthora will see to that."

"I've been thinking," she continued before Rowan turned away. "Would you be able to teach me Nordican?"

"What for?" His dark blue eyes held her fast, clearly curious.

"I want to put my best foot forward when I meet your superiors, and I don't think I'd be able to do that if I couldn't speak your language."

"You really want to?" He appeared skeptical.

"If I can at least *talk* to them in their native language they might give more weight to what I'm saying. And it'll help pass the time."

"We can try, I suppose." He sighed before returning his gaze to the cooking hunk of serpent, which was being pulled off the spit by some rather excited Celetors.

"If you don't want to, I—"

"No," said Rowan. "It's fine."

"You will like this very much." Nalu's cheery remark pulled their focus back to the meal. The Celetor, in obvious anticipation, had started cutting into the meat with his dagger. She supposed she wasn't the only hungry one among them. "It will give you much strength. Much strength."

She politely nodded, wondering just how much of that "strength" she could handle taking.

CHAPTER 4

IT'S OFTEN THIN THREADS THAT CONNECT ONE TO ANOTHER,
BUT IF YOU WEAVE THEM TOGETHER YOU'LL HAVE A STRONG ROPE.

—Old Tralodroen proverb

Gurthghol, the god of chaos and darkness, rested in his bed while a Lady of Darkness named Twila peered into his strange eyes from atop his naked, hairy chest. The god's long black hair had been left to flow free, framing his plum-colored flesh with an onyx mane that stood in contrast to Twila's own short black hair.

"So." Twila smiled, bringing a playful spark to her violet eyes. "Have I convinced you yet?" Her grayish-purple skin displayed the unique quality the Lords of Darkness had taken on since becoming masters of the cosmic element of darkness.

"To make you my favorite?" Gurthghol ran his hand down her back, his long black nails tracing out his fingers' path.

"I'm not going to give up." Twila's eyes flirted with mischief.

"I hope not," Gurthghol said, pulling the black silken sheets over his lover's body. "That would take you out of the running for sure." He focused again on her fair features. She was one of the many women in his harem.

He watched her study his eyes. They were one of the most unique sights in all of creation. Where they should be white, they were black, with a purple iris and black pupil. Twila wasn't alone in her fascination. None in the pantheon had ever grown accustomed to them.

"Have I mentioned how *determined* I am?" Twila said, scaling the god's shoulders and neck, lavishing his cheeks and mouth with kisses, and brushing across his long mustache in the process. Gurthghol had adopted the look in his youth, in part as an homage to his father, who'd worn the same style all his adult life.

Only the flicker of a few candles strewn randomly across the lavish room provided any light. The windows had all their drapes pulled tightly shut. Not that a great deal of light would spill in through them even if opened, given that Altearin, Gurthghol's realm, was a place of constant twilight. As Twila's kisses intensified, Gurthghol latched on to her shoulders and turned her on her back, falling on top of her as he began ravaging her lips with his own.

Before a fresh fire could be kindled, there arose a forceful knocking at the wrought iron–enforced door some ten yards from the bed. Neither paid it much heed at first as they continued to entangle themselves, but the knocking wouldn't be denied.

"My lord." A voice now accompanied the aggressive pounding. "There's an envoy who's arrived with an urgent message."

Gurthghol pulled back from Twila with a frustrated sigh.

"Just pretend you're asleep," she pleaded.

"Lord Gurthghol?" The pounding intensified, this time accompanied by a raised voice.

Gurthghol rose with another sigh and made his way to the door. His naked feet made no sound on the black marble floor, the same color as the silken pants he adjusted about his waist. "I'm coming." A moment later his hand was on the door's latch, yanking it open. "What is it?"

The figures behind the door were about half Gurthghol's size and looked like children in comparison to the towering god. One was a Tularin, a special class of paradisal incarnates who served the pantheon as messengers and honor guard of Thangaria; the other was Gurthghol's trusted Karduin chamberlain.

"Forgive me, sire." The Kardu, named Erdis, gave a bow of his oval head. It was shaved save for a brown ponytail at the back, allowing his pointed ears to be clearly seen. "I wouldn't have disturbed you if it wasn't urgent." The Kardu wore rich robes but had the look of a scholar compared with the martial qualities the Tularin embodied, even with his white robes and golden sash.

"Ganatar has called for a council," the Tularin said, making sure to keep his eyes focused on Gurthghol's, as was proper protocol.

"Why?" Gurthghol studied the paradisal incarnate closely. He was always interested in the way they never seemed to change. Every Tularin wore the same robes and sash and even had identical platinum hair. If not for the variation in skin tone there would be total uniformity among the race. He found it a strange way to live, let alone to perpetuate generation after generation.

"A lich named Cadrith Elanis has returned to Tralodren." The Tularin spoke with an emphasis conveying the greatest importance.

"So?"

"He was a wizard king . . . and it's come to Ganatar's attention that he's being backed by an old foe."

"Old foe?"

"I was told not to speak its name," the Tularin responded, "out of respect."

Gurthghol smirked. "Still standing on superstitious ceremony, I see." Yes, old fears and traditions didn't just run in Tularins, it seemed.

"This lich is making his way to Galba."

"Galba?" This stoked the god's interest. "You sure about that?"

"It's what I was told," said the incarnate. "He wants the pantheon to meet as soon as possible," he continued. "How soon can you alert the rest of the Dark Gods?"

"Soon enough." It was a safe answer. He didn't know how quickly he wanted to let Asorlok, Rheminas, and Khuthon know about what was going on. At least not until he had some time to mull the matter over a bit more himself. If something *really* was taking place with Galba, he had to be wise in what he did next—they *all* did.

The Tularin bowed. "I shall leave you to it then." He gave a flap of his white feathered wings, which elegantly lifted him off the ground as he skillfully turned and made his way down the large hallway.

Gurthghol returned his attention to Erdis. "Was there anything else?"

"No, my lord." The Kardu gave a bow of his head. "Again, my apologies for having disturbed you."

Gurthghol shut the door behind him.

"What is it?" Twila had wrapped a sheet around herself and crept his way. He supposed she'd heard enough to figure it out, but humored her nonetheless.

"A council's been called."

"You don't sound pleased."

"I'm not. Not if what the messenger said was true."

"And what did he say?"

Of all the women in his harem, Twila was the most inquisitive, and bold enough to speak her mind—even if it was in matters that didn't concern her. But Gurthghol enjoyed that about her . . . for now. "That an old enemy could very well have returned. Only now we don't have the throne to defend ourselves . . . or take our revenge."

Twila tried to soothe his dark mood, softly stroking his arm. "I'm sure you'll find a way to deal with it. There's nothing in the cosmos more powerful than the pantheon."

"That's what we'd have it believe." He abruptly turned and made his way to a purple-draped window. "I have to inform the other Dark Gods."

"I understand," Twila said sadly, watching him pass.

"You're close though." His words caused her head to swing and meet his small grin.

"To what?"

"To being my favorite."

"Then don't be too long in summoning me." Twila gave a familiar mischievous smirk Gurthghol had yet to grow tired of. "I'd like to continue where we left off."

"Then get some rest." He laid hold of the silky curtains with both hands, giving them a sharp tug and revealing the window beyond. "You'll need it." Twila saw herself out while Gurthghol delved deeper into his thoughts, placing his hands over the ornately carved wooden sill.

"A wizard king on his way to Galba . . ." The purple-black skies beyond the panes reflected his murky mind. There were so many possibilities muddying the water. He had to sort through them before he summoned the others. But he also had to think fast. The rest of the pantheon would be on Thangaria soon enough.

•●•

The first thing Cadrissa noticed was the sunlight piercing through the crosshatched pines above. The second was the rich scent of sap mingled with the aroma of fresh-cut wood. Following this was the sudden awareness of her stiff limbs and back crying for attention. Before she could tend to them, she had to wriggle free of the talon still wrapped around her body. Its grip had loosened with the roc's death, but it still held firm, making for an uncomfortable bed.

Though she had to grit her teeth more than a few times to put down the flares of pain, a mental inventory informed her she wasn't that bad off. Most of what she suffered was bruises and a few scrapes and cuts. No broken bones, and nothing else serious. To say it was a miracle was an understatement.

Once free and on her feet, Cadrissa began to study the landscape, amazed at the swath of destruction that greeted her. The roc had plowed through the pines for a good distance before finally coming to a stop. Furrows of earth dug by the roc's body as it skidded to its final resting place intersected with toppled and uprooted trees lying this way and that. A handful of these trees lay across the large bird's wings and body. Some of the pines had to be over one hundred feet tall. It was another miracle none of them had crushed her flat.

Noticing the roc's head, she was amazed by how large it was, especially now that she was so close to it. She surmised the width of the thing was close to that of a small tower, the golden beak able to snatch her up whole in one snap. When she saw the bird's empty socket, created by Cadrith's spell, she realized how easily she could slide inside. She shook such macabre thoughts away with a shudder. At least it was dead, while she was still alive—bright spots on an otherwise gloomy horizon.

"It seems you've taken enough rest." Cadrith's comment caused Cadrissa to spin quickly around. She'd completely forgotten about him, but it seemed he hadn't forgotten about her. Like her, he appeared to have a few scrapes, but nothing more. But unlike her, his wounds were only small tears in his flesh and brought forth no blood. Cadrissa thought if she could get close enough, she'd actually be able to peer beyond the tears into the various layers of whatever muscle and flesh remained on his bones. Another shudder cleared her thoughts.

"We've taken enough time as it is." Cadrith stepped closer. She did her best at suppressing the discomfort caused by his chilling aura.

"But what if Endarien—"

"He can't do anything now. None of the gods can. Now don't make me regret using that spell to save you."

She didn't know how to take the news, but did recall the spell that enveloped her before the roc made its final impact. He just as easily could have cast it for himself but had chosen to extend it to her as well. Whatever Cadrith was planning, he needed her alive for it. That was something, she supposed.

"Now come. We still have a good distance to go." He maneuvered over the toppled trees and debris with a steady rhythm. She knew he could keep that pace all day, probably longer; she couldn't say the same about herself.

"Aren't you going to cast another spell?"

"No. We're going to walk for a while."

She opened her mouth, then thought better of it. Instead, she forced her feet forward, doing her best to match the lich's pace.

"Now listen very carefully," Cadrith said, keeping his eyes locked on the path he now followed. "The gods might not be able to touch us, but that doesn't mean we won't be disturbed along the way. From here on, anyone we encounter should be considered an enemy."

"But from what I've read—"

"We're in Galba's land now, and she'll be standing against me every step of the way."

"So who is this Galba?"

"Haven't you read the Kosma or the Theogona?" Cadrith's tone mixed mockery with disbelief.

"I'm not really that religious," Cadrissa confessed sheepishly.

"No *true* wizard is. But you'd be wise to learn of your enemies and how things began."

"But the gods aren't our enemies."

"If you're truly going to amount to *anything*, they will be," said Cadrith. "They'll look to hold you back and keep you under their thumb."

She knew he was speaking about the path of power. Centuries ago, when wizards grew in skill and strength, many sought to walk one of two paths. One path was that of knowledge, which sought the way to enlightenment and understanding using magic and the insight gained by it. The other was the path of power, the pursuit of power and its accumulation for the sake of ownership and exploitation of that power.

The path of power was the most common path followed by wizard kings. As such it was no surprise to hear Cadrith speak as he did, but his understanding of the gods . . . that was something she'd never heard anyone express before. She might not have been too devout in honoring them, but she'd never say they were her enemy.

"But Dradin's the god who *gave* us magic. If anything, he's an *ally*."

Cadrith stopped and faced Cadrissa with a sneer. "Did you ever read of the Divine Vindication?"

"Y-yes." Cadrissa, like all mages, was aware of the time when magic was removed from the world. A time of darkness for every mage across the planet. She wouldn't have wanted to have been born in such a time or even in the centuries that followed. She couldn't imagine what she'd do without the ability to access and wield magic.

"Then where was Dradin?" he mocked. "I was there. I saw the gods move to stop what they feared: their creations being able to rival them as equals. And Dradin did *nothing* to stop it."

"But the wizard kings were . . ." Cadrissa heard the words coming out of her mouth before she could stop them.

"Were what?" Cadrith's humorless smile had Cadrissa biting her tongue. "None of you know *anything* about what it is to be a wizard king. You hold to some idea of *virtue*, while keeping from your *true* potential. You've shackled yourselves with false ideals and will *never* go further than your chain allows." This said, he resumed his brisk walk.

Cadrissa followed, debating the accusation he'd just leveled against her and all modern-day wizards. Was what he said true? You needed some sense of right and wrong to follow—some code of morality—it was the foundation for any civilization to flourish. Cadrissa had her own, which she'd adopted from the common religious and civic mores she'd been born into, adding to them what she'd learned at the academy. For magic was a discipline too. It required a sense of responsibility not just to yourself but to your fellow mages and the rest of the people around you. The wizard kings were famed for willingly shoving aside such concerns for purely selfish motives. They'd toss aside kingdoms and whole populations to get what they wanted.

Could it really be a weakness to hold to a moral code, to consider a more responsible take on magic? Was doing so really a leash like Cadrith said, strangling a mage's further development? No. Cadrith was speaking from the path of power and with the arrogance of the wizard kings. And if he was truly the last of them, he was, no doubt, the worst of them. And if that was so, she began dreading even more the fate awaiting her.

"Galba is a place and a person." Cadrith was calmer now, adopting the air of a sage instructing their pupil. "All of Arid Land is under her sway. And thanks to an ancient pact, the gods will no longer be able to interfere by keeping me from seeking her out.

"So keep up." He doubled his pace. "I don't plan on keeping her waiting."

Cadrissa let out a small huff as she urged her sore and bruised body to maintain a respectable gap between them. She didn't want to get too near and have to contend with his cold aura, nor did she want to stray too far behind and stir up more of his ire. It would be a challenging pace.

Already she could feel the first beads of sweat forming on her forehead, but the haunting experience in the tower with that tentacled mass was ever lurking in the back of her thoughts, motivating every step.

•●•

High on a mountain peak, the tranquil and majestic temple to Endarien and the community of Endari who kept it had long ago faded from memory. The ruins were now a home for birds and wild animals. Only the echoes of what had been and its sudden end nearly eight centuries before remained. The temple had been perched on one of the Pearl Islands, a region named for the numerous isles scattered about in the southern portion of the Western Lands and once thought to resemble a great collection of pearls flung into the Yoan Ocean.

While the name suggested an elegant beauty, the truth was darker than the ideal. In many places charred slashes remained, evidence of the fires that destroyed so much so long ago. Worse were the bones, strewn into small piles or flung across the rubble. What the scavengers had left was now bleached with age and just as silent as what still stood.

Into this environment descended a small breeze that twisted into a dust devil before just as quickly dissipating. In the dust devil's place stood a man covered head to foot in a storm-gray hooded cloak. Removing his hood revealed the features of a young, white-haired Telborian with yellow eyes: the common guise of Endarien, god of the sky.

The young god hawkishly surveyed the terrain before making his way to a partially toppled pillar that had once held up a massive pediment. The pediment itself had crashed to the ground long ago, dashed into a hundred worn fragments.

The area he walked about was once an approach to a fair-sized temple dedicated to his worship. Here priests would travel between its small rooms and the handful of other buildings that allowed them to remain self-sufficient for year after year. Until, that was, when the mages appeared . . . The temple had been a thing of beauty, and it was the only piece of architecture that remained even slightly intact—at least to the point of being recognizable and even serviceable in places. Endarien had seen to this preservation in anticipation for the day now close at hand. But for the moment, the sundered pillar would serve as a place to lean as he folded his arms across his chest and waited for the others to arrive.

"Not the place I'd expected you to choose." A new voice arose, startling Endarien, who quickly located the black-cloaked figure behind him.

"It's the last place anyone would think to look."

"And people think *I'm* morbid." Asorlok pulled back his hood, releasing his tan, bald head, hawk nose, and brilliant blue eyes from the dark shroud.

"She said we needed some place away from prying eyes," Endarien said by way of explanation. "You can't do much better than this." Asorlok didn't seem interested.

"So. Where *is* my sister?" The god of death strode through the debris. "She always has such an impeccable sense of timing." In this guise Asorlok had adopted a fine black shirt with dark brown pants, a stark contrast to the silvery white shirt and brown trousers worn by Endarien.

"Then you have no need to worry." A Celetoric woman stepped from behind a half-toppled statue that once had been an impressive rendering of a griffin raised on its hind legs. Her eyes were pure white, her head as bald as Asorlok's. Her skin possessed a light brown hue, smooth and clear like polished teak. Her neck and wrists were draped with a vast collection of bracelets, necklaces, and jewels. The rest of her frame was covered with an ornate lavender dress and silver cloak.

"Who said I was worried?" Asorlok greeted Saredhel's mortal guise with a smile.

"It was not what you said, but what was left unsaid." The goddess of fate and prophecy gave a passing nod to the god of death. Though she appeared blind, she could see just as well as any sighted being—even better, given her ability to see into the rivers of time and discern the fate of things to come.

"So now that we're here, what next?" Asorlok inquired as Endarien joined them in the middle of a more open area amid the ruins.

"Yes, what do you want?" There was a slight restlessness that crept into Endarien's voice. "You said it was urgent."

"And it is," said Saredhel. "First"—she directed her attention at Endarien—"how did your encounter with Cadrith go?"

Endarien did a terrible job of keeping his surprise from showing. "You were *spying* on me?"

"Tell me of your encounter."

"Why? If you already saw it—"

"Just tell her." Asorlok sighed.

"Cadrith and another wizard had managed to get to Arid Land, and so I called upon a roc to dispatch them."

"After your elemental failed." Saredhel was matter of fact.

Endarien's eyes narrowed. "Yes." He didn't like the reminder. The tower should have been weak with age, but it still resisted the assaults. He should have gone himself. But he'd a special fate planned for the lich, and now twice he'd failed to enact it. Never had he had such trouble dealing with a mortal, a fact that made Cadrith's destruction all the more desirable.

"And what happened with the roc?" Saredhel continued.

"They were able to escape."

"How?" Asorlok looked over Endarien carefully.

"Does it matter?"

"It might," countered Asorlok.

"Cadrith used his magic to free himself and the wizardess," he admitted.

"Impressive," Asorlok flatly mused.

"Frustrating," he corrected.

Asorlok's head tilted slightly to the side. "I'd expect Khuthon or Perlosa to let a handful of mortals get under their skin, but not you."

"It's a matter of justice," Endarien snapped back.

"Which is why you picked this place to meet," Saredhel continued. "The matter is heavy upon your mind."

"And why *shouldn't* it be?"

"Because you're never going to have what you seek as long as you go about it like you have." Saredhel's words stilled the rising storm of Endarien's anger. "And it's the same reason your priests will fail in their attempt to send the lich to Mortis."

It was Asorlok's turn to go wide eyed. "What are you talking about?"

"Your priests are no doubt getting ready to launch an assault on Cadrith, since he's defied the natural law. But if you let them go, they'll enter your gates well before him."

"Then speak." Asorlok's voice was as emotionless as the grave.

"Cadrith is not working alone. He's been aided by a patron whose shadow has crossed our paths before. And this is what you saw, Endarien, no doubt, in your last encounter."

Endarien gave a solemn nod. "There were hints of it, but I wasn't sure." He thought on the encounter in Arid Land—when he watched the events through the roc's eyes—right up until the bird's death. He hadn't been sure at first, but it became clear soon enough that there was a shadowy aura around the lich. Something that only a god or perhaps a well-trained divinity could spot, but it was there nonetheless.

"Then be sure," said Saredhel. "Our enemy has found a new pawn and is ready to start its game again. But it won't be able to succeed if we're able to stop it first."

"How?" asked Asorlok.

"Cadrith is seeking Galba."

Asorlok broke into a chuckle. "Then he'll save my priests their effort."

"Not from what I've seen." Saredhel stilled all present.

"And just what *have* you seen?" Endarien dared a step forward and glared at the goddess. "You never *do* share all of what you know, anyway."

"I've seen another great threat to the pantheon, and Cadrith is tied to it."

"And because we both have something against him, you've called us together." Asorlok smiled. "Sounds like you want to keep something from the others."

"They won't be able to help—not yet—but with your help we can prepare."

"You're aware of my oath and how I can't stray too far from it." Asorlok reminded Saredhel and Endarien of the less-than-comforting truth regarding his patron.

"Yet you're sending your priests to hunt him down . . . or are you planning something *else* instead?" Endarien's eyes narrowed. "Maybe we have *another* ally of our enemy in our midst."

"No." Saredhel was quick to counter. "We each have something unique to offer: thin threads that can be woven into a strong rope to hold Cadrith back. But we don't have much time to act. He's already on Arid Land, as Endarien has said."

"If he's headed for Galba, then the others will know it and call a council." Asorlok said what everyone else already surmised. "Which is why you've reached out now—before we gather. Impeccable timing, as always."

"We play a part of a larger plan." Saredhel continued, ignoring Asorlok's critique. "The others will find their place in the rest of it."

"I thought as much." Another cool smile traced Asorlok's lips.

"If the council finds out—"

"Are you going to tell them?" Asorlok interrupted Endarien.

"No, but—"

"Then they won't find out. Now let her speak."

"I've seen there will be a chance to stop Cadrith's patron before he rises to become a greater threat, but it will take place at Galba and with those who helped return him to Tralodren. That is why I've called for you. I can bring two threads together but won't be able to get the rest in time."

Asorlok rubbed his chin in thought. "The priests—you want to use them."

"Yes." Saredhel nodded. "To gather the others."

"Then why me?" Endarien asked. "If the Asorlins are going to get the rest, then you really don't need me for anything."

"You'll have your part to play," said Saredhel. Whether the comment was meant as ominous or encouraging, Endarien couldn't say.

CHAPTER 5

IT HAS BEEN DECREED THAT ALL SHALL DIE AND
THEN PASS ON TO ASORLOK FOR JUDGMENT.
ANYTHING ELSE IS AN ABOMINATION.

—The Scrolls of Dust

The empty chamber was silent as Cracius Evans and Tebow Narlsmith solemnly strode to its center. Both were priests of Asorlok, but they couldn't have been more different in appearance.

Cracius was the shorter. Clean shaven with red hair cropped close to his head and a youthful, medium complexion marking him as not more than twenty years, he had dark brown eyes that spoke of a dedication and understanding far beyond what his youth might suggest. The green-eyed Tebow was the older, with dark brown hair graying at the temples. His jaw was covered in stubble and his skin was tan and rugged like a woodsman's or a farmer's.

They were both dressed in simple garb: parchment-shaded robes and black leather boots, with blood-red sashes tied about their waists. Around their necks was the symbol of their faith: the Silver Cross, a pendant depicting two crossed sickles. Over all this each wore a black hooded cloak, the hoods left down.

A handful of torches scattered around the walls provided enough light to illuminate the general confines of the otherwise empty room. The chamber was part of a hidden temple dedicated to Asorlok. It was small but effective, crafted from simple stone shaped into tight, smooth walls, floor, and ceiling. The only object of note in the chamber was a round, black granite dais at its center. Stopping before the dais' steps, the two Asorlins turned to face the set of double doors through which they'd entered.

Through these doors appeared seven more Asorlins, dressed the same as Cracius and Tebow save that their black hoods were drawn, partially obscuring their faces. The priests made their way to the same dais. Six of their band formed a circle around it and Cracius and Tebow, while the seventh ascended the steps. Once the seventh had reached the top of the dais, the double doors were shut.

"The time has come," said the one atop the dais, who was the grand abbot of the order. Focusing on Cracius and Tebow, he asked, "Are you ready?"

"Yes," said Cracius.

"Yes," Tebow repeated.

Tebow and Cracius had served with the order for some time—Cracius since he was ten and Tebow since the age of twenty-eight, some twelve years ago. They belonged to a sect dedicated to the eradication of those who would cheat the god of death and the natural cycle. An unusual order who were just as hard to find as temples to Asorlok.

Not many on Tralodren had a favorable view of the god, who was seen in a negative light. Even though Asorlins would argue his rule over death wasn't as tyrannical or sinister as many thought—death just being the passage from this current life to the one beyond—few could bring themselves to accept this. Instead, death was seen as something terrible and evil, and so, by association, was Asorlok.

This meant, of course, those who served him were often suspect. It also didn't help that on various occasions small cults had arisen to worship the god of death in a less-than-positive manner. As such, all Asorlins were painted with the same brush. But regardless of public opinion, the priests of the temple dedicated to the Sovereign Lord of the Silent Slumber had a sacred task before them.

"Once more, another seeks to cheat Asorlok," the grand abbot continued. "And once more we must rise up and show him the error of his ways. Cadrith Elanis must not be allowed to mock Asorlok any longer."

"We're ready to serve as Asorlok wills," said Tebow with a slight bow.

"Then let us begin," the grand abbot said, raising his arms in prayer. "Oh Lord Asorlok, god of the outer world, and gatekeeper to the realms beyond, hear my prayer. We have assembled together once more to set out to teach those foolish enough to mock your laws the error of their ways.

"As with Rainier and all those who came after him, we've been faithful to carry out your will and plan. As the Scrolls of Dust say: 'Flesh is not eternal and shall one day fall away. It has been decreed that all shall die and then pass on to Asorlok for judgment. Anything else is an abomination.' And so shall it be with Cadrith Elanis."

Lowering his hands, the grand abbot continued. "Tebow and Cracius, you have been chosen to deal death to this lich's body so his spirit might finally reach Sheol's gates. Know that you journey under Asorlok's favor, who will watch over you until your task is complete.

"Bring forth the hammers." The grand abbot motioned to two priest's at the base of the dais, who revealed two hammers from under their cloaks. Their black walnut shafts were about as long as each priest's forearm. The silver, two-faced hammer heads were about a third of the shafts' length and connected by means of an intricately carved silver skull. This skull was also two faced, providing a leering visage on both sides of the hammer. The Asorlins holding the hammers bestowed them on Tebow and Cracius—handles first—who accepted them with great reverence.

"The hand of Asorlok is also upon these hammers," said the grand abbot. "Use them well." He extended his hands toward Tebow and Cracius, saying, "Now receive the blessing of our god. May you walk in the shadow of the lord of death's wings, may he make your way prosperous and your enemies fall before you."

"Into your will and spirit I walk, Asorlok." Tebow bowed his head.

"Into your will and spirit I walk, Asorlok," Cracius echoed.

"Now, my brothers," the grand abbot addressed the rest, "let's tend to the gate."

Tebow and Cracius raised their hoods as every Asorlin took part in a muted prayer that brought all the comfort of a dirge. Shortly after the prayer had begun, the grand abbot raised his arms, moving to face the blank stone wall behind him. As he did, an old wooden door appeared within the stone, growing from a small, dark speck into a fully formed and operational structure. It had the look of antiquity upon it but was sturdy enough to handle what was to follow.

"It now falls to you," said the grand abbot to both Tebow and Cracius. "You have my blessing and Asorlok's; do what needs to be done."

"We won't fail," Tebow said with assurance as he marched toward the door. Cracius joined him. As they progressed, their fellow Asorlins parted and the door silently swung open, revealing a blackness impenetrable by torch light.

Tebow motioned for Cracius to step through the doorway first. He did so with silent steps. The darkness swallowed him whole. Tebow followed, his black cloak blending into the utter darkness. Once they'd entered, the door swung shut and faded from view.

•●•

"This isn't the tower," said Tebow as he and Cracius entered a ring of standing stones. Each was solid, smooth, and about four feet wide. All were free from any sign of age, though both priests instinctually knew they'd been there for many centuries. The upright stones rose fifteen feet and had flat, one-foot-tall blocks of stone lying across and between them in a post-and-lintel design. The posts were arranged to allow twelve openings into the circle's center, where Tebow and Cracius now found themselves standing.

"One of Cadrith's tricks?" Cracius took a few paces into the center of the circle, which consisted of nothing but a flat lawn.

"Or a defense, perhaps . . ." Tebow turned back to where they'd entered. He saw the doorway he thought they'd walked through, but it wasn't the same doorway they'd entered in the temple. Instead, it was one of the twelve open areas between the stone posts. Looking to the other openings, he beheld various images inside them, scenes of different lands, mysterious places under the waves, and even patches of sky. All the images changed over time, flickering through a collection of scenes, with none of them repeating what had come before.

"I don't like this." Cracius rejoined Tebow. His grim expression mirrored what Tebow felt. They shouldn't be here—wherever *here* was. This wasn't right, but who had the power to derail them from their destination? Was this really the lich's work? If so, had he been expecting them?

"Just keep alert." Tebow was talking to himself as much as Cracius. "We'll sort this out."

"You think these are all portals?" Cracius said, scanning the shifting scenes flickering between the posts.

"They look to be." Tebow lifted his gaze, noting the sun and sky. "But we're still on Tralodren . . . just not where we're supposed to be."

"So what happened?" asked Cracius.

"*I* brought you here," a soft, disembodied voice replied. Unsettlingly, it wasn't distinct in its gender—a blending of both male and female voices creating a most unusual sound.

Cracius raised his hammer. "Show yourself."

There came a flash of white light that caused both priests to squeeze their eyes shut. Once it had passed, there was a new figure in their midst. She wore a white cloak draped over a long-sleeved gray gown. Her pale face was partially hidden by a deep, alabaster cowl.

"Welcome." This time there was no confusion in what they heard. This was most certainly a woman, one with a calm and inviting voice.

"And who are you?" Cracius asked, tightening his grip on his hammer.

"Galba," came her soft reply.

"Galba?" Tebow turned stiff as a plank.

"It's a trick," Cracius snapped. "One of the lich's distractions."

"No," Tebow said, taking a tentative step forward. "Cadrith wouldn't go to all this trouble. At least not with all this." He indicated the stones around them.

"It can't be real," Cracius said, shifting his weight.

"And why not?" asked the woman. "Haven't you read the Theogona or the Kosma?"

"Of course we have," said Tebow, "but this—this is—"

"If you're *really* Galba," Cracius piped up, "then where's the throne?"

"Safe for now. But that could change in the future, which is why I've brought you here."

"Why?" Tebow was still trying to make sense of all this. He'd read in the Kosma, as had just about any other priest on Tralodren, about the things that had come before recorded time, events that mentioned the pact between the gods and a being named Galba. But there weren't many details given about her. There was just mention of a stone circle and the throne. So far they only had the circle.

"I know of your mission and want to help make it a success," Galba said, moving to stand before Tebow. As she did, the elder priest found himself awestruck by what he could now see of the woman's face. Smooth, ageless skin flowed over gently defined cheekbones down to a slightly rounded chin. Only the small ruby island of her lips broke up the serene, porcelain sea that was her face.

"And how is diverting us from it going to help us achieve it?" Cracius joined Tebow's side, hammer kept at the ready.

"You don't think the saving of your life a *helpful* thing?" Galba looked Cracius full in the face. Both priests took note of the small emerald flashes beneath the hood—the most alluring sparkle of eyes they'd ever known.

"We have Asorlok on our side." Cracius was firm. "These hammers"—he gave his own a small lift—"have been blessed to finish the lich and anyone else who might get in our way. *We're* not the ones who are going to be dying today."

"You think your enemy is Cadrith," Galba continued, "but you're wrong."

"So Asorlok is *wrong*?" Cracius' growing discontent was evident. Before he could say more, Tebow's hand was upon his shoulder. Tebow could feel Cracius tighten like a spring, but some firm pressure kept the younger priest in check. They weren't going to get any answers if they took to swinging their hammers.

"So then who is our *real* enemy?" asked Tebow.

Galba gave a small wave of her hand. The action caused all the images inside the stone-framed doorways to darken into a deep well of pitch. Only it wasn't just empty darkness nestled between the stone posts. There was something in it. Something that slammed into the portals with a clapping thud, causing both priests to jump with fright. Each portal revealed the same scene: a twirling coil of black tentacles ending in a maw of vicious white teeth. Each tentacle and snapping mouth seemed to have a mind of its own, trying to break through the invisible barrier of the portals and spill into the open area beyond.

"*This* is what you're *really* facing." Galba motioned toward the dark entity.

"What is it?" Cracius couldn't take his eyes off the sight.

"Cadrith's patron."

"The lich isn't working with anyone," said Tebow. "He never has."

"He doesn't know he has one," said Galba. "His patron selected him long ago and has guided him to this present hour. In Cadrith's ignorance he assumed it to be his own greatness that has seen him rise to such heights, when in reality he's nothing more than a tool being used in a much larger plan."

"Which is?" Cracius snapped, turning toward Galba. He'd lowered his hammer about a hand's breadth, but still kept it ready to strike.

Another small wave of Galba's hand banished the darkness that had been battering the portals. Once again, tranquil scenes took hold, and Tebow was glad for it. "You said you've read the Kosma," said Galba. "Then you're aware that there are other forces in the cosmos besides the gods. Some of them even *greater* than the gods."

"What are you implying?" Cracius gave the circle another look. "That Cadrith's patron is more powerful than Asorlok?"

"Yes," came Galba's soft reply. "And if you're to defeat him and his patron, you're going to need help."

"Help?" Cracius spat out the word as if it was rancid meat. "We have all we need in Asorlok. As all his priests have proved for *centuries*."

"If I hadn't taken you aside, you wouldn't have faced Cadrith but rather his patron. It's protecting him and will destroy you outright if you try to do Cadrith harm. But together we stand a much better chance of success."

"You're asking a great deal of trust from us," Tebow said, shifting through the various angles of what was being presented to him. "You admit to abducting us, say we're going to fail if we try to press on, and then offer us your aid, all without giving any clear idea of what you really want."

"Just as Cadrith has a patron, so too do I," said Galba. "And just as Cadrith's patron wishes him to succeed, mine seeks to stop him."

"How?" asked Cracius.

"By assembling some others to join you in stopping him." Cracius gave Tebow an uncertain look. This was becoming more complex by the moment. "My patron will be behind them—and you—if you're willing to seek out two of their number and bring them here. My patron will take care of the rest."

"The Kosma didn't mention Galba having a patron—at least not that I recall." Tebow sought to get some answers as well as test the woman's claims. Impressive as this place was, he was having a hard time believing he was actually standing in a place said to be barred from the gods.

"I have my patron in much the same way your god has *his* patron."

And then Tebow understood. "It's the same patron, isn't it? Asorlok's and Cadrith's?"

"Yes."

"Then you're asking us to side with another god to fight our own," Cracius concluded.

"No." Galba gave a shake of her head. "He, like the rest of the pantheon, wouldn't stand for what Cadrith seeks."

"Which is?" Cracius pressed.

"This circle and the throne."

"But none have ever succeeded in taking the throne," said Tebow. "The Kosma makes it quite plain. It can't be done."

"You've seen his patron," Galba countered. "And if it's already more powerful than the gods, then what's the throne of the first god before it?"

"Then we need to kill him *now.*" Cracius raised his hammer with his voice. "If we hurry—"

"He's not at his tower. He's already on his way here."

"Then we'll wait for him," said Tebow, firmly planting his feet in the sward.

"And you'll still fail." Galba raised her delicate hand to silence any rebuttal. "I'm asking for an alliance in the place of my patron. It will take care of the others; you just need to see to the two who remain."

"Why us?" Cracius asked.

"Because you have a desire to put an end to Cadrith, as does Asorlok. We share a common goal, and together we can achieve it."

"And just who *are* these people?" Tebow inquired.

"The same who helped free Cadrith from the Abyss."

"Why them?" Cracius asked.

"Because they were chosen to free him."

"Chosen by *whom*?" Cracius continued.

Galba didn't answer.

"Poetic irony aside," said Tebow, "what do any of them have to offer that would give us an edge against Cadrith and his patron?"

"By themselves, not much. But together you'd all be backed by *my* patron, and once Cadrith steps into the circle he'll become vulnerable."

"*How* will he become vulnerable?" Cracius made no attempt to hide the doubt in his voice.

Again Galba didn't reply.

Undaunted, Tebow continued his quest for answers. "If what you say is true, why didn't the grand abbot or Asorlok inform us?" It was an obvious question, the one that was lurking just beneath this verbal sparring that was getting them nowhere, except further away from their small window to confront the lich.

"If you're priests, you can be expected to take some things on faith." Galba's reply didn't satisfy Tebow, who adopted more of Cracius' surly disposition.

"Asorlok we know and can trust, but you—"

"You doubt." Galba drew closer to Tebow. "I'm not about to explain everything to your satisfaction, but if you need proof in order to speed things along, you shall have it. Look into my eyes, if you can."

Tebow snorted at the comical notion that he could be so easily swayed to trust her over Asorlok. But if it sped things along, he'd do it. Every moment wasted gave Cadrith greater opportunity to slip through their grasp. Galba's green eyes dug deep into his spirit. Their subtle depths made his heart beat just a little bit faster, but there was something more behind them. Something that began to overwhelm him, making him grow weak in mind and body.

"Forgive me." He bowed before Galba, much to Cracius' amazement. All of Tebow's former doubts had been washed away as easily as a sand castle in a tidal wave.

"What are you doing?"

"Look into her eyes, Cracius. Look *fully* into her eyes and tell me what you see." Cracius hesitated but did as Tebow instructed. "You see it too, don't you? That kind of thing can't be faked—not by magic or anything else."

"Yes." Cracius had gone limp in voice and body. "She really *is* Galba."

"Which means all she's been saying is true."

Cracius faced Tebow. "Then why—"

"There isn't much more to tell. More importantly, we don't have much time to discuss the matter," said Galba, walking toward the image of a woodland grove nestled between the two stone posts across from them. "Should Cadrith arrive before you—"

"How much time do we have?" Tebow followed Galba.

"Enough to do your part." Galba's delicate fingers stroked the image between the posts, sending a ripple across it as if she'd touched a still pool. The scene quickly changed to what appeared to be the inside of a cavern, though not much more could be discerned from where Tebow stood.

"So we're *really* going to do this?" Cracius joined Tebow at his side.

"If Cadrith is really able to take the throne—would you want that on your conscience for all eternity?"

"Only two . . ." Tebow thought aloud as he stared into the image of the cavern surreally framed between the two stone posts. It could have just as easily been an incredible tapestry or a lifelike painting.

"Yes. A dwarf and a Telborian. The rest are being gathered through other channels."

"And how are we supposed to convince them to come along with us?" Cracius asked Tebow. "This is a wild-enough story for *me* to follow, let alone try and convince someone else it's true."

"Perhaps we could appeal to their baser nature," he suggested. "If we offer some sort of payment . . ."

"We don't have any coin. Just our hammers and robes."

"Then we'll have to keep our faith in Asorlok. If this is the only way to send the lich to Mortis, then Asorlok has truly guided our steps." Turning back to Galba, he asked, "What are their names, and how will we know them when we find them?"

"The first is named Vinder." Galba moved further away from the image as she beckoned the Asorlins to enter. "You'll find him through here."

"How do we get back?" asked Tebow.

"The same way you got here the first time. I'll make sure you're able to find your way inside again." It was as much as they were going to get, and Tebow knew it.

"You ready?" he asked, giving Cracius a once-over.

"I was ready the last time," he replied, sharing a weak smile.

"All you need do is walk through the portal. The rest will take care of itself."

"Keep your hammer ready," Tebow advised as he stepped toward the image. Pushing back a swelling sense of déjà vu, he passed through the portal.

Cracius followed.

CHAPTER 6

Free will is really more the working of other factors beyond your control.

—Baxter Natter, half-elven philosopher
1 BV–119 PV

On the western side of the Yoan Ocean, nestled in the Sea of Bithal's temperate waters, lay the Republic of Rexatoius, home of the Patrious elves. This idyllic land was awash with sun, greenery, elegant architectural wonders, and breathtaking landscapes. Rexatoius' rocky coastline gave way to soft, rolling hills, with thick forests and crystal-clear lakes, rivers, and streams, while a few snowcapped mountain chains raced across the land until finally collapsing into a bed of rich sward.

Delightful cities and charming small towns and villages were scattered about Rexatoius. Though they seemed disconnected, every town, village, and city was linked by wide cobblestone roads with wheel ruts worn so deep not a single blade of grass dared show itself. These roads—the arteries of the republic—crisscrossed the land en route to Clesethius, the heart of the Patrician republic. And it was to Clesethius that Gilban had taken Hadek.

It took the bald goblin a few moments to register what had happened to him. One moment he was standing in the jungle of Taka Lu Lama outside the crumbling ruins of an ancient dranoric city, and the next he found himself standing in what he later would learn was the Temple of the

Goddess of Mysteries, the chief temple dedicated to Saredhel in the nation's capital. He remembered feeling himself grow weightless for a moment and recalled how one landscape seemed to fade into another, but it had happened so fast—if he hadn't been there, he'd doubt it had even occurred.

He wasn't always knowledgeable about distances but knew something in the way of geography, having gained some insight from his time helping the priests and Valan. So it was even more amazing when he realized they had traveled very far very quickly—almost halfway around the world. And Gilban wasn't tired in the least after the journey.

But while the situation was amazing, Hadek soon sobered at the thought of this new reality—a reality he might have rather recklessly agreed to without fully thinking the matter through, though there hadn't been much time for consideration. The offer was presented and Hadek had accepted it, for better or for worse.

The following morning, he found himself covered in a rainbow of light that spilled from the stained glass windows of his modest room. The colored images depicted the history of the faith and how the temple was built. In one of them, a radiant woman touched the head of a kneeling Patrician man; around him a collage of multicolored glass gleamed.

Hadek stared at the windows, wishing he could understand them, but Gilban had been too busy to explain them. It wasn't that he was slow of wit; it was just that to him, the images were only images. The priests of Saredhel loved to study, speak in, and look for symbols and riddles. Hadek was fast learning that theirs was a language of figurative texts and revelatory concepts. The full meaning of their art and literature was, as a result, not always so easy to comprehend.

Upon their arrival, Gilban had informed the other priests of his desire for Hadek's safety. The priests understood and put the goblin in a small section of the great temple where he'd be safe from harm. But he really knew "safe from harm" meant "able to cause the least amount of harm to them, the temple, and its activities." Though Patrious elves, he was learning, were known to be more accepting than other Tralodroen races, they were still wary of creatures that had certain destructive and less civilized tendencies, such as Hadek's kin.

Goblins, along with hobgoblins and ogres, didn't have the best reputation. If Hadek left the confines of the temple, he might come to harm or find himself in a far worse predicament. The priests made sure to give him a simple chamber where he could rest from his journey, and allowed him to roam a small, little-used section of the temple that sat apart from the major areas.

Though if the priests had any worries about Hadek causing any trouble, it was for naught. He was far too tired to do much more than walk around the section in which he was confined. When he did, he often found himself revisiting his decision to join Gilban and leave his former world behind. As the hours dragged on, pondering—and at times regretting—his decision was just about all he *could* do. From what he understood, Gilban had left to report to his superiors, and then to the elucidator, about the mission's success. Hadek felt abandoned in the elf's absence.

Lost in a strange world, he sat on an old, worn chair in his room. It was the only ungilded thing he'd seen so far, and it felt strangely separate from the temple. He could relate. His simple brown tunic, pants, and boots blended well with the seasoned wood, while his lime-green skin seemed to complement it all the more. Rubbing a hand over his bald head, he sank deeper into thought.

The goblin had in him the spark of something great; at least, Gilban had told him that before he'd left the temple. He'd said so hurriedly, in passing, along with assurances he'd return shortly. He recalled hearing Gilban saying the same thing in the jungle before they left. The words hit something deep inside him, but Gilban didn't seem willing to elaborate any further. So if the small word of encouragement was supposed to help him feel better, it didn't.

He had no idea how he could have the spark of *anything* great in him. He was smarter than his kin, that he knew, but he wasn't much further along than the rest of them when it came to his station in life. So what did Gilban mean? More importantly, perhaps, why was he here now? Sure, he'd gotten away from his old life to—hopefully—a safer location, but what now? These were powerful thoughts he had to contend with, but if he wanted to move forward with his life, to make sense of what had happened, they needed to be confronted.

Hadek sank his head into his chest, heavy-lidded eyes closing in thought. He thought of his mistreatment by Boaz. Mistreatment he'd been freed from with his servitude to Valan. The aftermath of the punch he'd suffered for aiding the mad mage had also faded, like the rest of his past. Boaz was dead. The hobgoblian priests he once served were dead. Valan was dead. So what now?

Many of his kin would never come to this point in their lives, would never even be in such a wonderful land as this. So now that he was here, where should he go? What should he do? He used to dream of such a thing happening but knew he would have to first be free of Boaz and his tribe. And that never seemed likely. But now that he had this newfound life, he realized he'd never seen himself ever being truly free. It was far from encouraging, but it was the truth. Now, if he could just find the rest of the truth that was lurking about the recesses of his brain, and—

"Rise, Hadek," said a soft, inviting voice in Telboros, startling the goblin from his thoughts.

"Who's there?" He jumped up, hastily looking about.

The room appeared empty.

"I have a task for you," the voice continued. It was an almost feminine tone. Hadek circled the room with his eyes, finding nothing. From out of the empty air, a figure began forming. The shape seemed female, but he couldn't know for sure, as it was wrapped from head to toe in a long, hooded black cloak. Besides obscuring her frame, the cloak engulfed her face, shading it from view. Once fully materialized, the cloak took on an even stranger nature, shimmering with cold white specks of light, so that the garment appeared as a slice of night sky wrapped around the figure's frame.

"Saredhel?" he nervously questioned. After what he'd just been through, he thought it wasn't impossible for even the goddess of the temple to pay him a visit next.

"No," the voice calmly replied. "But you have nothing to fear. I'm not your enemy, simply a messenger."

"*Whose* messenger?" Hadek asked, tilting his head, trying to pierce the inky shadows of the figure's hood.

"Take this." A pale hand darted from the black cloak. In it was a red silk pouch.

He stared at the object intently. "What if I don't *want* to take it?" He attempted to peer again beyond the hood's shadows. She wasn't a Sarellianite, that much was clear. The dress was all wrong, and the way she carried herself—with a regal bearing—spoke against a priestly nature. So not a goddess or a priestess . . . Then there was that strange cloak . . . a wizard perhaps? He'd had his share of wizards, that was for sure.

"You'll need it in the future—*both* of you will."

He frowned. "*Both* of us?"

"I don't have time for questions. But Gilban will know what to do with this." She tossed the pouch toward Hadek's foot, where it hit the floor with a solid thud. Something hard and round was inside it. Looking up, Hadek noticed he was alone once more. The figure had vanished as quickly as it had appeared.

"Well," Hadek said to himself, backing up to get as far from the object as possible, "if Gilban's supposed to figure you out, you can just wait for *him* then." He retreated to the far corner of the room, where he sat with a huff.

"If they can't tell me *who* they are or who they're *speaking* for, then I don't want anything to do with them or their *gifts* either. I'm not dumb enough to start getting into another mess now—and in a temple of Saredhel no less." He attempted to find something else in the room more to his liking, but slowly his head returned to the pouch.

"Nope. I don't want anything to do with you." He decided to study the window again while he waited for Gilban. But try as he might, he couldn't endure more than a few brief moments of observation before he cast a cautious glance back at the pouch. He sighed. This was going to be a long wait.

•●•

Rheminas' Fingers could clearly be seen even from Antora's coast. Like massive fire pits, the volcanoes smoldered away, hinting at their far-from-dormant state, continually threatening a potentially devastating eruption.

The cluster of five volcanoes was named for the god of volcanoes, whose hand—seen with some imagination, each volcano forming a digit—was clawing its way up from the earth. And while the site was an interesting one, with some legends all its own, its most noteworthy claim to fame was as the place where the ancient linnorm Gorallis dwelled.

All of Tralodren knew of dragons and linnorms, but few had ever seen one in their lifetime—even generations of lifetimes. To see a linnorm, though, and survive was something from which myths were made. And of all the linnorms, Gorallis was the oldest and largest. Said to have been born when the world was young and mortalkind hadn't even begun to establish its hold over Tralodren, Gorallis was spoken of as an unstoppable force.

Scores of legends, stories, and myths had been told of him over the centuries. Many claimed he'd lived on every part of the world, moving as he grew larger, wealthier, and more powerful. Like most tales, it was hard to know what was true. But what was known for certain was for the last few centuries he'd made Rheminas' Fingers his home. Over those years he'd also gathered a great army to serve him.

Through the centuries he'd enlisted a band of cutthroats and petty thugs, turning them into the Red Guard—a feared and loathed band of warriors who scoured the lands of Tralodren looking for treasure their master had lost over the years of migrations . . . or simply coveted. They were relentless fanatics who hoped for nothing more than to die in their master's service, whom they worshiped as a god.

As the Red Guard changed through the generations, so, too, did their master. Gorallis was thought to be immortal. Some tales claimed Gurthghol created him as one of the first of his race. But if he was immortal, he was still showing some signs of age. Often he would sleep for years at a time before waking to demand the guard bring him more wealth and information about the world, which had changed while he'd been dreaming.

As the years passed, Gorallis' naps stretched into longer slumbers. Those of the current generation hadn't seen their master in their lifetimes. It proved to be the longest rest the linnorm had ever taken. None of the Red Guard was worried, however. They knew he would awaken at the right time, and when he did, they'd be ready to serve the glorious linnorm in whatever he called them to do.

This awesome worship had given rise to a small sect of Red Guards who set aside combat to form a priesthood. At first they were akin to scribes who kept records of the commands and life of Gorallis along with the workings of the Red Guard's growing community. In time, they developed rituals and an air of reverence that eventually turned into a functioning religion called the Order of the Flame.

One of the most devout priests of the order was a slender, middle-aged Celetor named Hilin. Unlike the Celetors who called the jungles and swamplands home, Hilin belonged to a desert-dwelling group that lived around the Southern Lands and some patches further north. He had a dark complexion, like all Celetors, but his was lighter than the shades found among the other pockets of the race. His hair was also straight, not the short, curly style common to his other kin, and his eyes were a soft brown.

Hilin's face was still young and fresh, which mirrored his untiring devotion to the order. He'd entered the priesthood shortly after his sixth year, but had felt an urge to be part of it since before he could remember. In the thirty years since he'd joined, he'd learned much of Gorallis and his nature, which helped increase his devotion with each passing day. His god had lived through the Shadow Years, the wizard kings with their four ages, and into modern times. Such a thing was unheard of for any mortal being, even a linnorm. Gorallis had lived longer than any creature Hilin had ever known. This alone was proof Gorallis was equal with the gods—if not one of them—and worthy of worship.

Hilin continued to work on the scrolls in his tent as service to the great Gorallis. Plans had been underway to construct a suitable temple, but so far nothing had been done. Many wanted to wait and get clear direction from Gorallis after he'd awakened. This meant that, apart from the largest of the five volcanoes in which Gorallis slumbered, their places of worship and study were still makeshift dwellings: crimson tents amid the slowly expanding village.

He had many speculations as to when his master would awake and used them to work out formulas and equations to try to find this truth. He'd yet to be successful. Every day he woke, hopeful and praying that it would be the day the great Gorallis rose from his slumber. He wanted to see it before his death, to be able to honor his god while he yet had strength and breath. He'd seen some priests fall into Mortis without ever knowing Gorallis face to face. He wasn't going to share such a fate, if he could help it.

Today, as with days previous, he reviewed his calculations and prayed to the Crimson Flame for insight about what to do next. As he prayed, he felt a presence enter his mind. With it came the sensation of all around him darkening as if a black cloth had suddenly descended. In the midst of this darkness came a shining light, a brilliant orange shimmering brighter than hundreds of torches. This orange light appeared near him as he stared, trying to discern what was making it.

"All has been made ready," a voice whispered in his ear as a figure emerged from the orange glow. As it grew clearer, he saw that the glow came from a globe held in an old, blind elf's hand. He assumed the elf was very poor—perhaps even a beggar—given his simple brown robe and hemp belt. If not for his reading and transcribing, Hilin never would have known the other's true racial heritage—he looked like a sickly elf, if anything. But it was clear from his pale gray skin the man was a Patrician elf, whose race made their home far to the west.

"I hold the key," the old elf informed him, "and I am bringing it with me." The vision fled just as suddenly as it had appeared, leaving Hilin pondering what he'd just experienced.

•●•

"So, Your Sagacity, the mission was a complete success." Gilban spoke in Pacolees, the language of the Patrious, as he addressed Diolices, the elucidator. "We not only retrieved the information and kept it from the Elyellium, but the ruins were totally destroyed. They're now out of the hands of the rest of the world as well." He paced before the elucidator, chest puffed out with pride.

Huge columns of black marble sprouted from the silver-veined gray marble floor. These veins pulsated with life, splitting and joining again before stopping at a great black stone dais that shimmered like fresh oil. The dais rose six feet from the floor and was covered with thin grapevines that caressed its steps, intertwining with onyx roses and thorns along its base.

Statuary of every size and shape skirted the room. Most were made of white marble or precious metals—some were even glass—and they deepened the room's profound richness. These statues of past elucidators, who'd served since the founding of the institution centuries before, spied all the corners of the audience chamber, not missing anything playing out before their lifeless eyes.

The throne on which Diolices sat had a back carved with a fan of palm leaves completely overlaid with gold. The arms were crafted of thick cedar in the shape of majestic griffins. Life seemed to be just a breath away from these carvings—as if at the slightest touch they'd snap open their beaks with a sharp, shrill cry. Between these creatures resided a thick red velvet cushion, beneath which the griffins' four golden talons held the whole seat off the ground.

Around the throne stood four guards garbed in polished-steel scale mail. Each was crowned with a pointed, open-faced, turban-clad helmet, and carried a tulwar and a long spear. Their swords were strapped to their waists, the spears gripped in their right hands. In their left each held a medium-sized shield emblazoned with the emblem of the republic: a silver spread eagle whose left-facing head glowed with a white nimbus, all against a green background.

"Praise the shade of Cleseth," Diolices said, smiling. The elucidator knew that by sitting on top of the dais, it seemed he was all that mattered in this world of columns and statues. He also knew all this splendor was lost on the blind seer.

Diolices was every bit the figure of a perfect Patrician elf. He was slightly smaller of frame than the rest of his kin, but his hair was a cascade of churning onyx, his eyes violet crystals against his angular face, which was forever set with a regal expression that had only deepened over the years. The light gray hue of his skin contrasted with his ornate, topaz-studded yellow robes of state.

He was of middle age and had seen many changes in the land of his ancestors during his tenure. Crowned not more than forty years prior, Diolices was proud of his reign thus far, and the people seemed to agree with him. His fellow kin praised him as the best to have held the throne since the days of Cleseth. A bold assertion, but Diolices still had a good many decades ahead of him to prove worthy of such accolades.

To help remind him of this, a larger-than-life, pure-white marble statue of the nation's first leader stood behind his seat. The figure looked strong but struck a pose of relaxed rule; its gentle, subtle smile and clear, clean gaze spoke of its self-assured power. Dressed in a simple flowing himation, the image expressed the noble ideals of a royal prince who relinquished his birthright to his fellow subjects, allowing them to control their own destinies. It also gave the appearance to all who came before Diolices that Cleseth was quite literally behind him, sanctioning his rule.

The Speakers of the Voice—the elected representative branch of the government—were absent for this debriefing. Diolices had requested it. He was the one who'd given Gilban leave to complete his task in the first place, and he didn't see the need to invite them for the initial report. He'd tell them the details soon enough, after he'd had time to digest it.

This wasn't totally out of character with the office, but it wasn't as things had once been, even only a few generations ago. The change was organic, kept in check by various political counterweights, but as the years progressed, these checks and balances were diminished and removed by a plethora of means, both minor and major. The voice of the people was still present, but with each new elucidator it grew softer in favor of a single enlightened ruler, subtly embracing more autocratic traits and tendencies with each new generation—the very thing that had caused their split from Colloni millennia ago.

Diolices watched Gilban closely. He was amazed by the path Gilban had chosen in life. He had given up his sight so that he might be blessed with the gift of prophetic insight from Saredhel. The seer had been old even when Diolices was a child. He didn't know of anyone who had known the priest with normal vision. Though he was blind and, to those who didn't know him, seemed feeble, Diolices knew the truth. More than once the priest had proven his worth.

His unique power of divine sight, more potent than that of his priestly equals, had saved the Patrious on many occasions. Twice before, attacks by wandering beasts had been halted. Gilban had even predicted a severe drought, allowing the republic time to prepare for and survive the potential disaster. So when Gilban came asking for the means to travel to the jungles of Taka Lu Lama and stop the Elyellium from getting dranoric knowledge long thought lost, Diolices didn't hesitate to support the seer's efforts. Upon hearing of his success, he knew he'd made the right choice. The republic would be safe for many more years—as would all of Tralodren—now that such knowledge was securely in their hands.

"The nation is pleased with the results, and Rexatoius remains safe from any Elyelmic threat," he said. "But where's Alara? You said she helped you every step of the way. Shouldn't she share in the honor?"

Gilban bowed his head. "She has decided to stay behind to mend some fences."

"Mend fences?" Diolices wasn't sure what he meant, as Gilban was known to speak in metaphors from time to time.

"With the Nordic knight I spoke of earlier," said Gilban. "He was quite insistent about taking the knowledge back with him to Valkoria."

"Which he didn't."

"I didn't give him much of an option."

"No, you didn't, did you?" Diolices smirked as he recalled Gilban's quick thinking. No doubt it had saved his life, along with the ancient knowledge.

"What I saw in my vision was quite clear," Gilban continued. "If we didn't retrieve the knowledge, it would have found its way to Elyelmic hands. Alara remained behind, of her own free will, to help break the news to Rowan's superiors."

"I doubt they'll be swayed by her efforts." Diolices released a sigh. "But what's done is done, I suppose. She won't come to harm, though, will she?"

"Not that I have foreseen."

"Strange, though, that she'd leave you so readily, and in the hands of a goblin, no less." Alara's separation from Gilban was the hardest part of the seer's report to fathom. From what he'd learned of Alara before she and Gilban had departed, she wasn't one to be so impulsive. But, as he said, there was nothing anyone could do about that now.

"I've been well provided for. Saredhel has seen to that."

"I'd have to agree," he said with a slight nod. "And speaking of him, I trust you and your fellow priests will inform me about your plans for him?"

"Once Saredhel has set a clear path before us, we will act accordingly," said Gilban. "Until then he'll be our guest."

Diolices nodded. There really wasn't much more he could do or say on the matter. If Saredhel had indeed brought him here, then she could be trusted to take care of him afterward. And he really didn't think either she or the priests would thrust him out onto the streets. Which meant the public sentiment would remain where it should be: focused on the recent success of Gilban's mission.

"Well, no doubt you can do with some more rest after all you've endured. You've certainly earned it," said Diolices. "And when you do, you can take heart in having done a great service to your nation."

Understanding he was being dismissed, Gilban bowed. "Blessings upon you," he said, before leaving the room as easily as any sighted person would. And once more, Diolices was amazed at the sight.

He knew word would spread—faster in some quarters than others—and that was good. The more the people knew of these developments—outside official channels—the better for him. Word of mouth always spread faster and was more readily believed than official proclamations. But this also meant the news couldn't be kept from the corridors of power. He only had a small window to fine-tune his official statement. It would be thorough but concise, with nothing to offend or disrupt the relationship that existed between the various political powers across the republic. He'd use what time remained to rehearse—polishing off any rough edges he might have missed.

•●•

"And that was when I awoke," Hilin finished informing the three similarly garbed men gathered around him. Like Hilin, they were all high priests, and had been summoned shortly after his vision. What he'd experienced was clearly a momentous thing and needed to be shared and discussed at the highest level of study, lest they missed what Gorallis was telling them.

They had taken to meeting in a common tent set aside for gathering the people to worship the Crimson Flame. The tent was large enough for three divisions. One, fitted with a makeshift altar, was for the common rank and file. Another room was set aside for the priests to study and maintain the needs of the altar. Then there was the smaller third area for gatherings of the high priests.

Simple and commonplace in appearance, the area contained only a circle of four wooden chairs—one for each of the four high priests in service to the ancient linnorm. The only light was the daylight filtering through the white cotton roof. A fainter glow emanated from the red-dyed outer walls.

"It's clear it was a sign," Nagal said, stroking his white beard as Hilin took his seat. He was the eldest of the priests, and as such was also the most revered in his understanding of Gorallis. "But of *what*?"

"His awakening," said the much younger Grell to his left. The clear-eyed Celetor was the youngest of the high priests, having entered the ranks just a few months prior. "It has to be. We all know the master must awaken soon—it's inevitable as the tide. And now he's given a taste of this truth to one of his high priests."

"Gorallis is not one to be so unclear with his meanings," counseled Aylan, a stout, bald-headed Celetor. "He's always been clear about his desires before. This vision of Hilin's isn't like him." As second eldest, his words carried great weight.

"And who of us ever had a vision from the Crimson Flame?" Nagal sought each of the others' faces with a serious eye. "None from my day, and certainly none after. So who are we to say how Gorallis can bless his priests with insight?" The question birthed a contemplative silence among the priests.

"I'm convinced it is a portent of things to come," Hilin softly continued. "It has to be."

"Then what do *you* think it means?" asked Aylan. "If it's from Gorallis, it wouldn't have been given without some means to understand it."

"It *must* have something to do with Gorallis' awakening," said Hilin. "All has been made ready. We must now look for the next step."

"Which is to await the arrival of an *elf*?" Aylan raised an eyebrow.

"I've been a servant of Gorallis long enough to know when something is spiritual and when it's not," said Nagal. "As have most of you, I should hope, else you wouldn't be serving the people. The question isn't if what was shared was real, but who sent it. And I, for one, believe it was from Gorallis." Nagal studied Hilin closely. "You said the globe had an orange light to it?"

"Yes," said Hilin, "a bright orange light."

"And was the object more like a globe or an egg?"

Grell's face beamed. "Yes! I see it now! An emerging of new life—a *rebirth*. It's like he's going to hatch again. Maybe even become something *greater* upon his return."

"Then what of the elf?" asked Aylan.

"I wouldn't be surprised if he brings the key to Gorallis with him," said Nagal.

"Or maybe the elf *is* the key," said Grell. "It's been a while since we've had a worthy sacrifice."

"Yes." Nagal gave a nod. "Another possibility. But the meaning is obvious. We need to be ready, watching for him to cross our path. The rest will be clear soon enough."

"A Patrious actually coming to help our lord." Aylan still couldn't believe such a thought.

"It wouldn't be the first time our lord has crossed their path," said Hilin. "And one of their kind aided him long ago, don't forget."

"And now it seems they will again." Nagal nodded in satisfaction. "We should tell the rest of the guard to keep alert. There wouldn't be a vision if things weren't soon to occur."

•●•

Dismissed from Diolices' presence, Gilban returned to his quarters. It felt good having a new staff in hand. He hadn't realized how much he relied on his previous one until he'd lost it in the jungle. He'd claimed a new one shortly after Hadek had been placed in suitable quarters and took to it instantly. Thinking on the goblin started him pondering anew. He had his doubts about how Hadek was doing and just what was going to happen to him now that he'd been taken to Rexatoius.

The more Gilban had gotten to know him since their return, the more he felt there was something odd about the goblin he couldn't quite place. He sensed the hand of Saredhel was powerfully upon Hadek in a very personal way. But it was in a way that he didn't quite understand. There was something else too . . . something even greater he couldn't yet fathom. It was almost a visible weight he could see in his mind's eye resting upon the goblin's shoulders—a compelling mystery he couldn't unravel. He trusted Saredhel would reveal these things, as she had others, in due time. He had enough to contemplate as it was.

As soon as he'd left the court, Gilban began to feel a strange sensation at the back of his mind. It felt like a person pulling the stuffing out of a pillow—and his mind was that pillow. It was a strange clawing sensation—not an attack, more an attempt to show him what was occurring around him, one piece at a time. As he made his way to the temple, the troubling quandary about the nature and source of the presence he'd felt on Hadek returned. What was Saredhel trying to tell him?

He silently strolled through the picturesque capital. He recalled, as he walked the familiar streets, what they'd looked like when he still had sight to behold their splendor, the wonderful aroma of fresh, exotic spices and cooking fish and lamb adding to the rich scenery. That had been over one hundred years ago, but those days seemed like yesterday. In his mind's eye he could see the tall spires of marble and granite sculpted to look like fluted columns seeming to support the very vault of heaven.

He remembered the outside of the Great Library, thinking back to the last time he made a visit before his vision had faded. The gigantic domed structure, capped in shimmering bronze and held up by solid granite and marble, was a sight to mist anyone's eyes. He recalled the eight caryatids holding the roof above the foundations as one entered through the massive gold leaf–covered cedar doors. He recalled being smitten with the lovely ladies—paragons of Patrician beauty in every sense of the word. The real wonder, though, was inside, and that was something he'd never enjoy again. For what use were books to a blind man?

He turned his thoughts from the library. Color exploded all around the blind elf. In his imagination, it was radiant. He thought about the bronze domes, capping off mighty buildings like inverted turnips. Dotting the landscape, they fought for recognition among the tall, colorful statues of heroes and shapely maidens of earthly delights; fabulously painted, frieze-covered arches built in homage to mighty wars and reigns of past elucidators; and fountains crafted as though the spouts and pools were alive, shimmering with the sun's reflection on their golden surfaces.

Soon enough, Gilban reached the temple he knew more intimately than his own body. Having counted the steps, learned the sounds, and memorized the familiar smells, he could gauge his location anywhere in the city. He carefully measured his footfalls to the grand staircase of the temple, then up the gray marble steps to the silver door carved with the Eye of Fate, the all-seeing eye of Saredhel, seer of all things that are and will come to pass.

He traced the sacred carving with his hand. It was smooth and warm to the touch, like living flesh. With a small effort, he opened the door. The temple was the largest in the world dedicated to Saredhel, but wasn't as highly trafficked as temples to other gods. There was a steady flow of those looking for answers to mundane personal dilemmas, but these were a mere trickle, given the overall population of the city. Only in dire need or perilous times of personal or national crisis would the steps become crowded with petitioners desperate for insight. During times of peace and tranquility, its marble steps were thinly populated.

Gilban was greeted with the soft aroma of lilac and honey, as the expensive incense, made specifically for the temple's use, was burned day and night for the pleasure of the goddess. Saredhel was the force behind the visions that the priests were granted. She held back the veil from the eyes of the worthy, offering a glance of what lay beyond. Without her efforts to help steward the curtain dividing the seen from the unseen, madness would ensue, as visions would propel themselves into the minds of those who were unable to stop them from coming, much less handle and interpret them.

Now that he had reported to his religious and secular superiors, Gilban would have time to speak with Hadek. He wanted to figure out the goblin's connection with all of this. He couldn't rush the matter, though; he'd learned that long ago. Impatience was a terrible companion, as Gilban knew all too well. His youth had been filled with a nervous energy unseemly for a member of his race. As he aged, though, he took in the fruit of patience as it ripened on the vine of years. His training with the priesthood additionally had taught him the benefit of maintaining a calm outlook. That lesson helped him greatly over the decades, even saving his life a good many times.

As he played absent-mindedly with his simple hemp rope belt, he thought about Alara's welfare. He took an unsentimental approach when he reported the matter to Diolices, but he'd have been lying if he said he wasn't concerned about her. Alara had done something even *Gilban* hadn't seen, but he trusted she'd find a way through it in the end. She had to, if his premonition about her safe return to Rexatoius was correct. But the future was always in motion and people still had free will.

He entered the temple courtyard, bowed to his fellow priests when he heard them draw near, and at last entered the temple's inner sanctum. Respected members of the order, in their own simple brown woolen robes and shaved heads, the priests greeted him as their equal. Gilban, while not the highest of the ranked priests, was certainly elevated and treated with much respect. In light of his recent success, his reputation was raised even higher.

Like him, the priests were impaired or maimed in some way in order to gain the blessings of Saredhel. Some were lame, others deaf or blind. Some had minor weakness of limbs, body, or a loss of other senses. They all had paid a price for the great blessing they now carried: the ability to peer beyond the veil and see deeper things than others could. Not one of them would claim that the exchange was unfair.

He continued making his way quietly through the long and smooth halls slick with gray marble and lit with small pools of light that trickled from lofty ceilings. Along with the brass and glass chandeliers, clear glass-paned windows honeycombed the walls. The hall grew silent and cold as he entered the older sections. Over the years, these sections had become less used, making them an ideal place to keep something or someone out of sight. He approached the door of Hadek's chamber. It was plain, totally unadorned. The handle was a simple wrought iron knob, which his hand easily found.

"Hadek," Gilban said, opening the door. He spoke in Telboros, the only language they both shared.

"Gilban?" The goblin's voice was calmer than he was used to, and there was something that seemed off in his tone.

"What happened?" he asked as he entered.

"How did you . . ." Gilban could imagine Hadek's amazed face. "Someone dropped something off for you."

"*Who* did?"

"I don't know." There was more hesitation in the goblin's voice. "I think it was a woman."

"You *think*?" He advanced further into the room.

"I didn't get a good look at her face, and she wouldn't tell me anything, only that you'd understand when you got it."

"Got what?" Gilban stopped.

"A pouch. She left it on the floor in front of you."

"Strange." Gilban tapped the ground before him with his staff. "Cloaked, you say . . ."

"With a black cloak."

"Then certainly not a priest."

"And she sort of appeared and disappeared too," Hadek added meekly.

"What do you mean?" Gilban directed his head at Hadek.

"She was here one moment and gone the next."

"Interesting." He returned to his stick poking. "Ah, here we are." His staff brushed up against what felt like the pouch.

"Are you sure you want to touch it?" Hadek sounded scared as Gilban bent to retrieve it. "I mean, who knows what it is?"

"Who knows, indeed?" Gilban took up the pouch and then stood tall once more. There was something with weight inside, and the pouch felt like fine silk. "But it wouldn't be anything to worry about. There are protective measures in place to safeguard against anything harmful intruding into the temple."

"Well, they didn't stop *her* from making an appearance," Hadek returned.

"They would have if she wasn't up to any good."

"You *sure* about that?"

"Is there something you aren't telling me, Hadek?"

"No."

There wasn't any deception in the goblin's voice. Fear, but no deception. "Then your visitor made quite the impression."

"She wanted to see *you*, not me," he explained.

"I don't think that's entirely true. I'm not that hard to find, and she didn't come to *my* quarters, but to yours. There had to be a reason for it. And this"—he gave the pouch a tiny shake—"is a large part of it."

"So perhaps what we have is an answer to a question we don't know yet." He wanted to say it could be an answer to the thoughts plaguing his mind since he'd left the elucidator, but didn't. Such a disclosure at this point in time would serve no purpose.

Instead he gently opened the pouch and put a hand inside. "Seems to be a pouch with a round object inside. It's like stone or—"

•●•

"Gilban?" Hadek didn't like this one bit. The seer's face had gone slack and his eyes had swelled to the size of walnuts. He took a step away from him, steeling himself for the worst.

"Gilban?" He skirted the priest's perimeter en route to the door. Just as suddenly, Gilban came to himself, causing the goblin to jump.

"We have to go to Antora." Gilban closed the pouch and affixed it to his belt in one smooth motion.

Hadek gave his head a shake, wondering if he'd heard correctly. "*We* have to?"

"I can't do it on my own. I need another set of eyes and there's no time to try and find someone else for this mission."

"What mission?" A knot was growing in the goblin's gut. "What are you talking about?"

"We have to take this pouch to Gorallis," Gilban said matter-of-factly, and started for the door.

"*Gorallis!*" Hadek's face turned ashen. "Gorallis, the Crimson Flame?" Even in the jungles of Taka Lu Lama, the linnorm's exploits were known. And none of them inspired anyone to hope for surviving even a *chance* encounter, let alone a *planned* one.

"Yes." Gilban stopped, remaining calm.

"So you want me to lead you to a linnorm?"

"Yes."

"Which is on Antora."

"We don't have much time, Hadek."

"And I'm not going with you." He crossed his arms.

Gilban faced him with a look of surprise. Had Gilban really thought he'd be eager to plunge after him like an excited pup? It hadn't been more than a few hours since he was running for his life from one life-threatening disaster. Why would he want to dash right into the path of another?

"You're free to make that choice," said Gilban, "but understand all who have been chosen cannot deny their purpose for long."

"What's that supposed to mean?"

"That you don't have much time to make up your mind."

Hadek paused. "You'd really go there on your own?"

"If that's what it came to."

"But that place is cursed! They even call it Doom Maker's Island. And Gorallis will roast you alive. Or worse."

"No, he won't. We'll be taking a gift in exchange for another item we'll need," said Gilban cryptically. "Once he has it, he'll be more than happy to let us continue on our mission."

Hadek's brow scrunched into a furrow of flesh. "What are you talking about?" Now he had a sore brain, in addition to his knotted stomach and panicked heart.

Gilban only smiled. "All will be revealed in time—that is, if you're there for the revealing."

Hadek hesitated.

"Make your choice, and quickly."

"You *are* coming right back after this is over, right?" He found it hard to withhold the concern in his throat. Gilban remained silent. "I mean, you're not just going to leave me here . . . right?"

"I can't say. Too much is in flux at the moment. But you're free to do whatever you wish. You're no one's slave."

Hadek let out a frustrated sigh. "But where would I go?"

"To Antora, if you're with me." Gilban slowly resumed his egress.

"What aren't you telling me?" Hadek inched after him. Gilban said nothing, pressing forward with all the speed of a turtle. "Back in the ruins you said something about me having a greater purpose," he said, trying a different tack. Gilban stopped, but kept his back to him. "Is this part of it?"

"I guess you won't know if you don't come along." Hadek didn't need to see the elf to know he was smirking as he spoke. He hated not knowing what was going on, but he didn't see another alternative. If he stayed what could he do in the temple while Gilban was away, or worse yet, if he never came back? But if he did accompany Gilban, what then? Assuming they actually weren't turned into a pile of blackened bones or worse, he supposed he *could* possibly find his way to some new locale. Maybe Gilban might even be willing to transport him somewhere else in the world—somewhere more hospitable for living out the rest of his days . . . But that was a *big* gamble—for either option.

And then it hit him. Gilban was supposedly able to see the future. If he didn't see Hadek's death, then things couldn't be all *that* bad. Well, not *all* that bad. He didn't think knocking on Gorallis' lair was going to be a simple, pleasant thing. He wasn't an idiot, but it was plausible . . . at least according to Gilban . . . So what would it hurt then if he went along? If anything it might actually speed things along with the seer, getting whatever was needed and back to the temple faster than if he tried blindly stumbling after it himself. And the sooner they got back, the sooner Hadek could move on with his life.

"All right," he said, releasing another sigh. "But just to Antora and back."

Gilban nodded. "Then we need to hurry," he said, continuing for the door, this time with more speed. "We need a few supplies, and I need to inform my superiors."

CHAPTER 7

TIME IS BUT A RIVER THAT CAN BE SAILED BY THOSE
WHO KNOW HOW TO NAVIGATE ITS CURRENTS.

—Old Sarellian saying

Gilban and Hadek sat quietly on a dark walnut bench outside the main doors to the temple's inner sanctuary. The doors, fashioned of a strong, dark-stained oak polished to a high shine, were unadorned save for the Eye of Fate on the two halves of the closed portal—the two parts of the eye met at the center. They had been sitting there for almost an hour. Silent and empty, the hallway outside the chamber did nothing to distract from the long wait for an audience with Gilban's fellow priests.

Gilban hadn't been any more open about what he was planning or what they were going to do since they'd left Hadek's room. He'd instructed the goblin to change his outfit, and he had. This after taking a quick bath during which he gave his head a fresh shave. Gilban also took a razor to his stubble while he waited for Hadek's preparations.

Hadek now wore a wool tunic dyed bright blue, short boots of black leather, and plain brown pants. The clothing came from a pile of donated goods the temple received. He assumed the original owner was a halfling or perhaps a gnome, given the garments' size. They'd also both packed some meager rations—enough for a few days' travel. Gilban said they wouldn't need more than that. When pressed for more information, the seer remained silent. Instead, he led Hadek to the bench, put his staff against the wooden seat, and sat down to await the audience he'd requested with the highest-ranking priests of the temple.

Hadek let out a loud sigh. They'd been sitting here for far too long. With Gilban not talking and no one else about in the empty, elaborate halls, he was getting pretty bored. Bored enough to scream. He peered up at the sightless seer. Maybe now he could get some more answers out of the old elf. Then again, maybe not. Gilban was proving to be pretty stubborn. At the very least they could have some conversation to help pass the time.

"How much longer is this going to take?" he finally asked.

"Patience, Hadek." Gilban continued his contemplation of the doors.

"Why do you have to talk to them again?"

"All will be revealed in time," he said, slouching a bit lower.

"You still don't want to tell me what this is about?" Hadek continued. "Why we have to go to Gorallis?"

Gilban said nothing.

Discouraged by the silence, Hadek scraped his boots across the stone floor. He was shorter than the races the bench was made for, but could still touch his toes to the stone if he leaned over far enough. "You think it'll be dangerous, don't you? That's why we're here." He kept his eyes on his boots. Perhaps keeping his gaze focused somewhere else would help. Maybe Gilban could sense him staring at him and didn't like it.

"One can never know these things with total certainty." Gilban slumped lower still on the bench. "Fate isn't a game, and the future can never be totally accurate in one's own assessment."

"Aha!" Hadek turned to the priest, his tactic forgotten. "Then we *will* die."

"You'll die just as I and everyone else will eventually die. There's no question about that. The better question to ask is *when*. But as I've told you already, we won't die on *this* undertaking."

"But if you did know the fate of someone's life, would you tell them even if they asked you?"

A grim humor played across the elf's face. "Many have asked me that question, and yet I never grow accustomed to it. Let us just say then, for the sake of argument, if I'd answer such a question, how would it benefit the person asking? Would that person still die?"

"Yes, but then he knows when."

"True. But how would it *help* that person?"

"It would just help him with life in general. He'd be better able to live his life." Hadek was losing his train of thought and growing confused.

"Help him *how*?" Gilban stared at the goblin, who thought the elf wasn't so much looking *at* him as *through* him.

"Like I said, you could get ready . . . *prepare* . . ." Hadek scratched his head, wrinkling his brow. "It would help to know so you could avoid it, I guess."

"Does anything on Tralodren live forever?"

"No," he replied sheepishly.

"How, then, could one avoid an event all share? You wouldn't be able to avoid your own death. That's the point. You'd spend countless days, weeks, months, or even *years* trying to *stop* the event from happening, pandering to your weaker, more selfish emotions. And life should be about living, not fearing death," said Gilban, setting his focus once more on the doors.

"Oh," Hadek said, renewing his interest in his swinging feet. "So you're *not* going to tell me when I'm going to die."

"No." Gilban adjusted himself again on the bench. "Everything will be fulfilled as it should be. Don't worry about things you can't control. Rest your mind. You will need it soon enough."

Denied answers on one mystery, Hadek tried for answers to another. "So what was in the pouch?"

Silence.

The goblin sighed, raised his tired, sore head, and stared at the strange and almost frightful Eye of Fate across from him. "You don't want to tell me what you meant about me having a great purpose either, do you?"

Gilban drew still for a moment, not even taking a breath. He seemed to actively be thinking the matter over—at least Hadek thought he was.

"I can't answer that yet. It hasn't become clear to me. Just still your mind and rest your spirit. All things will be revealed soon."

Hadek released another loud, bored sigh.

•●•

While Hadek grew more restless with the wait, Gilban appreciated the time to think. There were strange happenings of late. First, there was the threat of the hidden knowledge falling into the hands of the Elyellium, and now the matter that had brought him here. If time was progressive and not circular, as some philosophers and even some of his order claimed, then the challenges and threats would get deadlier and further reaching. But to what end? If there was some grander purpose behind these matters he'd yet to see it.

His hand went to his belt, where the pouch with the orb rested safely beside him. He pondered what fate it had tied him to. Not more than the size of an apple, the globe was smooth and hard, like marble. It was heavy too, like a lead weight, and gave off a great heat when in hand. He recalled how the orb felt like a stone that had sat too long under an angry sun when he'd first grabbed hold of it. That might not have been the wisest of actions, but he couldn't get any real answers without some physical contact with it—and the temple *did* have its precautions, as he'd pointed out to Hadek. The orb, though, was something of a puzzle.

As he sat quietly on the bench, he tried calling the orb to mind, but was unable. He repeated this exercise off and on while they sat, when he wasn't bombarded by the goblin's questions. Hadek wasn't the only one with questions. He too wanted to understand what this whole event, tied somehow to the orb, was about, but something he didn't understand was blocking him from discovering it. He wouldn't give up.

He obsessed over the orb not just because it was an intriguing mystery, but because of what it first revealed when he'd taken hold of it. In a vision of swirling light and sound, he saw a cloud of shimmering mist whose radiance was like a bank of clouds at daybreak. Silver and gold billows of dust mixed in the mist as a strange voice told him to seek Gorallis and give him the orb. In exchange he would receive an artifact from the time of the wizard kings, which he should take to Arid Land, and a place called Galba. When he asked why, he was told this would help to stop an advancing threat. He was also told he'd be joined at Galba by those from his previous mission.

When he asked exactly what the orb was and why it was such an item of interest, he was informed Gorallis would agree to anything for the orb, as it was his lost eye, plucked from his skull centuries before. Fascinated, he'd tried to figure out what preternatural traits the eye must possess to have survived all those years, passing through who knows how many hands until it reached his. To think he held in his grasp the very eye of a creature of legend, one who might indeed have seen the birth of Tralodren—as some legends say—was beyond astonishing.

He had wanted to ask more of the voice but was unable. Something held his tongue and stilled his mind. It still did whenever he tried to probe for more insight and understanding. Instead, he felt compelled to carry out the task just as he'd been instructed and trust the missing pieces would be revealed along the way. The vision was standard in that regard.

He'd experienced enough visions to know this one should be obeyed, even if he didn't understand who told him to take on this task. Saredhel had been faithful in aiding his discernment of true and false visions, as well as making him familiar with magical effects that could mimic them. With her help, he had quickly deduced what he'd received was genuine. Though he might not have been able to figure out who had given it to him, it had been allowed by Saredhel, of that much he was certain. And that was all he needed to know to round up Hadek, some supplies, and be on his way.

Whatever this threat was, he felt it close at hand. He also felt, as he sat waiting for his audience, that he should hide the orb. Something was going to happen in the near future, and he would do well to safeguard it. He supposed now was as good a time as any to do so. Taking the pouch around his belt and holding it in his hand, he whispered a soft prayer to Saredhel. As he prayed, he rolled the pouch and orb together in his hands. He felt the orb slowly growing smaller and smaller until it was no larger than a walnut, the pouch around it shrinking to match the new dimensions.

Gilban pushed the smaller pouch with the orb into one of the secret pockets in his robes. It swallowed the object whole. There wasn't even a bulge showing where the orb had gone. He felt better about the issue already. When he had need of it, the orb would be close at hand. Until then it would be hidden from any passing eyes or wandering hands.

The sound of the doors opening caught his attention.

"Finally," he heard Hadek mutter.

"We will see you now," said a young female voice in Pacolees.

•●•

Hadek had thought the temple and the city in which it resided were richly adorned, but they paled when compared to the sanctuary. The large circular room was engulfed in gilt. Gold and silver overlay covered a stylized relief of vines that crossed the room, bisecting it with a foot-wide stripe. On the bottom portion of the wall, under this stripe, ivory planks provided a smooth and delicate contrast to the opulent decor.

He craned his neck at the high ceiling that rose the entire height of the temple. Covering the concave surface of the concrete dome were minutely detailed painted figures. He couldn't make them out from such a great distance, and the upper reaches of the sanctuary were dim, despite the blaze from a hundred silver candles on an enormous brass candelabra descending from the dome's center that filled the spacious room below with a shimmering metallic glow.

The young priestess leading them limped a bit, favoring her right leg. Hadek noticed it as he took in the colorful polished stone mosaic beneath his feet. The floor was a sea of green and blue with a silver circular outline in its middle. Inside this circle stood four ornate silver pedestals, each standing in the center of a lavender tiled circle, with a larger fifth pedestal and additional lavender circle between them. A bright silver basin, filled with mercury, rested on each of the pedestals. Though he wasn't sure what to make of these, he was convinced from his time with the priests of his tribe that they might be used for some sort of divination.

The rest of the room was awash in rich murals of priests and visions, symbols and tales older than the temple itself. He wanted to take a closer look but didn't have the time. The other priests were waiting.

All five of the priests were Patrician and dressed in the same simple brown robe, leather sandals, and hemp belt as Gilban. Two were female. As far as Hadek could tell, the women were middle aged and seemed unimpaired. Beside them were three men: one young and two middle aged. The youngest of the three had a shriveled left arm that hung limply at his side like a dry strap of leather. Another of the men was blind. His companion didn't *seem* impaired, but Hadek noticed he favored his left leg when he moved. The young priestess who'd invited them in made her way to the priests, who were all standing outside the central lavender circle.

"Welcome, Gilban," said the blind priest in Telboros, which Hadek assumed was for his benefit, since they probably would have used their native language if he wasn't present.

"Thank you for your audience," Gilban replied in the same language.

"Are all the priests here like this?" Hadek whispered up to Gilban.

"Like what?" Gilban asked as they stopped outside the silver circle.

"You know . . ." Again he kept his voice just low enough for Gilban to hear. "Everyone I've seen since we've got here looks like—"

"An invalid?" Gilban interrupted, no longer whispering. "What one gives up for the ability to see beyond the veil is worth the sacrifice. To judge any of us by what we lack is to ignore what we have inside us and what we have to offer. That is the power of our faith and our goddess."

"Gilban speaks the truth," said the other blind priest. "I may lack sight, but my hearing is still good, and Saredhel's boon is worth the diminishing of my physical vision, as I'm sure Gilban would testify to as well."

"I'm sorry. I—"

"No need to apologize," said one of the middle-aged women in calming tones. "All are judged by some standard, but it is with Saredhel's we must find merit."

"We have prayed and meditated on your recent request and find ourselves in agreement to grant it," the younger male priest with the withered arm continued. "While this revelation is not from Saredhel directly, we sense her favor in seeking it out."

"What are they talking about?" Hadek asked Gilban.

"They will help us get to Antora." Gilban never let his attention leave the other priests.

"So they have a ship?"

"Something better." Gilban's lips curled into a subtle smile.

"Indeed," said the other blind priest. "Enter the circle."

Hadek cautiously joined Gilban in moving forward.

"As it has already been said," the blind priest continued, "we have come to the conclusion of our meditation. The time and place of your arrival has been set, and now you must journey to it. But what you have proposed is linked with a particular segment of time, in a very intimate fashion. Because of this, you both will have to travel some distance and emerge further downriver than where we currently tarry."

The middle-aged priest with the bad leg shifted his attention to Hadek, adding, "Do not be distracted by what you see. That would cause you to lose your focus. Should you lose your focus, your pathway to your destination will alter, and you'll end up in some other place and time."

"I don't want to mess anything up," Hadek said. "I'll just close my eyes."

"Your natural vision won't be of any concern in this journey. You'll be seeing with the eyes of your spirit, which don't need physical eyes to see."

"Oh." Hadek's shoulders dropped slightly.

"So be mindful of where your mind drifts," the other middle-aged woman chimed in, "and prepare as best you can."

"I have, as I know Hadek has as well." Gilban's reply struck Hadek with more than a little surprise, but he said nothing. If Gilban thought he was prepared, then he supposed he was probably as prepared as he was going to be.

"Then let us begin." The younger priest with the withered arm directed them to move into the space between the four lavender circles. "Stand in the midst of us."

Gilban stepped into the fifth lavender circle, as did Hadek, though more carefully than Gilban, whom he followed to within a few steps from the larger pedestal. Outside the circle, the six priests surrounded them. He sensed a shift in their manner as they prepared for their ritual.

The young priestess led the others in the invocation, speaking in Telboros while the others spoke in Pacolees. Her peaceful voice had a surreal, almost dream-like quality about it. "Here is the beginning. Here is the end. Spawn of Dreams, we ask your favor. We ask your presence. Send your favor upon this priest and goblin, we beseech you, oh great Saredhel. They embark on a journey birthed in mystery and tied to time. Show yourself in your great majesty through our petition and send these two beings to their destined location across time and distance. For what is time to you who mastered it long ago, and what is distance that you should be hindered by it when you sit above the world looking down upon all?

"Come now. Take these two into the river and guide them to the path they are meant to walk." The priests fell silent. Hadek noticed they'd closed their eyes and were swaying rhythmically as if to some music only they could hear. After a moment of this strange silence, Hadek started feeling odd. The whole chamber seemed to sway like he was about to faint, before everything was swallowed in lavender light.

It was a swimming sensation at first, like he was caught up in a tide he couldn't fight against; he could only struggle to stay afloat as it surged forward. But it wasn't water, just a force of something like it—something invisible yet powerful that compelled him beyond the lavender light and into a panorama of images.

"What's happening?" he shouted, though he didn't have to. Gilban was right beside him.

"Keep your mind focused on the task at hand," he instructed.

Hadek tried to keep his eyes clamped shut. It didn't do any good. Just as he'd been told, the images rushed through his head, blurring his mind. Images of forests and glades, caves and seas, many flying past his inner sight before he could bring them into focus.

"I can't keep them out!" he screamed, panicking.

"Don't focus on them," he heard Gilban say. "Just relax and let the current carry you."

He tried to relax his mind, but found the pictures only slowed down instead. He couldn't keep them from entering, and that prevented him from focusing on one image alone. He saw himself as he had been in the past, in the ruins before he'd escaped. No sooner was that image gone than a new one came to mind. This was of him just prior to where he found himself now: a small green creature amid the priests of Saredhel. This image moved slower than the first, and he felt drawn to it. It felt familiar and normal and it tugged him toward it, urging him to place himself back into that situation . . .

No! This wasn't where he was supposed to go.

The goblin shook his head, clearing his thoughts, only to have another image rush into view. This one was the strangest yet. In it, he saw a gray expanse stretching for miles. This expanse was littered with debris: stone, mostly, from broken columns and statues—endless ruins of buildings stretching as far as the eye could see. The longer he let his mind dwell there, the more clearly he could see a lone figure in the gray gloom. A figure he knew. It was the Telborian he'd met briefly in the jungles of Taka Lu Lama. What was his name again? Dugan. Hadek marveled at the strange outfit he wore and the flaming sword in his hand. And then there were the—

"Withdraw from the thought!" Gilban said, putting a hand on Hadek's shoulder. The touch returned him to his senses for a moment, disrupting the scene he'd been viewing like a pebble cast into a pond.

"You see the future, but you see it too far. That's not where we need to go." Gilban's words began to sound hypnotic to the goblin. "Focus on Antora and let yourself feel the current the others have laid for us to follow."

Hadek tried doing as Gilban said, but it was hard. The image of Dugan wanted to stay, swimming back and forth in his thoughts, going from blurry to clear, blurry to clear. It was a very strange and compelling image, but he knew if he were to keep focusing on it, that was where he'd most surely go . . . and he didn't want to be there. He scrunched his eyes tighter in concentration.

"Antora. Antora," he repeated to himself in a low whisper.

A few moments more and the image of Dugan amid that gray, gloomy desert of ruins was gone. The wild and untamed land of Antora materialized in its place. He found the land pulling him to it, willing his body to follow along as he concentrated on the location. He could almost smell the waves he saw hitting a beach and feel the warm air on his skin. Antora. Doom Maker's Island. The home of Gorallis. And the two of them were going right into his waiting talons.

CHAPTER 8

Ultimately, one walks this path alone.
Those who try to walk beside you are either
a hindrance or a tool for working your own ends.

—Malakin Keris, Telborian wizard king
Reigned 610 BV–572 BV

Night filtered through the pines which Cadrissa had been walking through with scant rest since she'd awakened in the roc's clutches. Sweat had become like a gown upon her skin, reminding her of the other difficult treks she'd made through the Marshes of Gondad and Taka Lu Lama just days earlier. At least she wasn't sloshing through water and jungles.

She'd stayed silent since their start, deep in thought and enjoying the unspoiled beauty around her. As in many things, reading about Arid Land was nowhere near the same as actually walking through it. Some things had to be experienced rather than explained. This line of thinking had caused her to ponder the life of an adventurer for a short while. But if she'd known saying yes to Gilban and Alara back in Haven would have led to all of this, she would have given the matter a greater amount of consideration.

"I need to rest," Cadrissa stated meekly.

"Again?" Cadrith was less than pleased. The lich slowed to a stop while spying the tops of the trees. "We should be there soon. The darkness will only help our efforts."

"Well, I'm going to need some rest before then." Cadrissa collapsed with her back against a nearby trunk. "I can't keep this up forever."

"You won't have to." Cadrith's comment was far from comforting.

"Just what do you need me to do anyway? If you're a wizard king, I can't really be of much help."

Cadrith slowly stepped toward Cadrissa, his unliving body no more the worse for wear from their long hike. One advantage to being a lich, she supposed. Another was his chilled aura that helped to cool her down.

"The sooner I reach Galba the sooner we can part ways."

"You never told me who Galba was."

"The last gatekeeper on my path."

"The path of power?"

"There's no other path to speak of, and in just a short while I'll claim the ultimate reward from it." A lone owl's hoot pierced the thickening night. "But that isn't the path you'll walk, is it?" Cadrith leaned forward on his staff with a glare that made her stomach turn. "You're the curious sort . . . bound to the path of knowledge just like *she* was . . ."

Revelation dawned on the wizardess. "The clothing in the tower—those other robes—and the baby clothes . . ." Her tongue stopped moving when her gaze drifted to the infant skull adorning the lich's staff.

"Which are nothing to you or me." Cadrith straightened to his full height, his face more stone-like than before.

"Then why keep them?" She bit her lip when she realized she'd spoken aloud.

Cadrith's eyes narrowed to slits. "Because at the time they had a purpose. But they, like *other* things, will soon outlive that purpose.

"You've rested enough," he said, turning on his heel. "If you keep your mouth shut for the next couple hours I might allow you to sleep for the night."

Cadrissa remained seated as she watched him depart. When he started to disappear amid the trunks and darkness, she forced herself to stand. Though throbbing and sore, she commanded her feet forward, hoping what Cadrith had said about sleep was true. If she was to be of any good to anyone—including herself—she needed to be as prepared as possible. That meant having her full strength and mental faculties about her. Which meant having to soldier through these next few hours. Dradin have mercy.

Somehow she persevered, and at last the two of them came to a halt. From what she could tell nothing really stood out from anything else she'd been seeing all day. She didn't think that was a good sign for gauging their progress, but was too tired to give the matter any further thought. Finding a rough patch of open earth, she fell like a sack of rocks.

Cadrith located a spot a few paces from her and took a seat, resting his staff atop his crossed legs. He wasn't far enough away to keep his cold aura at bay but at this point she didn't care. She worked her cloak into a suitable pillow and yanked her boots from her sorely vexed feet. Cadrith watched with mild interest, like a tree himself.

"How much further do you think it is?"

"We're close. You'll need to be ready."

"For what?" she asked, leaning on her elbow.

"Sleep fast. I want to be moving before first light."

She was too tired to press for more. Since a new day would be fast upon them, she lay down to take what slumber she could. She'd worry about the matter of food and water tomorrow. She didn't want to push more than she already had and knew even Cadrith would have to allow her some water—and maybe food—before long. He wanted her at or close to her best . . . at least for the time being. The only question was what spell did he think she was able to cast that could be of any help to him in getting to Galba?

The ability to wield magic was an inherited trait. Some believed it was passed on from the dranors, who many claimed were the forefathers of mortalkind. The handful of mortals who took the time to develop the talent for magic were able to wield influence and control over the sixteen cosmic elements. This was made possible by the strength of will, spirit, and inherited cistern of ability—often called a well—residing in each mage. It was this threefold force that made it possible to cast spells. However, the vessel that cast them was still given to the limitations of mortalkind. They also needed rest in order to recover from the pressures placed upon them during spellcasting.

Practice in making use of magic allowed a mage to grow in strength and ability. Their well was like a muscle in many ways: the more it was stretched—the more it was worked—the stronger it became, and the longer it could supply energy to the spells a wizard desired, for as long as their spirit and will could hold out. These, too, could be increased with continued effort, but it didn't come easily. That was why magic was so disciplined and regimentally focused in nature.

If one let their craft slip long enough, they'd find their grasp of what they once had known greatly diminished. Cadrissa had learned this lesson at the academy, as she watched too many students take time off from their studies only to return weaker than they'd been before they left. It was this revelation that made her resolve to always be a student. And this experience with Cadrith was certainly going to teach her much . . . if she was able to survive it.

•●•

"It feels more like a tomb than a temple," said Kendra. Cadrith had to agree. Of course both of them had had a hand in making it that way. Raston had sent them there earlier in search of some information, and they'd all eagerly complied. Well, most of them did. After the initial fighting, it was only he and Kendra who had remained to complete their mission. And because of that they were now able to make use of something else they'd discovered in the unique opening presented to them.

Endarien's mountaintop temple was unchanged since that last visit. The fires had long burned out, of course, but the dead remained just as they'd fallen. Most had rotted away or been picked clean by the birds that called the mountain home. Fed upon by the very creatures they once revered—a fitting irony, he supposed. The stench of death was still present, but not as strong as it could have been, thanks to the birds. An ashy dust coated a few places and tainted the air, but he didn't pay it much mind.

"Not too much of a surprise given how few hold to Endarien these days," he said, peering at the hole in the ceiling where the Storm Lord had cast a bolt of lightning that had killed one of their fellow mages during their previous visit. While it might have frightened the others with them, it hadn't stopped Cadrith from discovering the secret hidden in the chamber. "If this keeps up, it'll be even easier to raise in rank once we return."

He and Kendra had hurried to the temple and the hidden room where they'd first encountered the ancient dranoric knowledge and mosaic. Raston had coveted such insight and Cadrith had learned why. With his master away, and only Kendra and himself the last living beings inhabiting Raston's tower, he felt it was time to follow the final part of his path and claim the ultimate reward. The longer he stared at the opened wooden door behind the remains of what had once been a statue of the great Endarien, the better he felt about doing so.

"A dranoric artifact in a temple to Endarien," Kendra pondered aloud as she approached the door, enacting a spell that brought light to the previously hidden room. "It's still amazing to think about." Even from where they stood the two wizards could clearly see the circular mosaic on the wall facing them. "Imagine how long it's stood there, and now here we are before it," she said, clearing the threshold.

"Built in part to defy the gods," Cadrith said as he joined her. "Fitting, I suppose, that we seek to do the same." Everything was falling into place. He had command of the Mirdic Tome and knew how to operate the portal; and while he and Kendra waited, they'd grow in power before returning and laying claim to the throne.

"Just as you seek to defy your master." Cadrith and Kendra spun on their heels, surprised to see Raston glaring at them from the temple's battered entrance. Well . . . glaring as much as his ruined features could allow. He thought Raston's eyes would go any day now, as there wasn't much of anything left holding them in place. "So you've gone from *wizards* to *thieves*. But then I gave you ample opportunity to act, didn't I?"

"We didn't have time to wait." Cadrith did his best to make himself sound obedient. He'd become quite skilled at doing so over the years and found himself falling back into it rather easily. "We're closer to the end than ever."

"Indeed we are." The frigid chill that always flowed from the lich's core fell upon his former pupils as Raston passed between them en route to the mosaic. "That's why I wrapped up a few remaining things before I came here myself."

"Then we can all leave together." Cadrith noted the optimism on Kendra's face and pitied her. She was still hoping this would end well. He knew better. It was clear what was going to follow. The question was, what was he willing to do about it?

"While you'd like that, I can't allow it," said Raston. "You've both outlived your usefulness, and I won't permit any more competition."

"But we stayed with you all this time, put up with you and all your ways—even served you well." From the corner of his eye Cadrith watched Kendra's countenance fall. For a moment he wanted to reach out to her—to comfort her—but shoved the thought aside. This wasn't the time for such things. If they were going to achieve what they'd set out to do, it was time for each of them to look to a greater goal and put personal need aside. And right now that greater goal was surviving Raston's wrath.

"Yes, but I no longer have need of you." Raston focused his eyes on Cadrith as what flesh remained on his skull stretched into a smile. "Just as Cadrith thought to use me, so I've been using you—and it's paid off well. I've had my research advanced, making the progress needed to bring us all here. So now"—the lich stretched a gloved hand his way—"if you'll return what you stole from me, I *might* let you live."

Cadrith knew it was a lie. Just as he knew there was nothing under his master's gloves but frail, bony digits. He'd offer the same thing were he in Raston's position. He knew how valuable the Mirdic Tome was. Even the short study he'd made of it showed there were greater things to be discovered that would allow him to rise even higher than Raston in power and place.

"You really trust us alive with your tower?" Cadrith stalled for time.

"Even as I speak, all items of note are being taken into the Tarsu's charge, which I can retrieve after I've returned."

"So then all you want is the throne." Things were finally clear to Kendra. Good. The sooner she saw the truth, the easier it would be to help her embrace it, turn away from the foolish path of knowledge, and commit to the path of power—the only *true* path for any wizard to follow.

"That's all it's ever been about; all this—and you—were just a means to its end. Even my becoming a lich was only to buy time. Something you've both run out of." Cadrith watched the empty sockets on the infant skull atop Raston's staff glow with a strong purple light.

Before either of them could react they were enveloped with a flash of that same light and frozen in place. It was a simple spell, but cast from a powerful wizard. It would take Cadrith time to unravel it—if he could find a way to do so without being able to move or speak. As it was he could barely draw breath.

Raston raised his staff, beginning the spell to activate the mosaic. "Kelram Kor! Nuth-ral ackleem ishrem giltan giltan ock-roth!" Cadrith watched the tiles spin and turn with a violet light. He was going to do it. Raston was actually going to beat him. He'd open the portal, kill him and Kendra, take the tome, and leave them to rot. He'd been so close. So close.

A massive explosion suddenly shook the room, accompanied by a blinding white light. For a long moment all he could hear was the ringing in his ears. Eventually, his eyes focused. He found himself lying on the debris-strewn ground with bits of rock and other pieces of the room where he and Kendra had been standing scattered all around them.

He noticed a few cuts, scrapes, and bruises, but he could move again. Whatever had happened broke Raston's spell. Which meant he'd survived. But not for long if Raston was still about. Leaping to his feet, he immediately focused on Kendra, who lay prone a short distance from him.

"Kendra?" He raced to her side. "Can you hear me?"

Her eyes opened with a dazed flutter of lashes. "A-am I in Paradise?"

"Not yet. Are you hurt?" He cautiously helped her up, checking for anything that might show she was more wounded than she appeared. Miraculously, the two of them had survived the explosion in fair condition.

"I'll live," Kendra said, looking over Cadrith in turn. "And you?"

"The same."

"What happened?" Kendra made a study of the once hidden room. What remained was a fragmentary wall which did little to cloak the mosaic from view. It wasn't much use to anyone now. A large crack had torn across it like an open wound.

"Raston failed and destroyed our escape in the process."

"And Raston?"

"I don't see him." Cadrith couldn't find any sign of his former master.

"Do you think he's dead?"

"Probably."

"Then why didn't we join him?"

"I don't know." It was a good question. One he'd ponder later. Right now they had to refocus their plans.

"So . . . we're stuck here?"

"Only for the moment," he said, starting to leave. "But if what he said was true about the Tarsu at the tower, we have to get back before everything's gone." They didn't have a lot of time. He wasn't sure how long the Tarsu had been in the tower, and if they were of sufficient number, they'd pick the place cleaner than the birds did the bones scattered around the temple ruins.

"But why would he turn to the Tarsu?" Kendra followed.

"I don't know. But maybe we can strike a deal—"

"Hardly." Raston's voice drew Cadrith's attention to a pile of debris at his feet. There, nestled in some of the rubble, was a skull with red flaming sockets. He was amazed he'd missed such a thing in his previous sweep of the room. "You won't find the Tarsu to be that hospitable—at least not without *me* standing at your side."

"I think your days of standing at *anyone's* side are over." Cadrith tried to hide his amazement at the sight. He failed. Raston should have been dead, crumbled to bone and dust like the rest of his body, but yet here he was—part of him, anyway. It only made Cadrith want to devour more of the Mirdic Tome and lay hold of *all* its secrets. Not far from the skull was Raston's staff. Cadrith summoned it to his right hand while causing Raston's skull to hover before them with his left. "And you're hardly in any position, let alone *condition*, to worm your way into anything else."

"Don't be a fool, Cadrith!" The skull's jaw opened and closed as if it still had muscles and tendons working the bone. "You don't know everything—"

"Maybe not yet. But I will. And then—"

"It'll be too late. The Vindication will come. You'll be helpless before it."

"I'll *never* be as weak as you," he said and formed his left hand into a fist, tapping into his well with all his hate and wrath. No protest or scream escaped the lich's lipless mouth. The red tongues of flame simply winked out of existence as the old bones disintegrated into grainy dust, falling onto the debris-strewn floor below. He waited a moment, making sure there was nothing left of his former master—or anything else that would stand in his way.

Confident Raston was truly gone, he stormed from the temple, taking a strong hold on his new staff as he did so. It felt right to him, like it should have been his from the very beginning. Between the staff and the Mirdic Tome he'd have more than enough resources and power to tap into when the time came. He was now fully his own master, with a clear path to his final ascent into the highest ranks of power and glory.

•●•

Cadrith found himself again in Arid Land at night. He couldn't say he'd fallen asleep. He didn't need to anymore. It was more accurate to say he'd been lost in the past. It had been happening more often than he liked of late. He needed to be alert. While he might have been at the doorstep of triumph, it still wasn't guaranteed. That's why he made sure he'd kept his staff all these years. Taking it from Raston was one of the wisest things he'd ever done. It had helped keep him secure in the Abyss, after he'd weakened over the centuries. Now it would help make this final part of the process possible.

According to Raston, he'd created the staff from the skull of an infant godspawn. The offspring of a god or divinity and a mortal were rare, but there were many tales about them if you knew where to look. He'd thought it was mere boasting on Raston's part at first, but upon reading the Mirdic Tome discovered how such a thing was possible. Now, having wielded the staff for so long himself, he knew his former master's claims were true.

He'd never learned who sired the child, nor had he cared enough to investigate further than Raston's notes that gave a semblance of a story. A woman had come to him seeking money for the infant. Raston had enough sense to see the potential that was there. After using it for a few experiments, he took the godspawn's life and had its skull crafted into his new staff. While the staff resembled other enchanted objects of the age, it held a powerful secret that could be unleashed as a matter of last resort.

The godspawn had been killed in such a way as to tie its death throes and part of its potential power into the staff itself. When called upon, the staff could unleash the full fury of those throes and power on anyone or anything the wielder desired. Neither Raston nor Cadrith had used this raw power, since it would take the staff and possibly its wielder with it, but it was a suitable weapon against the most powerful of foes if and when needed. He'd been tempted a couple of times to tap into it but was glad he'd resisted. Doing so kept him free to use it with Galba when the time was right. He knew he wasn't going to take the throne without a fight, and the staff would make sure that fight was brief at best.

He watched Cadrissa sleeping, noting how well she'd fared so far. He'd pushed her hard, he knew, but he also understood he had to be wiser about doing so in the future, lest he risk her life too soon. Her questions were starting to become annoying, but he soldiered on. Once they got to Galba it wouldn't matter. She'd have served her purpose and he would finally have his prize. Contemplating the time to come and all the glory and power he'd soon embrace held his focus until the darkness faded into dawn.

"Get up," he said, giving Cadrissa a kick. When she was too slow to respond he thumped the end of his staff against her head.

"It can't be morning already," Cadrissa said as she rolled onto her back, putting a hand to her eyes to keep out the light.

"We're close now. We need to keep moving." He watched as she forced herself to her feet, standing as strong as she could, preparing for what was next.

"*How* close?" the wizardess asked, running a hand through her tangled hair and bringing another memory of Kendra to mind.

"Close enough," he said, stepping from Cadrissa's side. "I assume you've been taught how two wizards can combine their wells for greater effect?"

"I've been told it's dangerous."

"To fools, perhaps. But with skilled mages it can be a great boon." Cadrith watched her eyes widen as understanding of what he was proposing dawned across her features.

"You can't be serious. Why would a wizard king want to combine his well with someone so much weaker?"

"It's time for you to earn your keep. We're going to cast another spell that will take us right to Galba."

"I thought you did that before." She was getting bolder the longer she was with him. Hopefully, questioning was all she was being emboldened to do.

"We need to make better time. Now that I've seen the lay of the land I can better pinpoint where we need to go."

"I still don't see why you need me," she repeated. "You could have done all this on your own." Cadrith watched another epiphany flash across her face. "You can't cast any spells, can you?" She didn't even try to hide her glee. "You haven't cast one spell since we were attacked by the roc. Why else have we been walking all this time? If you were in such a hurry, you'd have cast another spell, and we'd have reached Galba a long time ago."

A very clever girl. "Just get ready for the spell."

"No," Cadrissa said, defiantly crossing her arms.

"What?" Icy rage rose from the lich.

"You need me," Cadrissa continued firmly, "and I want some answers."

"So this is your attempt at a threat?"

"A bargain. I want to know what's going on, why you abducted me to begin with, and why you're trying to get to Galba. In return—"

"I'll give you one more chance," he said, towering before her and making sure to lock his gaze on hers. It helped to have eyes again to do this, which he made sure were glaring with hints of danger if she continued this foolishness. He needed to be as dramatic as possible if he was going to bring her to heel and have done with this tantrum.

For a moment they just stared at each other, unflinching in their resolve. Cadrissa did her best to remain strong, but Cadrith knew she was bluffing. "Prepare yourself to combine a spell. If you do, you'll have all the answers you'll need." Cadrissa held his gaze for a moment longer before crumbling with a sigh. "You'll need to open your mind and focus on the center of power close by. Can you do that?"

"Yes." She sighed once more. "But this isn't a safe practice. If we—"

"Just do as I say." Cadrith masked most of his rage with a stoic but stern tone. He'd won; there was no need to risk stoking a new round of rebellion.

Cadrissa closed her eyes.

"Ready?"

"I think so."

He drew still, focusing on his own well while reaching out from it toward Cadrissa's. While he was blocked from casting any magic on Arid Land, as Cadrissa had deduced, he could still dip into the well of another to cast spells. She was right that it wasn't the safest of ventures—for either participant—but being the greater skilled and more powerful, he believed he could minimize any potential threat. The added natural benefit which Cadrissa brought into the equation only bolstered his confidence.

Reaching up and dipping into her well, he siphoned the energy he needed, first casting a simple location spell for Galba. It was easy enough to find. In a land where magic isn't known or practiced, there could be only one source for the swell of power he detected. They were closer than he thought! All the better. It would make for a less taxing spell, leaving Cadrissa available to tap into again once they'd arrived. Now that Galba had been located, he just needed to enact a transportation spell, which he began speaking. Both he and Cadrissa were enveloped in a violet aura before becoming transparent and fading away into nothingness.

Cadrith materialized a moment later with Cadrissa beside him. She had the look of one who'd been dealt a hard blow to the stomach—slightly hunched over, trying to catch her breath—but otherwise appeared fine. Once he fully materialized, Cadrith quickly sought Galba's stone circle. They must have materialized almost right on top of it. But all he saw were trees . . . some of which were vaguely familiar. It wasn't until he saw the outline of the dead roc, about a hundred yards behind him, that all the pieces fit into place.

He stabbed his staff at the earth with a murderous bellow.

"We're back where we started . . ." Cadrissa was confused as well as concerned.

"What did you do?" He glared at Cadrissa.

"N-nothing."

Grabbing her by the collar, he yanked her forward so they were face to face. "*What* did you do?" he said again, slowly and with more force.

"I just focused on the source of power, like you told me."

"Then we should be at the stone circle, not back where we started from!"

"I did everything you said," said Cadrissa defensively.

"So then tell me. How did we get here?"

"I don't know." Her face had grown even paler and her lips were as thin as knife blades.

He tossed her aside in disgust. He was so close. It was all in reach, and now this. It was Galba. It had to be. Cadrith had known she'd be a hindrance to his magic but thought to get around it with Cadrissa. It seemed Galba wouldn't be so easily conquered. And *he* wasn't going to be so easily defeated. He'd play her game if that was what it took. In the end he'd have his prize.

"Get up," he said, uprooting his staff. "We have a good day's march before us."

CHAPTER 9

If there is no enemy within, then the enemy outside can do no harm.

—Old Celetoric proverb

"That looks promising," said Vinder, pointing out the village in the distance. Together he and Dugan had been working their way through the Grasslands of Gondad. Though taking a different path than the one they'd originally traveled with the horses, they were doing their best at moving in the same general direction. With grasses rising over Vinder's head in places, it was easier to lose one's way than he'd thought. Even with Dugan's additional guidance, the uniformity of the terrain could make for some confusing traversing if one wasn't careful.

"You up for one more run?" Dugan asked from beside him. They'd been pushing themselves hard for the last few days, taking what water they could find in small pools or ponds they encountered along the way. They'd dined on wild game: more rabbit and some snake, cooked over what scraps of wood they could gather as they went. It was enough to keep them going. And it was free.

"Looks about just under a mile," Vinder replied. "We can make it."

Dugan started into a jog before increasing into a run. Even with his shorter gait, Vinder kept the pace beside him. As they drew nearer it became clear that this was really more of a small community—perhaps a multifamily settlement working its way into something larger with each ensuing generation. No matter, it was still a welcome sight. If there were some supplies they could purchase, bread and waterskins, they could better weather the days ahead.

They slowed to a trot as they reached the first building—a shack with two small windows on the wall facing them. A handful of Telborians watched them approach with a curious eye but no malice, as far as Vinder could tell. They were dressed in the common garb one might expect from such places, in limited earthen hues. But it wasn't rags, and they all appeared clean enough. Another good sign.

"Welcome," said a deeply tanned, stubble-faced man. He stood in front of the others and was most likely the one in charge of the community—a magistrate or just a locally accepted leader. "You look like you're in need of some refreshing."

"You could say that," said Dugan.

"How long have you been in the wild?" The other took them in from crown to heel.

"Longer than we should have been," said Vinder. "We have some coin if you have some supplies."

The man nodded. "It's not much, but it should help you on your way. Where you headed?"

"Elandor," said Vinder.

"Haven," said Dugan.

Both answers apparently pleased him. "Well, we have a blacksmith, a common shop, and even a public bath."

"I could do with the bath," said Vinder. "I can still feel parts of that marsh in my beard."

"How much is it?" Dugan's interest was clearly piqued.

"Three copper for the use of the tub and water," he replied.

"A fair price," Vinder mused. "What about horses? You have any for sale?"

"How much were you looking to pay?" Vinder didn't know if he liked the sudden sparkle in the man's eyes.

•●•

Rowan listened as Alara recited what he'd been sharing with her about Nordican. They'd done little else since leaving Nalu and the others, which was fine by him. It was a welcome distraction from his thoughts, and the less they had to talk about other subjects, or worse still, keep company in silence, the better.

"How was that?" she asked after finishing.

"Better. You're starting to make more sense." He stretched his shoulders. The weight of the shield resting over them wasn't much, but the burden grew as the day progressed. Thankfully, he was getting used to it.

"I wasn't expecting it to be so different from Telboros," she replied.

"You can see some similarities with all the human languages once you study them a while," he explained. "They all came from the same source, after all."

"And you really learned all of them?" Alara was still impressed with that detail he'd shared before their first lesson.

"If I need to represent and help humanity, I need to be able to speak with all of it."

Alara considered some fluttering birds as they continued making a path through the tall grasses dominating the landscape. "I think I'm starting to miss those horses."

"Just be thankful we've had a peaceful time. It could be a lot worse."

"Those lizardmen were bad enough."

"There are worse things out there than lizardmen," he continued.

"Like fiends and that skeletal monster." As Alara turned to face Rowan he felt the same troubling unease he'd been struggling with return. "It was still amazing what you did to that fiend."

"Panthora helped me." He refocused his thoughts and sights on the way ahead, searching the swaying grasses for some greater sense of achievement. They'd been walking for half the day already—and several days previous to that—with scant sense of any real progress.

"I guess she did," said Alara. "Between the two of us I don't think we could have been any real threat otherwise."

"I'm sure your own god would look after you." Rowan noticed Alara's features fall flat.

"Maybe . . ." She let her gaze drift back onto some chirping birds resting on the swaying stalks.

"Hello," said Rowan in Nordican, "what is your name?"

"My name is Alara," she replied in the same language. This part was always the smoothest. It was the simplest and now the most rehearsed phrase they'd been practicing.

"And why are you here?" he continued in the same tongue.

"I have come to speak to you about Rowan's mission," she continued with equal skill.

"I think you almost have that part memorized," he said in Telboros.

"I should hope so. We've been at it since leaving Nalu's camp."

"But that's just the introduction. What you share is going to be more complicated. And once they start asking questions . . ."

"It will work out." She placed a hand on his shoulder. A ripple of nervous energy fluttered across his body at the touch.

"So what *do* you plan on saying?"

"The truth."

Rowan waited, ready for her to share more. When she didn't, he nodded at her to continue.

"I suppose we'd better start by telling them why you don't have that information and backtrack from there," she said.

"Okay, so then you're going to want to . . ." He started putting together a new collection of phrases for her to learn, making sure they were as simple and straightforward as possible—not only to learn but also to understand. They didn't need any ambiguity or confusion when Alara started getting into the heart of her message.

•●•

The sun was setting as Dugan and Vinder brought their horses to rest. The grasslands had finally started to recede as farmland, game trails, and paths took over the landscape. Freshly bathed, with a full stomach and a slaked thirst, Dugan felt better than he had in weeks. And with a fresh horse and some supplies, his confidence was even higher.

"Looks like we've found the main road," said Vinder, pointing out a dark strip of hard-packed earth in the distance.

"The horses made good time." He gave his brown steed a soft pat on the neck.

"They better for how much they cost," Vinder grumbled.

"Well worth it," he replied. "I wasn't about to run all the way to Haven."

"Yeah, that might have raised some eyebrows." The dwarf shared a lopsided grin. "Not that you won't anyway with all those swords on your belt."

"Once I get to Haven it won't matter."

"You might not want to lighten your load too soon," said Vinder. "You might be tempted to spend it faster than you realize."

"Only on what's important."

Again Vinder shared another lopsided grin. "Depends on what someone considers important, I guess. And it's not much of my business anyway."

"You sure I don't owe you anything for the horse?" Dugan watched Vinder carefully as he spoke. When the dwarf first offered to purchase horses for both of them, Dugan was taken aback. And while he might have been able to find a way to pay for his own, having the animal provided for him made things much easier. The more coins he could keep for Haven, the better. Vinder never explained his motives for the sudden act of kindness, nor did Dugan probe too deeply into the matter. Though as they were close to parting ways, it just felt right to inquire one last time.

"We're fine," he replied. "If you don't ride it into the ground you might be able to get a decent price from someone in Haven. It might even be better than what I'll get in Elandor."

"I think you can drive a pretty hard bargain." Dugan smirked. They let the scattered chirps of crickets and birds fill the silence as each studied the road.

"So I guess this is where we part ways," said Dugan at last.

"You were better company than I thought." There was some honest appreciation in the dwarf's voice. "Take care of yourself."

"The best I can," he replied. "And a safe journey to your mountains."

"Yeah. Drued willing," Vinder muttered before peering back out over the road.

Another silent moment passed between them until finally Vinder moved into action. "Well, I better get moving." He urged his horse further east. "The sooner I can get to Elandor, the sooner I can get my money."

"I'm sure those Olthoans will be pleased to see you," Dugan called after him. He thought he actually heard the dwarf chuckle. He hadn't seen much, if any, mirth from him since they first met.

Dugan watched the gap between them widen, saying nothing. There really wasn't anything more that needed saying. Once again he found himself impressed with how well Vinder rode. Dwarves and horses, from what he understood, weren't always so common—the size difference between them often creating some challenges—but having watched him now all this time it was clear Vinder didn't have any difficulty with keeping things under control.

For a moment Dugan thought back to their travels through the marshes, slightly embarrassed about how he treated the dwarven mercenary when they shared the same horse. Of course he didn't know any better and he didn't plan any of the mission either. Still, he wondered how much Alara—and especially, Gilban—knew when putting everything together. But there was nothing he could do about any of it now, only let the past be the past.

Eventually, when Vinder had cleared quite a distance, Dugan guided his horse south and east. The first road would soon enough widen and give way to a paved thoroughfare, according to Vinder, which would lead him to Haven. Deciding to cover more distance Dugan urged the horse into a fast gallop, putting everything further behind him. There was only forward now. Forward and his future.

•●•

Though Rowan was asleep his mind wandered in a dream. A dream he'd been reliving every night since leaving Nalu's camp. In it he was in his armor, but without any weapons, and standing in an open green meadow with no one present for miles. As in nights previous, from out of nowhere an unseen force grabbed him. Once again, he struggled with his opponent until he could pull him to the ground. Like before, once subdued, his attacker's face was clearly made known. It was his own. Following this revelation he'd awake, sweaty and gasping for air. Fully alert, he'd clasp his knees to his chest until steeling himself into taking some more rest.

In tonight's dream, however, there were some changes. When he had discovered his attacker was himself, this time he'd remained in the dream, the figure he'd once sparred against fading like mist. Peering up from this disturbing sight, he discovered he was no longer alone. A woman was with him. Though she kept her face from him—only her cloaked back could be seen—the logic of dreams told him he knew her. The longer he stared, the more his awareness increased, until he knew full well who she was.

"My queen." In the dream, Rowan dropped to his knee.

"It's been a long journey," Panthora said, with an air of both tenderness and authority. "But how much longer will you allow yourself to suffer?"

"Suffer what?" Rowan asked, daring to look up at his goddess, but seeing only her back.

"This dream you've been having is a reflection of what's happening in your spirit and mind. How much longer will you endure this conflict?"

"Conflict?" He was still confused. "Like I'm struggling with myself?"

"*Within* yourself," the goddess corrected. "And you've been at war with yourself since before you left for Talatheal. Only now the strife grows greater, as you're forced to deal with other matters emphasizing these areas of conflict."

"I simply seek to serve you as best I can," he humbly returned. "I know I failed you with my first mission, but if—"

"Who said you failed?" Panthora was quick to interject.

Rowan wasn't sure he'd heard her correctly. "My mission was to keep the knowledge in those ruins from falling into elven hands. Obviously,

I didn't do that." He hung his head, again reliving the burning shame of his failure.

"The wrong hands," Panthora corrected. "You were to keep it out of the *wrong* hands."

"Yes," Rowan cautiously replied. "And I failed. And now I have an elf coming with me to announce that failure to everyone."

"Is that how you see it?" Panthora's question partially lifted Rowan's chin.

"It seemed to make sense at first," he confessed, "but the longer I've thought about it the less sense it makes. They're not going to believe her anyway, and if she does actually go through with it, she might end up getting hurt . . . or worse."

"If you're so worried about Alara coming back with you, then why haven't you told her she doesn't have to?"

He opened his mouth, then thought better of it. Nalu's words echoed across his thoughts: *Maybe they taught it to you in secret.*

Panthora broke the silence. "You won't be fit for my service if you continue to battle yourself."

"I don't wish to do anything to displease you. It's just your teachings—the teachings of the knighthood—hold me to a higher ideal." He lowered his gaze. "I'm still not fully able to stand in the light of your code. If there's any conflict, it's that I fight against my old nature to live up to the expectations of what you'd have me be as your knight."

"The conflict *is* between an old way and a new," Panthora acknowledged, turning her hooded head slightly, though nothing more of her face was revealed. "But it's really a war between your head and heart, your soul and spirit."

"Then what should I do?" He dared raise his gaze once more.

"Rise."

"I don't—"

"I said—rise." There was steel in her command, snapping him to his feet.

"Never forget you're my champion in light of your truest self, not what men would have you be. Understand that it wasn't by any great work of your own, but the potential I saw in you, that raised you to where you stand now.

"I've waited for someone like you for a great while." Rowan could feel the warmth of pleasure in the statement. "Someone who can come to know my heart on any matter, who can and would work out my purpose and plans across all of Tralodren."

"I'm not worthy of such a high honor." Rowan's chin dropped to his chest, humbled in the face of such praise. "Surely another knight—one with more experience—who's served you much better than—"

"Do you think I'm bound in one keep?" Panthora's words were soft, but stern.

"Forgive me, I didn't—"

"Do *you* think I'm bound in one keep?"

He swallowed hard. He didn't understand where this conversation was going and was fearful he'd done something wrong—said something insulting. "No. You're a goddess who has claimed humanity as your own. Your dominion is over *all* Tralodren."

"And," added Panthora, "though I didn't create you, I've claimed *you* as my own. My purposes for you are larger than any knighthood. But you delay and frustrate them by this endless strife within yourself. Let go and be free of it." Panthora's words struck him hard. "Let go and embrace the place and purpose I have for you."

"You *didn't* create me?" His face was awash with his confusion. "That goes against all I've learned. The Sacred Scrolls even say—"

"Understand this: it wasn't I who raised the keep in Valkoria, but the hands of men. It wasn't I who started the knighthood, but those same mortal men who called upon me. I answered them, for their intentions were pure and good in the beginning . . . but now there's coming a change.

"The day is fast approaching when I will raise up my *true* knights, and they will bring my will for all humanity to Tralodren. None will say there is a knighthood in Valkoria that speaks for only one race of humanity. The coming order will be a grand sight to behold: a new age ushering in the change I've fought to bring about since the beginning of my ascension.

"And you will be the champion of this cause. You will lead the first charge, for you are of the same mind and spirit as me, and it pleases me to see my will come to pass through you." Rowan experienced the warmth of Panthora's pleasure once again. He wished it would never end. It was like being covered in warm honey and cocooned in an aura of peace.

"But none of this will happen if you cling to internal division." Panthora turned and faced Rowan full on. He nearly stopped breathing. Before him wasn't the visage of a goddess, but that of Alara! Her silver hair shone in contrast to her pale gray skin as her violet eyes sank deep into his startled conscience.

"Your current struggle has roots in the larger one you've been waging since before you left the keep," Alara calmly informed him, though he knew Panthora's words were behind the elf's voice. "If you deal with your current conflict first, the other will quickly be resolved." Alara's eyes turned more serious. "But if you fail to deal with this, then you'll be of no use to me and instead be torn apart in the struggle."

Rowan woke from the dream. He didn't curl into a tight ball this time, but lay perfectly still in his roughly made bed. His heart raced and his breathing was hard, but not as in his previous awakenings. This was something different—a more peaceful feeling that had eluded him the previous nights. He was thankful for it.

His crumpled cloak had been used to cushion the hard ground. All was silent along the road to Elandor where he and Alara had sought rest underneath a tall oak. They'd managed to set up a simple but effective camp before falling fast asleep from the long day's journey.

He turned his head and saw the slumbering elf curled a short distance from him, twisting her own frame around the oak's fat roots and wide trunk. She looked so peaceful. The moonlight highlighted her silver hair and pale skin. While they'd started out on foot, wagon traffic on the outskirts of the marshes from nearby villages, various caravans, and other migrating groups allowed them a faster pace when they could find a ride. And once they got closer to the city the roads appeared, further easing their travel.

Rowan tried getting comfortable again. He laid his head back and began to stroke the shriveled panther paw necklace he kept hidden beneath his leather armor and tunic. He'd kept it there since he received it in the ruins of Gondad. He never let it into plain sight if he could help it, for he didn't really know what it would or could mean to others. He also didn't know what it might be capable of either. It could have been blessed by Panthora for all he knew, a holy relic or something else just as wondrous or powerful. It was another mystery amid a whole cloud of questions he didn't have the answers to. Not even Panthora seemed willing to shed any light on it. But she had said much tonight, hadn't she?

Only Rowan didn't want to face what Panthora had put her finger on. He'd hoped to try to sweep the whole matter under the rug—just endure it until he got to Valkoria, where he assumed he'd be done with it. But now that Panthora had told him to his face it needed to be resolved or he'd face an even greater failure than the one he already suffered, a hand was tightening around his heart. But that had only been *part* of what she shared.

Was Panthora telling him the knighthood wasn't where he needed to be? Nalu had thought the knighthood taught him some things that might not be true to their shared faith. Now there was this vision with similar words. Panthora had said the knighthood was built by men, not by her. She had honored it because it followed her and her teachings. But if she hadn't founded it, then who did, and why? And if she didn't form the knighthood, then what was still keeping it in her favor if she desired to form something new to replace it?

What was going on?

There were too many questions. And he'd had enough with questions and struggles for now. Deciding to take advantage of the night that remained, he closed his eyes. They'd be in Elandor by the following day and then it was off to the *Frost Giant* and the journey back home. He needed some more rest for what lay ahead.

He sighed. Even with these new revelations and questions he found it easier to relax his mind than in nights previous. Soon sleep claimed him, keeping a firm hold of him until dawn. And for the first night since leaving Nalu's camp, his slumber wasn't troubled.

CHAPTER 10

Before the gods, before time, or even reality itself,
there was nothing, and there was everything . . .

—The Kosma

Thangaria was a quiet, dead place. Once a fertile world that served as the center of an ever-expanding divine empire, it was now just a fragmentary expanse of rock. Only one sizable chunk, still called Thangaria, remained in the middle of the floating rubble. Like a ghost haunting the place of its death, the phantom sky enveloping it blocked all stars, light in the perpetual dim grayness permeating the horizon. Under this somber cloak stood the Hall of Vkar.

The hall rested on the center of the floating rock, climbing toward the tattered atmosphere. Ten stories tall, it was built of marble, gold, silver, gems, and granite, outlined by a jewel-encrusted, white marble curtain wall. The same wall was capped with spiked wrought iron and flowed a mile to the left and the right, forming a perfect square around the palace. The main gate was made of colossal silver doors detailed with an intricate scroll design. Tall towers, broad walls, and shapely turrets made the hall a surreal image of unimaginable beauty. Even the gods, when they came to the place, were awed by the sight of it.

The hall was smooth and simple yet still regal and assertive in its design. One look conveyed awe and fear, compassion and dominance. It was a fitting home for the first god, who once ruled from behind its walls. The courtyard beyond the silver gates was paved in smooth granite blocks. Once its pools and fountains had been filled with crystal-clear water and its groves of trees thrived and blossomed, but no more. Only the specter of time haunted the open space with echoes of past memories dancing amid petrified trunks and cracked pool basins.

The Hall of Vkar had become a sacred place where all the gods of the Tralodroen pantheon could meet on neutral ground in council. The council had been established to help maintain discourse among the divine family, providing each member with an equal voice on matters brought before its table, where they could debate any threat that clashed with the pantheon and their interests. Outside of the council, each god was free to rule their own realm and manage their own affairs as they saw fit, unless of course it birthed a conflict that required resolution from the council.

All the pantheon was barred from bearing arms while at the hall, as well as maintaining the presence of a personal guard, and even coming in their true form. Each god instead took on a weaker guise for the entirety of their meeting. By adhering to these rules, the peace had been maintained over many divine councils, allowing disputes and conversation to be just that: a warring of words and positions, not a place to vent disagreements in a physical manner. Though effective, the council wasn't always successful at stopping the flow of violent disputes from taking place outside the hall in the greater cosmos. But thankfully, the number of such actions could be counted on one hand since the council's inception.

With a new council called, the gods assembled inside the hall, each taking their assigned place around a long table in the center of the meeting chamber. Past the head of the table, granite steps rose to a dais. Upon this dais rested three titan-sized golden thrones, two positioned lower than the third, which rose between them. On these thrones sat Dradin, Gurthghol, and Ganatar, who claimed the highest throne.

"Are we ready to begin?" Ganatar was calm and composed. He wore a golden tunic and black pants. His tan, clean-shaven face and square-cut white mane of hair complemented his powder-blue eyes as they gazed over the gathered gods.

Gurthghol, seated at Ganatar's left, gave a nod. As with the others present, he kept his original size. His black hair was pulled back in a ponytail and his plum-hued frame was draped in a black tunic and pants with a rich purple cloak.

"Everything seems to be in place," said the green-robed Dradin. As in his true form, a close-cropped full beard matched his short white hair. Ganatar took a moment to observe his bookish brother. Like the rest of the pantheon, he was fascinated by Dradin's staff.

Even though the object he held was only a replica of the original, it was still a wonder. At the top of the shaft was an angular curve of gold, creating a large concave opening in its middle. In the center of this curve floated a crystal globe. About the size of a fist, the crystal continually glowed with a soft green light while a cloud of indecipherable whispers circled the staff.

"Let the council commence." Ganatar's voice dominated the room.

On the opposite end of the table sat the most recent additions to the pantheon: Panthora, Aerotripton—also called Aero—and Drued. Often referred to as Race Gods by those outside the pantheon, each resembled the mortal race from which they ascended. The only difference was their size: each stood twelve feet, making them the shortest of all gathered.

An elegant purple cape fell from Aero's shoulders, draping over a matching toga. The cape nearly hid the gold-trimmed white tunic underneath, but not quite. This contrasted with the more commonly attired Drued, whose deep blue eyes highlighted his white hair and chest-length, iron-gray beard, with twelve braids resting on top. Panthora appeared as a brown-eyed, chestnut-haired, dark-olive-skinned human with a panther-skin cape and medium-length leather dress.

"So we've been gathered together in fear of *one* mortal man?" Khuthon exclaimed with great disdain. He joined Asora, Asorlok, Olthon, and Saredhel on the left of the table's head.

"He isn't alone," said Olthon, Khuthon's sister. "That's why we're all here."

"But he's headed for Galba." Khuthon's brown eyes swept the faces of the others around the table. "He won't even make it close to the throne—even *with* his patron." The god of war sat back in his chair, arms crossed over the leather jerkin covering his muscular, olive-skinned chest.

"Things are not always as simple as they may seem." Olthon's blond hair fell in thick curls about her fair-skinned head and neck. A soft, sleeveless white gown hung from her shoulders. The garment had been specially made to allow for the white dove-like wings folded behind her back.

"Dead is dead," argued Khuthon, "and no mortal has ever sought out Galba and lived. It's more *simple* than you think." His wolfish grin added radiance to his thick, curly red hair and scruffy goatee.

Used to her husband's bravado, Asora sat in silence beside him. Her soft green eyes were filled with compassion. Her long reddish-brown locks outlined her sun-kissed skin with a simple elegance. She was also pregnant, which was clearly displayed in her current guise.

"So you'd have us do *what*, exactly? *Talk* with him—engage in some form of *diplomacy*?" Asorlok's eyes were a piercing blue, darting into everything like spear points. He was deeply tan, with a hawkish nose, a hairless head, and a body draped in rich clothing and jewels—mostly ruby and onyx.

"Obviously, you don't understand the forces at work here." Olthon's face grew more serious.

"Oh, I know them—better than any of you," continued Asorlok. "Which is why I know anything short of his total destruction won't do us any good."

"But is it true?" Causilla's gentle gray eyes sought out Ganatar. "Is the lich really backed by the same—"

"*Nuhl!*" Gurthghol spat out the name like a sour grape. "Its name is Nuhl. And there's no need for all this superstitious nonsense. It was beaten before and can be beaten again."

"Of course, we had the throne then," said Rheminas from beside Endarien. The leather harness, made of the same material making up his pants and boots, kept him from being completely bare chested. The coppery-red skin, bright yellow eyes, pointed ears, and fiery red hair and beard made him even harder to miss.

"Which we no longer have access to," Perlosa, Rheminas' sister, added from beside him. Her icy tone matched the coldness of the small crystal icicles dangling from the delicate silver chain around her neck.

"What are you implying?" Gurthghol glared at the goddess. Perlosa's bluish-green skin and cold blue eyes accented her long, shimmering white hair and snowy, low-cut dress.

"Nothing. Only stating a fact. If we were barely able to stop it before, when we had the throne, what chance do we have now?"

"Did you actually *fight* at our last encounter?" Rheminas asked scathingly, giving Perlosa a sideways glance. "I seem to remember things a bit differently."

"If you're finished." Ganatar raised his voice to stop the bickering. "I can confirm that Nuhl is indeed working alongside the lich. Why he's being driven to Galba, I don't know. But should he succeed—and do so with the backing of his patron . . . Well, I don't think I need to convince you what harm could come of it."

"It seems clear the effort alone would be daunting." Asora drew all eyes her way. "But can we be sure he could even complete such a venture? That seems to be the first matter to settle."

"It's not much of a question," said Rheminas. "No one's been able to get close enough to the throne to even come close to being a threat."

"But if he does have some additional support it might be possible." Dradin rubbed his beard in thought. "Though even then it still wouldn't be as easy as he *thinks* it could be. But he *was* a wizard king, and isn't a stranger to magic and power."

"Which is odd," Gurthghol commented, "since I thought all the wizard kings had been destroyed, or at least robbed of their power along with the rest of the wizards, during the Vindication." If Dradin noticed Gurthghol's probing glance he never acknowledged it.

"No matter how it happened," said Olthon, "it happened, and we have to deal with it. The longer we lose sight of the main issues, the less time we have to act."

"What about Galba?" Asora's eyes sought her husband's in a search for answers. "She could help us stand against Nuhl."

"She won't help." Khuthon's face grew as hard as steel. "She can't. She took that oath, remember? Don't expect her to lift a finger."

"Then we'd have to stop him *before* he gets to Galba," said Panthora.

"Only we can't," Endarien was quick to point out. He sat to the right of Causilla—yellow eyes scanning the gathered gods. "The pact with Galba forbids any god or divinity from stepping foot on Arid Land." His silvery white shirt matched his short hair while the brown trousers were the same shade as his hawk-like wings.

"Then how can Nuhl be there?" asked Drued.

"A good question," said Rheminas.

"With an easy answer," said Dradin. "Nuhl holds to an older pact and never made one with Galba. It's free to roam where it pleases, though I suspect it still wouldn't be allowed inside the circle."

"If so then the lich would be vulnerable if he makes it inside," Khuthon mused.

"Perhaps," Dradin continued, "but Nuhl just might find a way inside too. This lich could be just a diversion or even its carrier so it could claim the throne for itself."

"But why go after the throne?" Olthon asked Dradin, clearly not seeing a connection. "It hasn't been used for millennia and even when it was, Nuhl proved it was still stronger."

"But it still exists," said Khuthon. "Maybe it thinks someday one of us might get ahold of it again."

"I hope not," said Olthon. "We don't need to go back to those dark days again."

"Or do you think Nuhl might actually want to use the throne itself?" offered Asorlok. "Perhaps through this lich."

"You care to share something with us, Uncle?" Perlosa's eyes narrowed as she stared Asorlok down.

"Just a thought," he calmly replied. "I have no idea what Nuhl might be planning."

"No matter what it's planning, we won't be defenseless." A fresh confidence filled Khuthon's face and voice. "Father left us more than enough for one more fight."

"More than enough what?" Aero searched the other gods' faces, grasping for understanding.

"Pure divine power," said Khuthon with a smirk. "Enough to stand against anything."

"So you think." Olthon's comment was met with Khuthon's disapproving look. "I'd prefer to think of it as a final option. We have no idea how much remains, nor how well it'll fare after all these years."

"Again, *what* power?" Aerotripton asked, looking from Panthora to Drued, noting their own perplexed faces. "We thought Vkar's death left nothing but the throne."

"You were told what was needed at the time." Asorlok calmly addressed the elven god.

Drued bristled. "So what *else* have you been keeping from us?"

"Please." Olthon raised a hand. "This isn't helpful for anyone. It probably didn't come up because most of us simply haven't given it any thought until now."

"So . . . what is it?" Aero tried his best to read Olthon but failed.

"You already know about Thangaria's destruction and our parents' deaths," Olthon explained. "What you weren't told was that with their deaths we were able to use their remaining essence to heal and restore what we could. It took almost all that remained of them, but we stopped that first attack from destroying everything. Later, we tapped into it again and raised you three to godhood."

"So you *didn't* do it on your own?" Drued was a bit taken aback by the confession. Panthora and Aerotripton didn't fare much better. "Then why give the impression you did?"

"At the time we—"

"It's not important right now," said Khuthon, interrupting.

"Well *I* think it is," Drued continued. "We need to fully know what we're dealing with to make the right decisions. So if we're going to start speaking truth then let's have *all* of it on the table."

"I don't think the table's that strong," said Asorlok, "and we need to stay focused on the matter at hand. But in the interest of full disclosure none but Vkar has been able to elevate or create gods from lesser beings, and even then only with the throne. Which is why there haven't been any other gods before or since added to the pantheon from outside our happy family."

"How much of Vkar's essence remains?" Panthora inquired.

"More than enough." Khuthon was curt.

"You hope," said Olthon.

"I know," came Khuthon's stern reply.

"So where is it?" Aero pressed, but Khuthon held his tongue.

"Somewhere safe," Olthon quickly interjected.

Seeing that was all he was going to get, Aero relented, though it was clear neither Panthora nor Drued was entirely satisfied with the answer either.

"If it really can do as much as you say," said Panthora, "then we shouldn't have anything to worry about with this wizard."

"That's what you'd *think*," said Rheminas. "But things aren't always how they appear—especially with Nuhl. It could be going after the throne, trying to come after us again, having a go at destroying Tralodren, or even all three. Each has been a thorn in its side for millennia."

"Destroying Tralodren?" Aero's eyes went wide at the thought. "Why?"

"It's the way of things." There was no joy in Asorlok's reply, simply the dry stating of fact. "Nuhl seeks to destroy any world it can. If it had its way the whole cosmos would have been gone long ago. The only thing keeping it in existence is the ancient pact it made before the cosmic foundations were settled.

"Tralodren, like all worlds, must face Nuhl in the end. And, of course, finishing off the pantheon, who had a hand in creating the planet in the first place, would just be an added benefit."

"It really hates you that much?" Panthora was amazed and a little saddened.

"It hates all life," said Ganatar. "We're just higher in its sights because of Vkar. None of us would be here without him and his throne."

"Including us," added Drued, clearly mulling over the deeper implications of Ganatar's words.

"So it will want to kill us too?" Aero motioned to himself and the other Race Gods.

"Eventually, yes." Rheminas didn't mince any words. "Though you're probably lower on the list. We've been around more—caused it more issues it'd like to resolve." The elven god's countenance fell.

"You were the ones wanting more truth on the table," Asorlok quipped.

"And none of it is getting us anywhere," said Perlosa.

"So what do you propose?" Endarien turned Perlosa's way. "If Nuhl tries to go for Tralodren first—"

"Never." Drued pounded his fist on the table. "All of us would defend Tralodren with our lives."

"Easy to say." Endarien looked the dwarven god full in the face. "But you weren't here the last time we faced one of Nuhl's agents."

"And we're older too," added Asorlok. "Older and maybe even a little weaker . . ."

"Speak for yourself," Khuthon huffed.

"No matter what Nuhl is planning we doubt you would share the same fate as us, dear uncle." Perlosa's frosty attempt at affection rankled the god of death.

"I don't crave the end of the pantheon *or* Tralodren. But what comes will come eventually, as all things must. Though I'm in no hurry to speed things along."

"So what do we do?" The lines on Asora's face added weight to the growing exasperation in her voice. "The longer we wait, the more lives we place at risk."

"You've been silent, my dear." Dradin turned to Saredhel. "Share with us what you've seen."

Saredhel pondered for a moment more, reflective in deep inner thought. Like her true form, she was barefoot and awash in jewels and gems of all kinds. The opaline cowl covering her shaved, brown-skinned head snaked about a swan-like neck, draping her pure-white eyes in dim shade.

When she finally spoke it was with a soft, low voice. "If one of us is willing to make a great sacrifice, we would gain an advantage over this new threat."

"What *type* of sacrifice?" Endarien asked as both he and Asorlok watched each other from the corners of their eyes.

"To confront our enemy successfully will require something dear from the confronter as payment for success." Saredhel's answer was cryptic, but the pantheon was used to it. Everyone knew of her nature to give just enough of the future in vague shards of insight. Each individual had to wade through the meaning in their own mind. Sometimes this riddle of sayings was understood, and other times each came to their own interpretation. None knew for certain just what was meant until the end, though events played out around them all the while.

Khuthon leaned forward, focusing his full attention on the white-eyed seer. "Are you saying we have to give up our own lives to gain victory?"

"I have spoken what I have seen." And with that, all knew Saredhel was done speaking on the matter. It'd do no good trying to probe any further.

"And yet we still don't know what to do," said Rheminas.

"Confront this lich," said Khuthon. "I thought that was obvious."

"Is it?" Olthon asked of her brother. "And you're forgetting about the sacrifice. Maybe there's some way to contain the lich, or even hold back Nuhl's plans."

"And how could we contain Nuhl?" Shiril's alto timbre startled many of the gods. "It's woven into the very fabric of the cosmos." The last of the younger gods, few paid her much attention, which suited her just fine. She'd chosen the guise of a brown-skinned woman with golden hair and silver eyes. Her cloth-of-gold tunic dress was accented by a gemstone-studded black belt.

"She's right," Asorlok said with a sigh. "We need to focus on that lich. He's the weak link in all of this. We take him out and Nuhl will just have to find another agent to work its will. And that will buy us time."

"How *much* time?" asked Drued.

"A few millennia if the last confrontation is any gauge," answered Endarien.

"And you're *sure* that's all you've seen?" Olthon dared one more question of Saredhel, not noticing the stoic-faced Asorlok and Endarien glancing at each other from across the table.

Saredhel said nothing.

"Very well." Olthon's head fell with her soft sigh. "Then I guess we have nothing more to discuss."

"Other than how we'd confront him." Causilla's somberness sharply contrasted with her rainbow-hued gown.

"Why not do it now?" Khuthon put forth. "*Before* the lich makes it to Galba?"

"No," said Endarien. "Why do Galba's work for her? Let him try and get to the throne. If he succeeds—"

"Then we could be facing another *god* instead of a wizard. *Brilliant*." Khuthon shook his head. "We should take him out *now*, while we have the strength and numbers."

"But don't forget the sacrifice." Asorlok raised a finger. "We don't even know what might be required for success."

"I would've thought you'd be after this lich right away." Khuthon studied Asorlok with a curious eye. "He *is* defying your edicts, after all."

"I'm patient."

"I'm not," said Rheminas. "We need to put this to a vote and start planning our attack."

"Even if we confront the lich we're going to be facing Nuhl too." Asorlok stared Rheminas down. "If you're not careful you could very well be running into our own demise."

"Then we'd have our sacrifice," Gurthghol said with morbid humor.

"Or we can wait for a more opportune time and strategy," Asorlok countered.

"And what would you have us do in the meantime?" Khuthon roared, slamming the table with his fist. "Cower in our keeps like *rabbits*?"

"Wait and see *if* he succeeds, like I said. If he does, we move forward with the last of Vkar's essence." The others' faces grew slack at Asorlok's suggestion. "Let *that* be our sacrifice. With it any of us will be *more* than enough for a newly risen god *with* or *without* Nuhl's backing. And if we strike before he's had time to learn about his new self, we can crush him underfoot like an ant."

"But who of us would fight him?" asked Olthon.

"I will." Endarien sat up in his chair. "If I have Vkar's essence flowing through me the barrier around Tralodren wouldn't be a problem either. I could face him with full force and finally send him to Mortis before he could even begin to fathom his new divinity."

"Are you sure you'd want to do this?" Ganatar inquired with a calm intensity.

"If that's what it came down to, yes."

"I'd be happy to go in your place," Rheminas offered. "After all, it's about revenge, isn't it?"

"No." Endarien's voice grew cold. "This goes beyond revenge."

"We doubt it," Perlosa was quick to retort.

"Do you even have enough of Vkar's essence for this to work?" asked Drued. "From how you've been talking it sounds like you've got just a few handfuls left."

"We do," said Dradin, "but it should be enough to get one of us to Tralodren in our true form and provide enough time for a battle."

"To *win* the battle," Endarien corrected. "I'd be backed with enough power to render Cadrith's advantage into nothing more than a shadow. If the council agrees to the action, of course."

"If he's ready to do it, then let's just put it to a vote," Gurthghol advised Ganatar.

Sensing consensus, Ganatar rose from his throne. "It appears we've reached the end of the discussion. Who here supports making Endarien our champion against the lich, should he succeed?" All the gods, save Saredhel, Asora, and Olthon, raised a hand.

"Then it's decided. Endarien shall battle Cadrith, should he rise to godhood. We'll use the last of Vkar's essence to give him the time and abilities he needs to defeat the threat." Turning to Endarien, he added, "Be ready. If needed, you'll have to act quickly."

"I'll be ready." Endarien nodded.

"Yes," said Asorlok, mirroring Endarien's emotionless expression before turning to Saredhel. "We *all* will be."

•●•

As the council finished its session, Gurthghol's true form sat on an amethyst-studded black marble throne, absent-mindedly stroking the barghest sitting beside him. His symbol, the Black Sun, was affixed to the throne's back. The wrought iron circle had eight points radiating out of it. Resting above the god's seat of rule, it gave those who came near an impression of a sun rising behind the god of darkness and chaos. An odd thing to convey, perhaps, but Gurthghol had embraced it since being liberated from Vkar's throne centuries earlier.

He was clothed in a rich dark purple tunic whose sleeves had two black linnorms slithering for his shoulders. His black pants were equally rich, boasting a subtle design only seen upon close inspection in the low light of the room. His bare feet were hard to miss. He rarely wore footwear, preferring to keep his feet naked in just about all situations. Thick black leather bracers made to resemble a linnorm's head trying to devour each hand completed his outfit.

Giving the barghest one last scratch behind the ears, Gurthghol sat to his full height, eagerly awaiting Erdis' arrival, while the large, tailless black dog kept its black eyes fixed ahead, waiting and watching for any threat that might cross its field of vision. Soon enough, Erdis entered the throne room with a silent tread.

Now that Gurthghol was seated, the Karduin chamberlain didn't seem as short, but still Erdis knew his place, bowing to the god as he approached the throne. "I've found what you requested." He brought forth a rolled scroll from under his arm. It was clearly meant for someone larger; the old parchment was easily one and a half times the size of the scrolls the Kardu normally would have used.

Gurthghol seized it at once. "And no one else knows you took it from the library?"

"No, my lord." Erdis' oval face was the picture of total obedience. "I was sure the matter was kept hidden from all."

"Good." Gurthghol unrolled the parchment. "The less said the better. And with the council still in session, I don't want to raise any more eyebrows."

"I also made sure there were no copies," Erdis added. "As far as I know, this is the only one in the archive."

Gurthghol started to read the blocky script—an older version of Titan, the first great language of the cosmos. Others who sought to read the text might have had difficulty in the dim light cast by the low-burning torches and handful of small wrought iron braziers, but Gurthghol had adjusted to the darkness long ago. Like so many of the denizens that called Altearin home, he could read in the dark just as well as in daylight. The adoption of the low light to his realm and palace was a partial compromise to those who didn't hail from the ancient plane of Umbra, which the god had merged into his new realm millennia prior. It was also an old habit Gurthghol didn't want to give up just yet.

It seemed like yesterday that he'd been standing beside Galba with the rest of the pantheon as the pact was crafted. It had been so simple then: agree to keep the throne away from anyone who would dare crave it. Gurthghol had endured being its prisoner for too long. Worse still, he'd witnessed the undoing of the fledgling pantheon as the gods warred among themselves to take his place. If it wasn't for his plan to create Tralodren and the rest of its solar system, he might still be on Vkar's throne right now.

No matter how much the others would have thought it possible to pull him from it, he knew they wouldn't succeed. At times he'd been tempted to yield it to any challenger foolish enough to step forth but knew none of the others could do any better than he. If anything, he had been the *best* choice to take the throne, given the irony of how quickly he came to loathe it. But he was also the firstborn, which played some role in the matter, he supposed—in one set of theories, at least.

"Is there anything else, my lord?" Erdis pulled Gurthghol away from his reading. He'd almost forgotten the Kardu was there.

"Yes. Inform Shador and Mergis to assemble four of their best men. I want them ready to fight should I need them."

"Outfitted for war?" said Erdis, raising an eyebrow.

"Just have them ready," Gurthghol returned, dismissing the Kardu.

On his way out, Erdis remembered something. "Oh, and Lady Twila has been inquiring about another opportunity to see you." The Kardu did his best to hide his smile. "What do you wish me to tell her?"

"To practice her patience," said Gurthghol. "I don't wish to be disturbed."

"As you wish, my lord." Erdis resumed his egress as Gurthghol returned to his reading.

The pact was simple enough. It was crafted to be. Galba claimed a piece of land that would eventually become Arid Land after the Great Shaking, and they were to leave her to it. While he was initially opposed to the provision allowing any mortal who wished to take the seat a chance to win access to the throne, the clause was still included. He didn't see the wisdom in the matter then and still didn't now, but it was said to be in keeping with free will and so, after some debate, the motion was carried.

Until now things had worked out well. Throughout the long millennia none who tried to claim the throne had succeeded. But now with this lich he was starting to have doubts, doubts fanned all the more by the words Saredhel had spoken not so long ago. He could see where this was all going and what he'd have to face. He hoped he was wrong, but if a sacrifice was to be called for . . . Gurthghol continued reading, searching for anything he could use for the time ahead.

CHAPTER 11

And so he expelled his deadly flame;
the rest he did rend and maim.
Against such a monster who can stand?
There's not a woman, there's not a man.
If e'er Gorallis' frame or banner you see,
take wise counsel, friend, and flee.

—Ancient ballad

Gilban and Hadek emerged from the lavender light and found themselves on a brown sand beach. The air was heavy, humid, and hot—almost stifling—as they studied Antora's shoreline.

"Did we make it?" Hadek wasn't excited by what he was seeing.

"Yes," Gilban said, taking a step forward, his staff striking the beach like a poking finger. "This is Antora."

Hadek took it in with a short, uneasy glance. He didn't like the feel of the land. There was something off, though he couldn't quite place it. It felt as if the rocks, the sand of the beach—even the heavy air about them—were looking at them, watching them with suspicious eyes.

Ahead of them, he spied a tall spine of mountains after a seemingly endless expanse of dry, flat plains. He supposed these were Rheminas' Fingers—the lair of the Crimson Flame, as claimed by hundreds of stories. He squinted to better see the smoking mountains that released grayish-black plumes like chimneys. He didn't like that either.

"Where do we go now?" Hadek didn't want to do anything except follow Gilban's lead. He wasn't keen on leaving anything to chance. Chance could get him killed.

"Tell me, are there any mountains around?"

"Yes. They're far away, though."

"How far?"

"Pretty far." Hadek really didn't want to hear what Gilban was about to say: that they would have to walk into those very lava-churning mountains and then get face to face with a linnorm.

"Hadek." Gilban grew serious as he peered down at the goblin. "It's very important you give me your answer as best you can. How far do the mountains appear to be?"

Hadek put a hand across his brow to shield the sun's glare. "They look like five . . . no, seven . . . miles."

"Are you certain?" Gilban was fingering his staff rhythmically.

"Yes."

"Then take my hand." He held out his free hand to the goblin. As soon as he took hold of it, the seer's lips whispered a prayer to Saredhel. At once, Hadek felt a tingling sensation all over his body. It was like a carpet of furry caterpillars were crawling over his flesh—inside and out. He didn't mind, though, because with it came a mild peace he eagerly welcomed. The whispered petition continued, until he felt lightheaded; then he saw nothing. Everything went black. No light. No sound. No understanding of even his own body's existence.

"Where are we? What's happening?" He was tightly clutching Gilban's hand . . . or he thought he was. He couldn't be sure, because he couldn't feel anything.

"We travel on the wings of fate," Gilban returned dryly.

Hadek recognized part of the feeling from their recent journey, but this time the experience was different. It felt less overpowering than the prayer that brought them to Antora. He suspected it was because it was Gilban's faith alone that carried them, and not the collective faith of any other priests. Maybe it was also because the journey wasn't as far as Rexatoius to Antora. Whatever the case, he wasn't troubled by strange visions this time around, and that suited him just fine.

Before he had time to think further, they arrived at the base of Rheminas' Fingers, materializing out of the sticky air. The smoldering volcanoes towered above them. He smelled faint sulfuric fumes, and light specks of ash drifted about like snow. Farther along the mountain nearest him—he supposed it might have been the "thumb" of Rheminas' hand—Hadek spied a pathway cleared from the volcanic rock. It seemed to twist along the outside of the peaks before being swallowed up by them entirely.

"What do you see now?" asked Gilban.

"I think it's a path." He squinted. "It goes into the mountains."

"*Into* the mountains?" Gilban seemed worried about this, but the concern faded as quickly as it had risen.

"Yes."

"Then we have no choice but to follow it. I'd hoped we wouldn't get so close to the heat and his lair, but fate is with us. We'll be safe." He sensed Gilban really didn't believe what he'd just said, but put the thought from his mind. The less worrisome matters he contemplated, the better off he'd be.

"Let's go." Gilban drew his lips tight across his face in grim determination.

Ash clouds rose from the path as they walked, adding to the small flakes fluttering at odd intervals, covering their garments and bodies in gray dust. The ash soon turned to paste as sweat poured down their faces from the increasing heat. As they neared the volcanoes, their eyes began to water so much that Hadek had a hard time seeing and had to be led by Gilban at times, whose own eyes cried thick, charcoal-gray tears.

The journey was longer than it should have been and grew even longer as they stopped to ease their irritated throats and inflamed eyes. Yet they soldiered on. The air around them was like acid in his lungs. He was sure the back of his throat was dripping blood into his gut. Gilban, if he felt the same, was silent. His brow was furrowed in deep concentration, which was needed to place each step securely on the treacherous, rocky ground.

Hadek knew his role. He knew he had to help the seer get to where he needed to be and keep the old elf alive. He dreaded to think of himself being left here should anything happen to the priest. Maybe *this* was his greater purpose: to help Gilban. Only the longer he considered it the less likely it seemed. Being brought halfway around the world to help a blind elf navigate through some rough terrain didn't sound like much of a great calling to him. There had to be something else . . .

Finally, they managed to get between two of the taller peaks. As they passed through, a deep darkness fell, and only small, sputtering embers and odd patches of cracked rock illuminated their way in the dirty yellow-orange haze. The heat was more intense between the two "fingers" of rock, and it seemed as if the darkness was stifling them.

"Is there no one in front of us?" Gilban asked.

"No one." Hadek imagined his face as gray, looking more like melted rock, smeared with tears, with yellow slits for eyes. The ash had caked upon the grooves and depressions in his face, adding yet another irritant to his growing list.

"I don't like this." The concern in Gilban's voice gave Hadek pause. Suddenly, his ears picked up a falling rock at his side. This was followed by the sound of another descending rock, and then still more, so that it sounded like a small avalanche tumbling around them.

"What's happening?" Gilban asked worriedly as Hadek tried to find where the noise was coming from. It was almost on top of them. A heartbeat later, he felt a coil of rope wrap around his feet, tripping him as he tried stepping forward. The three round weights that smacked his ankles let him know he'd been ensnared by a bola. This revelation was quickly followed by a harder truth: the ground pounding into his face as he fell. He heard Gilban join him before pain bloomed in the back of his skull, sending him into dreamless slumber.

•●•

Hadek woke first.

His head ached and his eyes throbbed. Through blurred vision he could just make out the shape of Gilban beside him. The priest was tied with rough rope around his wrists and ankles. With some minor struggling, he discovered he was bound in similar fashion. He shook his head in hopes of clearing it. They were inside a cage crafted of iron bars, just large enough to accommodate their slumped forms. As more of his vision cleared, he saw a red-clad warrior standing by him, guarding the cage. This warrior appeared strong and possessed an aura Hadek found unsettling.

One good thing was the air had cleared, although the heat remained. The warrior guarding the cage seemed unaffected by the warmth, his scale mail vest fitting him like a second skin over his sleeveless tunic. Both dyed red, they matched his cherry, black-horned helmet, which was crafted to resemble a horrible linnormic face. He also wore scarlet-dyed pants and tall, matching leather boots. On his naked left shoulder was a tattoo of a tongue of flame embedded deep into his skin with a bright ruby ink.

Hadek could make out a village of some kind just beyond the warrior, small cooking fires dotting its center and scarlet banners and flags circling the perimeter. The homes were crafted of mud, stone, and wood. He noticed Celetors and Telborians—even a few half-elves—in the village. The guard himself, upon closer inspection, revealed a mix of Celetoric and Telborian ancestry.

"What's going on?" Hadek asked the guard in Telboros. The guard was silent, not even acknowledging his shout. He tried speaking to him in Goblin. Again the guard remained still as a statue.

"Gilban." Hadek kicked the slumped-over priest in frustration.

The seer awoke with a start. "What's going on? My hands—Hadek?"

"I'm here," said Hadek. "We're *both* here."

"Where are we?" Gilban's sightless eyes peered from the cage.

"We're stuck in a cage. Tied like hogs." He proceeded to gnaw on the bindings about his ankles with his teeth. He could just reach them if he strained his back, pulling his legs and thighs wide.

"I take it we're not alone." Gilban wiggled to sit up against the warm iron bars. "How many are there?"

"Lots," he said as he continued to work on the rope. It tasted old and was soured by a sulfuric aftertaste.

"We must take this next step very carefully," Gilban said, lowering his voice and cocking his head Hadek's way. "Something doesn't feel right. Can you see Gorallis anywhere?"

Something didn't feel right? That couldn't be a good sign. "No. Haven't seen him yet, thank the gods." Hadek managed to pull a small piece of the rope off the larger strand holding his ankles fast. He'd started to pull his head back and up, unraveling a continuous string of it, when the strand broke, causing a streak of Goblinish profanity.

"I'll ask for guidance, and then we'll seek the linnorm," Gilban said, closing his eyes.

"No hurry," said Hadek, spitting out more strands. A few fibers stubbornly dangled from between his teeth.

As Gilban prayed, Hadek observed a new Celetor approaching the cage. The stoic guard became alive, bowing to the other before stepping away from the cage entirely. The Celetor, whom Hadek assumed to be a priest of some sort, wore a headdress fashioned out of a large lizard's skull—possibly even a drake's skull—and draped with white and black strips of cloth. The bone hinted at a faint yet potent carmine shade.

"Who are you?" The Celetor addressed Gilban in Telboros. Hadek didn't know if he liked the strange and sudden interest the man showed in him. Maybe Celetors didn't like having priests from different gods around.

"Speak to me," the priest continued. "I have the power to keep you from death for trespassing on Lord Gorallis' lands."

"What do you wish of me?" Gilban opened his eyes.

"You're blind," the Celetor said, shocked.

"So I am." Gilban adjusted himself to sit higher against the back of the cage. "But you must have urgent need of me. I am now at your full disposal."

The Celetor said nothing for a long while, staring at Gilban as if trying to see through him. "Bring him to my quarters," he said, spinning with a ruby flourish, before returning back to the village.

The guard sprung into action, producing a silver key and opening the cell. Thrusting Hadek away with one hand, he grabbed Gilban with the other. He hefted the priest over his shoulder. A swift closing and locking of the cage with his other hand and Gilban was carried away, leaving the lone goblin to contemplate his fate. Hadek pressed his face between the bars as he watched Gilban's departure. He didn't like this one bit.

"Be at peace, Hadek," Gilban shouted from over the Celetor's shoulder. "I have a feeling you will be safe."

"Great," Hadek muttered, then spat more bitter rope from between his teeth.

A moment later, a similar guard came to take the post the other had vacated. He was a paler version of the first, but possessed an even more menacing air.

"Just great," he repeated.

•●•

The elf was carried into Hilin's tent before being dumped onto the dirt floor with a jerk of the guard's shoulders. Hilin, like most of the priests of the Red Guard, lived in a scarlet tent partitioned into various rooms. The tent was large enough to allow for storage and study of religious texts, along with rooms for slumber and priestly worship. Though large, it wasn't richly decorated, being fashioned from materials and structures that could easily be packed and transported at a moment's notice. The rough furniture seemed like the sort of thing one would expect in a hunter's tent, and the rest of the simple decor was equally sparse and plain.

"We've been waiting for you," Hilin said, searching the blind elf's face. The blind *Patrician* face.

"Have you, now?"

"Who are you?" Hilin asked, pulling the elf to his feet.

"My name is Gilban Polcrates, a priest of Saredhel. The goblin and I are on a mission seeking your master." Hilin stepped away from the elf, who tried to keep his balance on the hard, rocky surface; his tied ankles gave him some trouble, but he managed to remain upright.

Hilin couldn't believe it. Everything was falling right into place—just as the vision had conveyed. A Patrious elf was now before him and was even *looking* for Gorallis. All *truly* had been prepared for, like the vision had said. But where was the globe? And what of the key?

"What's this I hear—" Nagal made his way into Hilin's tent, only to fall silent upon catching sight of the blind elf. "The elf . . ." He rushed to stand beside Hilin. Grell and Aylan followed behind him.

"His name is Gilban," Hilin informed them, "and he seeks Gorallis."

"Praised be his name," Grell was quick to spout off. "His vision has come to pass."

"Vision?" Gilban brought all the priests' eyes hard upon him. "What sort of vision?"

"What concern is it of *yours*?" Aylan gruffly replied.

"I might be able to help make sense of it," said Gilban. "I *am* a priest of Saredhel."

Nagal shot Hilin a troubled glance. "The servant of another god here to help ours?"

"You're all priests then, I take it," said Gilban.

"What of it?" asked Aylan.

"And of Gorallis too, no less. Interesting."

"He was accompanied by a goblin," Hilin continued, briefing the priests. "He's being held until we decide what to do with the elf."

"Why are you here?" Aylan growled, taking a step closer.

"I already told you," said Gilban. "To seek Gorallis."

"For what purpose?" Aylan continued. "No outsider has ever sought the great Gorallis without wishing to do him harm."

"We don't seek to harm him, only to exchange an object which has great meaning to him for an item that has great meaning to us."

"And what *is* this item?" Nagal's eyes narrowed.

"Four of you then," said the elf, shifting his sightless orbs to the other's location with incredible accuracy. "Unless there's more who've yet to speak."

"What *is* this item?" Hilin inquired, drawing closer.

"I'll tell you, if you'd be so kind as to answer some of *my* questions first." Gilban calmly smiled.

"Is that your game?" Hilin crossed his arms. "Very well. We'll humor you."

"But only so far," Aylan added.

"So all of you are priests then?"

"Yes," said Nagal. "We're all servants of the great Gorallis."

"Which means you actually believe him to be a god."

"Gorallis is immortal!" Grell cried, jumping into the verbal fray. "What else *can* he be? He lives forever, and we are here to serve him. We see to it his name is praised and honored above all others of his kind."

"It's been a long time since I've heard any fresh tales about your master."

"Gorallis has slumbered since before I was born, and into my whole life thus far," Hilin offered. "There's a prophecy that states he will soon awaken, leading us into what will become the most glorious time of his reign."

"And apparently a vision to go with it," said Gilban. "A vision, it seems, that involves me."

"And now you're here before us," Hilin said, circling the bound seer. "I saw you appear, and with you an orb of orange light. Is this the item you brought? Is this the key we seek?"

"I suppose it could be—at least a key for me getting what I've come for. In truth, I never really thought about what it might resemble for you."

Hilin placed a hand upon Gilban's frail shoulder. "Do you have it?"

The elf's white eyes locked onto Hilin's, stirring unease deep in the priest's gut. "I have the one object Gorallis would want more than anything else in the world."

"Which is?" asked Nagal.

"His eye." The priests' jaws fell slack at Gilban's words.

"You *have* it?" Hilin was the first to regain control over his tongue. "But how?"

"It doesn't matter *how* it was retrieved." Gilban's voice grew steely. "Nor are you to see it. It's the property of Gorallis, and to him it must be presented. Now untie me so that I can do so."

"You"—Aylan didn't try to hide his mocking tone—"a priest of Saredhel, would come all this way to return the eye of Gorallis?"

"It's been a strange day for all of us," said Gilban. "But I'm speaking the truth. I was sent here to find Gorallis and return his eye. The sooner you untie me, the sooner I can do so."

"I'm willing to allow it," said Nagal after some thought. "Gorallis must have willed this. The vision is too close to reality, and if he *does* bring the key to Gorallis' awakening . . ."

"And if he doesn't, we can always make a fresh offering instead," Grell said, nodding. "Either way, he'll end up serving Gorallis."

Hilin withdrew the curved knife from his belt and cut the ropes around Gilban's ankles and wrists. "Come," he said, taking the elf's wrist. "Gorallis awaits."

CHAPTER 12

To Panthora and her order you now forever are bound.

—Knighting oath of the Valkorian Knights

"You've been pretty quiet," said Alara as the outskirts of Elandor rose into view. They'd been walking the cobblestone road leading into the port city since dawn.

"Just thinking," Rowan said, taking stock of the city walls as well as the wide assortment of people streaming toward the ironclad wooden doors of the city's gate. Outside the gate stood two studious and stout guardsmen, Elandor's rank-and-file protectors. These dark-haired Telborians warily watched the throng of folk filtering past, keeping a tight hand on their pole arms and looking quite stern in their banded mail armor.

"Is there anything I should know about this boat or its crew before we get to it?" Alara slowed behind the thickening line of people seeking entrance into the city.

"It's called the *Frost Giant.*" Rowan observed the two guards as they thoroughly examined a Telborian beggar before bringing a trader's wagon to a halt so they could search it. "They should be happy to see me. It means they'll be getting back that much sooner."

"So they should be in a good mood."

"We'll see." He moved ahead with the others, noticing how he was singled out already from the rest, the guards spying his leather armor, sword, and dragon-emblazoned shield slung over his back. They took an even greater interest in Alara, letting their gazes linger a bit too long on certain parts of her body. A flash of anger came over Rowan but quickly passed, leaving him surprised and confused.

"If you don't mind," said Alara, passing the guards, "I'd like to check on my ship first. If we're going to be gone for as long as you said, I'll need to make sure it'll be secure."

Though morning had dawned, Elandor was still coming to life. Most of the activity was on the docks where Alara and Rowan were headed. A handful of alert guardsmen on the other side of the doors gave them some notice before letting them flow into the throng heading to the city's streets and corridors.

"I didn't know you had a boat."

"It's how I brought the others to Elandor," she explained.

"If you have a boat, then you could go back to your people," Rowan said, peering into Alara's sapphire eyes.

"Except I'm going with you to Valkoria."

"But I thought Gilban had stranded you here. If you have a boat—"

Alara stopped in the middle of the street, causing Rowan to trip. "I asked if you were all right with me coming along before we left. Is there something you aren't telling me?" Rowan opened his mouth, but nothing would come out.

"I'm still committed to going back with you to Valkoria," she continued, "but only if you want me to." She stared directly into his eyes, and brought fresh pressure to his shoulders and chest. "Do you want me to come back with you?"

Did he want her to come back with him? What could he say? That part of him leapt at the idea while the other part was screaming no? The more he tried to come up with a reasonable reply, the more the divergent views widened in their opposition.

"I said it was fine," he replied and made for the docks. He was eager for release from the elf's gaze—and to put distance between himself and the conflict her question had stirred.

"Rowan?" Alara called out as she hurried after him.

"You think they'll let you keep it here until the end of the year?" He kept his focus on the path before him, away from Alara.

"I don't know," she said, "but we'll find out soon enough."

"Might as well take any supplies you had in there too," he suggested. "Less to steal or spoil."

"There it is," she said with a pointing hand. He could make out a fairly common and nondescript sloop. It might have been decent for navigating short trips on rivers and maybe even around the Talathealin coast, but on the open oceans? And with only one helmsman—since Gilban wouldn't be much help? That was *more* than a little foolish.

"You and Gilban sailed all the way from Rexatoius in *that*?"

"We didn't sail *all* the way," said Alara. "Gilban was able to find us a shortcut."

"Shortcut?"

"Let's just say we had some divine help," she replied.

Not wanting to pry any further, he resumed his study of the vessel as they drew near. "It doesn't look half bad. You might be able to find a buyer and save yourself the hassle of finding a safe dock for it."

"Maybe, but something tells me to hold on to it a while longer."

"You starting to see visions now too?" he teased.

"Probably just woman's intuition," she said, offering him a soft smile. They found their way to the sloop and went on deck. Rowan let Alara do what she wished while he did his best to keep out of her way. The longer he waited, the more he thought, which only made his internal conflict worse.

Part of him was ready to spin around from where he'd been peering off the side of the deck to tell her she could just leave now, just take her ship and go. But as soon as he made a move to do so, he found his legs rebelled. Just as strong as the force pressing him to rid himself of the elf was another urging him to keep her by his side—both for the upcoming trip and after that . . .

"You ready?" He jumped when Alara's hand alighted on his shoulder. She'd brought a few more things with her, adding them to a new pack she carried over her back. This joined a new dark blue tunic and brown cloak. He envied the fresh change of clothes. After these last few weeks he could do with a bit of refreshing—though the simple bath he'd managed in a village a few days back helped some.

"Yeah."

"Then I guess we'd better get going." Rowan watched Alara make her way off the sloop.

"So you're just going to leave it here?"

"For now."

"Woman's intuition?" he said, coming alongside her.

"We'll see." He found himself incapable of sharing the same soft smile.

•●•

"There it is," Rowan said, pointing out his vessel to Alara. The *Frost Giant* was an older caravel with two masts and deep blue sails striped vertically in a brownish-red shade that resembled dried blood. From some of the stories Alara heard about the Nordicans, she supposed it very well *could* be blood. The ship was moored to a stout, weathered post and was joined by a few other ships in that area of the docks.

"Let me do the talking," Rowan said, approaching the vessel with steady steps.

"Don't think I've learned enough yet?" she said tauntingly, knowing full well she wasn't nearly as proficient as she'd need to be. She'd been picking up some, but still needed more teaching and practice, which hopefully she would get on the rest of the trip.

"Just stay behind me." He pressed on. She could see a seriousness take hold of his features and was careful to give him distance. She followed him up the gangplank, where he was quickly greeted by a rather rotund captain. The flabby man at first was quite jovial, but he soured upon catching sight of Alara—as did the rest of the crew, who were staring at her in a manner that made her uncomfortable.

"Good to see you, lad," the captain said in Telboros, which Alara assumed was for her benefit. "We actually just finished packing up the last of the supplies."

"Glad to hear it," said Rowan. "I wonder if you'd mind taking on another guest for the trip back."

"You mean *her*?" the captain said with a grimace, pointing at Alara. His eyes took note of her sheathed sword before returning to Rowan. "Is this a joke?"

"No," Rowan said, tensing up. "She needs to get to Valkoria to speak to my superiors."

"Then she can take another ship," said the captain. "She can't ride on *my* vessel."

"She's important to my mission." Alara could hear the edge in Rowan's voice. "If you deny her, you're denying my mission, the knighthood, and *Panthora*, who sent me."

"She's an *elf*," the captain said, jabbing an accusing finger at Alara. "And she's not welcome on my vessel." The crew had stopped their duties to stare at her, clustering like kindling for a coming inferno.

"*You*, of all people, should know it was the Knights of Valkoria that *stopped* an elven invasion at the end of the Shadow Years and have kept us safe ever since."

"*Invasion?*" Alara muttered to herself. She didn't recall any Patrician invasions to the Northlands during the Shadows Years or any other time since then. Then the captain's meaning dawned on her. "Many people who aren't elves think that I'm Elyelmic, but I'm Patrious . . ." The last word died on her lips as she saw the hate glaring back at her.

"I can just get another ship to meet up with you," she flatly informed Rowan.

"No." Rowan shook his head, all the while glaring at the captain. "You won't know where to go, and I can't afford to wait for you to arrive—*if* you even arrive."

"Then we'll find another way." Alara took hold of Rowan's hand and tried her best to ease him away from the captain. "I still have the sloop. Maybe we can get enough money from it to buy passage elsewhere."

Rowan didn't budge. "We're not going to find any other ships going to the Northlands. This is our *only* way to Valkoria."

"There has got to be another," she said with another gentle tug. "And we'll find it."

"We *have* found it."

"Not with *her* you haven't." The captain crossed the two plump logs that served as his arms above his copious stomach. "*You* can come aboard. I have no quarrel with you or the knighthood, but no *elf* rides my boat. Never have, and they never will."

"This is important to the knighthood." Rowan's lips were as thin as a sword's edge. "If you let her come along, Panthora will favor you." This brought forth a wave of angry murmuring from the crew as their captain stood like a tall, fleshy oak rooted to the gangplank's lip.

"Panthora already favors me. I'm a human." The crew let loose a ruckus of riotous chuckling at the retort.

"Let's go." Alara tugged at Rowan's sword arm. It was tough and stiff, with his hand locked around his sword's pommel. For far too long for her liking, Rowan remained as stiff and unyielding as his arm. Then, in his ire, he turned on his heel and stomped down the gangplank, giving her hardly any time to clear out of his way as he stormed past. She cast the captain and crew one final look, making sure there'd be no further repercussions or retaliations, then followed after Rowan.

Alara and Rowan found a sea-pitted wooden bench to occupy after their exchange with the *Frost Giant*'s captain. From it they watched the day burn away until the sun nearly kissed the horizon. The fading light made Alara's silver locks explode like molten metal. Beside her Rowan was silent. Neither had really said much of anything since taking a seat. There wasn't anything to say. Just more time for Rowan to wrestle with his thoughts.

He'd removed his shield to rest beside his feet. It helped release some of the weight on his shoulders, but that wasn't everything weighing on him.

They'd watched the *Frost Giant* unmoor after its crew performed a minor offering to Perlosa by dropping a gold coin into the waves, then dwindle from sight. The only chance he had of returning to Valkoria and the keep was lost. If he thought he'd failed before, he'd now become a disgrace.

"I should have been on that boat," he muttered to himself. What had he been thinking? They would have taken him and he'd be safely on his way, but he had to go and push for Alara to join him. He had to try to force her on his fellow humans when he knew the knighthood wouldn't want to hear what she had to say anyway.

"I'm sorry," Alara said as her hand came to rest on his back. It was supposed to be a thing of comfort, he knew—of empathy—but instead it filled him with a rage that flared up and out of his mouth.

"It's all your fault!" he snarled, thrusting a finger in her face for good measure. "If you'd just gone with Gilban, like you were supposed to, none of this would have happened!" He glared at the docks, not wanting to look at her any further. "Maybe the captain was right," he said, more to himself, though loud enough for Alara to hear. "Maybe you elves *aren't* anything but trouble."

The sound of Alara's sudden departure drew Rowan's head. He watched her stride for the sunset. Part of him was glad to see her leave, but part of him was set to dash after her. He swung his head back to the waves with a sigh. This wasn't the way things should be, and this wasn't the way he should be acting. He knew better than to blame her for his woes. She was trying to help. He knew that. So where did all these troubling thoughts and feelings bubble up from?

Maybe they taught it to you in secret. Nalu's words echoed in his head.

It wasn't I who started the knighthood, but those same mortal men who called upon me . . . Panthora's words also haunted him.

"Show me the way, Panthora," he prayed before thinking about what Panthora had shown him since he started this mission. The necklace, the dream, Nalu's words . . . they all had a powerful part to play in his life, he knew. He was fighting a war, Panthora had said, a war with himself. A war whose first battle was over Alara.

Looking in the direction she'd gone, he saw her standing a good distance away, watching the lapping waves and seagulls scatter across the sky. He hadn't meant to hurt her. What he said wasn't really what he felt. Or was it? Part of it had felt real enough to him, even as part of him was sure it wasn't the whole truth either. He was frustrated with things, yes, but it wasn't Alara's, or anyone else's, fault. It was his alone.

He placed his hand over his heart and the hidden panther's paw that rested over it. His words were soft and humble. "Help me, Panthora. I don't know what else to do. I don't even know what to think anymore." A slight breeze ruffled his hair. His mind drifted for a few heartbeats and then returned as a shadow fell across his lap. Peering up, he discovered a lone Telborian sporting a congenial grin, soft greenish-blue eyes dancing above a patchy three-day-old beard.

"And why are you so crestfallen on such a lovely day?" the man asked with a gentle voice. He was no more than forty or so winters old, with short-cropped white hair and weathered features. Rowan was pretty sure he was a sailor, noticing his loose-fitting green pants and parchment-colored shirt for the first time. On his right shoulder a lone seagull perched. Its gray-white head was cocked in Alara's direction.

"You a Nordican?" The man's eyes squinted as if he was trying to see the finer details of Rowan's person.

"Yes."

"Then you're pretty far from home."

"And it looks like I might be here longer than I planned," said Rowan, gloomily.

"So you're stranded here then?"

"Unless I can find a ship headed to the Northlands," he replied.

"That's some pretty fancy armor." The sailor's eyes squinted again. "You a knight?"

"I'm a Knight of Valkoria, yes." The seagull on the Telborian's shoulder turned its head Rowan's way, as if suddenly interested in the conversation.

The sailor rubbed his stubbly chin. "Well, I'm headed to Arid Land," he said. "It isn't the Northlands but if—"

"*Arid Land?*"

The man smiled at Rowan's joyful outburst. "I have some business that needs attending there. If you like, I suppose I could find a place for you onboard." If he *liked*? It was almost too good to turn down. Once in Arid Land he could potentially find another ship that could take him back to the keep. Panthora be praised! This was truly a miracle.

"I don't have much coin." Rowan rose from the bench, working to temper his previous enthusiasm. He didn't want to appear too desperate and risk getting taken advantage of with any potential offer—miracle or not. "But I could—"

"I'm not a pirate." The other held up a warding hand. "I'm sure we can work out a simple-enough arrangement. That is, if you're open to the offer."

Rowan smiled. "I think you're an answer to my prayer." The seagull cocked its head sideways, almost as if it wasn't sure what to make of the comment.

"I don't know about that," said the sailor. "You might change your mind after a few days at sea."

"Well, if you'd have me, I'd be *very* thankful for the offer," said Rowan. "When do you leave?"

"We should be off soon enough. I'm just going to the boat now to get a few last things in order."

"What's your name, sir?"

"Brandon Dosone."

"Rowan Cortak." Rowan extended his hand for Brandon to shake. Then he noticed Alara in her lone vigil against the waves. "Does your offer allow room for one more?"

"I could handle one more, I suppose," said Brandon.

"You don't have a problem with them not being human, do you?" Rowan watched Brandon's face as their hands parted.

"As long as they aren't a goblin, hobgoblin, or ogre, then my crew and I are fine with whomever you bring with you." He followed Rowan's gaze.

"That her?" he asked, jabbing a thumb over his shoulder at Alara.

"Yeah." Rowan nodded.

"Then I think she'd be *more* than welcome." Brandon's smile widened. "You two been together long?"

"Yes—I mean—we've been *traveling* together for a short while now."

Brandon chuckled. "Not really much of my business anyway."

"Where's your vessel?" Rowan asked, eager for a change in topic. "I thought all the boats had sailed for the day. I didn't see any more on the docks."

"I'm docked a little ways further up, away from your line of sight. If you're ready, you can follow me to the boat, and once you're settled we can set sail."

•●•

Alara studied the sloshing waves of the Cerulean Sea, thinking of how their churning mirrored her own thoughts. She found herself wondering—*again*—if she shouldn't just head off on her own to return to Rexatoius, Rowan and any obligation she'd once felt toward him be damned. She knew Gilban had told her his insight into this situation, even sharing how they had a destiny together, but he'd said so much since the start of their journey, it was now all a jumble.

Rowan needed some space. She wasn't pleased at bearing the brunt of his anger, but knew that wasn't really him speaking—at least not entirely him speaking. She'd left because part of her had felt she really *was* guilty of what he'd accused her of.

It was true none of this would have happened if she had just gone back with Gilban. And if she had, she'd be home, spending time with her family and enjoying some well-deserved rest. She had turned away from that because . . . because of *what* exactly? She'd told Gilban it was her obligation to vouch for what he'd said—that the Patrious had no desire to go off and build an empire—but that was a half-truth, and she knew it. She was concerned about Cadrissa as well, but that wasn't it either. It was Rowan. She was confident Gilban knew it, and she was starting to believe that Rowan knew it too.

What was she doing chasing after some Nordic knight more than a decade her junior? Was this really what she was feeling? She admired him, true enough—he had great potential—but was this something more than admiration? The longer she'd traveled with him, the more she thought it very well *could* be something more. But the more time Alara kept company with him, the more trouble came. If the last encounter with his own people was any indication, there wasn't going to be much of a friendly welcome awaiting her in Valkoria.

Her selfishness was hurting his mission and had probably hampered Gilban's mission as well. She had basically thrust him into the arms of a strange goblin they'd only just met. That hardly sounded like a responsible thing to do, given that she'd been brought along to protect him in the first place. Yes, everything had been going relatively well until the two of them crossed paths. Maybe it *was* for the best if they just parted ways now and were done with it.

"Alara?" She heard a soft voice say her name. Behind her stood a rather penitent Rowan. "I'm sorry—about earlier, I mean. It's just—things haven't been going like I thought they would."

"You were right, though." Rowan was surprised by her reply. This wasn't the reaction he'd been expecting. "If I wasn't with you, you'd be on your way back to Valkoria. Maybe you should just go on without me. It might be easier . . . for both of us."

"And where would *you* go?"

"I could sell the sloop, then take the money to go as far west as it would get me."

"I've been with you long enough to know you don't really mean that."

Yes, he definitely had some potential. "Either way, looks like we're going to have to camp again tonight. I won't be able to sell anything now, and there aren't any boats left to sail until morning."

"I wouldn't be too sure of that." There was a hint of boyish mischief in Rowan's face and voice. He pointed at a white-haired Telborian some yards away from where they stood. The man gave a wave. "He's willing to take us on his ship, and he's leaving right now."

"Do you trust him?" Alara kept her focus on the Telborian, thinking.

"I do."

"How did you find him?"

"*He* found *me*, actually—by the grace of Panthora. And he says he can take us to Arid Land."

She found Rowan again as she sighed. "Well, it's the best option we have at the moment. And Arid Land's halfway, isn't it?" She still wasn't entirely clear on the distance between the Northlands and the Midlands and was making an informed guess.

"It's closer to the keep than we are now."

"Yeah, it is, isn't it?"

"Something wrong?" Rowan asked.

She paused. "It's—it's just a little strange having you two cross paths so quickly, is all." She tried putting her best spin on the matter, not wanting to entirely dissuade Rowan from what he clearly thought was a good thing.

Rowan smiled. "I told you, Panthora must have arranged it. She's still watching over me and guiding my way."

Alara gave a small nod. "Okay, so it looks like we have a possible ride to Arid Land. But is he letting us board for *free*?"

Rowan's face went slack. "How serious were you about selling that sloop?"

About an hour later Brandon, Alara, and Rowan were on the deck of a caravel. No decoration adorned its sides. No insignia or marker of any manner showed ownership of the vessel. The boat didn't even have a name. It was a silent form entirely, as quiet as the breeze blowing across the Yoan Ocean, over which they would soon travel. All the vessel had was a simple mast and a skeleton crew of Telborian males in their twenties. No one spoke to the new passengers, or even their captain, which made for a slightly surreal setting. But as long as the boat took them closer to Valkoria, it didn't really matter.

"So you're all set?" Brandon asked, playing with a few ropes along the riggings as he looked his new passengers over.

"We have all we need." Rowan's spirits had lifted considerably since the incident with the *Frost Giant*, which now seemed to have occurred days ago instead of mere hours. He and Alara traveled very light, having lost much in the hurried flight from the lizardmen in the marshes. Rowan had also left his chest on the *Frost Giant*. He'd had no desire for another confrontation with the captain over it. And he hadn't wanted to try toting it around the docks or anywhere else he might have wandered before he crossed Brandon's path. Besides, it was making its way back home anyway. They'd be sure to unload it when they arrived, and it would get back to his new room at the keep. Alara had already taken what she could salvage from the sloop. Whatever they had, they carried.

"And I have a nice new sloop." Brandon gave a small nod to Alara. "It will be well taken care of, rest assured."

"It wasn't going to do us any good anyway," she said.

Rowan thought Brandon had made a fair offer. He'd taken the sloop in exchange for transporting them to Arid Land. Fair in the sense of their present need, that was. He couldn't really speak for Alara. But it wasn't his ship to sell and so whatever she had wanted to do with it was her choice. He'd just been glad she'd decided to sell it, or they would be watching yet another ship—and possibly their last best option—passing into the sunset.

"So you must be in a great hurry to get to Valkoria." Brandon finished with the riggings before sizing up each crewman square in the eye.

"More than you know," said Rowan.

"Well, hopefully, you'll find more help once you get to Arid Land." A seagull's squawk lifted Brandon's head to the topmast, where the same bird Rowan had seen perched on Brandon's shoulder earlier kept a lone vigil amid the riggings above.

"So when do we leave?" Alara asked.

A soft wind tickled the sails. "How does *now* strike you?" Brandon said with a grin, marching for the wheel. "Heave, lads!" he bellowed to his crew. "We'd best take this spurt while we can!"

The silent hands responded rapidly, swarming like hornets about the boat, letting loose the sails that swallowed the winds with a ravenous gulp.

The boat was off with an incredible speed across the harbor. It glided into open waters, churning the waves before its prow like a plow in the field.

"We'll be in Valkoria before we know it," said Rowan, pleased with their already rapid progress, fully expecting it to continue until they reached the Arid Sea.

CHAPTER 13

HAIL THE CRIMSON FLAME!
ALL GLORY TO HIS NAME!
BENEATH HIS SHADE LET ALL GIVE KNEE,
FOR GREAT IS OUR MASTER, AS ALL SOON SHALL SEE.

—"An Ode to Gorallis, the Crimson Flame"

Hilin found himself with the rest of the high priests at the head of a small procession consisting of a handful of lesser priests accompanied by the Red Guard. He'd taken to keeping watch over Gilban, leading him where he needed to go. A fitting gesture, since Hilin had been the one given the vision that had brought this all to pass. The warriors with them carried one black and one white banner with a gout of red flame at the center of each.

The procession passed through the town in which the Red Guard lived, which was at the base of Rheminas' Fingers: close enough to be near their god, who lived in the "thumb" of the "hand," without risking too many of the dangers posed by an active volcano. Those who saw the procession looked on with murmuring lips and excited eyes. Already rumors of something great—something about Gorallis—had spread among the people. Those of the population not dressed in red tunics, pants, or dresses wore red scale mail, red capes, or horned helmets, and carried deadly long swords.

At first the Red Guard had lived in the volcanic valleys around Gorallis' lair, forming small camps while always practicing their martial skills. They wanted to be ready when their master called upon them. As centuries passed, women began filling their ranks, and soon whole generations of children were born knowing no other reality than that of being a servant to the great Crimson Flame. It was with this influx of children that the camps slowly became homesteads, and in the present era formed what could be called a town.

"How far is it?" Gilban asked.

"If you can keep the pace we'll be there soon enough," said Hilin. The elf was actually doing quite well, in spite of just having his staff to aid him. He hadn't stumbled once since they began the procession. All the easier for Hilin.

"You were the one who had the vision, correct?"

"Yes." Hilin focused on the large volcano rising ahead of them. There was a path weaving through the rocky terrain, created from past eruptions, that would lead to a large cavern at the base. From there, they'd ascend until they reached the heart of the volcano and the slumbering Gorallis.

"What's your name?"

"Hilin."

It didn't take long for the warm air to grow even more so, adding a metallic tang that began coating and agitating the throats of those present. As they neared the cavern's mouth, the procession came to a stop. The opening was quite large. No one had ever really measured it, since few dared to get so near their god, save the priests. Even to them being this close was a rare occurrence. As long as Gorallis slumbered there wasn't much need for them to venture that often into his lair.

The cavern's mouth was dark, illuminated weakly here and there by the veins of lava bubbling through the broken rocks, briefly pouring out before crawling back beneath the earth that spawned it. Magma sizzled like meat on a spit. The sound was nearly everywhere. The hair on their hands, eyebrows, and nostrils was singed—even the very hair on their heads felt like flaming straw.

"Wait here," Nagal said, addressing the accompanying guardsmen. "We shouldn't be long. Only the priests are to accompany us further." The group split, leaving the guardsmen at the cavern's mouth while the priests encircled Gilban.

"We're at the mouth of the cavern," Hilin informed the elf.

"I gathered as much from the heat." Gilban leaned heavily on his staff. Sweat covered his face, just as it did the other priests', like fine linen. "How much farther now?"

"It'll be a bit longer until we actually near the volcano's heart," Hilin answered.

"Then Saredhel preserve me from this furnace," Gilban wheezed as Aylan waved them all forward.

From that point on no one spoke. This was holy ground. Together they walked up an incline, turning up and around the volcano. As they marched, the darkness was overcome by the searing glow and heat of an awesome inferno. A few paces later, the tunnel took a sharp right, placing them before the volcano's heart.

"We're here," Hilin said as he joined those gaping at the enormous open space. It was at least an eighth of a mile in diameter, rising another half mile above them, where a tiny dot served as the vent for the eye-watering fumes and smoke that continuously rose from the lake of magma.

Once again the elf had done well navigating the terrain. He was even more sure footed than some of the priests, who'd stumbled a time or two along the way. His endurance was remarkable, too. Hilin was barely holding his own. He couldn't imagine what the frail elf was having to endure. He just had to keep drawing breath for a little while longer. After that, Hilin didn't care if he fell dead on his face. All that mattered was getting Gorallis his eye.

"Just us now from this point forward," Nagal instructed the other priests, who gave a bow before retreating from the high priests. While they might have been eager, Hilin noticed some were pleased at the reprieve.

"Watch your step," Hilin said, laying hold of Gilban's sleeve and pulling him forward until they reached a ledge. It was thin but solid, enough to keep them from the seething lake of magma just a hundred feet below. "We're in the very center of his holy lair. The heat of his presence overpowers us. And yet he's merely sleeping." His hand became tight as a talon on Gilban's shoulder. "Now, awaken him, so we might be called to his side and the Crimson Flame can consume all."

"I hear the magma," said Gilban as he stared off into space. "How far are we from it?"

"It's about a hundred feet below us," said Hilin. "Safe enough for now."

"Unless you prove to be lying," Aylan added.

"The eye!" Hilin nearly choked on the words. "We've done our part. Now you do yours."

Gilban reached into the spot of his robe where he'd hidden a red silk pouch. As he retrieved it, the elf shed the fine silk covering, revealing a familiar orb.

"Just as I've foreseen," said Hilin, wide eyed, as Gilban brought the orb to his chest. It was like he was in another vision.

"Gorallis shall arise!" Grell was beside himself with joy.

"And when he does, the world will tremble!" Aylan added in obvious delight.

"Sadly," Gilban acknowledged, "I think you're right. I can only hope what I'm about to do will outweigh any evil your master brings." He placed the small orb to his lips and whispered something over it. The orb swelled while taking on a bright orange aura. The orange illumination quickly encompassed Gilban before shooting a beam into the deep center of the writhing magmatic lake. The orange light shot through the liquid rock with blinding speed, digging into it like a rabid mole. The flash of the beam was instantaneous, dimming from the bright orange to its original red hue within an eyeblink.

Hilin dropped to his knees. "It has come to pass. Gorallis shall arise."

"Hail the Crimson Flame," said the other high priests, who followed Hilin's lead in the honor and worship of their god.

A stillness hovered over the area, like a gentle, gauzy breath. It was as if the world had stopped in anticipation of what would come next. Slowly, the lake changed. Its boiling slowed before stopping completely, becoming like freshly molten glass whose serenity was disrupted by a large rock emerging from its center in a continuous fluid motion. As it rose, smaller rocks budded around it. These stones transformed into small horns on a great reptilian face, the first rock forming part of a large snout.

The emerging head was longer than a catapult, and wider than three war horses lined end to end. It rose high into the domed sky with the aid of a long, thick neck of crimson scales, and was studded on its back with black spikes as tall as a Nordican. Two massive forelimbs, acting as arms, erupted from the steaming magma, and dug into the earth before and below Gilban and Hilin, causing the ground to tremble and Gilban to nearly fall over. The arms were like ruby towers, sturdy and immense; their talons dug long scars deep into the rocky ledge.

The linnorm seemed to match the color of the lava from which it had risen. A fiery orange-red body glowed amid a smattering of cold, black scales. If one used his imagination, it would seem like the whole linnorm could have been crafted from magma. Hilin instantly lowered his head as a large yellow reptilian eye moved his way. While not filling the whole lake, Gorallis was still a massive and awe-inspiring sight. Just how large he really was, no one presently living knew, but it was common lore linnorms never stopped growing.

Gorallis' lone right eye spied the form of Gilban and hovered over him for a moment. His left eye socket was scabbed over, covered in tiny scales with a deep scar running from the top of the socket to the bottom. The scar itself was wide enough to serve as a footpath or game trail in some wood.

"Who has awakened me?" Gorallis' deep voice spoke Telboros. It was so strong the walls of the volcano shook, causing small chunks of debris to fall into the pool below.

"I have," Gilban answered in Telboros, craning his head as high as his neck would allow. "Gilban Polcrates."

"Why?"

"I have come, great Gorallis," Gilban said, his manner diplomatic, "to ask for an exchange. I wish to collect the Scepter of Night to hinder a growing threat I've been commissioned to stop. In return, I will give you your eye."

Gorallis' massive head silently swung to observe the other prostrate priests. His lone eye, which was bisected with a vertical black pupil, contracted as he scanned the elven seer. "And why should I give you anything when I could slay you and take what you have for myself?"

"Because to hinder me would be to anger those who sent me."

Gorallis' eye narrowed. "And *who* has sent you to me?"

"A vision compelled me," Gilban declared. "A vision sanctioned by my goddess, Saredhel."

"And what did this vision reveal?" Gorallis' head retreated a short distance from the blind seer, taking the heat that had been radiating off it with him, for which Hilin and the others were grateful. Feeling brave, Hilin dared to lift his head enough to get a clearer view. If he was able he wasn't going to miss a single part of this historic event.

"That I'll have need of this scepter to stem a rising threat, as I've already stated," said Gilban.

"That's all?"

"That was all I was told." Hilin was amazed at Gilban's boldness before the face of a god.

"Such blind trust in things you know nothing about." Gorallis' nostrils flared as he inhaled a deep breath. "You must be a fool or indeed a true man of faith to brave my lair in the hopes of rousing me for this parley."

"I only do as I'm led to do. Nothing more."

Gorallis drew further from Gilban, fixing his focus on the still-prostrate priests. Hilin made sure to lower himself to his former subservient pose. "And it seems my priests have led you to me. Rise." They did as bidden, keeping their eyes low and the sockets of their bone headdresses level with their god's studious stare.

Hilin ventured an explanation. "It was all on behalf of your vision, Lord Gorallis."

"Vision . . ." The linnorm slid the word across his lips.

"Yes," he continued. "The vision you sent. The one proclaiming your awakening. Everything you've shown me has come to pass." Gorallis paused. Hilin wasn't sure if that was good or bad but wasn't about to dare another look for clarification.

"You did well in bringing this elf to me." Hilin basked in his god's praise.

"We live to serve you, my lord," said Aylan, who was equally great in his admiration.

"As well you should," replied Gorallis. "And do you wish to serve me now?"

"Oh yes, my lord!" Aylan said, popping his head up in his excitement.

"I hunger." Aylan disappeared into Gorallis' lightning-fast jaws as he swallowed the priest whole. Too fast for a scream, too quick for regrets, the Celetor was chewed twice before becoming one with his deity. The action immediately brought the high priests who remained into sudden prostration.

"All hail the Crimson Flame! All praise his name!" Hilin, Nagal, and Grell recited until the initial shock of the action had faded.

"My love for gods is probably not what it should be," Gorallis informed Gilban, "and I care nothing for your so-called *threat*. But I do owe a debt to the children of Cleseth, and it would be good to finally be able to repay it. And so I shall, by granting your request instead of roasting you alive."

"A very wise and charitable decision," Gilban replied, with a small bow of his head.

"What is the date?" Gorallis said, lowering his head for a closer view of Gilban and the orb clutched at his side.

"It's the first day of Asoria, seven hundred fifty-three years since the Vindication," Gilban informed him.

"So I've slept for more than forty years?" Gorallis' whisper echoed like the rumble of distant thunder in the cavernous chamber. "Before we proceed, I want a closer look at the eye."

Hilin dared another peek, watching Gilban hold the orb for inspection. Gorallis' huge nostrils, which could swallow a man in their own right, sniffed at it, while his eye scrutinized every facet of it like a jeweler deciding how best to cut a diamond.

"Where did you find it?"

"That's of little concern." Gilban returned the orb to his side.

"Bold words for a blind priest in a linnorm's lair." Gorallis snorted a hot gust. "You realize I could take it from you at any time."

"I am trusting you to be an honorable being." The words brought a smile to Gorallis' scaly lips. Hilin thought if the elf could see just how frightful that smile truly was, he might not be so confident.

"Then you won't be disappointed," said Gorallis as he rose slightly higher, stretching his neck and serpentine body. "The Scepter of Night. I thought the world might have forgotten about it by now. It's been so long since I found it. Do you even know how to work it?"

"Not yet," Gilban admitted. He had to crane his neck as far back as it would go to look up at Gorallis, though why he did so was beyond Hilin, since the elf couldn't see anything anyway. "I trust you can provide such information as part of the exchange."

Gorallis again sunk lower into the magma, bringing his head even with the ledge on which Gilban stood. "Whatever you plan on doing with it, the scepter can only be used once in your lifetime. Once, and no more."

"I understand."

"Good." The linnorm turned his palm to the seer. "Now hand it over."

Hilin held his breath. Here was the moment of truth. He wasn't going to miss any of it, and turned more to his side, allowing a full, unhindered view of the action. He was confident he was going to witness a powerful miracle of which future legends would arise. Legends in which he himself might actually have a small part.

After a simple check with his staff, Gilban bent low and placed the orb in Gorallis' palm. The orange light blazed once more from the orb's center, and the apple-sized globe swelled first to the size of a grapefruit, then a head of cabbage, before Gorallis closed his claw and brought it up to his snout. With the orange light still shining from between his claws, he slammed his palm into the left side of his face, right over the scarred empty socket. This motion was followed by a mighty roar that erupted with such force that it flung Gilban against the stone wall behind him, where he dropped to the ground, winded but conscious.

Rocks fell from above, splashing huge puddles of lava far into the air and narrowly missing Gilban and the kneeling high priests, who, thankfully, had not been thrown by the roar. An explosive flash of amber and orange filled the chamber, flying up and out of the opening at the volcano's roof. In its wake was a powerful linnorm with two yellow, black-slit eyes glaring at the fallen seer. Fire danced amid their gleam above a smile that was the most terrible yet.

"Great is Gorallis," Hilin whispered in awe.

"You've done well." Gorallis chuckled. More sprays of pebble-sized debris rained down upon him, shaken loose by the linnorm's thunderous mirth. "Yes, quite well. And now you shall be rewarded."

•●•

Hadek scratched the old metal floor of his cell with his fingers. He didn't like being left alone for so long. Things had taken far too long for his liking. He had to prepare for the worst. And that meant he needed a plan. If he was truly on his own now, he had to set about trying to get himself away from these red-clothed fanatics before their mood changed and his throat found its way to a dagger's edge.

He'd managed to free himself from his bindings shortly after Gilban left, and now watched the guard in front of his cage with hardened focus. He was good, too good. He wasn't expecting that. Used to being hardly acknowledged at all, the guard's incredible devotion to his task was unsettling . . . and frustrating. If he was going to find a way out of this mess he needed to think harder. *Think.*

He looked around the cage. There was nothing to help him—nothing at all. He squirmed to the back of the cell, letting his head rest against the bars. When he did, he heard a faint clunk and thought he felt a bar move slightly. Amazed, he gently pressed the bar again. It gave some but still held securely. If the guard heard anything, he didn't react, remaining as still as a statue.

Silently and swiftly, Hadek wiggled the metal rod like it was a rotten tooth, twisting and tugging, pulling and pushing. It seemed to be loose where the bar met the metal floor of the cell. The more he played with the bar, the more a thin layer of decayed flakes of crumb-like debris appeared around its base. He steadily—and quietly—continued to work the metal rod, taking the debris brought forth as a positive sign of his success.

After some more finagling, he'd managed to work the bar loose enough so he could push it outward at a forty-five-degree angle. In very little time he was able to push the bar out of the top slot holding it in place.

This created an opening just wide enough to squeeze his small frame through. He made a last check on the guard. Amazingly, his captor remained still. Maybe he was finally getting a little lazy. Hadek exhaled a deep breath, then shimmied through the opening. He was out of the cage and running free in a heartbeat.

He got no more than thirty yards before he wondered where he should go next. Did he dare risk trying to find out what happened to Gilban or just look out for himself? He supposed he could do both—at least for a while.

He slowly maneuvered into a shadowed area close to an outcropping of rock that marked the beginning of the pathway between the volcanoes where he and Gilban had been captured. It would keep him hidden long enough to get his bearings and focus. He let out a slow breath, which he discovered he'd been holding for some time. He hoped he might find something that could tell him Gilban's whereabouts, but it was a slim hope at best. Still, if the elf could get them both out of here with a simple prayer, it behooved Hadek to at least make sure that option was totally lost to him before moving on with his own plans.

Eventually, his breathing and his heart slowed. He wanted to make sure he had full control of his body and mind before he continued. Keeping to the shadows was a very consuming effort. And he should know; he'd used it effectively against Boaz more than once. He knew he probably had only a moment to rest before someone noticed he was missing. He was surprised the alarm hadn't been raised already. Maybe the guard really was getting a little lazy.

Hadek managed to sneak around the outskirts of the village, keeping to the volcanic rock as much as possible in order to avoid detection. He searched for any signs of Gilban, anything to help him figure out where he'd been taken. For the better part of an hour he searched, but found nothing. Disheartened, but not wanting to press his luck any further, he decided to make his way to the beach where they'd first arrived. He mentally cursed himself for wasting so much time and not putting enough distance between himself and his captors when he heard some rocks tumble behind him.

He froze.

Slow footsteps followed. *Think!* He had nothing. No weapons. No Gilban. No help. No hope. It was over. Letting out a deep breath that sounded more like a shivering sigh, he turned and faced his enemy, hoping to die fast. But when he spun around, he was caught by surprise.

"Gilban?"

"Ah, there you are," the blind elf said to the rather stunned goblin. "I've been looking all over for you." He gingerly stepped down the last bit of incline on the rocky ledge and stopped at Hadek's feet. Gilban seemed as whole and sound as ever. The only thing different Hadek could see was a silver scepter that hung at his side.

"*You* were looking for *me*?" He wasn't sure Gilban even grasped the irony of his statement.

"Yes. And you certainly wandered from where we last parted ways."

"I thought you were dead," said Hadek, still unsure he was really seeing everything correctly.

"Did you?" There was a small lopsided grin on Gilban's lips as he spoke. "I told you it would be all right. And Gorallis was most helpful."

Hadek glanced again at the scepter. It was a brilliant but elegantly simple object, in sharp contrast to the seer's humble attire. He was surprised at how strongly the urge rose up within him to take hold of it. He swiftly trampled it back down. The less he had to do with all of this, the sooner he could find a normal life for himself.

"Now, if you're through exploring," Gilban continued, "we should be off."

"Just like that?" Hadek asked. "These fanatics are just going to let us go?"

"Yes," Gilban replied. He kept his face and answer devoid of emotion. "Gorallis will be quite happy with his new eye for a while, and I've been given his word we have safe passage. He's still an honorable creature, and his followers see him as a god. They'll let us pass unharmed."

"Then let's get moving," he said, taking hold of Gilban's hand.

Gilban submitted to the goblin's lead. "So where did you think you were going?"

"What do you mean?" Hadek helped Gilban over the last of the ledge and onto the flatter ground.

"You escaped the cage, but where were you escaping *to*?"

"Just away from here, I guess," he said, glancing over his shoulder. "I *was* trying to find you for a while."

"Were you, now?" A sardonic smile played on Gilban's face. "Then I'm glad you achieved your goal."

"Let's just get out of here," Hadek said and began making his way forward again. "It's going to be a long walk back to the beach."

"No, not by foot." Gilban put his hand on Hadek's shoulder, keeping him from progressing any further. "We have to travel the same way we came. I merely wanted to be out of Gorallis' aura in order to keep my prayers free from any contamination."

"Contamination?"

Gilban didn't explain any further. Instead, he asked, "Are you ready?"

"I guess."

Gilban grabbed the Eye of Fate around his neck and whispered a prayer to Saredhel. He and Hadek faded from sight. A moment later, they reappeared on the beach where they'd first arrived—facing the Sea of Shadows. It felt better being farther from the volcanoes, but it would be even better when they were back in Rexatoius.

"So all this trouble was for *that*?" Hadek said, pointing to the scepter. "It must be really important." He continued staring at it, uncertain of what to think. It was plain with a slender shaft and a round head about the size of a plum, but at the same time incredibly fascinating.

"Yes, it is. If it works as well as I was told, and I believe it will, then it's imperative we get to our final destination."

"So it's back to Rexatoius."

"Arid Land, actually."

"*Arid Land?* I thought we'd just get this scepter and be done with it all!"

"Did you?" asked Gilban as his attention flowed back to the waves and the sun now sinking into the horizon.

Hadek gruffly crossed his arms. "So what else did you lie to me about?"

"I meant no deception, Hadek. I *did* tell you we were going to Antora."

"Right, and *that* was it." Hadek furrowed his brow and scowled.

"Well, things have to go a bit farther," Gilban said, adopting a fatherly tone. "You're welcome to come along if you wish . . . or you can stay here. The choice has been, and still is, up to you."

"*Some* choice," he muttered under his breath. He was beginning to wonder if that wasn't more a joke than an affirmation.

"So is *this* part of my greater destiny?"

"We don't have much time, Hadek. Tell me now how you would have it. Either come with me or stay here."

"You can't send me back to Rexatoius?"

"No—at least, not until we've been able to complete what needs to be done in Arid Land."

"Would you actually come back for me if I chose to stay?"

"That depends on what happens in Arid Land." Gilban closed his eyes in concentration. "I can't foresee anything at this point in time, but the future is always in flux . . ."

"So we'll just call that a no," Hadek said, releasing a frustrated sigh. "Why do I have the feeling you're *still* not telling me everything?"

Gilban opened his eyes but said nothing.

"Fine, I'll go with you." He didn't have much of a plan for when they got back from Antora anyway. And part of him had wondered if they'd even return in the first place. So, in a way, going with Gilban made sense. He didn't want to feel like he was being used for ends he knew nothing about, although he already was to some small, but growing, degree. So at this point what difference did it really make anyway?

"I'm not *that* stupid to stay here alone."

"You *were* willing to do so before, if I recall." Gilban's voice flirted with sarcasm once more.

"Let's just leave. I want to be done with linnorms and scepters and all the rest of this."

"Very well. Then prepare to focus on Arid Land."

"Don't we need more priests to get there?" Hadek watched as Gilban grabbed hold of his pendant.

"No, that was a much more powerful petition. It spanned time as well as a great distance. We're to remain in the same time frame now, so the task is much easier."

"Oh . . . wait, did you say we moved through time? How—"

"Ready?" Gilban interrupted, not waiting for a response. He prayed in his native language under his breath as he grasped the Eye of Fate. In just a few breaths Hadek experienced the familiar swimming sensation he'd felt back at the temple before he saw the lavender light envelop him.

"Remember to focus on Arid Land" were the last words Hadek heard as his consciousness failed him.

CHAPTER 14

Enter the darkness dreaming and you'll never awake.

—Old Tralodroen proverb

Dugan stood across from the only bards bold enough to enter the Tempter's District after dark. In the hopes of garnering some coin, they'd set up and performed for more than an hour, managing to gather a small crowd about them off Tempter's Way. The only main through street bisected the rundown district as it snaked along the worn plaster-faced wooden buildings and aged brick structures. The street's tributaries were nothing more than alleyways, littered with refuse and other things best kept out of immediate sight and mind.

The street was so named for being by far the worst area in the entire city of Haven. Behind its walls and more pleasant avenues lurked deadly characters. Brothels and gambling halls lined whole blocks, behind temples and other respectable places, like sickly shadows. As in most cities, Haven was built outward—like an expanding puddle—with the oldest sections in the center and the newest outside ready to lure the innocents in like a spider lures its prey. The oldest part was called the Tempter's District, named for all the temptations that assailed anyone who simply passed through it.

These four bards, however, didn't seem to show any concern for personal peril as they each enacted some special feat for the enjoyment of the twenty or so onlookers. One of them performed with lit torches, eating the flames and spitting them out again in fiery bursts. Another juggled four colored balls while moving back and forth. Still another conducted acrobatic maneuvers, like standing on his head and walking about on his hands. The last of their company piped a merry tune, a drunken ballad often heard in taverns and inns where the occasional handful of patrons would sing the refrain whenever so moved.

Though the gathering crowd was far from impressed, the variety of the entertainment—and the lingering effects of copious amounts of alcohol—saw them willing to part with a few of their coins. Dugan wasn't one of them. Instead, he kept his green eyes fixed on the antics while his mind wandered somewhere else. He shot his head up sharply when a robust man bumped into him while clapping ecstatically—a drunken glaze in his eyes. The former gladiator scowled before returning to his thoughts as his mind fixed on the fire eater, recalling his own past and the fire that ate him.

He'd thought about his past almost incessantly since arriving in the city. The money he'd collected from the ruins had helped him enjoy his newfound freedom, but now that coin was almost gone. He'd spent it like water, enjoying the life he'd been denied for so many years. As Vinder had warned, the temptation to overindulge had been too strong a pull, and now he forced himself to grow more tightfisted with what remained.

He departed the crowd. It had grown late and the entertainment ceased being the distraction he desired. What coin remained would afford him a room for at least one more night. Then he'd have to start sleeping in the streets or wandering outside the city. Until then he'd try his best to move faster than his thoughts, and hope he could outrun them by morning light.

The night had grown cold over the shops and alleys, and the stench of urine, spoiled food, and fetid mud was still strong despite the soft breeze. Barking dogs, groaning victims, and cries of death mixed to form an odd and fitting song. It was the song of the hopeless. A song he was beginning to think might be his new anthem. The illumination from the stars and first-quarter moon aided his walk. He spied vagrants and miscreants behind every shadowy corner and nook. They reminded him of rats, with their mischievous eyes.

He kept his hand on the pommel of the sword at his left hip, ready for anything. Once arriving in Haven, he'd traded the two weapons he gained from the ruins, along with the gladius he'd commandeered from the hunters, for a single blade. The merchant who had done the transaction told him the broadsword he now carried was able to do incredible feats of wonder in the right wielder's hand. Just what those feats were the man didn't specify, but after testing the weapon Dugan noticed it felt like something more than a common sword. As for coaxing any further wonders from the blade, he'd been unable.

The horse was the first thing he'd sold upon entering the city. He'd no need of it any more and wasn't about to pay for its upkeep. He probably didn't get too fair of a price for it but didn't care. The extra coin had helped him really get to see and enjoy more of the city than he otherwise would have.

He'd also traded his armor for a simple breastplate of polished steel attached to studded leather pauldrons. He didn't feel the need to stay as heavily armed and armored now that he was in the city. He didn't plan on going on any more adventures and wasn't really looking for any more fights. He discovered the citizens of Haven didn't mind armed men in their cities. They'd a strong, able-bodied guard to handle any uprising—a virtual army in its own right. Besides, most sane folk knew it was wise to keep a dagger, a mace, or even a simple club in their homes for protection. From what he'd seen, the largest—and possibly most dangerous—army in Haven, should they ever be given cause for assembling, was the citizens themselves.

The largest and most diverse city on Tralodren, Haven itself was said to be the reason why Talatheal, the land on which it rested, had earned the nickname "the Island of the Masses." It was in Haven that all races, creeds, and faiths were allowed. They even had an academy of magic where Cadrissa had supposedly studied. They also had all manner of temples and shrines. And that, more than anything, had called him like a moth to flame.

What he was able to find in the way of shrines and temples en route to Haven offered him scant comfort. Causilla, Endarien, Shiril, and Asora could only bless him and send him further on a journey that he felt was going nowhere fast. When he reached Haven, he sought out the major powers of the Tralodroen pantheon: Ganatar, Gurthghol, and Dradin. All failed him. The day prior, he'd finished with the last of the gods: Asorlok, Khuthon, Olthon, and Saredhel. All had left him peering sadly into a dim and murky future of grievous uncertainty.

He wandered through the rat-speckled roads, looking for any sign or person who could lead him to his desired end. The further he traveled, the less he saw. Now, not even alley cats and their bulbous prey scurried through the rank puddles. The hours passed until dawn's fingers caressed the stars. He'd passed through the old center of Haven without encountering so much as a wandering drunk. Tired and in need of rest, he was ready to call it a night when a cloaked figure, much shorter than him, appeared from the shadows.

"Your name's Dugan, right?"

Dugan drew his sword. "Who are you?"

"If you still want to find what you seek, you must come this way." The figure moved into a lone alleyway across from him.

"And what am I seeking?" Dugan stood his ground.

"I've watched you for days. You've traveled from temple to temple, looking and pleading for release from your dark pact with Rheminas. I've heard you ask the priests about it. But you're asking the wrong people."

"You've been *watching* me?" Dugan's eyes narrowed.

"Oh yes, I have known about you since the time you first entered Haven. The others have too."

"Others?" Dugan asked, intrigued. He took a few steps to follow the man into the alleyway.

"We're the eyes and ears of this city," said the figure as he melted further into the shadows. "Nothing happens here we don't know about." His voice then took on a soft satin quality as he said, "There is much to tell you, but it can't be spoken here. Too much can be overheard; we're not the only eyes and ears about. Come with me and you'll be given the answers to all your questions. You may even find a purpose for your newfound freedom."

"You want me to trust you after you just said you were spying on me?"

"Yes." He tried to get a better view of the figure other than his dark outline but was unsuccessful. "It won't take long. You can hear our proposal and decide if you want to accept it."

"You're offering me a job?" Dugan tightened the grip on his sword. He didn't know where this was going but it smacked of some shading of the truth.

"Your coin is just about gone, isn't it? And you aren't going to get the freedom you seek from the other gods, that's for sure. So why not at least hear the offer? I think you'll be pleasantly surprised."

"More than I am at you spying on me?" He continued searching for the other's face beneath his shadowy cowl. "You a wizard?"

"No." When the other man saw that Dugan wasn't going to say or do anything else, he took a step forward, adding, "We'll be able to answer all your questions. Just not here."

"If you're trying to rob me—"

"No," the man said, holding up his hand. "We want to offer you an opportunity to help us, and in turn, we'll help you."

Dugan searched the shadows, asking, "How many are you?"

"Come and see. You and I both know there isn't much more hope out there for you, and if you enjoy the idea of sleeping in the gutter, well, I suppose you're welcome to it. But why not hear us out first?"

Dugan hated to admit it, but the man had a point. He couldn't keep this up forever and knew his options were dwindling by the day. What else did he really have left to hope for? While he had some reservations, it was still a fresh option to explore—a rare thing these days. And he'd never know for sure if it was worthwhile if he didn't at least look into it.

"All right," he said, lowering his sword. "But this better be good."

"Follow me." The figure completely disappeared into the shadows. Dugan was quickly lost as they twisted and turned through an arena of alleys, walls, and secret areas none seemed to know about, save the mysterious man leading him. Finally, they came to a dead end. Dugan scanned the area, ready for anything that might leap out at him. He'd never sheathed his sword, keeping a tight grip the whole time. He might be open to exploring new options, but he still wasn't about to let his guard down—especially not when being led through such a maze.

"You really won't need the sword," the man said, staring at him from under the hood that always masked his features, no matter how many times Dugan tried taking a peek.

Dugan didn't move.

"From here on out, you'd do yourself a service to follow my command," the man continued while turning to the wall. "Where I'm about to lead you is thick with protective devices. One wrong step and you'll be a faint memory." The figure pressed a section of brick wall. Dugan wouldn't have noticed it was any different if the man hadn't revealed it with his action.

A section of the wall smoothly fell into a pitch-black doorway smelling of moisture and rot. The man motioned for Dugan to step through and smiled, revealing his yellowed teeth. "Enter, but step on every other step, or you'll be in for trouble."

He wondered how many of these secret areas dotted the city. How many people had access to them? He saw clearly how this man, and others as well, could follow him or anyone else from anywhere in Haven. It was unnerving. Haven did indeed have some very large rats—intelligent and potentially dangerous rats—scurrying between its walls.

"You go first," said Dugan, motioning with his weapon.

The man bowed, then began the descent. "Remember to step on every other stair. If you so much as brush the top of the wrong stair, your life is over."

Dugan sheathed his sword and followed. The weapon wouldn't be of much use to him in the dark. Their trek down the stairs was very quiet and slow. He didn't want to even come close to the steps he was told to avoid. He'd seen many strange and dangerous devices in the arena, invented to slaughter and ensnare. He stopped for only a moment to see if the man who was supposed to be in front of him still was, or if he had blended into the darkness, leaving him to fend for himself. A few breaths later Dugan heard a soft rustle of fabric in front of him.

"Why have you stopped?"

He still couldn't see him, or anything else for that matter, though his eyes were adjusting to the darkness.

"How much farther?"

"Not much."

"How can you even see where you're going?" He grunted as he tried securing his foot on the next step.

"You'll get used to it." The man's silken voice floated out of the darkness. "For now just trust your instinct and step after me.

"When you enter the next room, you'll meet the others. They'll give you the information you seek, but you must let me do most of the talking. They don't take kindly to strangers entering their most sacred chambers."

"I thought you said they wanted to talk with me."

"They do. It's just that they're always cautious when meeting new people."

"If they threaten me—"

"Then your last breath will be in their presence." Dugan thought he could make out the hooded man's outline. His vision was finally adjusting to the darkness of the tunnels. "We are ardent defenders of our faith."

Dugan was going to say something more, but he could see the man had raised his hand. He stilled his step. It was still black around him but at least he could make out the basic structure of a room. A room with no door, though he could sense walls close by. One of them was behind his cloaked guide.

"Now, beyond that door is the room I spoke of."

"What door?" asked Dugan.

"Be careful and let me do most of the talking." The man's words were sharp and forceful. "Understood?"

Dugan clenched his jaw.

"Good."

He watched as what seemed to be a solid section of wall was pushed by his guide with only the slightest of effort. Illumination, fainter than torch light, wafted from beyond the secret doorway.

"Please be so kind as to enter." The other motioned Dugan to the opening. For the first time he saw the man's face. It looked long and narrow and slightly rodent-like. Fitting, he supposed.

He continued eyeing the man as he entered the doorway. Though he'd just seen a good deal of his face, Dugan found it hard to recall—the image blurred as he tried to focus upon it. The smell of food and exotic spices pushed this thought aside. The further he traveled the brighter it grew.

The first increase of the light was like a searing poker jabbed straight into his eyes, but he found himself able to focus well enough to make out a tunnel created by dry gray bricks that had seen the years pass cruelly over them. He didn't think they'd hold up the ceiling for much longer. Even as he walked past he saw a small chunk to his left fall with a heavy thud. Continuing on, they came to a large room covered in candles, torches, and braziers, with a fireplace roaring from the wall opposite him.

The room was large, created from the same decaying bricks as the hall but painted a deep red, making the room appear to shift and squirm in the flickering light. No more than ten feet in front of him was a long wooden table covered with food. Breads, meat, and mounds of fruits and vegetables were spread over the oaken surface, making a rather foreign sight to his eyes. But the smell and display were intoxicating and inviting.

As he made his approach, eager to take his fill, scores of black-robed figures emerged from the walls like ants or flies to a carcass. His hand was wrapped around his sword's hilt before he took another breath.

"Hold, Dugan!" came his guide's warning voice from behind. "You're in no danger. These are all followers of Shador." Coming up beside the Telborian, he added, "It's time for us to eat. And you are our guest."

Dugan observed the forms shifting in their dark robes. They gathered around the table, quietly taking whatever victuals met their fancy. He noticed they had neither plates nor any cutlery—tearing and taking whatever they wanted by hand. He found that odd for civilized folk, but having been raised in the arena of Remolos, he didn't make too much of it. No one else seemed to notice, or if they did, didn't bring it to anyone's attention. As they feasted in silence, Dugan studied the room. It was well lit. He made a quick count of the men and discovered they numbered about one hundred fifty, with a few more he thought he could see skulking in the shadows outside the circle of torch light.

After the numbers at the table had thinned, Dugan drew near, taking a turkey leg with great interest. The night of drowning his sorrows was over and he didn't know when he might eat this well again. He waited for the rest to finish in silence. When all had supped, the multitude thinned to a faint shadow of its former count, but Dugan spied on those who remained with predatory eyes. He began catching glimpses of faces when the light peeked into the shadowy pool of their hoods. He could make out elven features, those of humans, and even a few dwarves.

He watched as his guide whispered to a larger man whose racial heritage Dugan couldn't discern. This man was dressed in rich finery dripping with gold, silver, and jewels that was a stark contrast with his black cape and garb. As his guide continued whispering, the larger man's hooded face showed the white sheen of a smile. The pearl-like semblance was eerie and unnatural in the hood's inky pool. He seemed to be in flux: cold and distant one moment and then radiating fatherly warmth the next.

"Welcome, Dugan," the larger man said as he approached. Behind him two other priests followed, each man carrying a wooden chair which they proceeded to set at the table.

"Please," said the other as he motioned to the chair placed before Dugan. "You will come to no harm. We are a peaceful people."

Dugan sat, prompting the man to do likewise. "I was told you'd answer my questions," he informed his would-be host.

"Of course. Let us begin with your most pressing concern. I'm the leader of this religious sect—head priest—and as such, I have direct access to our god, Shador."

"All hail Shador," the others present in the room droned.

"He has told me of your plight, and your need to be rid of your curse." The head priest folded his hands. "He has taken pity upon you and wishes to free you. But for such favor you must partake in a simple matter for his cause."

"A simple matter?" Dugan struggled to make out more of the head priest's features but was unable to see past the flickering shadows.

"Well, simple for someone of *your* skills." For a moment Dugan thought he saw bushy eyebrows, like brown caterpillars crawling over pale flesh.

"How do I know you're telling the truth? I've already dealt with fake priests before . . . and cultists."

"Yes, you have, haven't you?" the head priest declared more than inquired. "But it's given you some wisdom, helping you ask a good question. And you're wise to ask it. This all has to be done in good faith. We with you, and you with us."

"If you don't trust me, why bring me here?" he asked.

"It's not a matter of trust, but what each of us can provide the other."

"Like what?" Dugan didn't like the pointless back-and-forth. Why not just say it plain and clear and get it over with?

"If you'll take on a small task for us, our god will free you from your curse." The priest smiled, a crescent moon in the hood's darkness.

"I want proof."

"I thought we might meet such an impasse." The priest's tone fell flat, but his smile remained. "I've prepared something to help alleviate your fears." He turned to address those behind him. "Bring it in."

A handful in the background parted, allowing another robed figure access into the room. In this new figure's hands was a wrought iron globe the size of a skull, belching dark smoke. The thick vapors moved like an ebony tide, trying to secure anything near it in its sooty grip. It reminded Dugan of the previous visions he'd seen . . . the hungry black tentacles lunging to ensnare him. He shook such memories from his mind, refocusing on everything around him. That was the past, and it was behind him. This was the present and his future.

"Remove the sacred knife of Shador," the head priest instructed.

"All hail Shador" was the response as two more cloaked men approached the globe, lifted off the lid, and drew forth a small, black-hilted knife. The one who withdrew the knife walked to the head priest, handing it to him hilt first. Dugan grew restless. His muscles became tight, and his right hand descended to the hilt of his sword.

"Behold, the power of our god and his valid promises to those who follow him as he bids." The head priest held the knife high over his head and said a word that sounded ancient to Dugan's ears. As he spoke, a thin bolt of azure light struck Dugan's left shoulder. He felt a pinch, then nothing.

"What did you do?" he growled.

"Be calm." The head priest returned the knife to the priest who'd handed it over. The knife was replaced in the globe and then the one holding it left the room. "Shador has shown you his favor. He's removed the mark of your physical slavery, making you free while you live in this world. He'll remove the final piece of your slavery—your *spiritual* slavery—when you complete the task. Then you will *truly* be free."

"I don't believe you," said Dugan coolly.

"Naturally." The head priest pointed at Dugan's left shoulder. "Look for yourself."

He uncovered the metal-studded leather and cloth hiding the section of meaty muscle faster than a hungry hound dashes at a bone. On his shoulder, once marred with the dark designs of imperial branding, the mark of the Elyelmic republic was gone. All that remained was firm, tanned flesh, unmarked and untouched but for time and his own hand as he ran it over his shoulder.

"See this, and know the truth," said the head priest with a small sliver of joy. "Who among the other gods could have done this for you? Asora, the very goddess of healing herself, couldn't even grant you this. Nor could any of the others you petitioned." His voice was a mixture of theatrical charm and religious piety. "It's only with *our* god that your wishes can be granted. You'll be blessed with the life you deserve. All this has been made possible through Shador."

"All praise Shador," the priests repeated.

"Will you listen *now*?" the head priest asked, leaning closer. "Will you *trust* now?" He folded his hands in his robes. "Will you ready yourself to undertake the will of Shador in order that you may *forever* be free?"

Dugan needed only a moment to consider. With this last glimmering of hope, he knew that he wanted to—*had* to—grab it. Even if there was more he wasn't being told, he couldn't let it pass. It seemed he'd have to be another's mercenary yet again in order to gain his freedom. Though he recognized the pattern, he swore to himself it would be the last time he'd repeat it. It had to be.

"Yes."

"Excellent." A faint sparkle of two eyes shimmered from beneath the head priest's hood. "You've made a wise decision, Dugan."

"So what do you want me to do?"

CHAPTER 15

He who shuns his heritage is like gold that's lost its luster,
but he who honors it shines like polished brass.

—The Iron Tablet

The Diamant Mountains scraped the cool, cloudless sky like broken claws. Under the bright morning sun the jagged peaks made Vinder's frame seem like a mouse before giants. He'd taken rest against a boulder nestled in the cover of a small plateau, soaking it all in with a misty eye. The mountains—his homeland—were beautiful. He'd thought he'd never see the sight again. He'd thought he'd tired of them and the whole vision of the rising rock, the snowcapped peaks, the gentle veins of pure water flowing from deep within the mountain's heart. Even the clean, crisp air caused his stomach to turn with homesickness. How wrong he'd been.

Having freshly bathed, he'd trimmed his hair and beard, letting it flow free. He was about to make petition to his clan, family, and god. Tradition held that a dwarf wishing to do so should be humble, without adornment of any kind, so that he should be as pure and natural as the unworked rock itself.

A few feet away rested the cart and the mule he'd taken with him. Both cart and beast had endured the journey well, the mountains being the most challenging part, even with the paths crisscrossing the valleys and peaks.

He also kept a close eye on the chain-wrapped chest inside the cart. He'd kept it covered for most of his journey with a simple burlap cloth, creating the illusion of it being a mound of common hay rather than a collection of riches. The chest itself was quite the sight, close to half Vinder's own height and twice as wide. A sturdy padlock held the chains together. The square clump of steel bore the crest of Olthon. The laurel wreath opened at the bottom, encircling a dove who held a coin purse in one foot and an olive branch in the other. The cart also held his armor and axe, both of which he wouldn't be needing from here on out . . . and hopefully never would again.

He carefully removed the necklace Heinrick had given him in Elandor from under his tunic. It brought him much comfort, filling him with hope of what could be. He took it as a sign that things could be better than he expected upon his return. Now that he was here, and ready to face whatever was coming, he prayed it was so.

Two decades had come and gone since his feet had touched this safe, pure landscape. He'd been a fool, a hotheaded fool. Clan Diamant and his religion demanded a lot from him in the way of penance; he only hoped he had enough. Tradition called for a priest of Drued to meet with the penitent soul before he could be granted entrance into the clan for judgment. Then he would need to be forgiven by his family, his faith, and finally, the clan in a public ceremony. If just one of those groups or persons failed to forgive the trespass, he was forever banned. There was no hope of a second chance. Tradition, honor, and family were the discipline that held the dwarven culture together. He drew his worth from them and was held captive by their edicts, for good or ill.

When Vinder had neared the mountains, he'd sent word through the first watchman he'd encountered to find a priest to perform the rites of remission. The watchman was one of many dwarves who dedicated their lives to the protection and sanctity of Clan Diamant's mountain home. They were the only dwarves allowed to interact with the outside world—though on a limited basis—serving as traders, scouts, and protectors of the Diamantic way of life. Some were even granted leave to trade with the communities around them for the few items the clan couldn't produce or get on their own. This was how Vinder had met Heinrick in Elandor.

The watchman had departed, allowing Vinder to climb the mountain as he sought his peace. That had been quite a while ago now, and he was starting to wonder what had happened. Had the priest not seen him as worthy? Was he being left alone in the mountains to waste away as punishment? All he could do was hold on to the small icon of Drued clutched tightly in his hand and continue his silent prayers. After some time, a noise came from behind him. He hid the necklace in his pocket before turning to see an older figure come up beside him.

This figure was also a dwarf, albeit more regal and refined, even though time had wrinkled his frame. His dark purple eyes shimmered in the daylight and his snowy white beard was divided into three braids held with golden clasps in the shapes of hammers and axes. The braids ended at the same length as Vinder's own newly trimmed beard. The dwarf's skin was a gray tone common to the race, though lighter than Vinder's, which had been darkened by his travels.

The priest wore a silver robe with gold trim also adorned with hammers around the hem and cuffs and a white sash with small golden hammer pendants attached to the ends that tied around his waist. A white stole marked by two crossed golden hammers at each end was draped about his neck, swaying in the soft breeze as he came closer. Vinder wondered how he'd arrived so silently, but put the thought aside. Tradition declared he couldn't ask such things during the rite. He was to remain silent until he was given leave to speak the litany, which had now begun.

"Brother dwarf, wayward son, you have returned." This was the traditional greeting of a priest to an outcast. It was spoken in Dwarfish, which would be spoken exclusively by all from then onward. This too, as tradition decreed. "You have come looking for forgiveness but are not yet pure."

Vinder faced the priest squarely, but didn't look directly at him, staring at the ground beneath his feet instead. "I have come to regain my pride and honor." Vinder was sober in his statement. "Forgiveness is what I seek, holy priest of Drued, my example and my god. I have come on forlorn feet seeking to be forgiven. Cleanse me from my foolishness and selfishness."

The priest took a pouch of sand from his belt and proceeded to dump it onto Vinder's head. "Like the sand, you have forsaken the path of your ancestors. You have broken from that path and are great with fault. Like sand, you have lost the strength of the knowledge that you were formed from the toughest stones in all the world under Drued's mighty hand.

"Drued is great in his mercy, however, and will forgive you for all your foolishness, and welcome your return to the fold of his clansmen."

Vinder dared to look upon a face that hadn't changed a great deal in over twenty years. The stony exterior remained, but he was comforted in knowing he could take this process of repentance a bit further.

"Honorable priest, I seek now your forgiveness. I have been too long from the ways of my clan and my home. Will you show the joy of a father whose lost son has found his way home?"

The priest's stone face crumpled into one of warmth and openness, a thin smile parting the old dwarf's dry lips. "Son, I forgive you. Your time of wandering is at an end."

Tears flowed from the corner of Vinder's eye as he hugged the priest. "Thank you, Father. I've been so stupid and selfish. You were right, and I couldn't see it. I've missed you and Mother these long years."

"We all have," Heimrick, Vinder's father, sobbed as he returned his son's embrace. "Your mother will want to see you, as well as your sister. Come. They're eager for your presence." Looking to the cart and its cargo, he added, "I'll send others for your cart. The chest will need to be evaluated before it's presented to Stephen."

"I know." Vinder gave it and the mule a final contemplative inspection. "I just hope I have enough."

"Come," Heimrick said, beckoning Vinder to follow.

He did so, saying, "Before you arrived I was starting to think I might end up forsaken. But receiving the rite and through *you* of all people . . . it's given me renewed hope." They made their way toward the city, which was still a fair distance from them.

"I had a dream of your return, and took it for a good omen." Heimrick peered over his shoulder. "It seems Drued still favors you after all these years." His father's smile eased whatever fears might have remained. "I was waiting for the news and set out to find you as soon as it came."

"Which you could have easily ignored," said Vinder. "So thank you for your forgiveness and your mercy."

"Drued is merciful to the truly penitent," said Heimrick. "Who am I to try and be anything less?"

Vinder followed his father through the various tunnels, hidden passages, and trails winding toward the secluded dwellings of his clansmen. While his father and Drued had welcomed him there was still much expected of him. The rest of his family, his clan, and his king still waited. He couldn't afford to be seen as anything less than a penitent man.

The guards they passed grew more numerous as they got closer to the capital, but they only acknowledged Heimrick. Vinder tried to do his best to avoid their gazes, which let him relax a little. The guards' actions were all part of the process.

The dwarves of the mountain clans weren't like their kin who dwelled in the hills. The mountain was forbidding and strong. It welcomed no one. Every dwarf that chose to remain in the clan must be the same. He hadn't agreed with this tradition and cultural law. He'd been seen, therefore, as siding with his "lesser kin": the hill dwarves, who welcomed friendship and interactions with the other races. This was what caused the exile from his home, with every hair on his head and face shaved off. That had been twenty years ago. Twenty years of looking for a way back into the home he'd left. And all because he'd shared pleasantries with a Telborian explorer and thought the life he lived in the world below the peaks was more interesting and meaningful than the life Vinder was living in them.

Putting these thoughts behind him, Vinder instead dwelled on the strong faith and religious power his father now held. When he'd last seen him, he was just a common priest of the order. Now he was a high-ranking priest of great distinction. Aside from his father's station, however, nothing else he'd seen so far had changed from how he remembered it. It was like he'd walked into a strange world where the sun hadn't moved in the sky since he was expelled.

Vinder's home—or rather, his parents' home—came into view. It was the first of many solid structures dominating the landscape on the mountains: a sturdy box of a building that blended well into the surrounding rocky reaches and edifices. Its strong walls were built right into the mountain. Its narrow windows allowed a little light to enter and air to flow, but the persistent and harsh mountain wind could not gain easy access.

His family's house was just one of many buildings now visible throughout the mountaintops and crevices, as they'd entered Diam, the capital of Clan Diamant. Some buildings were underground, like the temple of Shiril. But some, like the king's palace, were aboveground, and massive. For beings that weren't known for their staggering size, dwarven architects liked to build things on a grand scale. The palace was clearly the focal point of the landscape. Built in terraces on top of the tallest peak in the area, the palace had shallow lakes of snow just dusting its peaked spires and roof.

All of the buildings in the city had solid square bases and slanted roofs, which helped keep the snow from piling too high, but the palace had been constructed another story above the tallest of these lesser buildings. No one could build anything higher than the king's palace. It represented the mountain upon which they lived—the symbolic source that their government was rooted in. The strength of honorable tradition.

Besides being taller than all other structures, the palace was decorated with the best of stones, hewed out of the sturdiest rocks to fashion a dwelling fit for the king. Fat granite pillars, as smooth as a newborn's lips, lifted the overhanging rock in a stoic colonnade at least three times the height of any dwarf. Iron doors, studded with blond, white, and black diamonds, made the common dwarven guards who stood watch before them look even smaller.

The exterior walls were dressed in relief carvings from the floor to the high roofline above. The history of the clan, from its founding to the present, could be found in their images. The roof was shingled in onyx, the rising towers varying in size, coordinating with the tall peak of stone that the entire palace had been built into. The whole of the structure dug into and enveloped the peak, with dozens of tunnels built within the ancient building.

Vinder studied the lower-level entrance to the palace a moment longer before turning to the less splendorous dwelling of his own family. Squat and plain, but practical, with a few geometrical and runic decorations, his home seemed more splendid than the most glorious of palaces. Though harsh feelings and dark memories might have plagued him throughout his journey, when he reached the threshold of his family home, Vinder's heart lifted. As his father gently pushed on the thick wooden door, it opened, as he knew it would—just like it had before he left, and he knew it would continue doing so even after his family had entered Mortis.

Behind the door his mother, Gilda, stood attentively with a warm smile and open arms. "Vinder!" She ran to him faster than a storm-birthed gale, taking him in her embrace. She was old by dwarven standards—both his parents having started their family later in life—and stood shorter than her son. Her long gray-streaked hair sported patches of black and white which blended into a shade of furnace-cast metal.

"Thank Drued you're alive!" Her eyes were a clear gray, beaming with love as they flooded with tears. "Your father told me of his dream and I . . . I just hoped it was true."

"Mother—do you forgive me?" The question momentarily interrupted her joy, but tradition called for Vinder to ask.

Gilda stepped back and looked at him with slick eyes and a tear-washed face. As she stared at her son—the child she hadn't seen for two decades—with maternal eyes, emotions pulled at her heart, but she had to do her duty both to her family . . . and herself. Years of training and discipline called for nothing less.

"You have left your family, your home, and your parents. Selfishness and shame followed you into the corrupt and failing world, and you want to bring it back with you now?" He watched her fight the conflicting emotions. It was hard, but she managed, as he knew she would and expected her to do.

Vinder bowed his head with shame while his father looked on sternly, just as custom decreed. "I've returned, humbled and broken. I have seen the world outside, and it offers nothing. Its promises are hollow. It is with my family and my clan that I am given truth, and find my purpose and meaning."

Gilda's face brightened into a smile so deeply filled with emotion that it flourished across her face like a field of wildflowers. "Then welcome back, Vinder. I've missed you so much!" She ran to catch him in another powerful embrace.

"I've forgotten how much I missed you—missed this *place*," he said, shedding a few more tears of joy. "It's been too long."

Gilda looked at her son's face, her own hair becoming tangled in his beard. Her eyes narrowed as if she was seeing him for the first time, the ideal image fading into the reality standing before her. "You look so much older than you should, and—by Drued—what happened to your eye?"

"I'd like to know that, too," said Heimrick.

Vinder gently withdrew from his mother's arms while Heimrick joined his wife's side. He sighed deeply before staring into his parents' faces. "I lost it in a battle with a band of brigands I met at the beginning of my banishment.

"I was hungry and alone. I looked to them for aid, but instead found cold steel—and it nearly claimed my life. Thank Drued it only took *one* of my eyes. But I've become stronger because of it, and I've come to know where my place really is."

"You've come back to stay then? You're *sure*?" Gilda eyed Vinder closely. "Once you've reconciled to the clan, you can't be taken back should you decide to leave again."

"There'll be no need." Vinder's timbre echoed the sincerity of his heart. "I'm home, and I can accept that." Looking to his father, he asked, "Where's Gretta?"

"At work." Heimrick's chest rose with pride. "Your sister's a fine blacksmith now. A mighty talented craftsman and weaponsmith to boot. She's even found a suitor."

"When will she be home?" he asked. " 'Tradition is a fool for no one.' And if she hasn't forgiven me, then it'd be pointless to move forward in the process."

"Vinder." Heimrick's voice became small. "Your sister was the first to forgive you the moment you left. She told both your mother and me when you were exiled. We told her to be quiet about it, since she was so young and we thought she didn't fully understand, but she never wavered. She loves you and forgave you long ago."

Vinder's lip quivered before he was able to contain it. "Well then," he said, coughing away any remaining emotion. "I suppose we should notify the clan of the ceremony."

•●•

Vinder viewed the tall marble walls glimmering with the flickering flames of torches, candles, and braziers. Thick tapestries, almost as old as the stones they covered, dominated the walls. Their bright colors were undamaged by time's passage and showcased the true pride of the dwarven nation, as well as the honor of Clan Diamant. The multitude of assembled dwarves looked like a field of statues. This was the clan—his clan, or at least those of any great rank or importance in the clan: the heads of families with their wives. They had been called together with the news of his return. He'd been forgiven for his lack of faith and the betrayal of his family. Now he would ask forgiveness of his clan and king.

All of the dwarves were dressed in their best for the occasion. Tunics and trousers of heavy twill for the men, dresses on the women. The cloth came in a myriad of earthen hues, browns and greens, beiges and creams, and black. Leather boots shod their feet, and polished stones and gems covered them in the form of rings, necklaces, earrings, and bracers.

The men were freshly combed, their beards neatened. This was an important and solemn time, and their appearance was just as important as Vinder's. This meant even their beard braids were on fine display. Upon reaching adulthood, each male gained the right to wear a single braid. The second was allowed upon reaching fifty years of age, with another added for every fifty years after that. Most men dyed the tips of these braids various colors. And those gathered here were no exception. Shades of blue, red, green, orange, and saffron stood out amid the assembly. But all of this paled in comparison to the *real* focus of the room.

Stephen Pram, king of Clan Diamant, was a middle-aged dwarf with a regal manner. He sat on an elegant, ancient throne, a replica of the first one used by the kings of old who once ruled in mighty Druelandia. Resting on a circular dais of smooth white marble, the polished granite seat spoke of the power and authority that had ruled in an unbroken line of kings since the clan's formation millennia ago. He wore a golden gown of state and a silver crown. His medium-length hair and beard were a deep black with two blue-tipped braids falling to the top of his collarbone.

Behind Stephen's throne a white banner fell from ceiling to floor. At its center were three black triangular mountains—the one in the center the largest of the three—that rested over a powder-blue oval whose black outline set it off from the sea of white around it. This was the great symbol for the clan—an ancient crest that had remained unchanged for generations. In front of the banner, standing behind the throne in a semicircle, the priests of Drued watched silently.

Vinder had noticed the priesthood was represented by the chief priest and another eight elected priests—his father among them. Four to the left and four to the right of the throne, with the chief priest on the king's right. All of the priests wore the same attire as Heimrick had when he'd first greeted Vinder, except for the addition of a white cape hemmed with gold in the same hammer motif found on their robes.

Neither Stephen nor the priests looked Vinder in the eye. He lacked honor. They wouldn't give him the benefit of dignified recognition. An additional nine elder men of the clan—the council of elders—stood even more stoically in another semicircle at the dais' base, facing Vinder. These, he knew, would be the toughest bunch to convince—following Stephen—to accept his plea.

As was the custom, Vinder remained silent and kept his head low. Beside him was the chest he'd lugged from Elandor. He knew it had been emptied, weighed, and put to the strictest of evaluations. He'd amassed a great deal of coin to pay the clan, for he was a valued member of society—as were all dwarves—and his contribution would have meant profit and abundance in certain areas. The clan had suffered financially with his loss. In order to procure the sum, he'd found all sorts of means over the last few years to collect an amount he hoped would help pay off the debt he'd incurred while away from his clansmen.

He wasn't always proud of what he had to do to get the coin, but he consoled himself by recalling that what had been taken from those fallen in battle could rightfully be claimed as spoil. He also took heart that some of the money was payment for services he rendered as a mercenary on previous adventures, and thus, he'd avoided less honorable ways of procurement. Between these two channels he'd found a balance he could live with. In the end, though, it would come down to what Stephen thought.

The silence in which he waited was suffocating. For a room filled with people there should have been some sort of sound—instead it was as if he stood in a graveyard whose lifeless tombstones were glaring at him. Finally, when he could bear it no more, and when his silent and desperate pleas for Drued's aid were all but exhausted, Stephen spoke.

"Shame upon you, you worthless pile of sand," the king's voice bellowed, vibrating throughout the chamber. "Disgrace and disobedience to our clan, your family, and our god: these things you bring with you, and declare your unworthiness. You have no place here. Yet you return and wish for us to acknowledge you. Why would you dare come before our presence?"

Vinder kept his head low, his mind and heart true to the cause at hand. He needed his full concentration, as the priests were reading his intention and the clansmen judged his character every moment he stood before them.

"I've come, oh great and honorable king, to beg forgiveness from you and my clansmen, whom I have dishonored and shamed. My selfishness and pride took me from the land of my birth, my people, and my heritage, and brought me to the lands of those who do not hold such high virtues as we are commanded to by law and creed. I ask only for the chance to offer compensation for this great transgression."

"Has your family forgiven your shame?" The king's comment was dry and formal as Stephen focused on the opposite end of the hall, avoiding Vinder's figure.

"His family has forgiven all that has been done to them by his foolishness, and his pleas are sincere," Heimrick answered from behind Stephen, though he looked beyond his son and into the far end of the chamber when he spoke, as custom decreed.

"Has the great Lord of the Dwarves forgiven him, according to his priests?" Stephen asked, continuing the traditional dialogue.

Again Heimrick responded in kind. "He too has forgiven, and vindication of past faults has been undertaken."

"Then it is by sacred custom that we honor the god of this clan—and *all* clans—while the final verdict is rendered."

As one, the priests began to sing a song in praise of Drued. The melody was deep and strong, like the everlasting rock, a mix of baritone and tenor voices that echoed in the chamber. It felt as though the very air around them pulsated with an energy and strength all its own.

Vinder took a deep breath. He felt the eyes of all around him burrow deep inside him as the song progressed. He could feel the waves of emotion flowing from them as the sacred song continued. Anger and regret clamped his shoulders as the waves of forgiveness and sorrow flooded his mind and heart. He wanted to speak against these unspoken accusations but didn't dare do so. To risk it all now by spouting off quick words would ruin everything he'd set out to do.

He clenched his jaw and clasped his hands into fists as the sweat began to bead across his forehead. His eye twitched with the rhythm of his heart, which was fast and uncontrolled with the strain. He needed to hold out for only a few moments more before he'd be free to offer his plea and the gift to buy his redemption. The song was almost over. The process almost through.

Silence fell once more.

"What, then, do you think you can do to gain back your honor?" Stephen's tone was combative. "You have been allowed to speak for this answer and this alone."

Vinder breathed deeply, and said, "I offer this chest of riches. It's taken me a great time to amass them, but as each coin was placed in the pile, it was done with a deep and thorough understanding of my shame."

He made his way to the great chest and opened it, letting the sheen of the gold, silver, and other treasures light the eyes of those present.

"I offer up what possessions I have. I beg, in the name of Drued, that it pleases you, and will permit you to forgive my past rebellion."

Vinder didn't dare look up. He heard Stephen's footfalls approach. From his limited field of vision, he could make out Stephen pawing through the treasure like a rodent digging a burrow. The rustling of coins lasted only a moment before he rendered his verdict. "This is hardly enough to make us forget your failings."

He felt a stone block drop on his neck while his heart was torn from his chest. Stephen began his slow return to the throne by saying, "Your trespass was great. To compensate, you must do something equally great for the clan. You must rid the world of that troublesome Troll Cael."

An invisible hand punched Vinder in the gut as the block on his back grew into a mountain. A *Troll*? How was he to fight a Troll by himself and *live*? But he really didn't have a choice. Not if he wanted to win back his place in the clan.

"Slay Cael," Stephen said as he took his seat, "and you'll have proven your worth to the clan. It would be an action that is as beneficial as your initial action was destructive. In one hour I will send you the information you need to seek him out. With this knowledge you'll be taken to the giant's lair to prove your worth. If death should take you, then honor would be satisfied. You will be given a hero's burial."

"So be it," Vinder said with a nod that sealed his fate. If Drued had gotten him this far, then he would just have to trust he'd see him through, or take him to New Druelandia instead. Either way, his fate was in Drued's hands. May he continue to have mercy.

CHAPTER 16

Blessed be the human who seeks Panthora with a whole heart.
Blessed be the human who keeps to her ways.
Blessed be the human who honors her,
for he too shall be honored.

—A Paninian blessing

Rowan sat in the swaying hammock in which he'd been sleeping. It took him a moment to remember he was on Brandon's ship, in the simple lodging room he and Alara had been allowed to share with some of the crew and the assorted goods hanging from the ceiling among the handful of hammocks.

The room was empty. The crew was always busy, and had never spoken the whole time he and Alara had been onboard. Compared with how things were on the *Frost Giant* it was a stark contrast, but perhaps Brandon just ran a more disciplined ship.

Alara was no doubt on deck, which was just as well for him. Since joining Brandon's ship, he'd begun to sweat every time she was near, so unsure of himself it felt as if she were judging his every action. He wanted to think that wasn't the case but the longer they journeyed, the more he found these feelings growing. More than once he'd caught sight of Alara staring at him, to the point where he was pressed to turn his head.

Naturally, this made his lessons with Alara all the more challenging, but he somehow managed. Whether or not she noticed this difficulty was another matter. For her part she seemed amiable. And she was making some progress speaking Nordican. She could almost carry on a simple conversation without any prompting, which was impressive given how brief her time of instruction was. But this teaching wasn't the only matter occupying his day.

During his private time, he returned to his persistent thoughts: the words of Panthora, the necklace, and even his shield—wondering if it too had meaning he couldn't yet fathom. The dream that had endured since leaving the ruins hadn't returned after Panthora had spoken to him outside Elandor, but the questions racing through his mind during the day had, every day.

He was beginning to think the questions didn't have answers . . . or that he didn't *want* to know the answers. The closer to home he got, the more he realized how homesick he really was. Each day away only added to that growing sense of loss. It wasn't just the loss of his family or tribe but the loss of a part of himself. He'd left behind all he had known—all he thought he was—to journey further south than most Nordicans dared. And where was the knighthood now? Still far away in the Northlands. He was the only piece of that institution—the only piece of his tribe and family—in these strange lands. If this was his future, he didn't know if he'd be able to endure it.

It was all self-willed out here. He had to fuel his own exploits, get support and purpose from internal desire rather than outside sources. There was no journey knight here to crack the whip. If it wasn't for his faith in Panthora, he'd be totally alone. And though his prayers brought him comfort, Panthora hadn't answered him in the way she had outside Elandor. Instead, she remained silent, leaving only questions—a *myriad* of questions—to ponder.

Would his fellow knights help him find the answers, or would they see his introspection as a sign of weakness, perhaps even unworthiness to the order? What if news spread about his previous exchange with the captain of the *Frost Giant* when it made port in Valkoria? Panthora had at least told him he was worthy of being a knight and that he had a higher calling. But if that was so, why did returning home fill him with so much unease?

Again, Panthora's words haunted him. She hadn't founded the knighthood; someone else had. Other men. Men with their own ideas. What if those ideas were not totally in keeping with Panthora's intent? What if—he stopped himself. He didn't want to entertain the thought. Not now. He would have to deal with it soon enough, he knew, and when he did . . .

He dropped his feet to the floor and made his way out the door, hopeful that fresh air and breakfast would brighten his mood. As he got through the door, Rowan found Brandon.

"Up at last, I see."

"I couldn't sleep all day," Rowan playfully returned.

"Didn't stop you from trying," he teased.

Rowan had come to like Brandon. He was even kind enough to let Alara and Rowan dine with him in his quarters each night. It wasn't stately fare, but the food was decent enough, and it kept them alive. He very much appreciated that, since neither he nor Alara had any food of their own. From these dinners and other moments of private conversation, he discovered Brandon was quite wise for someone not yet old enough to be an elder. Rowan was also fascinated that the man seemed to be oblivious to the insight he possessed, as though he was really just a simple man with no life lessons to impart.

From these short conversations, he'd built up some rapport with the sailor. Their exchanges soon became a fun time for him as he gleaned knowledge that would help him as he continued his journey into manhood. Besides, he felt a great peace whenever the two spoke. It was like a gentle breath of reassurance blown over him, scattering the troublesome matters constantly fluttering over his person while they talked.

More than once Rowan had thought of asking Brandon for his advice on the matters troubling him about Panthora. But whenever he tried to bring it up, an uneasiness pooled in his stomach. He didn't take such a thing as a good sign and so found other topics to occupy his time with the older sailor.

"So how far off are we now?" he asked.

"We're making good time. Endarien has chosen to bless us with favorable winds. I'd say just a couple more days, maybe less."

"Those *are* some favorable winds. That's the fastest I've ever heard of someone making it to Arid Land. We'd be cutting the trip by a fourth at least."

"Thanks be to Endarien," Brandon was quick to return.

"Well it's nothing short of a miracle," said Rowan. "I've never seen or heard of anything like it before."

Brandon shared a simple smile. "Endarien just favors me, I guess."

"He must. I've noticed your men don't pay homage to Perlosa like men from my land do."

"No, we don't. Nor will we ever," Brandon said with a powerful conviction. "We pay homage only to Endarien, and it looks as though he has shown us the rewards for doing so." Brandon's voice lowered, adding, "You'd be wise, though, not to bring up the goddess of the waves around the crew. They're not too keen on her."

"I'm sorry. I meant no harm."

"None taken." Brandon's wide smile banished any uneasiness the topic had brought.

"Endarien isn't worshiped that much in the Northlands," Rowan said. "How do you and your men worship him? I haven't seen many of your rituals."

"We pay homage to him by thanking him for his gales and breezes"—Brandon gestured to the clouds—"by offering incense into the air so that he may smell it, be pleased with us, and show us favor. As you can see, it's been most beneficial. Now, if you will excuse me," he said as he hurried off to his cabin, where he often resided for most of the day. "I have some other matters calling me."

Rowan periodically wondered what he did in there. It shouldn't take all day to plot a course and to make sure the boat was still on it. An internal voice urged him to stop with the rooting for reasons and be thankful they even had a way to Arid Land. He could just as easily still be stranded in Elandor, searching for options. Perhaps the man just liked to be alone and think. After all, he did seem something of a philosopher. Maybe he was a budding poet or chronicler of tales. And was that really any of Rowan's business? As long as they got to Arid Land, Rowan could leave well enough alone.

He spied Alara at the bow of the boat and decided to make his way over to her. During the last ten days on Brandon's ship, Rowan had begun allowing himself to think more highly of her, even if some parts of him still felt displeasure for doing so. And it wasn't just his growing admiration of her quick mind in picking up new languages, but other good traits he was slowly acknowledging within her. It took work at first but he started to move beyond toleration and into appreciation. But that appreciation was deepening into something else, and he wasn't sure how to handle it.

In some ways she was the exotic breeze blowing through his ordered world, upsetting all his former beliefs. Panthora had told him in not so many words that perhaps not all of what he had been taught to believe was trustworthy. But what, then, did he hold to? He needed to have an answer—a strong answer—to that question before they reached Valkoria. It wouldn't do facing his superiors internally questioning the very things he'd sworn to uphold and promote. If only Panthora would speak to him . . .

•●•

Alara stood at the bow of the ship, contemplating the bobbing waves of the Yoan Ocean.

Their travels had flown by. The weather had been—and still was—unbelievable, a good gust constantly pushing them along. It almost reminded her of the spell Cadrissa had used to speed their own progress from Altorbia to Elandor what felt like months ago now. She was sure they were making even better time while she and Rowan slept, but couldn't prove it. The wind never seemed to vary as it guided the nameless vessel through the calm waters, helping them on their journey.

The only ones who spoke at all were Rowan and Alara, both during and after the few small tasks they were assigned. It was really more volunteer work, which both she and Rowan gladly accepted once they realized just how beneficial it was to have something else to do to help pass the time. They could only practice speaking Nordican for so long and none of the crew were apparently that interested in any sort of personal interaction.

Occasionally, they were able to talk with Brandon when he wasn't in his quarters or working his men, but other than that a hushed, almost reverential, silence clung to the vessel tighter than any barnacle. Trying to strike up a conversation with the sailors was fruitless. Both she and Rowan thought it very odd, but tried not to let it bother them. Maybe they didn't take well to new people. Whatever the reason, she and Rowan had transport. The crew wasn't hostile, just a bit rude. She could put up with it; she'd dealt with worse.

Brandon seemed simple enough. He was definitely a naval man, and loved the openness of the sea. He was strangely philosophical too; that was showcased each night when she and Rowan got to dine with him. During the day Brandon gave them simple food to keep up their strength, saving the evening meal for something more involved like stew or fresh fish. While they never asked for it, Brandon's kindness in sharing his table was just another thing that deepened her fondness for the man.

She couldn't recall ever seeing the crew eat, oddly enough. Even those Rowan and she shared a room with never took any bread or even water. She was sure they had to at some time, but so far she'd never actually seen them do it. Odd, but then they weren't the only ones acting strange. Rowan had taken to being even more confusing of late, one moment helpful, congenial, and open, the next closed, brusque, and distant.

This vacillation in mood made for some interesting personal interactions, but she was able to work through them. And for her efforts she was rewarded with more lessons on Nordican, which was proving to be a fairly interesting language. Simple on some levels, it was also fairly complex in terms of multiple meanings of words and getting the context right when using them. But she was learning. When she'd ever need to use it again after their meeting with Rowan's superiors, she hadn't a clue, but if it helped smooth things over between them and Rexatoius, so much the better.

As to the reason for Rowan's alteration of moods she had her suspicions, but it wasn't until the last few days she'd finally figured out the truth. She was certain he was starting to take more of a romantic interest in her. She'd snatch glimpses of him from time to time where it was clear. He'd stare at her, only to divert his eyes when caught. Only the other day, she'd realized how much she was starting to enjoy it. While she had dabbled with the thought before boarding Brandon's ship, it was now front and center: she was falling in love with the young knight.

She'd tried shrugging it off with all the excuses she could come up with: the stress of the trip, the close quarters, or any other cause. But still, the feelings wouldn't go away. Her body continued to tell her what she didn't want to believe. She dreaded the feeling, and what it might mean for the future. It wasn't good for elves and humans to become romantically entwined. Though they were compatible—the only two different races on Tralodren who could successfully reproduce—their offspring and other strains on the relationship were often more a curse than a blessing. And although Rowan was younger than her, elves could live up to twice as long as humans.

But she had a choice in this. At least Alara was sure Gilban would tell her she did. Despite what the poets and bards might say, one didn't have to be a slave to one's emotions. Things could be resisted. Logic and reason could prevail. She'd given her word to aid Rowan, and now she was en route to do so. She needed to stay true to that purpose. The reality before her told her to stop acting like some young girl with her first infatuation. She didn't have time to be a moonstruck fool. There was still Valkoria. She didn't need this. She needed to remain focused.

"Brandon says we're to be in Arid Land in just a couple more days," Rowan said from behind her.

"Better than we thought, huh?" Alara saw Rowan duck from her gaze. She could imagine, in part, what he must be enduring himself. From what she'd learned of him so far, she didn't think such an attraction was highly favored by his order.

"It's better progress than what I would have made on the *Frost Giant*," offered the knight.

"But it's still only halfway." She realized too late how pessimistic her words sounded and was pained by the drop in Rowan's features. Thankfully, he quickly recovered.

"We'll find a ship in Vanhyrm."

"I hope so. I wouldn't want to be stranded there." She found herself staring into Rowan's dark blue eyes before she knew what was happening.

"Why? There are worse places to get stuck."

"Maybe for you, but you're not an elf. And if that encounter on the *Frost Giant* is any indication, I'm not expecting too warm a reception."

"At least now you'll be able to understand them a bit better. You're making good progress."

"I must have a good teacher." He gave a nod and then fell silent.

"I never did thank you," he said, keeping his focus on the waves.

"For what?"

"For agreeing to go with me—to Valkoria." He faced her with a truly grateful expression.

It had been the first time she'd heard him say anything of his appreciation and she was lost on how to respond. After some furious mental gymnastics, she pushed out an anemic "Sure." Realizing how halfhearted it sounded she quickly added, "Thank you for letting me come along."

Again, he nodded before drifting into a pondering silence.

"You're still thinking about Cadrissa, aren't you?" The question caught him off guard.

"Among other things," he replied. "I wonder why that thing took her in the first place."

"For nothing good, I'm sure." She made a survey of the sailors among them. Each kept to their task, maintaining a taciturnity that made her and Rowan's conversation seem all the louder. For a moment, she wondered if they were listening in.

"I still don't know why she cast that spell," she confessed. "If she hadn't, she'd never have been taken." Alara shivered at the memory of the event. Such a terrible outcome, especially for the bookish Cadrissa. And it had happened under her leadership. Maybe if she—no. She stopped herself in midthought. Everyone made their own choices by coming along. No one was forced. Everyone had a choice—free will—and Cadrissa made her own choices. They all had.

"Maybe she didn't do it on purpose."

"What do you mean?" The comment brought her back to the present.

Rowan paused before continuing, with some hesitation. "When we faced those lizardmen, before Cadrissa cast her spell, there was something different about her. Like she wasn't the same person." He stared right into her eyes, emphasizing the conviction in his voice. "I could even have sworn her eyes changed color."

"She's a wizard." Alara was trying to convince herself as much as Rowan. "Maybe it was part of the spell."

"Except she acted the same way right before she cast the spell on that column in the ruins."

"So what are you implying?"

"I don't know." His gaze retreated back to the waves, and he sighed. "There's just so much to think about and do . . ."

Alara found her hand on Rowan's shoulder before she knew what she was doing. He seemed surprised by the gesture but not as much as he might have been even a few days ago. "Faith and patience," she heard herself say. "It just takes faith and patience. We'll take this one step at a time." Once she said it, the moment turned awkward, and Alara withdrew her hand.

"So who do *you* pray to?" asked Rowan.

Alara paused. "I haven't settled on anyone in particular. Each has their place."

"But isn't that confusing?" She could see he was on more comfortable footing. His demeanor was calmer. "If you had just one, you'd know who to follow and where you'd go when you died. And how could you please *all* those gods, when one might oppose another?"

"It wasn't always that way," she replied. "In times past people held to more than one god; some even worshiped the whole pantheon."

"Not since the Imperial Wars," he replied. "They helped define things better for everyone."

"Maybe. I guess I'm just not as dedicated as you are." She gave a polite smile, hoping he'd take the hint.

"But you could be." It seemed he was slow to catch on.

"After we meet with your superiors, what then?" she asked, forcing a change in subject.

"I suppose I'll get another assignment—assuming they let me stay after losing the information."

"I'll do my best to make sure that happens."

"Then you're going to need some more lessons before then," said Rowan.

"I'm ready when you are." The reply birthed a flash of something she thought might have been excitement across his eyes. But it was so short lived she wasn't sure.

"Okay. Then I suppose it's time we start talking more about the order itself, getting some of the terms right. You don't want to address someone the wrong way . . ."

CHAPTER 17

Sing now we true of honorable things,
Of commoners, priests, and kings.
Long may they shine in Drued's great hall,
An example, forever, to all.

—Old dwarven ballad

Cael had been slumbering on a stone slab in his cave when he was awakened by the smell of dwarven flesh. At first only his clawed fingers and toes twitched when he caught the scent, but soon the rest of him came alive as well. Even as he was roused from slumber, he maintained the illusion of being asleep, hairy shoulders reclining on the stone and his shaggy chest rising and falling with a slow rhythm.

Trolls were a race of giants spawned by the dark machinations of a fiendish prince foolishly summoned to Tralodren when titans still roamed the world. Corrupted, disliked, and mistrusted by other giants, Trolls led a solitary life and were content to make the best of their lives for as long as they could. In this, Cael was no exception to his race.

He sniffed the air with his wide nostrils. Yes, it was definitely a dwarf. One dwarf standing in front of his lair. The Troll's bright yellow eyes widened with anticipation. His sharp, jagged teeth seemed to mimic the thick ram horns curled into fat dollops of beige bone on either side of his head. It was laughable—totally laughable—to think a fool would throw away his life so heedlessly.

Cael, like most Trolls, hated just about every race outside of giantkind—the latter only being tolerated—but he hated dwarves like no other. They represented the foolishness of the gods: shorter than practicality would have a race be, bent on tradition to the point of stagnation, and pesky as cockroaches that burrowed from their homes in endless lines. One day he would be free of them and this region of the mountains would be his once and for all. Until then, he'd have to put up with these occasional encounters.

Even as he rose from his slab, he was drawn away from the cave's mouth and the dwarf outside it by a tingling sensation to his left. It had the feel of magic about it—no, divine power, and it was coming toward him. A flanking attack? Perhaps the dwarf wasn't as stupid as he'd first thought.

Cael didn't know what to expect, but it didn't matter. Whatever they'd planned, they'd all die in moments, allowing him to eat. Being so close to a handful of dwarves made his stomach leap with joy. He'd grown hungry in spite of the meager pickings he'd been able to find the past week. It'd be good to have something more filling and satisfying for a change.

The sensation on his left grew stronger as he saw a vortex of swirling white mist. What were they playing at? It wasn't like a dwarf to get clever. They often just charged into battle head on. As he watched, a door appeared out of the mists. A double-hinged, metal-reinforced wooden door. This was the last thing he was expecting. It opened toward him, and appeared to hold something behind it, though he knew nothing *could* be behind it, except more of his lair. From the door came an even stranger sight: two priests—Telborians from their look and smell.

Very strange.

He decided to play with them a bit. He kept to the shadows, watching, all the while focused on the lair's entrance, waiting for an opportunity to act against them. The Telborians were dressed in the garb common to Asorlins. He smirked—his rough, cracked lips curling up and over his yellowed teeth. A lone dwarf at the door and two Asorlins in his lair. It was certainly working out to be *quite* a festive platter. He slunk deeper into the shadows as they drew closer.

•●•

"All right," the emerging Cracius said, making a quick study of what appeared to be, and definitely smelled like, some sort of animal's lair. "Where's the dwarf?"

"He can't be far," Tebow replied, slowing his pace as the door closed behind him and then vanished. "Keep your eyes open for any animals." He wrinkled his nose. "Smells like something's close by."

"Something *dead* for sure," Cracius said with a cough. "I can't see any dwarf looking to stay in this place—even if he *is* a mercenary." Cracius motioned with his hammer to the light streaming in from the cave's mouth. "That way looks promising."

"Still—"

Tebow was interrupted by a dark shape that leapt before them. "Troll!" he shouted.

The priests raised their weapons in unison. Cracius prayed as he readied to face an opponent nearly twice his size. A massive claw drew back, ready to eviscerate the pair, but a swift blow from Cracius' hammer landed hard upon the giant's beefy chest with a crack before the Troll could finish his swing.

The Troll bellowed.

A ripple of darkness emanated from the impact site, rapidly pulsating over the Troll's entire body like a bitumen tide. It was a sickly thing to see, moving with the intent of an obvious intelligence focused on injuring all it crossed. The Troll gave it a moment's consideration, before lunging forward with a roar. Another hammer strike, this one from Tebow, hit the Troll's stomach—right above his breechcloth. The impact sent more ripples over the giant's body as it slashed at the scattering priests. Tebow's billowing cloak was shredded to tatters as he dashed away.

Both priests kept a tight focus on their opponent, who fought defiantly against the ailment Cracius knew would soon overtake him. As the Troll took another step forward, he stopped with a jerk, stumbling and short of breath. He leaned on a nearby wall, trying to keep himself from toppling to the floor. His skin was darkened by smoky tendrils bubbling underneath his flesh like bulging varicose veins.

Cracius watched the giant observe his swelling hand, which was turning a putrid shade of plum. His reddish-brown skin was now a deep black, and Cracius knew the Troll could feel a burning sensation all about his flesh. The final stages of Asorlok's touch were upon him, approaching their deadly completion.

The Troll appeared to mouth some words but no sound emerged. Then the trembling came—a frenzied series of tremors that shook the giant's body from head to toe. Trying to quell some of the agony, he violently clawed the ceiling and walls, sending chunks of debris across most of the cavern in the process. Choking bursts of dusty clouds drifted outside the cave. The Troll toppled immediately after the loud thunder of a man-sized piece of rock dropped from the ceiling near the stone slab that had been the giant's bed.

Cracius and Tebow waited for the remaining dust to settle before wiping it from their eyes and carefully observing the fallen giant. Only a few black serpentine coils remained, wrapped around the odd bone or two of the skeleton that had fallen to the ground like a crumbled marionette. The bones had been bleached, though they still clung to each other as they sprawled about the debris-strewn cavern floor. Even the Troll's malicious jaw was frozen in a silent scream of agony.

The priests gingerly stepped nearer to the fallen form. The air had grown silent and cold—so silent that when the dwarven warrior's battle scream rushed into the cavern, they turned their full attention to it with wide-eyed surprise.

•●•

The stench of Cael's lair overwhelmed Vinder, but that was the least of his problems. Shortly after the ceremony reached its conclusion, he'd been ushered into a back chamber, where he was told what he had to do to kill the Troll. The same Troll that not even the bravest of heroes had been able to dispatch since the prodigal dwarf had been a child. But if this was what was needed to reclaim his honor, then so be it.

Fear overtook him like nothing he'd ever experienced before as he made his way to a wild pocket in the mountains where Cael resided. He tried to remember the tales of the giant he'd heard in his childhood. Cael was already making his name when Vinder was young, if the stories he'd just been told were to be fully trusted. Though no one had ever heard of a Troll dying of old age, no one thought they were immortal, either. And while Cael might be older, he would be far from infirm. Rather, the opposite was true of his race, who were said to grow stronger with age, not weaker. This only added to Vinder's growing apprehension.

He continued to mull over these dismal thoughts as he neared a cave hung with threatening stalactites and littered with carrion, charred rock, and earth. The stench became overwhelming as rotting matter—both vegetable and meat—mixed in his nostrils. He squinted as the foul odor hit him, the acidic breeze stinging like a thousand needles.

Stopping just short of the darkness inside the jagged portal, he gripped his axe with both hands. The only thing driving him was a desire to keep some honor in this situation. But when he stared into the dimness of the cave he saw the face of Asorlok return his gaze. Thoughts, words, and deeds flooded over him—his whole life traveling through his mind like a rising wave, cresting, and then falling into the present, reminding him of his mortality.

Was he sure this was what he wanted, that there was no other way? He couldn't help but smile weakly at the thought. His time away had certainly made him something different than he once was: questioning and reasoning as he looked at things from different angles. But all that had passed—it had to, if he wished to reclaim what he'd given up long ago. It was time to think once again like a mountain dwarf. Black and white. Clear boundaries and parameters.

He shook his head in an effort to stir up some more courage. He was sure he wanted this. Sure he *needed* it, to prove his worth and reassure his mind and heart that had been in torment since his exile. He'd been deluded with his selfish pursuits. He'd gained access to the world but had lost himself and what he'd loved along the way.

Honor. Family. Tradition. These echoed with every beat of his heart. It wasn't hard and demanding. No, that was how he had let himself see it once. But now he could clearly see it was gentle and soft, like the touch of a young child: love in the den of hate he was about to enter.

Taking a deep breath, he stepped forward, but he got no further than that step before a violent tremor overtook the area, and threw him on his back. A peppering of small rocks rained on him as clouds of dust flooded his vision. The eruption of noise that followed was deafening. When it subsided, the silence was even more consuming than the explosion. What in Drued's name was going on?

He hurried to sit up, brushing the dust from his chest, beard, and face. He scraped debris from his eye and mouth, spitting out a gray, chalky paste in frustration. Taking a breath, he tried to make sense of what he saw before him, but failed. All he could see was a lingering cloud of dust spilling out of the cave's mouth. Had there been a collapse? An avalanche of some sort?

"I won't be denied," Vinder growled defiantly as he stood. He gripped his axe with both hands again. "Do you hear me?" He ran straight for the cave with a war cry on his lips.

He ran into Cael's lair at full speed, his body filled with adrenaline and fear. He knew he was going to die but he was going to do it valiantly, on *his* terms. When his brain finally registered what his eye was seeing, he couldn't believe it. He stopped in midstride, the war cry dying in his throat. Before him were the skeletal remains of the very Troll he was there to kill. The scene held him spellbound, until he noticed other beings in the cave's murky depths.

"What are *you* doing here?" Vinder addressed the two Telborians in their native tongue as they emerged from the shadows. Both of them carried silver hammers adorned with a skull motif and took him in with the same puzzled gaze he assumed his own face was making. Telborians weren't supposed to be this far into the mountains. This was dwarven territory. A sick feeling started swirling in the pit of Vinder's stomach.

"I think we've found him," said the older of the two.

"*Asorlins?*" Vinder planted his legs in the rock as soon as he made out their garb. The sickening feeling only worsened. If this was an omen, it couldn't be good. "What in the name of Shiril and Drued is going on here?"

The younger of the priests stared intently at him. "Peace. We're here to help you."

"Help me do what?" he asked with a huff. "Get back. I said get back! You just keep yourself where I can see you. Now, what's going on? What happened to Cael?"

"Cael?" The older priest seemed lost.

"The Troll," Vinder said, pointing out the giant's breechcloth-clad remains with his axe.

"Well, if *that's* Cael," the older priest continued with a gentle demeanor, "then he's been slain."

"So *you* killed him?" Vinder wasn't making any sense of this. Asorlins in a Troll's lair killing the very Troll he was sent to kill? Yes, definitely not a good omen.

"It was either him or us," the younger priest stated matter-of-factly.

"Why are you even *here*?" Vinder inquired while biting back the rising pool of rage in his throat. The sort of rage that would have had him slashing the priests' guts wide open. But it was hard to get answers from corpses.

"To find *you*, actually," said the older priest as he took a step forward. "Assuming you're Vinder."

Vinder brought his axe before him with a white-knuckled grip. "And who in the Abyss are you?"

"Tebow Narlsmith," said the elder priest, "and this is Cracius Evans." Tebow motioned to the young priest beside him.

"Death priests." His gaze went from Tebow to Cracius as he felt the swelling rage beginning to mingle with confusion and frustration. "Death priests in a Troll's lair in the Diamant Mountains. And they just *happened* to kill the same Troll I was sent after." Vinder's eye narrowed. "Why?"

"As we said"—Tebow motioned for Cracius to bring his hammer to his side—"it was self-defense. We came here looking for you."

"And what do a couple of Asorlins want with me while I'm still alive? You want to kill me, too? Rip off my skin and make me like him? This some sort of *game* you people play?"

"We've been sent to find you," Tebow calmly repeated.

"By who?" Vinder was only half focused on the conversation. His mind was trying to find some way—*any* way—to get through the mess he found himself in. Cael was his only way back into the clan. And now Cael was dead without him even getting in a swing of his own. This wasn't right. He had Drued's blessing, he'd been forgiven by his family and religion. If not for this final task he could have been welcome back with open arms. And now this . . .

"If you'll come with us—"

"So did you do it out of *spite*?" He glared at the Troll's mocking bones. "I can't *lie* about what you've done," he continued. "It'd be a hollow victory, and I'd get *no* honor for my family or might." His glare was an angry jab straight into Tebow's face.

"We're sorry," Tebow said with a bow. "We didn't mean to—"

"Well, you have," he barked, "and there's little I can do about it now."

"Please," said Tebow, stepping closer, which further stiffened Vinder's spine. "We haven't much time. We need your help—"

"Well, I don't need *yours*. Unless you can bring *him* back to life."

"No." Cracius shook his head. "Asorlok doesn't deal with life, only death."

"You still haven't given me any answers. Why are you here? Who put you up to this? Was it Stephen? Did he want to be sure I failed? Were you sent to kill me too?"

"We came here because we were told you could help us defeat Cadrith Elanis," said Tebow, calmly.

"Who?"

"The lich—that skeletal mage—you and your previous companions recently helped release," Cracius explained.

"I have nothing to do with that," he said with a growl. "That's all behind me now. I have a new life here . . ." He sighed, trying to dig a scrap of hope from Cael's bones. "Or at least I *would* have."

"You were looking to face a Troll on your own?" Cracius asked. "I think you and I both know you wouldn't have much of a life to live after that."

"Oh, and you're offering me something better, is that it?" He snorted. "You come all this way to accuse me of something I didn't do, then take my only chance at being accepted back into my clan from me, and *then* try to pull me away so I can follow you on some *fool's* errand?"

"We can't do it without you," said Tebow.

"And what great cause is it now?" Anger and sarcasm flowed out of Vinder's mouth in thick torrents. "Another *great* tragedy that's going to destroy the world or some such thing? I'm done with all of that—would have been finished by now, too, if you two hadn't stepped in."

"Please." Tebow was even calmer and more diplomatic than before. "Let me finish. There's a great threat to all of us. Cadrith is seeking an object that will give him enough power to not only put an end to Tralodren but the entire pantheon as well."

"Right." Vinder smirked.

"Listen." Cracius stepped forward with such sudden speed Vinder nearly cleft him in two with his axe. "This dead Troll, your honor—even your clan—won't matter if the lich is successful. There'll be nothing left."

"Then I suppose you'll like it," Vinder pertly replied. "More death for you to revel in."

"But are *you* prepared to live with the consequences?" Cracius pressed. "You helped free him, and now you have a chance to help stop him. Together, we can keep millions of innocents from dying."

"Asorlins wanting to *save* lives?" he chuckled. "Now I *know* you're both mad. Just get out of here. I don't have much time as it is to sort this mess out."

"No, you don't." Tebow dropped his hammer head first to the ground, letting it rest on the rocky earth beside him. "None of us do. We need your help, Vinder. If you're truly concerned about honor—about completing your obligations—then you'll see your place is beside us and the others who are being called to stop Cadrith."

"Others?"

"The rest of the mercenaries you traveled with when you freed Cadrith," Tebow continued. "They're being gathered together as we speak."

"I didn't *free* anything." He was growing tired of the priest's accusations. "It was *Cadrissa* who opened the portal, not me. So if anyone is guilty of anything, it's *her*. Now, get out." Vinder thrust his axe at the cave's entrance in case they didn't know the way.

"What if we can promise you'd still have your honor?" Cracius' question gave the dwarf pause.

"How?"

"If you help us, we'll help you," the priest continued.

"How?"

Tebow exchanged a glance with Cracius before speaking. "You weren't looking for *honor* here so much as an honorable death. That's why you're upset. You see us as taking it from you."

"How did you—"

"You've already made it more than clear to those who know how to look and listen," said Tebow.

"Well, if you know that, then you can see why I'm not too willing to come with you."

"Not even if we could promise you what you're seeking?" Vinder didn't like the way Tebow's gaze fixed upon him.

Vinder took a few steps back. "What, you're going to kill me?"

"Not death, but honor." Tebow's strong stare worked its way deep into Vinder's heart like a spear point. "You said it yourself: there's no honor here for you. By joining us you could win your honor on a much larger scale."

"And how would the clan know?" Vinder sheathed his axe. He didn't have need of it now, seeing as the priests were more talk than threat. "And if they did . . . why would they accept anything else I did? I was told to face Cael, not go toe to toe with rotting mages."

"Do you still want your honor?" Tebow was relentless.

"Mighty convenient how you set all this up where I have little choice."

"We've told you the truth," said Tebow. "We had no idea about the Troll or any of what happened to bring you here, only that we were to find you and bring you with us."

"And who sent you?"

"Not Asorlok, if that's what you're after," said Cracius.

"Are you with us or not?" Tebow clearly desired to hurry the conversation along.

Vinder let his thoughts and attention drift to Cael's skeletal remains. Did he really have another plan, other than rushing in the cave, hoping he got a few swipes in before he found himself in New Druelandia? What if these Asorlins were right? What if this *was* his only hope? What if Drued was showing him still *more* mercy—even if it had to come through two Asorlins? Could he really afford to toss this all aside and hope for the best? Who was he fooling? There was nothing better to hope for.

"All right," he said at last. "Just where exactly are you planning on taking me?"

Both priests took up their hammers as a wooden door, outlined with white light, materialized at the back of the cave. It was as sturdy and sound as any door should be, except that it hadn't been there a moment before and looked rather odd in the back of a Troll's lair.

"Through there," Tebow said, pointing. As the door started to open, it spilled a pale mist and bright white light.

"Come on," said Cracius, motioning for him to follow.

"May Drued continue to have mercy." Vinder surrendered a small sigh before joining them.

CHAPTER 18

All this talk of a spirit is for naught.
There is no such thing, only soul and body.
These two and these two alone. All else is a lie.
There is only this life and what we make of it.

—Cyrin, dranoric philosopher

Dugan awoke on his simple bed. The sparse look gave him scant comfort, though his mattress was soft and covered with black silk sheets. The elegance in an otherwise simple room intrigued him. The cult appeared to him to be very well to do, and were ardent lovers of silk, among other luxuries. He wondered why, if they lived among pleasures, they hid in these decaying tunnels and warrens. Another secret they probably weren't willing to share.

He'd shed his armor to take his rest, which left him with his gray, short-sleeved tunic and studded leather pants. The breastplate rested beside the bed, close at hand. Soft firelight radiated from a single brazier in the far corner of his room. Not enough to bring total brightness to his surroundings, but enough to keep him from total darkness. He'd slept better than he thought he would, given where he was and what these cultists were asking him to do. He just told himself this would be the last time he'd be used to kill.

He found it ironic when the head priest had told him they wanted Dugan to kill the mayor of Haven. Killing another man to win his freedom. Many would have frowned on such an idea, but he knew this was his last chance. Yet, no matter how hard he tried to uproot a growing sense of discomfort, the more often another bout would arise, until he was now contending with a quickly growing field of ponderings. With these ponderings came the thought that he'd never be free.

Though the cult had promised him freedom, their promise seemed hollow. How many would he have to kill for his freedom? Was it worth having murder over his head? The word intrigued him; he'd never seen killing another man as murder before. His whole life was kill or be killed—it was survival. Yet, with only a limited view of freedom, his outlook changed.

He found his left shoulder. It was still smooth. Still clear. It was almost like a dream. Only he knew it wasn't. This was the closest he'd ever come to finding his freedom—the entirety of it—both in this life and the next. He was so close. Just one more task. Just one more . . .

He tried using the brazier's flickering flames as a point of serenity and escape from the chaos inside him. The metal object glowed with a dirty orange hue. He watched the flickering shadows it produced on the wall. It was the only source of light he'd encountered in the cult's secret lair, outside of the room where he'd first met the high priest. It seemed they thrived on darkness.

As he stared at the dancing display of shadow and light, his mind continued to wander. Gradually, he became unaware of his surroundings. It was a simple-enough exercise. The focus wasn't on the flames themselves but what they signified. As his mind wrestled with ethical and emotional matters, tiny sparks fell from the brazier. At first they drifted down like a light snow, then became a flurry of flakes. Finally, they poured onto the floor and pooled at the bottom of the wall, forming a stout figure no more than two feet in height and less than a foot across at the shoulders.

Dugan jumped as he realized what had happened. The ash-born creature smiled at him with carbon-covered teeth as jagged and uneven as broken columns in an ancient ruin. Its eyes glowed with a faint reddish glare that reminded him of dying embers. It looked like a very ugly and short goblin—a pile of soot, with claws ending the unnaturally long arms that stuck out of a dirty and worn hooded cloak.

"Greetings," the creature said, in perfect Telboros, though with a dry, raspy voice that reminded Dugan of stone scraping across bone.

"What do you want?" Dugan was off the bed in an instant, sword in hand.

"I mean you no harm. I bring a message from my lord, Rheminas." The strange creature bowed its head. As it did a thin, wispy cloud of ash floated up from it like the last gasps of a dying fire.

"Rheminas?" Dugan asked, strangling the sword tighter.

"I wish you no harm. I only seek to relay the message I was given and then will trouble you no more."

"You'll die and return to your master!" He swung his sword in a deadly arc, slicing the creature in half. A monstrous cloud of dust and embers immediately filled the room, flying into his face, digging into his throat, eyes, and nose and bringing him to his knees as he coughed with searing pain. As quickly as it was released, the gray cloud re-formed itself into the creature again, its eyes glowing a gentle amber in what could have been amusement.

"That was unwise." The creature's words grated on Dugan's ears. "Now listen to the words of Rheminas."

Dugan glared at the creature through his burning, watery eyes. He could taste bitterness from the ash still in his throat and feel the gummy tears streaming down his face. And he could feel the layer of ash covering his whole body with black.

"He has my *soul*, what else does he want?" Dugan spat at the creature with disgust. The reddish-black projectile struck the creature on the chest, then rolled down his rough, grimy cloak in an oily black ball.

If any offense was taken, the creature kept it well hidden. "What you seek is in vain, for none can free you from our pact. What you find here is false hope—false security."

"Is that what he sent you for?" He glared at the creature. "To gloat?"

"My lord continues," said the small creature while straightening its frame. "His advice is that you'd be much better off slaying these cultists now than letting them continue to pull your strings."

Dugan snorted. "Throw away my one chance for hope?"

"It's a false hope, and a vain thing that's hoped for. 'You are forever mine,' says Rheminas. Slaying them now will spare you a great heartache that's yet to come."

A grim joy flooded Dugan's face. "Sounds like Rheminas is worried. Like maybe I've found a way of escape."

"In this matter Rheminas is certain," the sooty messenger continued. "Future events, should you continue on this path, will end most sorrowfully for you."

"Since when did *any* god, *especially* Rheminas, care about me? I'm tired of your master's lies," said Dugan, clenching his jaw. He hated to be played for a fool. He wanted desperately to be free of the whole experience—to be free from it *all*. But the more he fought, the less free he felt, and the more anxious and angry he became.

Instead, he found himself thinking things through very carefully. Rheminas was either playing with him again or . . . or this creature could be speaking the truth. He glanced down at his left shoulder. The branding mark was still absent. That was real . . . wasn't it? Of course it was real. It was solid and tangible. And none had been able to do such a thing for him until now. No priest. No religion. No one.

He'd wait the other's speech out and then be done with both it and him. He was free enough to make up his own mind. It would take a lot more convincing to win him over, and he doubted he'd hear anything else as tangible as what the cultists gave him. Still, he might be able to use this opportunity to get a better idea of what Rheminas was playing at.

"Why does Rheminas want them dead?"

"Cults are permitted for a season. And that season has now passed. My lord has chosen *you* as the means to enact this judgment. It is an honor and a blessing, for he is sparing you from future disappointment."

"Where's your proof?"

"I'm not in the business of debating that which was spoken, only of relaying what has been said. And that is all that my lord has spoken."

"He's lied to me from the start. Why should I trust him now?"

"Then what should I tell my master?"

"Tell him to go to the Abyss with his false promises!"

"As you wish." The being's frame started rapidly disintegrating, turning into a pile of inert dust. Dugan studied the debris for a moment before stomping his foot upon the ashen pile, scattering it further under heel until it wasn't more than a memory.

"Dugan?" The door to his room opened, allowing a cloaked cultist full view of what Dugan assumed was a very odd scene indeed: a soot-sprayed Telborian looming over a pile of ash.

"I-I thought I heard shouting."

"It's over now."

"What's over?" The cultist looked from corner to corner, finally settling on the circle of soot under Dugan's heel.

Looking to change the subject, he asked, "We still set to leave tonight?"

"Yes." The cultist's uncertainty vanished. "After the evening meal. Having second thoughts?"

"No," Dugan replied curtly. "I'll be ready."

"Good." The cultist paused before returning to the door. "You'd be better served using the greasepaint over the ash, but do what you think best." He quietly closed the door behind him. Dugan began wiping what he could of the soot and ash from his face. He didn't think he could do any more sleeping. That just left him alone with his thoughts. Taking a seat on his bed, he let his eyes rest on the brazier once more.

•●•

Dugan, dressed in black pants and tunic, stood before a stone wall. His hands were wrapped in dark gloves and his face covered in a silken mask that rested over the bridge of his nose, encircling his eyes with a band of darkness. The rest of his face was smeared with an inky greasepaint, particularly around his eyes where the mask didn't cover, as well as his chin and jowls. The black substance had been applied in stripes of varying lengths and thicknesses, breaking up the contours of his face. The job had been so well done that if he didn't move at all he could blend right into the gloom about him—the perfect living shade. He wore his sword strapped to his back, over his armor, along with a belt holstering four daggers across his chest, which were also smeared with a black gel to prevent any sheen from revealing them.

Next to him were three similarly dressed persons. Unlike Dugan these were thin, sinewy beings who appeared more nimble by nature. Unlike Dugan's mask, theirs covered the whole top half of their head—hair and all—allowing only their chins and mouths to be seen. Each carried at their side an onyx-hilt dagger smeared with the same black gel and wore thin black shoes crafted of leather and cloth.

He'd been told these three would be there to protect him and secure the area while Dugan lay in wait to kill the mayor. He ignored the gnawing pang in his gut and the anxious energy jolting through his muscles as he wondered why he needed to be protected. He could see the reason for a guide, since he didn't know the way, but added protection for something that was presented as fairly straightforward seemed slightly off to him.

"Are you ready?" one of his companions asked in a small whisper.

"Yeah."

"Remember—kill him quickly. We don't want the guards to rush in and overwhelm us. We'll protect you, like we said . . . however, we've been informed we are to secure the room more tightly than before. We might be occupied in certain areas as we determine its safety, so don't be alarmed. We need your strength and experience to kill the mayor, and you need our talents to protect you and guide you to him."

"That was the deal," Dugan said, barely registering the conversation. His mind had drifted to thoughts of a better life far away from here, away from Rheminas and the suffering and killing on the whim of another man or god. The other men grew still as the first of their number pressed a hidden stone in the wall in front of them. A three-foot-wide section of the wall separated itself from the structure and sunk deep into an opening behind it without a sound.

"We should be off," said the leader.

The cultists and their assassin sped through the twisting, lightless corridors. Sometimes Dugan had to struggle through an opening no more than a foot across. On other occasions he charged through halls that could have held a chariot race. The understreets of Haven were more vast and confusing than their surface counterparts. Hordes of folk could live all their lives beneath the noses of those above. He could see why the cultists had thrived as long as they had.

As he ran, he thought about the pathways and secret openings the cult had provided him access to, and wondered why they needed him at all. They could carry out their own assassination with minimal risk. A troubling sensation had been rising in his gut since they started. He couldn't place the feeling, but it grew the longer they traveled.

He had to concentrate harder as he approached the area designated by a cultist; he still didn't know their names. His silent run slowed to a gentle trot when he saw the faint glow of a dagger painted onto the wall to his left. It possessed a soft luminescence that was like moonlight to his eyes. The sign had been placed to mark the mayor's room, or so Dugan had been told. All he had to do now was slip in, kill the mayor, and leave the same way he came. Easy enough. He took a deep breath and waited.

"It's time," one of the cultists whispered.

Dugan released the last of his breath through clenched teeth.

"We'll be watching, making sure your escape is assured," the disembodied voice informed him.

He took another deep breath before slowly pushing the section of wall in front of him. It moved forward an inch, then stopped. He pushed it slowly to the right. It glided effortlessly. Just as had been described to him, he found a tapestry that kept the secret entrance into the mayor's chambers from being seen. It was a perfect hiding spot.

Like a shadow, he slid from the hidden doorway and behind the tapestry, sword in hand. He was poised to unleash the full extent of his strength as he neared the end of the wall hanging and dared a covert look around its soft edges. Beyond the tapestry was a sparsely decorated room framed in deep brown wooden planks.

Unlit torches and candles lined the rest of the walls and a long painting hung on the wall opposite Dugan, depicting the view of Haven from outside the city. A large glass window to his left shed starlight across the area, which kept him from having to grope across the room. In the faint light he made a quick study of the painting. He guessed it showed how Haven appeared some time ago, as the city was smaller and the buildings that were now old and rundown appeared new. If he had to hazard a guess, he'd say Haven had more than doubled in size since the painting had been completed.

He'd emerged on the far wall, opposite the door into the hallway. To his left was the mayor's unoccupied bed. To his right was a wooden chest and a simple closet containing the elected ruler's personal effects. Nothing he need concern himself with. After he'd become familiar with the room and was sure there was no immediate danger, he darted back to the covered darkness of the hidden passageway.

"He isn't here!"

"Our reports said he frequents his room at this hour," one whispered defensively.

"Could they be wrong?" another asked.

"No. We're just early or he's a little late. Dugan, set yourself behind the door while we search the room for any dangers or hidden ways a guard could enter."

Dugan trod softly upon the hardwood floor covered with bearskins and wonderfully patterned woven rugs. Taking his sword, he stood next to the door, crouched in anticipation of the mayor's arrival. The other cult members crept in, drifted toward various corners, and searched with trained eyes and hands.

"Over here! Quickly!" one of them whispered as he approached the picture of the ancient city. "I've found the strongbox. It's behind the painting."

Together they lifted the picture from the wall. Behind it was a one-foot-square metal door latched and closed with a hard iron lock. Swift as predators, the cultists pulled out a lock pick and began to work on the device with the skill and grace of fine artisans. Dugan paid them little mind. He figured they were just securing the room. Since he'd never seen a room secured before, he didn't know what was involved or what traps or secret doors the room might contain.

The lock sprung open with a click.

Swifter than the wind, the cultists' hands were inside the opening, pawing at the interior. The activity intensified as they pulled out a small steel box about a foot in length. Dugan was drawn to it.

"What are you doing?" His uneasiness increased.

One turned. "Keep your watch on the door. Tell us the moment you hear anything. The mayor can't be too far away."

Dugan's brow furrowed. He watched as the cultists withdrew a silver necklace with a matching pendant about the size of a plum. In the pendant's center was a lapis lazuli stone, cut in a brilliant circle that sparkled with a life of its own.

"We finally have it," the leader declared with an awe-filled reverence.

"Is it the real one?" another questioned as his fingers reached for the gem.

"Yes. It has the markings," the leader replied. "He'll be pleased." The three men shifted their focus toward Dugan.

"He suspects now," one whispered.

"It's best we should go."

"Make sure the distraction is taken care of," the third responded in a frigid tone.

The shadowy group split up. Two made their way back to the tapestry with the necklace; the other neared Dugan.

"What's going on?" Malice and mistrust weighed heavy upon his breath.

"The room is secure," the cultist said as the two others vanished behind the tapestry. "You only need me here to help you make your escape."

"You didn't tell me about the jewelry." Dugan's attention faded from the door.

"Just trust me, Dugan. We have no reason for bickering. What we do here isn't connected to you or your goals. You'll still be freed from your suffering." The figure slowly walked toward the window next to the large tapestry.

"What are you doing now?"

"Stay down," the cultist ordered harshly. "I'm just looking to see what's going on outside." He dared a look out the window. "The mayor is late, and I don't like that. Rest easy, but stay vigilant. He could appear at any time."

"Do you see him?" Dugan asked as his eyes darted to the dark opening behind the tapestry.

"No—"

The words were drowned by a crash of glass and footsteps. "Farewell, fool! May the arms of Rheminas welcome you!"

Dugan had trouble processing what had happened. The cultist had thrown the metal box through the window, where it shattered in a deafening crash. The noise brought commotion and shouts from the hallway. In the confusion, the cultist fled behind the tapestry. He heard a click above the rising clamor, and then everything fell into place.

"You'll be the first to greet him!" Anger seized him as he lunged at the tapestry, tearing it down to reveal a solid wall. He couldn't tell where the opening started and the wall ended, but that didn't stop him pounding on the stone like an ogre, shouting his rage. The very next moment the door flew open and ten armed, armored men rushed into the room.

Before he knew what was happening, Dugan was surrounded by five Telborians who were barking orders and questions all at once. He didn't care to answer the questions nor obey the commands, showing his contempt for such things with the blade of his sword. All five men had their bodies slashed in one powerful movement. It appeared their chain mail shirts hadn't been enough for Dugan's full-fledged fury. They tried to stem the flow of blood and innards, but were unsuccessful in their attempts. They dropped their swords, along with a torch one of them carried, to tend their wounds.

Dugan didn't stop for a second swing and galloped to the window. As he did, the remaining five men moved in and took aim with their crossbows. He managed to avoid four of the bolts, but one sliced his left shoulder as he turned. He cursed as he leaped, head first, from the window.

The drop wasn't great, and he managed to tumble to the ground unharmed. Even as he stood up, he heard the alarm being called and the whole complex rising to oppose him. Trapped in a strange location he knew nothing about, hunted like a dog, and now wounded, he realized escape was unlikely, let alone survival.

Why did this seem so familiar?

Taking in the broken window, Dugan saw the bedroom was on the third floor of a very richly decorated stone mansion in an enclosed complex. The guards shouted curses at him as they lobbed more bolts upon him. He managed to dance around these while cursing himself beneath his breath. How could he have been so stupid?

The night air was filled with bobbing torches and activity. All around him he could see pinpricks of light growing larger by the moment. He knew he'd be surrounded soon enough. All he could think about was getting revenge on the people who brought him here—brought him to *this*.

He felt every muscle tighten and every nerve in his body—every part of his being—lock in rage. He tore the cut sleeve from his left arm and examined his wounded shoulder. With a grunt, he pulled the bolt out of his flesh. The blood washed away any and all lingering doubts on what was truth and what was lies. As surely as it had been there before, the mark of his enslavement—the branding of Colloni—had returned.

So *stupid*.

Furious, Dugan released a howl of rage. His last hope had been nothing but a lie. And Rheminas had actually forewarned him. The fury was hot in him, boiling what was left of his reason. He'd played right into the cultists' hands—played their puppet and pet so they could get what they wanted, and he could get his reward: death. But he wasn't about to give them satisfaction. If he was to be condemned to Rheminas' flames, he'd send all those who played him for a fool to Mortis first.

Removing his mask, Dugan wrapped it around his wounded arm. He noted the torches had moved much closer. They drifted in the sea of night from behind the manicured garden that surrounded the mayor's estate. The soft green bushes and artistically pruned trees would only hold back his pursuers' eyes for so long. He retreated further into the garden, rapidly searching for an escape plan.

This way, Dugan!

He spun and found nothing but the guards' growing light setting the night ablaze. It seemed, though, that he could make out another light growing closer with each passing breath.

"Turn to me and claim your revenge," the voice said from this new light.

The closer it got the more Dugan saw it resembled a ball of swirling flame about the size of a man's fist, hovering three feet from the ground. The closer it came the more it grew, and at a rapid rate: it took on the width of a man within a few wild heartbeats. He was awestruck and frightened at the same time. He knew what the fiery globe represented.

"You want me to kill these cultists?" A fierce grin birthed of blood lust and retribution swelled his cheeks. "For once, we're in agreement."

"Rheminas will give you revenge against your enemies once more, if you just step into the flames. You'll be given all the power you need to kill and make suffer those who have deceived you." The flames sang a maddening music to his ears, making it all the easier to surrender to his fate with fatalistic resolution. "Step into the flame. Be free to commit your revenge. Or you can stay here . . . and be killed." The flaming messenger approached, holding out its hand.

Dugan closed his eyes. The irony of his life filled him with such sorrow and rage he couldn't take it anymore. It was time to stop fighting his fate. It was time to accept the one into whose hands he had sold his soul. All his fighting had gotten him nothing. His whole life he'd been the slave of someone else. Nothing of freedom was ever known to him. Even if he was free from Colloni, he was never free from his past. It shook him to the bone. His demons wouldn't let him go, and he'd grown tired of fighting them.

Like the tired general who knows he's outnumbered and the battle's lost, Dugan made his choice to die on *his* terms and be done with it all. If he could send these cultists—these liars—into the Abyss in his final act in life, he'd be content. Fighting and bloodletting had been all he'd known. It was fitting he'd end his days in the midst of it. At least it wasn't a cross.

He reached for the messenger's flaming hand. It didn't burn, just as he knew it wouldn't. The figure moved forward and the two became one; flesh and fire mingled before vanishing entirely. All that remained was a puff of curling, greasy black smoke, befuddling the guards who found it.

CHAPTER 19

All of life is a journey. And every journey has its end.

—The Scrolls of Dust

A thick silence descended from the secret chamber's wooden rafters like an invisible sheet onto the cultists below. They'd gathered deep beneath the city, pooled in a semicircle around a dais that held the head priest and his throne. The massive room was lit only by the light of the wrought iron sconces that jutted out of the brick walls in a straight line that traced the room. Each cupped a reddish liquid that kept alive a single tongue of flickering flame. Combined, the flames were enough to reveal some old tapestries on either side of the chamber. Each depicted night scenes in a wilderness setting. There were dark-clothed figures doing something in them as well, but the light wasn't great enough to reveal just what that might be.

From behind the gathered cultists three forms approached the head priest's dais with measured strides. These were those who'd been sent with Dugan, hooded and cloaked once more in their ceremonial regalia. The head priest's throne, a rough black stone seat covered by black silk, rested on top of the three tiers like a tombstone. Given his dark attire, an illusion was created while he was seated, wherein the head priest and the throne appeared one and the same, each flowing out of the other.

The centermost of the advancing cultists held a claret silken cushion, which cupped the stolen necklace. As they drew near, the other dark-clad bodies in the room and around the dais quietly parted, allowing full access to the throne.

"You've done well," the head priest said, addressing the three with pride. "What of Dugan?"

"He's been left as a scapegoat and sacrifice for the great Shador," said the centermost cultist as the trio reached the foot of the dais.

"Excellent." The head priest raised a hand. "Praise Shador."

"Praise Shador," the room echoed.

"Bring it forth," the head priest said, beckoning.

They did as they were ordered, the one who held the cushion stepping up to the throne, where he then knelt in a presentation of his gift. The necklace, once in the head priest's hands, glowed with a faint bronze illumination. "At last, the desire of Shador's heart has been satisfied. Now he shall favor us even more. Great is our god and great is his benevolence to those who serve him!"

"Hail Shador!" the group shouted in unison.

"Begin the ceremony!" The head priest clapped his hands together. The chamber became filled with dry, low chanting in a language that none of the priests truly understood. It pulsed with an eldritch power, flooding the stone walls and floor, seeping into the cultists' inky cloaks, and causing the very air to tingle with energy.

"Hail the Lord of Shadows, our master and our god!" The group fell prostrate as the prayer began.

"Shador," the head priest said, raising his hands above his head, keeping the glowing necklace grasped in his left hand all the while. "I call you forth, great lord. Appear to us. Make known your will."

The room began skittering between the realms of the spirit and matter. From this divide a great inky coil shot out like a bolt of lightning, striking the ground between the prostrate followers and their leader. The image that followed was unclear and shaky, ethereal and transient as it blurred, then resolved itself, before settling with a type of watery clarity. Never more than a moment in a sharp, true image, the vision stood seven feet tall and swam with a shadowy form of a violet-eyed man.

"I have come," Shador said in Telboros. His voice was deep and booming. Dust from all the corners of the room fell around him with his echoing thunder.

"Praise Shador!" the cultists chanted.

"Great god of shadow." The head priest fell prostrate before his god, kneeling on the top step of his dais a short distance from his throne. "I'm humbled to present this token. As you have requested, we have retrieved the necklace."

Shador stared at the head priest, with his blazing eyes giving the impression of twin violet stars burning in the night. "You've done well." A slit of white tore across the darkness of his face.

"Thank you, lord." The head priest let his head fall to his chest.

Shador extended his hand. "Give it to me."

The head priest held the necklace up, averting his eyes so as to not fully look upon the shifting form of his god. As Shador took hold of the necklace, a change came to the air of the chamber. It was an incredible increase in heat to such a degree that the air in the chamber exploded in a violent fireball. Flame shot from the center of the room, burning many of the cultists where they kneeled while illuminating everything else with a brilliant flash of light.

Commotion overtook the fervent worshipers as flaming cultists scattered like grain in the wind, expelling pain-soaked screams as their garments blazed and skin melted away. The explosion also sparked smaller fires, which pooled and slithered around the room seeking objects to devour; tapestries and similar material burst into flame.

In the aftermath, a shape could be seen in the center of the room, where the explosion had arisen. Unaffected by fire or even heat, this figure rose from its crouched position with one even motion. By his hand a long sword appeared as the figure marched toward Shador's flickering image and the trembling cultists who still remained unharmed from the flames.

"Who dares defile my temple?" Shador snarled at the man approaching.

"Retribution." While still dressed in the dark garb Dugan had worn to kill the mayor, he'd been transformed into a vessel for revenge: a reflection of the god that burned inside of him.

His face had become a frightening thing: twisting and pulling against his flesh with unchallenged rage and lust for revenge. His hair also pulsated with life, sparking with odd tongues of flame that didn't burn as they danced around his ashen blond locks like snakes amid tall grass. These same tongues of flames flared out from his body in short bursts of self-contained combustion. Others wrapped around his muscular frame like veins, a sign of the gift from Rheminas, who'd transported him to the cultists' chamber.

"You have the Flame Lord's mantle upon you," Shador said, cringing. "I'll not challenge Rheminas today." Shador's murky shape dissipated as quickly as warm breath in winter, leaving his followers to their fate.

•●•

"Great lord!" The head priest desperately reached for the lingering black mist, only to lay hold of nothing.

"Your god seems as reliable as your promises." Dugan gritted his teeth and ran right for the center of the priests. Tiny gouts of flame trailed behind him as he raised his flaming sword high. The helpless cultists scattered before him. They'd lost their arrogance—secrecy fell away like a simple puff of smoke. Fear and the need for survival took its place.

Dugan pulled a dagger and threw it into the back of one of the fleeing cultists. The weapon burst into flame when it hit the air before it ate into its victim's flesh. He threw a second, taking grim delight at how it lodged in the pale-skinned throat of another. His victim turned so violently that his hood fell, revealing the face of a middle-aged, balding Telborian. For a moment his eyes flared wide before the flaming dagger sliced his neck, spilling and spraying blood in an explosive fountain. The pale man stood a moment more, swaying on his heels, before he crumbled to the floor, his body to be trampled by the fleeing cultists.

"Who's next?" Dugan roared. As much as part of him knew what was to follow this bloody work, he did his best to revel in the massive swell of power, pure anger, and hatred flowing through his veins. He'd never feel such freedom and power again.

Speechless and unable to act, the cultists knew the deepest and most gripping kind of horror. Dugan watched with delight as his weapon did its work. Flames still flickered from his body and he felt the heated breath of his master upon him. Rheminas wouldn't leave him until he'd drunk deep of the Vengeful One's cup.

Like stalks of corn at the farmer's blade, the priests of Shador fell. Amid the blood and black cloth, crunching bone, bursts of flame, and flesh-rending screams, death latched hold of all. How many fell by Dugan's blade he'd never know. It was just a macabre dance in which he decapitated, disemboweled, and maimed his victims with a malevolent lust and skilled hand. His weapon shattered their frames within moments of contact, sending them howling to Asorlok's gates.

In a very short span of time the room was littered with cultists who had either fallen by Dugan's fiery blade or been overcome by the smoke or heat of the swelling fire. The others fled down the various hallways like the rats they were. The fallen bodies started to burn as tentacles of fire crept farther into the room, ever hungry for more to devour.

The fire, left unchecked when it was first spawned by Dugan's entrance, had grown so much that the room was alight. Smoke curled around the corners of the ceiling and slithered out of open doorways, hovering at head level as it tried to claw its way away from the growing inferno. A few heartbeats more and the flames would have conquered all. But a few heartbeats were all he would need.

He'd saved the head priest for last, who could do nothing but watch Dugan sprint up the dais. His god had left him, his fellow cultists were dead or had fled, and now he realized his own life was forfeit. The priest reached for the dagger he kept in his belt, but the action was in vain. Dugan's searing blade plunged into his flesh the same moment he pulled the dagger free. Burgundy blood seeped in small waves from his gut, pumping out of him with a sporadic rhythm. Dugan himself was covered in a fine mist of it as he continued his deadly assault, maddened by the slaughter and satisfaction of retribution.

In response to the attack, the leader stabbed Dugan's chest. The wounded priest was unable to pull the dagger back out, his body already too weak to stand. The blade dug deep into Dugan's left breast, near his heart, but he didn't cry out in pain. Even as the rivers of crimson flowed from the wound, his mind was set on only one resolution.

"I'm tired of being lied to and cheated," Dugan snarled as he locked on to the dying head priest's dimming eyes. "You're all liars. *All* of you!" He yanked his sword free with a savage growl. With a mighty downward thrust he lopped off the priest's left arm. Raw sinew dangled from the laceration, drooling blood. The priest could do nothing, not even voice his own agony. His arm tumbled helpless to the floor, where its fingers twitched in spastic throes.

Dugan watched with a heaving chest, coughing bloody phlegm amid the thickening smoke from the growing inferno. The priest's life faded away, dwindling to a faint trickle, before leaving him as cold and empty as the flagstone floor upon which he fell.

Satisfied, he welcomed his own end. Throwing his sword at the base of the dais, he ripped the dagger from his chest. The wound flared to life, releasing greater streams of blood that grew into raging rivers. He didn't care. He'd done what he had come to do, and now it was over. He lifted his face and arms above him.

"I'm ready now," he shouted amid syrupy coughs. "I've nothing left. Nowhere to go. No one to help.

"Take me if I'm yours, then!" He stumbled down the dais, falling to the floor beside it to land hard on his lower back. To his right he noticed his blood-painted sword. The ravenous flames enveloping it had left. The weapon was now lifeless and cold, like he'd be in a few more breaths.

He felt lightheaded, his vision blurred. No matter. All around him the fire raged, smoke drawing a tight stranglehold over his throat. The heat had cracked and shattered many of the bricks of the room, causing the ceiling to creak and groan in protest. His doom was fast approaching, and he welcomed it with open arms. Flattened by the roof, burned alive, or drained of blood—either way he'd join Rheminas soon enough.

•●•

What Dugan failed to notice as his vision dimmed was the black door that had appeared in the corner of the room. A door of fine wrought iron, crafted into a solid image devoid of hinges that opened to spill pure daylight into the hellish chamber. Out of the door came Cracius and Tebow.

"Over there." Tebow pointed to a crumbled mass. "That must be him."

"Did *he* do all this?" Cracius cried over the roaring flames.

"Hurry." Tebow did his best to sprint through the fallen bodies and flames between him and Dugan. "We don't have much time."

Cracius followed the elder priest's lead, joining him at Dugan's side.

"Can you walk?" Tebow asked the battered and confused Telborian.

Dugan didn't respond.

"Can you walk?" Cracius asked again, this time covering his nose and mouth with his cloak to keep back the smoke that was already causing his eyes to stream.

Tebow joined him in covering his face, saying, "Asorlok's hand is heavy upon him."

Cracius coughed. "Then we better get out of here, unless we want to perish in this inferno too."

"Be at peace." Tebow placed a hand upon Dugan's shoulder. Dugan took hold of Tebow's hand with a vise-like grip. His face was ablaze in rage.

"No more priests," he said, his voice rough and gravelly amid the gurgling in the back of his throat.

"We come in peace," Cracius pleaded.

"Liars!" Dugan snarled. "You're all just *liars*." He fell into a fit of coughing that rocked him to the point of collapse and sent blood flailing all about.

"He's mad," said Cracius. "Leave him. He can only be a danger to himself and others. Let him die in peace and with some dignity."

"We need him," Tebow countered. "Remember what Galba said: we'll need *all* of them."

A burned wooden beam toppled a short distance from them, scattering embers in a blazing splash. They jumped away, using their cloaks to shield them, but they wouldn't be able to shield themselves from the whole ceiling collapsing. The entire chamber began to moan and wail.

Tebow held his hand before Dugan's face. "By the will of Asorlok, sleep." For a moment nothing happened, then the god's touch overtook him, and Dugan fell to the floor in a heap. "We'll have to sort this out later." Tebow assessed Dugan's injury. "The wound is a hard one, but not too grave to remedy. If we can get him out of here, he'll live." He motioned with his head toward the open wrought iron door. "We'll have to carry him through the portal."

Another groan from above filled their ears. Wasting no time, the priests took hold of Dugan—Cracius his feet, Tebow under his arms—and rushed for their door.

"The sword." Tebow motioned to the weapon as they passed it. "He'll need it, I should think."

Cracius retrieved it. A small pile of flaming bricks tumbled onto the dais and throne. A moment later, fueled by the spirit of their god and pure adrenaline, the Asorlins reached their doorway. As soon as the door closed behind them the ceiling fell, releasing a cascading pile of cinder, flame, timber, and ash.

CHAPTER 20

Strangers often have a strange way of doing some strange things at the strangest of times.

—Elliott Midon, Telborian bard
(420 PV–500 PV)

"This wasn't exactly what I was expecting." An olive-skinned human woman emerged from behind a ruined statue, calmly striding through the rotting wreckage of centuries past. Her hair was long, shiny, and black, her eyes a deep brown. She wore a gown made of hides with matching boots. Though crafted from raw and savage materials, they'd been worked into an elegant set of items that accented their wearer's simple beauty. Around her waist was a thin leather belt, to which a dagger was sheathed.

"Not the best, perhaps." Endarien's guise greeted Panthora's in the mountaintop ruins of one of his decimated temples. "But it will work for now." They found themselves in an open area that had been a simple courtyard centuries before. He appeared as a Telborian man with short white hair and yellow eyes. The rest of his garb was simple: a brown tunic and black pair of pants and boots.

"I still don't see why you had to call me all the way out here," she said. "We could have spoken at Thangaria." Of course, that was ruins too in a way, though not so ramshackle as this place. Besides the general disarray common to most ruins, there was the added displeasure of dry bones and other signs of the long dead strewn about the area. The whole place, in fact, felt more graveyard than temple.

"Too many ears," Endarien explained. "I wanted to share what I have to say in private."

"I see." After her apotheosis, Panthora had quickly learned how the pantheon dealt with each other. Hidden meetings and plots were far too common for her liking, and she thought this behavior beneath beings who were supposed to be so much better than everyone else. In fact, the more she'd seen, the more she was amazed at how much like mortalkind the gods were. Or perhaps mortalkind were more like the gods, learning such things from their creators.

"So what is it you wish to share with me?" she asked.

"I need your help."

"For what?"

"To stop something bad from happening."

"Bad for whom?"

"All of us—even Tralodren—if left to go too far."

"I thought we just had this conversation in the council."

"We did." He paused. "But this is a little different."

"Then the council should be addressed, and together we can—"

"We're working *outside* the council."

"We?" She wondered who might be teamed up now. And with Endarien. He was a Gray God, so perhaps another of their number . . . More plots and twists she was less than fond of. Sometimes she wondered why the council was even used at all; so many of the pantheon seemed to form their own ad hoc ones whenever needed.

"Asorlok, Saredhel, and myself."

"Really?" She did her best to keep her amazement from showing.

Endarien sighed. "Look, we're going off of a vision from Saredhel."

"We all are," said Panthora. "You heard what she said in the council."

"Yes." Again there was another pause. Far too long for her liking. It spoke of needing time to better present what came next. And given what she'd learned from both her mortal and now her divine life, that rarely spoke well of what followed.

"Well, this is another vision," Endarien said at last. "One she shared only with Asorlok and me. We're supposed to help bring the same people who helped free Cadrith from the Abyss together to stand against him once more."

"Why?" None of this was making any sense. And she didn't see a part for herself in it.

"Because they're supposed to be the ones who are going to stop him before things could get any worse."

"But Saredhel said—"

"Don't try and understand everything." Endarien was curt. "You'll just get a headache."

"But why would Saredhel give two different prophecies?"

"Look, we're working toward the same end." Endarien was clearly interested in keeping out of any debate.

"Is that what *Saredhel* said, or what *you* took her to mean?"

"I am getting ready to face Cadrith, in case you've forgotten." There was a slight edge to Endarien's voice.

"So then why bring me here?" Panthora persisted for answers.

"Because I believe what she said to Asorlok and me." He sighed. "And now that I've heard her other prophecy in the council I can see how both can fit together."

"Even if what you said was so, I still don't see what help I can be to you."

"Rowan Cortak." The Nordican's name got her attention.

"What of him?" She did her best to keep her face neutral. She had invested much into him of late and had larger plans for him ahead. It wouldn't do altering things too much now—not when she almost had everything she'd always wanted and worked toward finally coming into alignment.

"I've managed to help get him and the elf with him closer to Arid Land, but I don't think they'll follow through on the rest of what's needed once making landfall."

"Which is?"

"Joining the others at Galba's circle." He spoke as if the matter should have been common knowledge.

Now it was beginning to make sense. "And since Rowan is a Knight of Valkoria you thought to turn to me to, what—*force* him into your plan?"

"*Guide* him, that's all." There was too much emphasis on that word for Panthora's liking.

"You really need to share what you're doing with the council," she said. "You're talking about breaking ancient rules and pacts."

"*We're* not going to Galba; they are. Mortals are free to come and go there as they please. We need Rowan and Alara there with the others. If *you* told him to seek out Galba, he'd go there in a heartbeat."

"Because he trusts me and is one of my most loyal followers," said Panthora. "And for good reason. I'd never lie to him, or any who call upon me."

"You're not *lying*," Endarien insisted. "You're just having him go to Galba. It's nothing deceptive." She remained motionless, staring him in the face. "All right, how about this?" he continued. "I know Rowan's still interested in finding that mage Cadrith captured."

"And how do you know that?" She was becoming less comfortable with how much detail Endarien knew about her affairs. Secretive spying spoke to how little one trusted another. Hardly a strong foundation to build anything long lasting.

"A little bird told me." He smirked. "Cadrissa is with the lich, who's making his way to Galba. So by going there Rowan would be getting to save the mage. And while he's there, he can deal with the other matter as well."

"*If* I told Rowan anything, I wouldn't force him to do anything. I would give him a choice. And if he decided against going, neither you nor Asorlok nor Saredhel could try and change his mind."

"All right," Endarien returned with some resignation. "I guess I can respect that. But you're still going to have to tell him then. Are you willing to do that?"

"Only if you're willing to tell me everything you know about all of this," said Panthora. "I'm not about to send anyone into some foolhardy venture."

"Fine." Endarien sighed. "But I'm going to need you to keep this to yourself."

Panthora said nothing, merely listened.

•●•

Brandon navigated the deck of his nameless vessel with only the fading stars and moon to guide his feet. Dawn flared on the horizon. It was time to finish this. The silent sailors still said nothing, engrossed in their tasks, pointless though they were. He'd kept this masquerade up as long as he could stand. There were more important things afoot than playing captain to those two. He'd done his job, at least as far as he had been told. Time to get back to focusing his effort on the greater threat.

"You've done well." He spoke to no one in particular. "You can return to Avion."

The sailors, who had once been the semblance of men, fluttered like ripples in a pond before fading away, leaving the deck devoid of anyone save Brandon. He craned his neck to the crow's nest and the seagull perched upon it.

"You can go too." The seagull gave a squawk, fluttered its wings, and aimed for the rising dawn. Closing his eyes, he took a deep breath before exhaling a stream of white fog from his lips. He continued blowing far longer than any normal human could, expanding the thickening cloud until the ship was swaddled in it, and the water and sky were completely hidden from view. When he'd finished, he opened his eyes to consider his work. Satisfied, he made his way back to his quarters, leaving the fog to rule the ship.

•●•

As Rowan slept, images of light and color played in his mind. Sounds and smells ushered him to places that could only exist in the world of dreams. He felt himself being whisked away by soft winds as tender as a lover's caress. Gently, the breezes cradled him across the great expanse of land beneath his floating body. Suddenly, his eyes passed through a veil of misty clouds. His vision was impaired, but he continued to float peacefully through his dreamscape.

He began to hear soft laughter that drew him forward in wonder. The noise was distant at first, but grew in volume as he drew closer. In the universal understanding of dreams, he knew it as the sound of his lover. Her voice was a bird's song—playful and musical. It brought with it all the gentle and alluring feminine tones he enjoyed.

As the laughter neared, the cloud parted. What the scene revealed was breathtaking and also hauntingly familiar. Before him was Alara, though not as he knew her in the real world. As is often the case in dreams, she was more fantastic than in the normal light of day. She wore a flowing stola and palla that draped her curves, the diaphanous material barely covering her supple skin. Her silver hair gleamed like fine strands of polished pewter.

She stood in a peaceful glade filled with young saplings, a gentle brook running beside her; soft flowing grass the color of emerald was all around her. There was a soft, silvery blue fog floating through the air like gauze. He stepped into the setting with outstretched arms. Alara entered his embrace and he crushed her to himself.

He felt compelled to touch her—to kiss her, hold her until the days themselves ended. He felt a jab of fear enter his heart as the thought came, a sense he was about to commit an unnatural act, but the illicitness of it made him crave it all the more. It fired a passion that drove him to seek Alara's silken lips. The thrill of battle and his love for Panthora were nothing compared to her touch. The wanting grew within him—an inescapable longing to be with this woman. Even as these emotions fueled him, a dark specter plagued him. It spoke of elven treachery and evils, should he continue.

"My husband," Alara whispered as she ran her fingers across Rowan's face.

Thunderstruck, he stared helplessly at her. Passionate thoughts, unknown to him until this moment, flooded every inch of his body. His hands moved to her smooth, bare shoulders as he became intoxicated with her aroma—a sweet and fragrant mix of spring breezes and summer blossoms that filled him with vigor. He reached to remove the gauzy material covering her body, but before he could the curtain glided over his vision once more and he was left alone with his troubled thoughts. Thoughts telling him the love he felt for an elf was unnatural and filthy.

•●•

Rowan woke to the sound of Alara entering the room. "There's a thick fog out there. I couldn't see anything. Not even the crew." He said nothing, trying to keep himself from looking as shaken as he was. The dream was bad enough, but to have her here, right before him, as the first thing he saw upon waking? He willed himself to take control. They were almost to Arid Land. Once they were out of these cramped quarters and had solid land under their feet, things would start to smooth out.

"You sleep okay?"

"Fine." Rowan hopped to the floor. Alara nodded. She was standing a short distance between him and the door.

"Well, now that you're up, I suppose we can get some breakfast. You're going to have to be careful on deck though—I couldn't see anything in front of me. We might even have to hold hands to get across."

"I'll manage." He was fixated on reaching the door.

"You sure you're all right?" Alara watched him, concerned.

"I'm fine."

Before he could reach the door, he found himself running into Brandon, who entered the room with a cheery grin. "Ah, good. You're both up. Makes things all the easier. You might want to start packing. We've just crossed into the Arid Sea. We should be within sight of the beach soon."

"How do you even know, with all that fog?" asked Alara.

"I have my ways."

"But it's thicker than—"

"Top of the crow's nest," Brandon interrupted. "You can see above and beyond it. Besides, it's thinning some. Should be mostly cleared up by the time we reach the beach."

"The Arid Sea. That's amazing." Rowan saw Alara shared his disbelief. "If I hadn't experienced it myself, I probably wouldn't believe it."

"Well you have, and we did," Brandon said with a small smirk. "Like I said. Endarien has really favored us."

"I guess," Alara said warily, as she made her way to collect her personal items.

"Go on then," Brandon said, encouraging Rowan to do the same. "I thought you had some urgent business to be about. The sooner you get to land the sooner you can be about it." Brandon watched them for a moment more before stepping back onto the deck, affording them some small privacy in their preparations.

A short while later Alara and Rowan were on deck. Like Alara, Rowan had donned what gear he could and packed up the rest, which, given how light they traveled, meant slinging his shield over his back and attaching his purse, with its handful of remaining coin, to his belt. True to Brandon's words, the fog had dissipated some—at least, according to Alara it had—allowing them to see across the bow. But there was still plenty about, obscuring their vision.

"Where's the crew?" Alara asked, shifting her head this way and that.

"Staying out of trouble," said Brandon. "There's not much can be done until the fog clears. It's just thinning at the bow." He pointed out the area again. "And there's the beach." He showed them the gray sand. Though still a few hundred yards from them, it was a welcome sight amid the near-endless craggy mountains lining Arid Land's coasts.

"And there's Vanhyrm," Rowan said, pointing to the Nordic settlement.

There was only one beach and safe harbor on all of Arid Land, and it was here where the Nordicans had constructed their trading post and settlement. Strong and defiant, Vanhyrm dominated the landscape for miles. Resting about a quarter mile inland from the soft, gray shore, it was surrounded by massive walls constructed of fieldstone and fat tree trunks sharpened to a point at their tops. Additional trees and underbrush had been cleared and cut around the settlement and a rough road, made of crushed stone, flowed toward a set of iron-reinforced wooden doors that served as the great gate.

"Wait a moment," said Alara, finding Brandon. "How can it be so close to sunset? It was still morning when you came to tell us about Arid Land."

"You were probably confused by the fog," he offered.

"No, it was morning." Alara was certain, as was Rowan, who was confident he'd awakened not more than a few moments ago.

"That's close enough," Brandon shouted into the mist. "Drop anchor here."

The splash of the anchor in the Arid Sea stirred the growing confusion inside the young knight. "What are you doing? We haven't even gotten close to the beach."

"This is as far as I go," said Brandon.

"What?" Rowan's eyes went from Brandon to Alara, then back to Brandon. "You said you were going to Arid Land on business."

"I *do* have business, and *you're* it." His eyes sparkled. "I brought you as far as I can go." Rowan noticed the fog starting to thicken. "You'll just have to make do with the rest."

"I think you owe us some answers—about *several* things." There was fresh fire in Alara's eyes, a fire Rowan was beginning to share.

"I don't owe you anything," said Brandon. "You needed help getting to Arid Land and I decided to provide it. I just can't get you to the *land* part of Arid Land, that's all." The fog rose, obscuring the "window" at the ship's bow, wrapping them in a plump cloud. "But you're *near* Arid Land now, aren't you?"

"No." Rowan rose to his full height. "You're going to take us to the harbor."

"Afraid not, son. You'll understand soon enough. I'm not about to waste time with explanations. Don't have enough as it is these days." Brandon pointed in the direction of the ship's bow. They saw nothing but a thick curtain of mist rolling in. "The water's probably not too warm, but if you hurry you'll still have the day."

"You can't expect us to *swim* to shore," said Rowan.

"I don't think you have much of a choice." Brandon withdrew into the fog, disappearing from sight.

"Hey!" Alara followed, but got no more than a few steps before she dropped into the waves with a splash.

"Alara?" Rowan barely managed her name before the deck faded into mist beneath him, blending with the fog, and he, too, fell through. He hit the cold water hard, shocking him to his senses.

"Rowan?" Alara yelled.

"I'm right here." He treaded water while fumbling with his shield. After a brief period of awkward aquatic acrobatics, it was free and in the water, the convex side making a suitable buoy.

"So where's the beach?" No sooner had she asked than a patch of fog lifted. "Convenient, wouldn't you say?"

"It's better than swimming in circles." He began paddling for the stretch of gray sand. Alara followed.

After a hard push, they reached the shore. While they hadn't been stranded in the middle of the Arid Sea, it was still a good swim, and their armor and clothing were heavier when wet. It was quite a challenge to reach land without falling into Perlosa's embrace. The fog seemed to have retreated from them as they neared the narrow beach, allowing him to see a handful of docked Nordic vessels to his left, but little else.

They emerged from the sea dripping wet and clinging to the dry land. Once he'd managed to stand, Rowan sought Brandon's boat in the nearly evaporated mist.

"It's gone. How can it just be gone?" He sloshed his hair back as if it were some wet kelp and suddenly realized how tired he felt. It was as if he'd lived a whole day in just a handful of moments. "What's going on?"

"One thing at a time." Alara wrung water from her hair and cloak. "Let's focus on getting someplace warm and dry first."

"Then we need to get behind those walls," he said, sliding his shield over his back. They headed to the crushed stone road that led to Vanhyrm's gates. Alara drew up her wet hood as they went.

"Let's just hope this isn't a prelude of things to come."

"You tired too?"

"More than I should be, since I thought we just woke up," said Alara.

So he wasn't just imagining things. "He must have been a wizard. He probably used magic to move the boat and that crew—they probably weren't even real."

"Maybe."

"But why go to all the trouble of helping us get here?"

"I don't know if that matters anymore," said Alara. "We're here now . . . and soaking wet."

"Not for much longer once we find a decent fire."

"I trust you're going to do the talking?"

"It'll be easier," he said, looking over his shoulder. "And I don't have an elven accent."

"Fair enough," said Alara. "What are we going to tell them, if they ask about me? I don't plan on drawing attention, but just in case . . . it'll be good to have a story to fall back on."

Rowan focused on the tall timber walls. He was studying the impressive ironclad gate when the idea came to him. "We can say you're my retainer."

"*Retainer?*"

"It's either that or my slave. But that would be a lie."

"And me being a retainer isn't?" Stopping to face him a few yards from the gate, she made perfectly clear what she thought of the idea.

"You said you came to help me," he pointed out.

"To *vouch* for you with your superiors. Not to be your personal slave."

"I didn't say I think of you as my slave."

"Then how *do* you think of me?" Rowan reined in his eyes, stopping them from popping wide open. But Alara wasn't done. "As *less* than your equal, your equal, or something else?"

He didn't know what to say, or if he even *should* say anything. His thoughts were awash with disappearing ships, failed missions, cautious joy at having returned to his people—not to mention the constant swirl of emotions regarding the elven woman before him. Why couldn't at least *one* thing be simple for a change?

"I-I'm sorry." A calmer Alara spoke. "I didn't mean that. It's just that sometimes . . ." She began taking an intense interest in the gate. "Sometimes you get me so—"

She snapped back to Rowan, her attention and focus solely businesslike again.

"We need to get you out of those clothes," Rowan heard himself say. Once he realized how that sounded, he added, "I mean *both* of us—we *both* need to get out of these clothes." This didn't sound any better, so he amended it even further by adding: "And in front of a fire—to warm up."

Alara smirked. "You *sure* you want to do the talking?"

"Let's just take this one step at a time," he said, returning to the gate. The thick timbers loomed over them, watching their advance. They kept a steady pace, the crushed rock road rustling beneath their steps.

"You'll do fine," Alara said, placing her hand upon Rowan's sopping shoulder. He felt a gentle warmth flush over his body when she did so. He both fought and welcomed it at the same time.

"Hello," Rowan shouted at the gate, in his native tongue.

Alara drew her hood tighter as time ticked away. Just as he was going to give another shout, they heard a noise from behind the wall. With a heavy grinding sound a vertical panel on one of the doors was removed. Two stern eyes topped with thick eyebrows appeared behind the opening.

"Who goes there?" It was Nordican, spoken in a deep, raspy voice.

"Rowan Cortak, Knight of Valkoria."

"What's your business here? We didn't hear of your arrival. We've closed the gates for the evening."

"We've come seeking some shelter for the night. It's been a long journey with still more before us."

"Where's your vessel and crew?" The eyes darted back and forth like a wolf sizing up its prey. "We never saw any sign of new sails."

"We're the only ones here, I'm afraid."

"So am I. Two people don't just show up out of nowhere without some means of transport. What did you do, *swim* here? Who's she?" The eyes darted to Alara, who wrapped her sopping cloak even tighter.

"She's my . . . retainer."

"So, you want to come in then?" The eyes continued their diligent search of the duo.

"Yes, we do, and if you don't start being a bit more hospitable it'll be hard to keep being so diplomatic. Is this how you treat members of the knighthood?" Rowan's blood began to boil. Why were they acting in such a manner to their own flesh and blood—even more so, to a Knight of Valkoria? "We're tired and wet from a long journey. We would like to warm ourselves by your fire and rest for the time ahead. Now, will you let us in?"

"Relax, Rowan," the voice behind the door said with a chuckle. "You always were able to give me a laugh." A playful air replaced the formerly stern tones. "Just like your mother, you are. So tightly wound up."

"Erland Sorenson?" Rowan said with a grin, finally recognizing the voice. "You're still alive?" He trod briskly for the door.

"Who's he?" Alara asked, following and speaking in Nordican with hushed tones.

"Erland was one of the men I used to listen to when I was younger," he returned in Telboros. "He's a great storyteller, traveler, and adventurer. He used to tell me tales when he returned from his travels. They'd be full of adventure and—"

He stopped when he realized he was about to say "treacherous elves." Suddenly that didn't sit right with him—as if he'd eaten something off and it had just hit his stomach. "And he's a friend."

"The man was just trying to get you riled up enough to break down the door and attack him. Doesn't sound like he's much of a friend."

"He really didn't mean any harm." Rowan grabbed Alara's arm. "Come on." He pulled her forward. He heard the sounds of great bolts and barricades unlatching before the sturdy gate opened.

"You young hound." The voice of Erland Sorenson crept from behind the massive timber gate. "The waves have brought you back safe and sound, eh?"

Erland appeared from behind the door. He wasn't a normal Nordican in the least. His left hand had been replaced by a metal fist. His right leg was a wooden peg below the knee. The crowning mark was his face. It was pitted and pocked from various diseases that had ravaged his skin in his youth. But these assaults hadn't taken his life. They only left their mark with the rest of his stitched scars. His smile, though, was genuine and whole.

White hair mingled with blond strands, and silver-gray splotches covered his thick mustache that hung past his chin. Blue eyes as sharp and clear as crystal took in everything, guiding the slightly bent, though still hearty, frame of the Nordic adventurer forward.

"I heard you left for your first mission already," he said to Rowan, keeping the conversation in Nordican.

"I did." Rowan took pride in the slap Erland gave his back with his good hand.

Erland gave Rowan and Alara a surveying glance. "I wasn't kidding when I said we didn't see any new sails. Did you *both* swim in?"

"Yes and no," said Rowan. "It's a long story."

"I bet it is." Erland's smile widened. "So. Any scars from your first mission?"

"No." He had dropped his defenses. It felt good to be back among his people and even better to be around a familiar face. It was almost enough to push aside the discomfort of the past few weeks. Almost. "Of course, I'm not done yet either. We still have to get back to the keep."

"So why are you *here* then?"

"I'd prefer not to say at the moment."

"Some sort of knighthood thing, eh?"

"You could say that."

"Sorry I wasn't able to make your ceremony. I'm stuck here with my duties for the rest of the year. Been looking for some treasure in my off hours, though. You just know them elves have something hidden here. So come on in then. You're soaked, and are catching something deadly for sure. These elves fill the air with disease—I'm sure of it." Erland led them inside the walls. "Mark my words, Rowan. One day those elves will be the death of this place, and us. You can never trust an elf. Isn't that what I taught you?"

"Yes." Rowan risked glancing at Alara, who remained silent and seemingly emotionless.

Again he felt that unpleasant pang in his gut as Nalu's words echoed through his mind.

Maybe they taught it to you in secret.

"Sound advice, I say." Erland's lower lip stuck out as he gave a solid nod of approval. "Just look at what they did to me."

"So you're a guard here?" asked Rowan.

"I help here and there," he replied. "Today just happened to be my time to watch the gate. No doubt Panthora saw to that so I could be one of the first to welcome you back."

Ordinarily, Rowan would have been tempted to affirm such statements but instead let the matter pass without comment. He wasn't entirely confident in stating what might and might not be Panthora's will at the moment. Hopefully, that would change after he'd had some time for rest and prayer.

As they made their way down a wooden plank road—the main road for Vanhyrm—Erland turned to Rowan. "So how are your mother and father doing?"

"They're fine." Rowan watched the people and booths pass by as the road grew narrower until finally the shops disappeared altogether and small, hard-packed dirt walkways took over. There were only taverns and a single large inn now, more communal than anything else. From his training, he'd learned such places acted as a combined boarding house, tavern, and general supply store. A sign painted in the Nordic tongue said it was called Skull Splitter. A simple picture made it clear for those that couldn't read: a lone skull with an axe wedged deep into the bone.

From the lack of general activity it was clear nothing of interest was happening in the streets. The sun would be gone soon, and it would be getting dark even sooner due to the tall walls casting a great shadow over the town's interior.

"I bet you're looking forward to seeing them again."

"You could say that."

"You can relax, Rowan. There's no one here who'll hurt you." Erland's tone softened. "We're lively enough, but the old feuds and ways don't mean much around here. If we were fighting all the time, we wouldn't have any food or make any money, now, would we?" Erland laughed as he slapped Rowan's back again with his good hand. Rowan wanted to trust the old man, but something wouldn't let him. It was an odd feeling that spoke in slivers of icy fear and twinges of mistrust, still swirling about his gut.

"So why do you have a retainer?" Erland asked with a glint of mischief in his eye. "And such a pretty one, from what I can see under that hood."

"Like I said, she's here to help in my mission."

"You *sure* you can't tell me anything about it?" Erland stopped in the path, facing the duo with an inquisitive but still cheery expression. "I'm just so excited about you getting through the dedication and into the knighthood. You must have at least a *few* stories to share."

Rowan observed Alara's shoulders tensing ever so slightly. "I'd rather not say right now. And we'll just be staying for the night. We have to be in Valkoria as soon as we can. It's vital for the cause I'm championing."

"I'm sure it is, lad. Defending humanity is a very worthy task. Just keeping a human woman out of trouble, for common men like myself, is a full-time effort." Erland's eyes were alight with mischief. "Seems they're some wild ones being raised up in the Lynx Tribe, stories say. Causing many a headache for all the men—and their mothers, no doubt. That's why I say it's best to keep a woman pregnant and in the kitchen, where you can keep an eye on them. Ain't too many evils lurking near the oven, now, are there?" A deep chuckle rolled up from his gut.

"Isn't that right?" The mirth-filled Nordican gave Alara's shoulder a hearty pat.

Alara went rigid.

"Don't say much, do you? Course"—he found Rowan once again—"a silent woman isn't a bad thing, now, is it? Gods, what a world it would be if women yapped only half as much as they do." Rowan chuckled nervously while Erland released another deep belly laugh.

"Well, you better get going." Erland motioned to the Skull Splitter. "I'll see you later if I can." He headed in the opposite direction, back to his post. "You'll find all you'll need in the inn."

"Thank you." Rowan nodded.

Erland waved farewell with his good hand, then ambled into the growing shadows.

"What an interesting man," Alara commented, returning to Telboros.

"He was just happy to see me again, that's all," he replied in the same tongue while scanning the direction Erland had headed. The seasoned warrior continued making his way from them. Rowan was surprised at the small weight that lifted from his chest.

"Come on," said Alara.

The Skull Splitter was the only place in Vanhyrm that provided hospitality to traders and common men denied elsewhere in the wilderness and the private houses, businesses, and small halls making up the rest of the settlement. Vanhyrm wasn't made to house a large long-term population and served mostly as a place of transient migration for people and goods. The halls and buildings that did exist were practical. No one would ever call the settlement a village. Maybe an outpost or trading center, but not much else.

Rowan pushed open the sturdy oak door, releasing a welcome blast of heat. Though the young knight had found a community in the knighthood, nothing could compete with the true kinship he felt when he was with a common gathering of his own people. It was a funny thing, but the more he lingered away from the knighthood, the better he felt, as if he was more alive.

They entered without attracting much notice. The men inside were too into their mead and ale to pay Rowan or Alara much mind. The large room was built out of strong wooden timber and thick rope. The poles had been roughly hacked from trees; bark-covered pillars shooting up to the roof groaned, both from the weight they bore and the elements they had to endure, inside and out. The light came from a large fire pit in the center of the building surrounded by fieldstone and soot-black iron bars. On these bars were large cooking pots and steaming kettles. From here wonderful smells of fresh stew and porridge greeted the travelers.

Tall-backed wooden chairs were scattered amid rectangular pine tables. This was where the Nordicans sat, half-drunk, shouting to their friends and singing off-key sagas of valor and blood lust. Traders and sailors were here too, but kept to themselves, or gathered in gaggles of like-minded fellows for their own brand of discourse. Amid the common rabble were men of learning. Some sages from various Nordic tribes were decked out in beast-cat-teeth necklaces and furs. He even spotted a few shamans, holding to the manners and dress common to each tribe's totem.

Erland was right when he said Vanhyrm was a great mixing point for all Nordicans. It was just such a thing the knighthood and Panthora were trying to establish throughout the Northlands. But even with Panthora's influence there were still pockets where the old ways dominated. Blood feuds and small battles were not that uncommon. Here, though, things were different. The image of many different tribes being civil to one another was an oddity to his eyes, though his training claimed all humanity should unite and be peaceful to each other.

Around the walls of the inn and on the upper level were small shelves and shops selling herbs and spices, clothing, seed, grain, and staple goods. Some even boasted magical elixirs, if their signs could be believed. Also on the upper level, and further on into the deep recesses of the building, signs and doorways spoke of rooms to rent, access to the kitchen, a place to bathe, and other areas catering to traders and travelers.

In the corners and dark points in the room, elves were serving food and removing empty plates and mugs. These elves weren't as expansionistic as the Elyellium, having kept to Arid Land for the entire history of their race. They called themselves Syvani. And to hear some tell it, that was one of their few redeeming traits: the less elves there were in the wider world, the better.

Each elf was clothed in a simple tunic and chained at the hands and feet. Their red hair was matted, and their flesh bruised and dirty. Though their bodies were strong and lean, they appeared gaunt. And then there were the marks of abuse—some old and scarred and others more recent.

As Rowan and Alara neared the fire, one of the Syvani looked at her. Unlike the rest of the elves, her doe-like face had some Nordic features that were hard to miss. She was obviously a half-elf, the product of the union of a Syvani and a Nordican—often a rape. She couldn't have been more than fourteen years old. A glint of fear touched her eyes when she saw what Alara's hood struggled to conceal.

"What can I do for you?" She spoke in fluent Nordican.

"We're looking for a room for the night," said Rowan. "A *warm* room."

"This way." She led them through a corridor behind a door that opened to a wider hall lined with still more pine doors, each emblazoned with an icon. These icons were painted in reddish-black paint, and resembled various animals common to the Northlands. Rowan couldn't miss the image of a panther clearly marking one door's surface. The same door the elf was leading them to.

"The panther room is open," she said, without raising her eyes. "Would you like to stay there?"

"Why aren't you chained, like the others?" Alara asked the half-elf in Nordican.

"What are—"

"Why do you wear no chains?" Alara spoke over Rowan's protest.

The young half-elf raised her head to look Alara full in the face. Her eyes were a beautiful deep green, like a dew-covered meadow. "I am a half-elf, and so am only *half*-savage. I am permitted to work for a small wage." Her tone was hushed and humble. "Does the room not suit you?"

"No, the room will be fine," Alara replied softly.

"Then may you have a pleasant evening." She bowed before leaving. Alara made her way in first, followed by Rowan, who shut the door behind them.

A set of two small square windows on the wall opposite were large enough to allow for light and fresh air but too small for anyone to crawl through. They had matching shutters to keep out colder air during winter. The rest of the room was clean and decent. The large pine bed in the center of the room had four posts, supporting a thick curtain along each timber to keep any drafts from the windows away. Rowan noticed the bed could hold up to two people comfortably and seemed filled with down, wool, or some other soft material.

On the left side of the bed was a pine cabinet, allowing for the storage of extra goods and clothing. At the bed's foot was a large cedar chest for more storage. On the right of the bed a plain ash table held a pitcher of water, a copper basin, and a folded towel. Next to this table was a sturdy oak chair and a pine stool. It was a simple affair but more than he'd been expecting for such a short stay.

"What was *that* about?" he said as he made his way to the table.

"You really don't know?"

"If I knew I wouldn't be asking." He draped his wet cloak over the chair to dry.

"And that's the problem," Alara mumbled to herself as she threw off her own cloak and hung it from one of the shutters.

"What is?" He watched her wring out the garment with obvious frustration.

"Nothing." She proceeded to remove her waterlogged boots.

"What are you doing?"

"Getting out of these clothes."

"Right *here*? In *front* of me?" He could feel the blood warming his cheeks and forehead.

"We can't afford two rooms, and we're only going to be here for one night anyway, right?"

"But . . . it's just that we have one bed, so—"

"Don't even think about it." Alara worked on the other boot. "*I* get the bed. *You* can have the chair."

"The fairest thing would be to cast lots to—"

Rowan was silenced by one of Alara's boots striking him in the face. The small puddle inside splashed onto his head and cheek before the boot fell to the ground.

"Fair enough." He wiped his face.

Alara approached the bed, drawing the curtains around it before climbing inside. "And if you even *think* of trying to get a peek or try to sneak into the bed later, then you might be in for some *further* regrets. Just get some sleep so we can be ready for tomorrow."

"Fine," he muttered, flopping onto the chair. It wouldn't do any good to argue and he was too tired anyway. Silently he began shedding his own clothing as modestly as possible.

CHAPTER 21

Not every path that seems the best in the beginning ends up being that good in the end.

—Old Tralodroen proverb

Cadrissa's muscles not only burned but screamed in protest while she juggled excuses to rest from what had been a harsh, hard march. She didn't know what went wrong with the spell. She hadn't intended to interfere, but *had* warned Cadrith about the danger of tapping into another's well. She hoped she'd never have to endure that sort of thing again, but doubted the lich would be so easily deterred.

The sensation had been similar to having someone reach inside and pull out part of her very core one moment, and then deal a punch to her stomach the next. There was also the unpleasant, lingering feeling of being violated. And she'd endured all that for what? To add more misery to her situation by angering Cadrith further. Worse still, she was no closer to getting any answers about what was going on.

She tried to keep her shoulders back and straight but it was no use. She was wilting from the constant exertion. If she didn't get some water and rest soon . . . Her thoughts suddenly stopped as she glimpsed movement on her left. She saw it again. She was sure of it. A soft rustling in the distance and a form between the trunks of two trees. What was it? More importantly, did Cadrith see it too? Surely not animal life. It looked too humanoid for that. A Syvani? If so . . . what was he doing? And was he friend or foe?

From what she'd read at the tower, the elves were a simple but barbarous people. If that were the case, they were in more danger than she'd first thought. She prayed some god, somewhere, would show mercy. She saw another form move around her. Another. Then another. They were appearing in droves, like jackals drawn to a fresh kill. Cloaked in the afternoon shadows, they were visible only in a hint of ginger hair and tanned, leather-and-hide-covered bodies. Cadrissa could sense a shift in the air with their presence. It was harsh and heavy upon her throat and chest, crushing what remained of her spirit and filling her with dread.

"Do you know we're being followed?" she asked as softly as she could.

"They're of no consequence," Cadrith said, dismissively.

Cadrissa disagreed. "I've counted more than twenty, but it looks like they're growing."

"Keep moving and keep quiet."

A strange noise like a rush of wind passed Cadrissa's right ear. Cadrith stopped. His attention was focused on his stubborn left foot, which resisted his commands to keep moving. When she reached his side, she saw a green-fletched shaft pinning the lich's foot to the ground.

She took a fresh count of the figures in the woods. "They're more than forty now."

"Prepare yourself for another spell," Cadrith said, pulling the arrow from his boot with a stiff jerk. If he felt any pain, he didn't show it.

A great crack of tendon and wood filled the forest. Green-fletched arrows began to rain upon the two wizards like a shower of death. The sky above and the spaces between screamed for their demise. Scores of arrows sailed at them, competing with their brothers for their lives. Cadrissa felt the blood drain from her face as she stared at the onslaught, unable to move or even think. She could only watch as the arrows raced near. Another strong punch hit her in the stomach, and she doubled over. She could hear Cadrith growling in heated frustration.

"Kelrap oltan geptari," he said, flinging his right arm over his head as he spoke the words that completed the spell and birthed a shimmering violet sphere of light that surrounded them. Cadrissa flinched as the arrows struck the protective barrier with a sound like birds flying into a glass window. As each arrow struck, it shattered into tiny bits of debris before sliding down the sphere's slope.

"Gnats," Cadrith cursed. He broke the arrow he'd taken from his foot in two. A moment later the other arrows that had been pelting the violet dome with a steady percussion stopped.

"Get ready." This time Cadrissa tried preparing herself for another tapping of her well that was sure to come. But her preparation was stopped before it even got started as she watched in horror as a gang of armed Syvani emerged out of the sprawling pines. Now that they were out in the open she was better able to do a head count, seeing at least fifty: a swarm of red-haired death charging toward them with bloody cries. She couldn't move. Her heart knocked against her rib cage. Though she knew the dome would hold their attackers back, it was head knowledge. Her emotions were the ones presently in charge.

Cadrith didn't move more than one small step to stand before the onslaught of hollering elves. She was aware of him crossing his arms and staring at the elves in perfect stillness like some arrogant statue. The first wave smacked face first into the violet globe. Those behind them rammed into the first wave, and so on in a tidal wave.

After they had a chance to right themselves, the warriors—who Cadrissa could now see were all men—swarmed around the glowing globe and proceeded to attack it with their axes and spears. Now that they were closer, she could see their faces, and the savage anger playing about their tanned skin. Most had wild, coppery-red hair, some spiked all over with a white substance she thought might be lime.

Blue face paint had been applied to others who howled and wailed as they hammered at the barrier with their axes and, in some cases, their fists. Others were tattooed with black swirling designs with knotted loops and other geometric patterns she actually found quite lovely. They wore little more than tunics with some assorted hide and leather accessories. Finely worked bronze jewelry in the way of bracers, necklaces, torcs, rings, and belts completed the rest of their attire.

A heavy thumping drew her focus upward, where the dome rose to its peak some three feet above her head. There she saw the dirty bare feet of Syvani jumping up and down on the dome in hopes of breaking through. Other Syvani had climbed on the shoulders of their fellows and were pounding away with the ends of their spears, even butting the barrier with their heads from time to time for added emphasis. But all their attacks were nothing against the dome. Yet they fought on with the tenacity of wild dogs intent upon taking down their prey.

"Idiots," said Cadrith, his voice soaked with malice. "Let's go."

Cadrissa flinched from the swift kick to her gut as Cadrith again drew from her well. The Syvani, gathered on and around the dome, flew away with a violent eruption of force that scattered them in all directions. Some hit hard against tree trunks, others toppled over onto their fellow warriors behind them, and still others bypassed their comrades and pine trees to land upon the solid earth between. Cadrith resumed his walk. The dome followed them as they traveled, molding itself into spaces between trees and other obstacles like an unbreakable soap bubble.

Cadrissa followed Cadrith with a determined gait; the brief rest had restored some of her strength, though not enough to last a whole day. Behind them the beleaguered elves were regrouping. Some had taken to firing arrows again, while their brothers in arms shook their heads to clear them of their throbbing headaches.

When next she looked, the elves had all ceased their actions and stood among the trees, watching the two wizards depart. When she looked over her shoulder again, after she and Cadrith had gained still more ground, she noticed the Syvani had parted to form a path for a single figure making his way between them. This figure wore the brown hooded cloak of a traveler and held a pine branch that served as a walking staff.

A moment later, she saw the cloaked elf raising his hands in the air, chanting something she was unable to decipher. The others around him remained silent in homage.

"I thought there weren't any wizards here," she said.

"There aren't. He's a shaman."

A shaman, as Cadrissa understood, followed his religion by honoring nature and the workings of its inhabitants: animals and plants. To a shaman, a tree was a sacred shrine and an animal a holy object in a godhead that was visible in the natural world while also interconnected with the invisible workings of the spirit realm in and around them. It was a different religion for sure, and no one outside of it knew much about it. Every shaman and his followers were said to interpret things a bit differently. As to where the power of their invocations came from, none knew. It wasn't from a divine source, though, as any priest of any Tralodroen god could have told the common observer.

Many other people saw this power as evil at worst or misplaced faith at best. These skeptics wanted the hard facts, the sense of reality the gods brought them. Beings you could touch and see in their temples—the presence of a power that could govern the world in ways they could understand. This preference was one of the major reasons shamanism was almost completely unknown in Tralodren, save for isolated pockets like Arid Land.

However his power was collected, the Syvanic shaman was bringing forth a petition of his own, which he flung at the two wizards with obvious effort. A large hawk, made of white flaming light, soared straight for them. Its high, shrill screech brought memories of their encounter with the roc, sending a shiver down Cadrissa's spine. Before she could react, the mystically created bird struck the violet sphere. The flaming hawk shattered the dome into a shimmer of gold dust and silver shards that fell around the mages like sparkling rain.

"Impressive," Cadrith said, stopping.

Seeing their success, the Syvani renewed their campaign with a rumbling yell, racing for the wizards.

"They're going to kill us!" she cried, running to Cadrith and trying to hide behind him as best she could. She quickly discovered he made for a terrible shield. "What are you waiting for?"

The Syvani were gaining ground and would soon overtake them. They were only ten, maybe fifteen yards away. She could feel the wild blood lust that was rising in them. They wanted to go hand to hand, face to face with their enemies. Never mind that Cadrissa wasn't their enemy.

She felt the now-familiar forceful punch as Cadrith tapped into her well for yet another spell. Before the first frenetic Syvani could jab his spear into them, Cadrith had extended his hand, shooting out the raw energy of death itself into the faces of the attacking elves. The crackling charcoal-gray lightning struck the nearest Syvani, then branched out, continuing its path to those around him. Once struck, the Syvani became the center of another dispersal of the same terrible energy into those elves nearest them, and so on, and so on, like deadly dominoes, until the gray energy stopped with the shaman, who, a second after being struck, joined the lifeless bodies littering the forest floor.

Cadrissa was speechless. She'd known magic was powerful and could do great things, but this was something she'd never seen before. Sure, she'd caused some harm in the previous altercations with Alara and the others—even using a similar type of spell herself—but that had been self-defense. This was something much different. There was a vindictiveness to it—a sense of showing one's supremacy against someone much weaker. And then there was the faint understanding of the spell having been crafted to cause as much pain as possible.

It was outright slaughter. And she had a hand in it. But no matter what she felt she wasn't in any position to confront Cadrith—not that he'd listen even if she did find the courage. But besides a twinge to her conscience the spell also stirred up something else inside her: a curious wonder. While Cadrith had cast the spell it still had come from her own well. And that was what amazed her the most: the strength of her potential. Just how much was there?

"I doubt there'll be any more for a while," said Cadrith as he prodded one of the bodies with his staff.

"So then can we take some rest?"

"You should find some water and food on them," he replied, retreating a few yards before stopping beside a pine. "Take your fill, but we won't be staying for long."

Cadrissa hurried to exploit the opening afforded her. While she didn't feel right pillaging the dead, if they had any food or water, it wasn't any use to them anymore.

"I've never seen that spell before," she said, examining the nearest elf. Like all of the others, his face was frozen in a painful grimace as if someone had reached inside and crushed his heart. That probably wasn't too far from the truth; she didn't see any sign of external injuries.

"You'll see more still if you continue to prove yourself useful," said the lich.

Cadrissa's eyes fell upon a small skin container hanging from a nearby Syvani's belt. She pulled out the wooden plug and sniffed at its contents. Water. She guzzled it down.

"We'll camp again at nightfall," Cadrith said as she scavenged stray hunks of bread, smoked meat and fish, and what she assumed was cheese. She shoved it into her mouth with ravenous speed. Now that she had at least something inside her, she started to feel more like her old self again. Cadrith allowed more of a respite than she thought he would. It still wasn't a long span of time—a little over a quarter hour at the most—but it was enough. She even had time to pack up what remained.

"Come," said the lich as he resumed his trek. He said nothing further until nightfall, which couldn't come fast enough for Cadrissa. Eager for rest, she now had the added boon of food and water, for which she was incredibly grateful.

They again had no fire to alert anyone of their location. No need to stir up more hornets; the trek was painful enough. She removed her boots while Cadrith sat a short distance across from her, leaning against a tree trunk. It was as if they'd never left the last camp they kept. She wondered if he saw the irony.

But Cadrith was otherwise occupied, searching the heavens. The stars and moon could clearly be seen through the canopy of trees, and helped make their rest much more bearable. The crickets, owls, and other nocturnal animals about them added to the peaceful environment, though there was still the threat of the unknown lurking just outside her vision. Cadrissa had just finished the last bit of water from one of the five small waterskins she carried when she noticed Cadrith staring at her.

"You're sure you didn't do anything to that translocation spell?"

She forced her hands to occupy themselves, putting away a half-empty waterskin. "I wasn't the one who cast it, so how could I do anything to it?"

Cadrith stared for another lingering moment before thrusting his finger into the sky. "What do you make of that?"

Cadrissa cautiously lifted her head. "The stars?"

"Take a look at the constellations. Tell me what you see."

"The Warrior is on the decline, the Boar on the rise. Both contend with the Two Lovers." She lowered a shocked gaze to Cadrith. "But that isn't right. We've only been here two days."

"Look at the moon."

Cadrissa was filled with confusion. "That can't be right."

"And yet there it is," said the lich. "A new moon that shouldn't be a new moon. We've been here for weeks, by my reckoning."

"Then you know I had nothing to do with it," she said. "I have no idea nor training on how to change time."

"Galba," said Cadrith. "It's one of her defenses."

"But only the gods can alter time." The wheels were really turning in Cadrissa's head. "Everybody knows that."

"Then you don't know everything."

"Who is she?" Cadrissa hoped for an answer to at least one of the riddles cluttering her thoughts.

"She's mentioned briefly in the Theogona and then again in the Kosma as the one Gurthghol entrusted Vkar's throne to, after the gods created Tralodren."

"I thought that was a myth."

"It is to many. But Galba took and guarded the throne from the rest of the pantheon, as well as anyone on Tralodren—or elsewhere—who'd try to take it. She knew, as did the pantheon, that if they'd risen to such heights of power *with* the throne, then anyone else who made it their own could do the same—and possibly even find a way to destroy them."

Everything clicked into place. It was so clear to her now: the final logical step on the path of power. "You want to become a god."

Cadrith smiled.

"But that's—"

"Impossible? You have no idea what *true* power is. The best of your mages today would be nothing but toddlers compared to those who once ruled the world. And yet the one who takes the throne would make *them* all into mere children."

"And you really think the throne's in Arid Land?"

"It took me a while to find it, but yes. It's here."

She thought a moment. "But why Arid Land?"

"You still think too small. If you hope to do anything of note, you're going to have to learn to see the *whole* picture—everything and its process. Arid Land didn't exist when Tralodren was created. It was just one large landmass. But when the Great Shaking came—"

"The modern lands were formed," Cadrissa finished, nodding.

"And it's been guarded by Galba ever since. No god can set foot here—in any form. That was their ancient pact, according to the Kosma."

"And she's keeping you out as well," she reasoned. "That's why you need me: to get you to Galba."

"And you've proved useful so far."

"Assuming we reach her, what then?" Cadrissa wasn't sure she wanted the answer but wanted to take advantage of his talkative mood while it lasted.

"That remains to be seen," the lich replied, his eyes hooded. "What do *you* plan to do once we get there?"

What was *she* planning to do? Run as fast and far away from the lich and his insane plans as she could . . . only, where would she run? And would she really want to turn back from seeing such a sight as Vkar's throne? If this really *was* the throne—the very seat Vkar used to become a god—could she refuse to see it for herself? And then there was the slight temptation to see if becoming a god was even possible. She had no idea how Cadrith planned to do it, but to see something of that magnitude up close . . . well, that would almost make this whole experience worthwhile. Almost.

Her thoughts stopped when she caught Cadrith smiling at her. It was almost smug, as if he knew her better than she knew herself. "You can't help yourself, can you? You have to see it for yourself. The path of knowledge really *is* ingrained in you, isn't it? Just like it was with her."

"With who? Galba?" The question wiped the grin from his face, replaced with his more familiar tight-lipped expression.

"You'll need your strength if you're going to continue to prove useful. We leave at first light."

Cadrissa knew when to leave well enough alone. She contented herself with this new information. It kept her pondering until sleep at last found her.

•●•

"Get up." Cadrith's boot prodded Cadrissa's shoulder. The pink dawn wasn't as welcome a sight as she'd thought it would be. Another day meant another hike. She was beginning to think they might not ever find Galba, instead continuing in circles like a confused dog trying to bite its tail.

Rising, she heard a low rumble. It was still in the distance but inching ever forward. She put a hand above her eyes as she stared east. Sure enough there was a bank of dark clouds growing as it swam across the sky. If she didn't know better she'd blame Endarien, but since he, like the rest of the gods, was banned from Arid Land, she supposed it was just an average storm.

"We should be close now," Cadrith said as he adjusted his hood and continued his trek through the forest.

She drew up her own hood and followed. She hoped he was right. She wasn't looking forward to trudging about in the rain for who knew how long in the middle of a strange forest. The sky brightened a bit before it was swallowed by the slate-gray clouds that began drenching the land. Soon enough, Cadrissa could not have been any wetter if bands of people were sitting in the branches, dumping buckets of water on her as she passed beneath.

Then came the snarling wind that swayed the trees and branches. In the darkness it brought, she could just see enough of Cadrith to know he wasn't stopping, no matter how much his clothing clung to him like a second skin as the water splashed over him. She wondered if he could even feel the rain like he did when he was alive. To give up so much, and for power . . . it was almost beyond her—or it would be, if she couldn't relate on some level. After all, she had a similar drive when it came to the pursuit of knowledge. Did that make the two of them alike?

Lightning flared, illuminating the landscape with a brilliant flash of white. The outline of a stone outcropping was visible for a few heartbeats before all went dark with the echoing boom of thunder.

"That's it!" Cadrith shouted. "That's Galba! We've made it."

"That's it?" Cadrissa couldn't hide her dismay. It didn't look like something created to house the throne of the first god.

"Yes," Cadrith said, spinning on his heel to face her. She didn't like his cold, serious eyes, locked firmly upon hers. "And now that we're here . . . you've served your purpose."

There arose a terrible sound, like trees crashing behind them. Her mind fled to the thought of another roc, but when she turned to investigate, she was filled with panic of an even greater magnitude. Though it was still dark, she could see something swaying in the trees. Something she'd seen before and had tried to put out of her mind forever.

"You did your job well," said Cadrith. "You got me to Galba. And now here is your reward." Another flash of lightning outlined the black tentacles that were only a few yards from her. Each one possessed a collection of sharp-toothed mouths, every one of them snapping in eager hope of sinking themselves into her tender flesh.

"You can't," she cried, pleading with Cadrith, but the lich had already moved on, trudging toward the stone structure. "I helped you! That's what it wanted. I did what it wanted."

"Yes." A familiar voice addressed her from behind. She didn't want to turn around, fearful of facing the one who spoke. "You did well."

"Then let me go," she said defiantly.

"And where would you go?" the voice asked as a ropy tentacle slithered around her waist. "Embrace your fate, like the rest of this world." She could barely take in a breath as the tentacle lifted her with such force she didn't know what had happened until a moment later, when she felt scores of mouths tearing into her skin and gown. Blood mingled with the rain as the razor-sharp teeth shredded muscle and bone as though slicing through cloth. She tried to scream, but no sooner did her mouth open than another tentacle slid down her throat, biting off her tongue in one smooth and painful action.

•●•

"Get up." Cadrissa awoke with a start. Snapping into a sitting position, she put a hand to her throat and said a prayer of thanks that it yet remained, along with the rest of her body. The pink dawn wasn't a welcome sight. With it came confusion and a rising dread. Was it all a dream, or was it a vision of things to come, as Gilban might have said?

"We should be close now," said Cadrith.

Cadrissa stood with a small sigh.

A dull echo of thunder rolled across the heavens, and she looked up to the brightening sky. Nothing. No clouds in sight, no darkness on the horizon. Maybe it *had* just been a nightmare. Another peal of thunder—still distant and weak—found her chasing Cadrith, who'd already secured a solid lead.

CHAPTER 22

Often what we don't want to see is the truth standing right in front of us.

—Abigail Ronas, Elyelmic sage
(50 PV–220 PV)

Rowan had been awake for a while, fingering the panther paw he'd pulled from around his neck. The morning sun streaming in the small windows provided enough light for the room without being bright enough to awaken Alara. The room looked like a washerwoman's residence, with clothing draped over the furniture and shutters. Some of Alara's clothing was flung over the drawn curtains around the bed. At least it had dried. Well, *his* clothing had. He didn't feel right checking on Alara's.

He still had no clue what had happened with Brandon and his ship. He knew it was real, that he didn't dream it, because here he was in Arid Land. So if it was real, then . . . what had happened? Was it a wizard, like he thought, a priest, or . . . could this be the work of Panthora? She was known to help Panians and humans in need. The Sacred Scrolls made it clear these things were possible. He was going in circles. Alara was counting on him to get them to Valkoria. He didn't want to tell her he wasn't sure he could. There might have been some vessels in the dock, but that didn't mean anything.

He supposed he might be able to find some local merchant to help, but if what happened with the *Frost Giant* repeated itself they could very well end up stuck on Arid Land for quite some time. He didn't know of any Telborians in Vanhyrm—though there could be some, he supposed. He needed to be sure before moving forward. He was still on a mission. He needed to do his best, no matter how many twists and turns crossed his path.

His gaze fell to his feet and the shield that lay beside them. He pondered the gold two-headed dragon emblazoned upon its black background. His eyes traced the bronze flames that spewed from the mouths of the dragon's heads, each head intent on harming the other. An interesting symbol. If only he knew what it was trying to tell him. It was like everything else in his life of late: just too much to take in. If there was a larger picture in any of this, he didn't see it.

Life wasn't supposed to be so complicated—so uncertain—was it? The world had seemed so balanced, so . . . *straightforward* to him before. Now chaos ran amok in the lands south of his homeland. Did he really think he could take Alara with him without some trouble? He imagined the response she'd received on the *Frost Giant* repeated over the entire population. And she'd be on her own when Rowan was reporting to his superiors. No, this wasn't good at all.

He shifted, noting how his lower back and shoulders ached with fatigue. He'd barely managed to get any sleep during the night, being forced to push his shoulders forward, his lower back outward, bowing his frame in an awkward manner. The result was stiff joints and an achy body when he should've had restful slumber upon comfy down-stuffed pillows. He'd stripped to his gray undertunic and off-white braies to sleep, leaving only his forearms and legs exposed. Thankfully, his sleep had been dreamless. But it didn't change the fact that he needed to know what to do next. He knew of only one person to ask for answers.

"Panthora," he prayed, "what do you want me to do? You've gotten us this far, but what do I do next?" His eyes glimpsed a strange glow about his neck. Investigating, he spied the shriveled paw glowing a gentle white. He was transfixed by the illumination as the rest of the room faded from view.

•●•

He knew he was experiencing another vision. His whole body felt light, as if nothing else existed save his mind and spirit amid a milky gray fog.

Rowan.

The voice was Panthora's. He was sure of it.

"Where are you?" he said, though he knew he wasn't speaking with his lips, but with his spirit instead.

You've been a faithful knight, Rowan.

"I don't feel like it."

Feelings don't have anything to do with faith. You have been faithful even with the doubts in your head and shifting emotions in your soul. You've begun to learn from my words. You have learned to take new steps. And you're right. I have favored you this far, and I will do so still.

I'm also aware of your desire to help Cadrissa. And if you search for Galba you shall find her.

"*Galba?*" Rowan stopped himself from saying anything further when he realized he'd interrupted.

Find Galba, and you will find Cadrissa, or you can continue on to Valkoria and keep to your original mission. The choice is yours.

"I don't understand. What are you saying? Am I supposed to seek Cadrissa instead of returning to Valkoria? Or do you want me to do both? Why are you telling me this?"

You decide what's best.

He found himself tongue tied at the thought. *Him* decide? Why would Panthora put this before him unless . . . "Is this a test?"

It's a choice. One you're free to make.

"But what's the *right* decision? I don't want to neglect the right thing in favor of something else. All I want to do is honor you in what I do."

Then decide what you will do and do it.

Rowan hurried through his thoughts, following what logic he could. "Forgive me, my queen, but how can I make a correct decision when I don't even know where Galba is located?"

On Arid Land . . . The mist started fading.

"Wait," he hurriedly called out, "that boat and Brandon—were they from you?"

The mist finished fading and the room came fully into view.

•●•

Rowan shook his head as he returned to the waking world. While he should have been amazed—even joyful—at the divine encounter, his eyes instead found the draped bed and the outline of the figure still resting in it.

What was happening?

Only a few weeks ago he was eager for his first mission and now . . . now he was in the midst of such a mess. What would he tell Alara? Panthora had given him two sure choices but said nothing about Alara being a part of either. Only . . . she was going to Valkoria, wasn't she? That had been the plan . . . or was that *his* plan, and not Panthora's? Why did this have to be so difficult? Things were so much simpler before he'd joined the order.

Panthora had said he'd been faithful. And if he *had* pleased her, then he was doing something right. Wasn't that the most important thing: pleasing Panthora? Wasn't that what he had been striving for since the very beginning? If so, he had a choice to make . . . and the longer he mulled it over, the more it didn't seem right to make the decision on his own.

He breathed a heavy sigh and placed the paw beneath his undershirt. "Alara," he whispered.

There was no response.

"Alara," he said again, at full volume this time.

"Is it morning already?" she asked in a sleepy voice.

"Yeah."

"Have you been awake long?" He watched as the clothing she'd draped over the canopy's curtains vanished one by one.

"For a while." He quickly donned his own clothing as he spoke. He'd leave his armor here for the time being. He wouldn't have need of it right now anyway, and wanted to be sure it was fully dry to keep it from damage.

Soon enough Alara drew the drapes. "You survived the night all right." She ran a hand through her hair, causing it to shimmer in the light.

"Better than some," he said.

"You hungry? Hopefully, we can find something for a decent price—"

"I just had a vision," he blurted.

"A vision." Alara's sapphire eyes locked tight on him.

"Yes."

"Well. Are you going to share it with me?"

"Y-you *believe* me?"

"I'm used to people having visions."

"Oh, right." He felt like a complete idiot. "You and Gilban." Overcoming his foolishness, he continued. "Panthora gave me a choice. I can either continue to Valkoria, or find someone named Galba and they'll lead me to Cadrissa."

"*Cadrissa?*" Alara was more than a little amazed at the prospect.

"That's what she said."

"Did she tell you where Galba was?"

"Somewhere on Arid Land."

"So Cadrissa's on Arid Land?" Alara tried putting everything together.

"Maybe. She didn't say Cadrissa was on Arid Land, only that Galba was and they would lead me to Cadrissa."

"From what I saw, Arid Land looks like a pretty big place," said Alara. "And if you don't know who you're searching for—"

"It could take some time," said Rowan. "I know."

"Does this mean you aren't going to Valkoria now?" Alara eyed him carefully. He could sense the growing concern flowing from her.

"It means I have to make a choice," he replied.

"And what are you going to do?"

"I don't know," he confessed. "I just wanted to tell you. So you could make up your mind too."

"I thought I already had."

"You said you wanted to go to Valkoria. But if I decided to go find Galba—"

"I tend to think better on a full stomach. How about you?" she asked. "If they don't charge us an arm and a leg, we should have enough for breakfast and a few supplies." She tugged on her belt as she straightened her garb, then went to pick up her cloak, which had completely dried during the night.

"Food would be good," he said, grateful for a familiar path he could walk for a while. "It shouldn't be too bad." He moved for the door. "They're not looking to gouge fellow Nordicans, so—"

They stopped when each reached for the handle at the same time, their fingers touching in the process. The act brought his nervous eyes firmly into Alara's gaze.

It was clear the moment was awkward for her as well. "After you." She removed her hand from the handle and pulled up her hood, leaving Rowan to open the door.

Returning to the common room, they found a group of Nordicans having their morning meal: traders, hunters, and workers of various crafts filled the tables. Peppered among them were half-elven and elven slaves tending to various tasks. No one took much notice of the new pair in their midst.

Alara scouted out the room for a secluded table, where they took their seats. Rowan noted one fat Nordican who reminded him of the captain of the *Frost Giant*. For a moment he thought they'd crossed paths again until the other man turned more Rowan's way, revealing his different features. A sense of relief flooded over him.

"What would you have?" asked a familiar voice. It was the same half-elf they'd seen the night before.

"Porridge," he said as he got more comfortable on his chair.

"And you?" the half-elf asked, turning to Alara.

"Your name," Alara replied in Nordican.

"I'm unimportant," she replied with a soft, subservient voice, nervously looking about to see if anyone else heard their conversation. "Please tell me what you want and I'll go and fetch it."

"First, tell me your name," Alara persisted.

Rowan watched Alara with a perplexed face. "Just order your food," he said, switching to Telboros, his voice low, "before you cause a scene."

"Name," Alara repeated.

"Tana," the Syvani replied meekly.

"There, now. That wasn't so hard, now was it? Well, Tana, I think porridge sounds good to me too."

Tana bowed before returning to the kitchen.

"What was *that* about?" Rowan asked as he gave a passing glance to the retreating half-elf.

"I only asked for her name," Alara explained.

"Why?"

"Because I wanted to treat her better than she has been."

"You don't *know* how she's been treated."

"No . . . but I can make a pretty good guess."

"Just be careful." He sighed. "I don't want to deal with any more trouble."

"So you think I'm trouble?" He thought Alara was teasing him, but he wasn't sure and would rather just be done with the whole matter. There wasn't anything more to be done about it anyway.

"Are you really sure you want to come with me to Valkoria?" The question brought a solemn air to the table.

"Rowan, I gave you my word."

"And I'm releasing you from it. If you want to leave, you can. No matter what I decide, I'll have to go back to the keep. And when I do I'll have to bear the grand champion's judgment."

"It won't be that harsh. Not after I tell them the truth."

"It's not going to work. I've known it from the start." His heart sank a few notches as he watched Alara's face fall. "They're not going to trust anything you say."

"Because I'm an elf." There was some resignation in her voice . . . and a hint of accusation.

"You'll be safer this way," he added. "You won't even have to set foot on Valkoria."

"This doesn't look that safe to me." She gestured at the other people in the room.

"I'm just sharing some ideas—"

"Which it sounds like you've had for a while." Alara had become unreadable, which birthed a fresh ball of worry rolling about his gut. He didn't want to hurt her more than he supposed he already had. "If you felt this way before, why didn't you tell me earlier?"

"I-I don't know."

"I thought you said Knights of Valkoria are supposed to always tell the truth."

"I—they are."

"Then why are you lying now?"

"I'm not." A burst of steely fire flared up his spine. "I *have* told you the truth—since we first met."

"Really?"

"Yes."

"Even to yourself?"

Instantly his mind returned to his dream, the one that haunted him from Taka Lu Lama to Elandor. The one where he saw Panthora turn to face him, only to reveal herself as Alara instead.

You've been at war with yourself since before you left for Talatheal. Only now the strife grows greater, as you're forced to deal with other matters emphasizing these areas of conflict. The conflict is between an old way and a new. But it's really a war between your head and heart, your soul and spirit. If you deal with your current conflict first, the other will quickly be resolved.

"Rowan . . ." Alara's voice broke through his thoughts. "It's time we talk about the *real* issue between us."

"We *are* talking." A nervous smile crossed his lips. He found his hands taking on a life of their own, flopping about the tabletop like fish pulled from water. "What do you mean?"

"You know what I mean." Alara seemed paler than usual. Rowan wanted to jump out of the chair, but he forced himself to remain seated. He needed to get through this, for himself *and* for Alara. "Rowan. It's pretty clear we have feelings for each other. We both know it."

So she'd finally said it. How long had she known? Wait. Did she just say she felt the same way? What did *that* mean? He cleared his throat before asking, "So how do you think we should deal with them?"

"Talk."

"Talk?" He raised an eyebrow.

"Yes, talk. We talk about our feelings."

"Why? Can't we just ignore them?" He forced his restless body to stay firmly planted in his seat.

"No. Because if we keep ignoring them, we'll end up doing more harm than good." Alara took a long, slow breath. "Let's just get this thing out in the open and be done with it."

He was speechless—unable to do anything but stare at her like she was a relic from some long-forgotten age.

"Okay," Alara said with another small sigh. "I'll go first. I've come to realize that I have some feelings for you." She paused for just a moment before adding, "And I can honestly say that in these last few weeks I've become more and more attracted to you in a romantic way."

Run! Now! his mind screamed. His heart was racing. He'd even started to break out in a cold sweat. This was the last thing he was expecting . . . and wanting . . . to deal with. But he knew, deep down, it had to be dealt with before anything more could be done. Panthora herself had told him as much. So he willed his body to keep seated, listening, while his mind and heart continued swirling.

"So . . . What do you have to say to that?"

"I . . . ah . . . understand you're an attractive woman, and I can appreciate that, but you're an *elf*, and I'm a *human*."

"Yes, Rowan, you're human and I'm an elf," she said, exasperated. "It isn't impossible for our two races to have feelings for one another." Alara took another deep, slow breath before continuing. "But if we're *sharing* the same feelings—and it seems like we are—I think it's also time we talk some about your attitude toward elves and other nonhuman races in general."

Rowan's eyes widened. He felt a fresh layer of chilled perspiration manifesting across his brow and back. Was his conflict so obvious to everyone or just Alara?

"I've come to see that you—and the rest of the Nordicans I've encountered—hate all other races but humans—"

"I-I don't hate them," he quickly retorted.

"Really?" Alara motioned for him to take another look around the room. "You don't seem to have a problem with how *these* elves are treated."

Rowan did so, being sure to note how many elves were about. It was more than he'd first thought. "There's nothing I can do about it. It's the way of my people and I have orders from the knighthood—"

"Orders which you're disobeying if you decide to go after Cadrissa."

"That's different. Panthora *told* me to go after her."

"I thought you said she gave you a *choice*? That's not the same as an order. And did she tell you and your knights and priests to despise all those who aren't human, too?" He winced, but Alara didn't relent. "Did she tell you to hate me and every other elf on Tralodren?"

"I don't hate you, Alara—I love you." He felt his mouth drop open once the words were out. "W-what I mean is—"

"It's okay." She placed her hand upon his upturned palm. "I feel the same way. The question is *why* do you have all these other feelings? You can't hate and love the same thing. It's impossible."

"I'm just speaking my mind." Instantly, he regretted the words. As soon as they had left his mouth, they surrounded him with a sick aura of unpleasantness. The uneasiness of the situation overcame him—an intense warm pang of confusion and anguish. Alara's eyes grew cold and her face took on a sullen pallor.

"Somehow I find that hard to believe."

"I-I don't mean to." He mentally stumbled about like a drunk weaving between the road and the gutter. "It was just how I was raised."

"Even *if* Nordicans share an uneasiness with nonhuman races, you're better than that, Rowan. It's what makes you different . . . what makes me love you." Those last two words trailed into a whisper as tears welled in the corner of her eyes.

"I can't change who I am. I'm a Knight of Valkoria, a Nordican from the Panther Tribe of Valkoria. Nothing can change that."

"No, you're wrong. You're Rowan Cortak, a man of the Northlands who can make up his *own* mind, who can choose who *he* wants to be, *what* he wants to become apart from his race, religion, and anything anyone else has told him." The tears had started flowing, resembling tiny streams of liquid glass.

Nalu's words haunted his memory more than ever: *Maybe they taught it to you in secret* . . . The visions of Panthora joined them: *You won't be fit for my service if you continue to battle yourself* . . . *It's really a war between your head and heart, your soul and spirit* . . . *Let go and be free of it.* Something was turning inside him, like the tumbler in a lock.

"You don't have to be like the worst of your people, Rowan," Alara continued. "You can be better than that. You *are* better than that. Let go of the past and embrace a better future. Together, we can get through it. Together, we can overcome anything." Her tears had stopped, but the serious demeanor—the yearning for him to *understand*—remained.

Eager for release from this building pressure, Rowan let his head drop. "I've wondered about my feelings for you." He forced himself to face her as he spoke—to look her in the eyes. "I've wondered about them since before we left the ruins. You're like no other woman I've ever known. You're brave, strong, intelligent, and beautiful. But at the same time I have these feelings for you I have a voice telling me why it's wrong."

"Is it *your* voice?"

"No."

"Is it the voice of Panthora?"

He paused. He wanted to say yes but realized that wasn't true. It *sounded* like Panthora, but he realized it was the knighthood claiming to speak for her. Having heard the real thing more than once, the distinction was quite clear.

"No." Another tumbler moved inside him.

"Then ignore it," Alara insisted softly. "If it isn't your goddess or your own voice, then it's not of any concern. You should listen to your goddess and seek to do her will—that's why you're a knight—but you shouldn't listen to any other voice. That would be betraying both yourself *and* your goddess."

A smile traced Rowan's lips, before quickly bubbling over into a full grin. "I haven't been able to make sense of anything until now, but with what you just said . . . everything gets so clear . . . I *know* it does. I can *feel* it does." The final tumbler turned, opening the lock. "It's like a weight's lifted off me." His eyes grew moist, though no tears fell.

A few breaths later, Tana returned with their porridge. When she caught sight of Rowan's grin she lowered her eyes, putting the two wooden bowls on the table before quickly turning to leave.

"Thank you, Tana." Alara addressed the young half-elf in the Nordic tongue.

"Yeah, thanks," Rowan repeated. More of that feeling of release tingled all over his body when he spoke. He felt freer than he'd been in a long while.

Tana stopped for a moment, then half turned back to the knight with a shy grin. "You're welcome." It was more of a question couched in soft tones. Once said she fled back into the kitchen.

"See." Alara was obviously pleased. "You *can* do it."

"It wasn't as hard as I thought it would be," he confided. "But I still have to push past some things to get there."

"It will come in time. And I'll be here to help you through it." Her encouraging words brought new life to his soul. "No matter what you decide."

"If that's your decision." He started stirring his porridge.

"It is. Now you need to make yours." Alara started eating her porridge.

"I just can't help feeling I'm missing something somewhere," he said after taking his first spoonful.

"I know," said Alara. "A stranger who brings us within sight of Arid Land and then has his whole boat fade into mist, a vision from Panthora saying there's someone here who can lead us to Cadrissa . . . seems a bit *too* coincidental."

"Or maybe it's divine guidance," said Rowan.

"Maybe." Alara wasn't so convinced.

"One thing at a time, right?" Rowan continued, shoveling another spoonful of porridge into his mouth. He'd had better, but it was far from the worst thing he'd ever eaten. "It would help if we knew where this

Galba was. If they were close by maybe I could do both—find Cadrissa and *then* head back to Valkoria."

"Assuming Cadrissa's close by," Alara countered. "We don't know where she is or where she's going."

"Galba . . ." he mused aloud. "That doesn't sound Nordic. Which means they might be Syvanic."

"It would make sense if they're supposed to be on Arid Land," Alara agreed.

"Which might mean Galba is an elf," Rowan mused.

"Wouldn't that be ironic after everything we've just discussed?"

"Or perhaps Panthora is preparing me to make the right choice," said Rowan.

They were interrupted by Tana setting a fresh loaf of bread between them. Her appearance sparked a new course of action in Rowan's mind.

"Tana, have you ever heard of anyone named Galba before?"

The half-elf paused, seemingly unsure of just how to reply. "Galba is known among my people," she finally said.

"Really?" It was hard keeping the excitement out of his voice. "Are they close by?"

"You don't really want to see Galba," said Tana. "Even the shamans leave her alone."

"Her?" Alara stepped into the conversation. "So Galba's a woman? An elf?"

"She is a woman, but not a Syvani." Tana had started growing more uncomfortable with the discourse.

"Does she live close to Vanhyrm?" asked Rowan.

"I really should get back to my work," said Tana. "Was there anything else you needed?"

"No," said Alara. "You've been very helpful. Thank you."

Tana eagerly returned to the kitchen.

"Panthora never said I had to go after Cadrissa right away," said Rowan. "If Galba knows where Cadrissa is, I could find her *after* I reported on my mission too."

"I still think neither of us is getting the full truth on anything yet."

"But Panthora wouldn't lie," Rowan countered. He was sure of at least that fact.

"Maybe not, but she might not be sharing everything either," said Alara, tearing off a piece of bread for herself.

"Which means if we find Galba we might have some more answers, which I could share in my report." He could see how this all was weaving itself into a plan he could follow. But was it the right plan? The right choice?

"Which means we're going to have to find a guide—if that's what you decide to do—I'm still not trying to lead you in any way in this," said Alara.

"No, you aren't, but it seems everything else has been," he returned. "It doesn't make sense passing up this opportunity. And if Panthora is already for it, I'm sure we'll both be safe."

"I have your word on that?" Alara half teased.

"I have faith in Panthora."

"Then we're back to finding a guide, and that will take some money—which neither of us has too much of at the moment. Unless you know of someone who'd be willing to do it for free."

"Erland Sorenson!" Rowan nearly jumped from his chair when the revelation hit him.

Alara wasn't as enthusiastic about the suggestion. "Maybe not the best choice."

"And why not?"

"We'd be going into elven lands. And it sounds like neither he nor the elves like each other that much. And who's to say if Galba would be any friendlier with him?" She paused. "And then he doesn't know I'm an elf too, but he would soon enough once we got into the wild."

"Okay . . ." Rowan could see the logic there, and wasn't about to argue. "But do you have someone better?"

Alara's attention focused across the room. "Maybe I do."

Curious, he turned around to follow her gaze. It led straight to Tana.

CHAPTER 23

Oh, his flame is everlasting,
Let it burn true inside of you.
Oh, his flame is everlasting,
Let it burn you through and through.

—A Remanic hymn

The cold water splashed over Dugan's head, jolting him to his senses. He blearily noticed Balus leering down at him. Dugan took small delight in the elf's bandaged right hand, but that was all he was afforded as two elven guards forced him to his feet. Sore from his troubled night of painful slumber, he jerked and twitched as the two men forced him to stand.

He watched Balus look him over, taking him in from head to toe like a cow at market. He should have been used to it by now but it still stoked feelings of anger even after all these years, especially given his previous encounter with the branding iron. The mark it had left throbbed relentlessly but Dugan tried to push the pain to the farthest part of his mind. There was no telling what new ordeal awaited him. He needed his focus there.

"You've made it through the night well enough," Balus said with a nod to the two elves, "but today's a new day." He felt the chains grow slack before realizing the guards had removed his shackles. Unsure about what was going on, he stood before the elven captain, barefoot in nothing but a breechcloth. In all his life, this might be the lowest he'd fallen. As he took in the full measure of the dark glint in Balus' eye, he knew the worst was yet to come.

"You can take a good beating." Balus' statement was almost complimentary. "But you have to learn how to deal out better than what you can withstand. And that brings us to your training." Dugan stared at the wooden gladius Balus extended to him "blade" first. "You're going to need this." It was almost comical. The object looked more like a child's toy than anything that could cause any serious harm.

"You have some laundry that needs whacking?" Dugan's voice was gravelly, sore, and bitter.

"Still defiant, I see." The malevolence in the elf's eyes only deepened with his smile. "A lot of you are when you begin. The smart ones learn to take to their lessons."

"And the others?" He coldly stared Balus down.

"They go to Mortis sooner than the rest. Their ashes are scattered and their lives are just as quickly forgotten." Balus shoved the wooden sword forward but Dugan did nothing with it.

Undeterred, he tossed the gladius at Dugan's feet. "Gilthanius, your master, thinks you're going to be a strong attraction for the people. I have my doubts."

"Then why are you here?"

"He's given me permission to oversee your training, *personally*." Dugan didn't like the way Balus' face lit up when he'd said that last word. It made him think of a butcher eager to hack into a cow. And Dugan wasn't looking to be anyone's cow. At least not for arena fighting. Manual labor was one thing—there could be something honorable in that—but to become a source of entertainment at the cost of his own life . . . that was another thing entirely.

"And what if I don't want your training?"

"You're going to go out in that arena soon enough," Balus said as he crossed his arms. "It'd suit me fine if you died your first time out, but Gilthanius wants to make some profit . . . and for that you'll need training. And I did make you a promise. Since I said I'd make sure you'd be treated worse than the hounds, I think that's where we'll start." Balus turned to the door. "They're often hungry, so you'd better take up your gladius. Unless you think your defiance is a better weapon."

The two elves on either side latched hold of Dugan's wrists, but he shook them free, causing them to put their hands to the hilts of their swords. Dugan squatted to retrieve the wooden sword—all while Balus opened the cell door and made ready to leave, caring nothing for what was happening behind him.

Once his weapon was in hand, Dugan straightened, the guards watching every inch of his ascent. "So what happens when I survive?" Dugan's question brought Balus' head over his shoulder.

"Then next time we'll have more dogs."

•●•

Reality shook Dugan awake, causing his eyes to bolt open. He expected to be surrounded by carnage and flames. Instead, he was in a forest glade. Upon sitting up, he saw tall pines creeping in on the outskirts of a peaceful area. The elderly wood huddled around the edge of the glade like giants, not daring to send a single root into the soft tendrils of grass that formed the sage circle in which he lay.

Unlike the forests of Colloni, here there were no birds singing or small creatures rustling in the underbrush. It felt artificial—unnatural—and he sensed no comfort in it. Despite losing his sword and being knocked about, he was alive, able to move and fight should he have to.

Placing a hand to his chest where the cult leader had jabbed his dagger, he found the wound gone. The tear and bloodstain were the attack's only echo. He hurriedly loosed the binding from around his shoulder while further investigating the rest of his body. All the other wounds, cuts, and scrapes were gone. Only his clothing revealed the carnage he'd wrought and apparently now lived through. A gruesome thought gripped him. What if this was Mortis? The longer he sat in isolated silence, however, the more his brain revealed the truth. He was still very much alive.

He knew Rheminas laid claim to his soul, and he was the god of fire, among other things. Dugan couldn't see, hear, or smell any fires anywhere.

Further, he still drew breath, and could feel his heart beating. He placed a hand over his chest once more. The familiar thumping doused the last flames of fear. So if he wasn't in Helii or Mortis, where was he?

"So you drug him along too, huh?" A familiar voice grated his ear. Dugan leapt to his feet and found Vinder and the two priests he'd seen in the burning cultists' chamber earlier. They didn't have their hammers, instead letting them rest head first on the grass a few yards from them—silver surfaces reflecting the light in glistening sparkles.

"Vinder?" Dugan studied the three figures as he cautiously drew near.

"It's me."

"What's going on?"

The dwarf crossed his arms. "Looks like they got you in the middle of something interesting." He let loose a lopsided grin. "The blood I can understand, but I didn't think you were so keen on greasepaint and dark clothing." Noticing Vinder's interest in the mask dangling from Dugan's left hand he hurriedly shoved it into a nearby pocket.

"Hello, Dugan," said the older of the two Telborians standing behind Vinder. Both were dressed in parchment-colored robes with red sashes about their waists and hooded black cloaks falling from their shoulders. Their hoods were down, however, allowing him to see their faces. It was a welcome change from his recent dealings with the cultists. He noticed the silver pendants that formed crossed sickles around each of the priests' necks. From his time in Haven he knew what the symbol was meant to represent.

"You're Asorlins?"

"Yes," said the older Telborian. "I'm Tebow Narlsmith."

"Cracius," the younger said with a nod.

"You're the priests that were in that chamber—the ones who . . ." Dugan reflexively went for his sword, only to be reminded of its absence. "What did you do?"

"We were trying to save you," said Cracius.

"So where am I?" He tried to wipe away some of the greasepaint with his sleeve.

"Galba," said Tebow.

"Where's that?" Dugan sought answers from Vinder.

"No idea."

"So they kidnapped you too?" Dugan reassessed his surroundings: a strange glade, Vinder, and the two priests—nothing that made any sense.

"No," said Vinder.

"Then why are *you* here?"

"It doesn't matter." Vinder clearly wanted to put the matter to bed. "I'm here now, and so are you."

"Why?" Dugan searched the two priests again, eager for answers.

"There's something that has to be done—for *all* of us to do," Tebow replied calmly.

"No," Dugan said, crossing his arms over his chest. "I'm done with priests and their gods."

"But they aren't done with you. Or *us*, it seems," came Cracius' gentle reply.

"What's he talking about?" Dugan again looked to Vinder for clarity.

"We're supposed to take on a lich."

"Lich?"

"That thing that took Cadrissa. It's some sort of dead wizard."

"Dead wizard." He repeated the words, making sure he'd heard them correctly. "How's that even possible?"

"Magic, I guess." Vinder jabbed a thumb over his shoulder, adding, "These two want to send him back to Mortis."

Dugan nodded, going over everything carefully in his mind. "So when do death priests heal a dying man?" He peered straight into Tebow's eyes.

"We were going to bind the wound," Tebow began, "but when we set you on the ground we discovered you'd been healed. Not by us, but the one who brought us all together." Tebow's face was as clear as his words. "Asorlok doesn't heal."

"What's really going on, Vinder?" He'd had his fill of priests and their enigmatic ways. He wanted something solid he could stand upon.

"It's true—all of it. We're here to fight that lich."

"What? All *four* of us? Last time the six of us couldn't even take on a *living* wizard—what chance do we have against a dead one?"

"Things will be different this time." Dugan didn't like the simple assurance Cracius was trying to feed him.

"Yeah." Dugan tried wiping away more of the greasepaint. He could tell he was just smearing it around more than removing it, and so gave up. "There'll be less of us."

"No," said Tebow. "The others will be joining us soon."

"Why?"

"Because of Galba," said Cracius.

"I thought you said Galba was a place, that *this*"—Dugan stomped his foot into the sward—"is Galba."

"She's both." Cracius' answer only made Dugan's brow furrow.

"Turn around," Tebow insisted, "and you'll see."

Slowly, Dugan did as instructed, and saw the most amazing thing he'd ever seen. He couldn't believe he'd missed it in the first place. It was huge: a large circle of gray stones, arranged in post-and-lintel formation, dominated the circular glade. Through the doorways created by the circle's design, he could see that inside the monument there was nothing except green grass. Somehow, though, he knew this wasn't totally true. Something was hidden from view. Something that escaped his ability to describe it. Something that was beyond even his mind's ability to comprehend.

"The others will be here soon," Tebow continued. "As will Cadrith."

"The lich," Vinder clarified.

"Then you'd better get ready for him."

Dugan felt Tebow's hand come to rest on his back. A thought had the former gladiator imagining the claw of some carrion bird eager to fill its gullet. "We *all* have a part to play, Dugan."

"What about your *Galba*?" He wildly indicated the stone circle.

"Galba cannot help us," said Cracius.

"*Can't* or *won't*?" Vinder gave Cracius a hard stare.

"She's said she can't break her oath by lending us any aid in the battle to come," Tebow explained.

"But she can *heal* me?" Dugan pointed out the tear in his shirt to emphasize the point. "Doesn't make sense—course, none of what you priests say does."

"Galba has led us to you for a reason." Tebow was consistent with his message; he had to give him that. "Your healing is proof enough of that."

"Now I see." Revelation dawned on Dugan. "You're just puppets. Your *master* has the real answers." With this new insight, he started marching for the standing stones.

"No, wait," Cracius began, but was stopped by Tebow.

"He must learn to respect what's before him if he is going to be of any benefit to us."

Dugan might have been angry and beleaguered, but he wasn't stupid. He'd learned from past encounters with priests and their ilk not to trust everything he was told or saw. He'd have his answers. And that meant getting inside that stone circle. He intended to walk right through an opening, entering into the center of the stone ring, but wasn't sure if he could.

The stones smacked of rules outside of his perception of reality. He never would have guessed they held such energy at first sight, for they seemed so plain, so simple in their design: tall posts of stone and nothing more. Yet there *was* something about them that made his gut squirm. Something that made his pulse quicken, mouth go dry, and fingers quake.

Tentatively, he stretched his left hand out for the nearest post. It had to be more than five feet across and at least ten feet tall. Before his fingers could reach the stone they struck an invisible barrier that shook his body to the bone. From his hand, thick serpentine currents raced up his arm, then across his shoulder and into his chest and neck, spreading like fire to the other half of his body and into his head. He felt the force fling him into the air with enough strength that he landed more than ten feet from the circle, where he convulsed from the pain.

Blood ran in tiny streams from his nose, ears, and mouth. His left hand was numb and speckled with light patches of discolored skin, which looked like a cheetah's pelt, pale white spots playing across his normally tan hue.

"Dugan!" Vinder ran to his side. The dwarf's fingers wrapped around the Telborian's wrist. It was still warm and twitched with the pressure of Vinder's hand. Dugan's eyes fluttered open, pupils wide. A soft groan escaped his lips.

"He's alive," Vinder said to the others, before Dugan jerked up into a sitting position.

"What happened?" he asked, eyes wildly scanning his surroundings.

"You didn't make it through."

Dugan sneered at Tebow's sarcasm. He stood, wiping blood from his face with his sleeve. He didn't feel as bad as he knew he must look, but even so he was rattled from the incident. Still, he wasn't going to be denied.

"Galba?" Dugan shouted at the top of his lungs. "I want some answers!"

A soft white light shone from between the stones, spreading and enveloping the group. In the blink of an eye they were first near the stone circle and then gone altogether—the white light swallowing them whole, hammers included.

It didn't take Dugan long to figure out what had happened. He stood slightly away from the others and wasn't too impressed by what he beheld. Inside the circle of stones was nothing really of note: a green carpet of grass and the stone circle itself, just as he had seen from outside. However, when he peered closer at one of the openings created by the stones, he found it displayed a scene from somewhere else. It was the image of a desert, where a harsh wind blew the hot sand about like an angry cloud of wasps.

A curious look at the portal next to it revealed the depths of a sea where fish swam right by him as if he were underwater himself. All twelve openings held some strange image of a land far away: high mountaintops, forests, jungles, large cities bustling with commerce and citizens. Each scene hung between the posts like a faint gossamer tapestry, flickering and wavering like a candle's flame in the wind.

But something else caught Dugan's attention. A glance at his hand revealed the markings of his previous encounter with the stones had vanished. He was once more healthy and whole.

"Galba?" Dugan tried again, this time less combative.

"I'm here." The voice was pure ecstasy as it slid into his ears.

"Where are you?" He scanned the empty expanse with his level gaze. "Show yourself." A blinding flash of light shook the air around him.

Dugan fell to his stomach with the force of the blast, unable to see anything but flares of white before his eyes.

"You can't talk that way to her," Vinder said as he helped Dugan to stand. "You've got to show her some respect. Even *I* know that much, and I'm not a priest."

"I've lost my respect for gods," Dugan said as he rose on wobbly legs. The blindness was still there, though weakening with each passing heartbeat. At least it wasn't permanent.

"I know your plight and sorrow." Dugan searched for the presence he knew was behind the calm, feminine voice. "But it wasn't the words of a god that have troubled you. Only your own."

"It's *my* fault?" he asked, angrily throwing off Vinder's supportive arm and drunkenly stumbling in search of his accuser. Tiny bits of color had managed to seep back into his vision, but he still couldn't see clearly.

"No one held a sword to your throat to force you to take it," the voice said, as calmly as it had before. "The decision was yours and yours alone."

"Where are you?" Forms had started to appear but they were still blurry.

"See and be made whole."

Dugan's vision was instantly restored, allowing him to take full sight of Galba, who he learned was right in front of him—possibly had been this whole time. Her willowy body, draped in a clinging long-sleeved gray gown, made his heart dance with delight. Under the garment her body was firm and toned: a warrior's frame if ever there was one, but balanced with a poise and grace that spoke of the deep allure of the feminine form. Alabaster skin shone like the morning dawn, creating a nimbus of soft illumination about her. He found himself drawn into her deep green eyes framed by luxurious serpentine, bright red curls.

Her ruby lips parted to speak and Dugan could do nothing but wait eagerly as though they were raindrops from heaven in a desert land. He was speechless before her—powerless to do anything but listen. He didn't know what happened or how, but he noticed he'd become ensnared by his own reflection in Galba's eyes. When he saw himself it was as if he was doing it for the first time, and the truth of what Galba had said dropped like an anchor deep inside him.

It was so clear. What he'd done, what had led him to Rheminas again and again like a dog returning to its vomit: Fear. Fear of dying as the property of another. Fear of not being able to live a life of freedom once he'd been freed from his slavery. Fear. That was the master he was trying to break free of, and instead he was ensnared by everything else he'd encountered along the way. Fear. The cruelest master of all, but one men would trade all they could to be free from, including their souls . . .

"Forgive me." Dugan fell to his knees. "I see now. I see everything."

"Dugan?" Vinder asked, shocked.

"He's finally seen the truth, and that insight has liberated him." Galba drew closer to the humbled Telborian. "Rise, Dugan, and live a while longer." As he rose, he noticed the weight pressing constantly on his shoulders was gone. He'd gotten so used to its presence he'd forgotten it had been there at all. It didn't change what he'd already done, but it was a taste of the truest freedom anyone could ever hope for. And he would enjoy it for as long as he could.

"The others will be here soon," said Galba. "As will Cadrith."

"So what does he want?" asked Vinder.

"Vkar's throne," Galba replied. "He wishes to become a god."

Vinder snorted. "Then he's a fool. No one can become a god—not on their own. Even Drued had help."

"And so does Cadrith." Galba's soft eyes rested upon Dugan. "He has another helping him he doesn't know about. One I think you've encountered before."

"The black tentacles . . ." Dugan muttered his sudden epiphany.

Galba nodded.

"So if *he's* getting help," Vinder continued, "why can't *you* help us? Sounds like we're going to need all we can get."

"I've sworn an oath that I shall not directly interfere. I can lead and influence to some degree, but never overstep the bounds of the oath. This is not my fight; I cannot take part."

"But you healed me," Dugan reiterated. "Isn't that getting involved?"

"Prepare while you can; your confrontation will come faster than you think." Galba faded from sight. With her departure, each who remained looked to the other. A commonality of purpose was clearly seen on their faces. But it'd do little good if they didn't have some sort of plan.

"So I take it you're with us now?" Cracius asked Dugan.

He replied with a solemn nod.

Cracius pulled back his cloak, revealing Dugan's long sword resting behind the priest's crimson sash. "Here." He withdrew the weapon and handed it to him hilt first. "We thought you might need it."

"It's a start." Dugan took the weapon, trying not to remember the flames it once bore and the incredible exhilaration he felt while wielding it in Rheminas' service.

"Now we just need about a thousand more and some hands to wield them," said Vinder dryly.

CHAPTER 24

GRAND IS HER GLADE, GREAT ARE HER WAYS.
KEEPER OF POWER, LONG BE HER DAYS.

—Syvanic hymn

Alara adjusted her hood while Rowan led the way with Tana between them. Together, they neared Vanhyrm's rear gate. Beyond the wooden portcullis-like barrier were the wilds of Arid Land. People had begun to go about their business, but not so much that they didn't notice the group of strangers in their midst.

Once they'd managed to convince Tana to serve as guide to Galba, things had gotten easier. She'd been hesitant to aid them at first but when Alara put forth their terms—which Rowan had to quickly come to grips with himself—her attitude quickly changed. It proved even easier getting Tana to the outskirts of the settlement walls. A simple explanation about needing her as a guide, along with Rowan's clout as a Knight of Valkoria, sufficed for the innkeeper. Being a knight also gained him free room and board, saving what meager coin remained. Truly Panthora continued showing him her favor. It increased his confidence that he was making the right choice. From there they'd wrapped Tana in a brown cloak, put together the rest of their belongings, and headed for the gate.

The rear gate was different from the front, crafted from trees that had been debarked, delimbed, and sharpened to a point at the top of their fifteen-foot lengths. These were bolted together with metal rods, then tied with thick rope at the top and bottom: a sturdy barrier to any outside aggression. Guarded by two watchful chain mail–clad warriors, it would be hard to pass through. The gate was always watched, opened only for raids or trading expeditions.

"Halt!" one of the guards shouted when they'd gotten within a few yards. The bulky man was more muscle than fat and possessed a long brown mustache that flowed over his lip to the bottom of his chin, matching his long brown hair.

"Who are you and what are you doing here?" His pale blue eyes ran over their bodies while the other guard, slender and clean shaven, squinted at them.

"Rowan Cortak, Knight of Valkoria." Rowan straightened under the scrutiny of the guards' gaze. "I have urgent business outside these walls."

"Is that right?" The mustached guardsman moved closer to Rowan.

"And who are these with you?" He motioned to Alara and Tana.

"One's a Syvani I've taken up to help my cause. The other is my retainer."

"Telling the truth today?" The slender guard moved closer behind them as the bulkier guard stared Rowan dead in the eyes. His face was as hard as the wooden wall they guarded.

"A Knight of Valkoria is a man to be trusted," Rowan said, returning the other's stare.

"Can't see why the knighthood would be interested in going out *there*." The guardsman stroked his mustache. "There's nothing but savages for miles."

"The way and will of Panthora is not always for us to understand," Rowan replied.

"And it's not wise to kick a hornet's nest either," the guard replied. "So if you go and rile up these savages against us—"

"I'm going to do what Panthora tells me," said Rowan. "Nothing less. Nothing more. And the longer we wait here, the more you frustrate her will."

"It's not wise to upset a goddess, Bjorn," the slender guard told the other as he moved up beside him.

"Very well, if it's a goddess' work to be done." Bjorn stepped aside. "Then be off with you."

"Thank you," Rowan said with a bow. In a dignified but hurried manner, all three made their way to the gate, which was opened by means of a thick rope, squealing on pulleys. Rowan observed two of the watchmen assigned to the wall, grunting in their efforts with the various ropes and wheels. It didn't look like it was something they did that often. After a few agonizing moments, the gate was finally raised.

"Panthora be with you," he said as all three passed through the opening.

Bjorn grunted as the other guardsman nodded at the blessing.

"Keep moving at the same pace," Rowan whispered.

"Once we get past the trees, I will lead the way," said Tana.

"Sounds good."

Looking across to Alara, Tana asked, "Am I really to be free once I've helped you?"

"That's what we agreed to. And it's the least we can do. You're a person. You should be able to make your own destiny, to think for and rule yourself. You're not chattel to be bought and sold."

"Do all your people think this way?" Tana asked.

"I can't speak for all of them," said Alara, "but I'm confident the majority of them do."

"Then I would very much like to meet your people someday." Tana smiled.

"Maybe one day you will."

•●•

"We have to move through these woods for a while, then we'll be in the heartland of my people."

Tana led Rowan and Alara through tall pines that appeared to go on forever. They'd been running for some time, since letting Tana take the lead. The further they went, the more ancient the forest became. The slashed stumps left behind by Nordic loggers had dwindled as nature regained its hold. They were now surrounded with the rich body of wood, untamed and untapped since the foundations of the world.

"So how far until we reach Galba?" Rowan asked.

"A few hours, if we can keep this pace, and don't run into any surprises." Tana ran effortlessly, like a doe, through the thick pine pillars.

"What *kind* of surprises?" inquired Alara, following with a steady pace.

"Usually it's Nordic trappers and loggers. Sometimes it's wild animals."

"What *kind* of wild animals?" Rowan asked through heavy panting. He wasn't sure he could keep this up for a full two hours.

"Griffins, for one."

"They actually *live* here?" he asked, shocked. "I've only heard about them in stories."

"We have a land *full* of deep mysteries and hidden beauty, and we like to keep it that way." Tana suddenly stopped.

"What's wrong?" asked Alara, slowing to a stop herself.

"I thought we could do with a rest." She wasn't even winded from the run. In fact, she seemed invigorated by it.

"Good idea." Rowan huffed as he bent over, placing his hands on his knees. Sweat dripped from his forehead and his face was flushed.

"Are you sure we can be to Galba that soon?" Alara had taken a beating from the run as well, but had fared better than Rowan. Only a thin layer of perspiration shone across her features, and her breathing wasn't as labored.

"It depends on how well you two hold up," said Tana.

"You think you can make it?" Alara joined Tana in examining the breathless Rowan.

"I haven't come this far to quit now," he said, straightening his back and ignoring the blood rushing to his head.

"If you need more time to rest—"

"No," Rowan interrupted Tana. "The sooner we get to Galba, the sooner we get to Cadrissa."

"It's okay if you—" Alara began.

"Let's keep going." He took a deep breath and slowly released it, letting Tana know she should lead on. They resumed their run without another word. As the hours passed, they alternated between jogging and running. The trees grew thinner and rough hills rose to meet them like giants. The grassy mounds were spotted with trees and smothered in rock like scales, making it harder and harder for green to flourish amid the grays, browns, and blacks of the rocky soil. When they'd reached the highest of the hills, they stopped.

"Galba is over that mountain," Tana said, pointing to the massive peak ahead of them.

"I thought you said we could be there by nightfall?" Rowan's face, like the rest of his body, was drenched in sweat. "There's no way we can get there short of a week. That mountain has to be the tallest thing I've ever seen."

"We'll be able to get there." Tana smiled coyly. "Just not in the way you might think."

"What do you mean?" Alara asked, huffing. She too was slick with sweat, but she was still in better shape than Rowan. He didn't know how she did it, but he was impressed with her endurance.

"Look around you," Tana instructed. "No. At the ground."

Rowan and Alara saw only wildflowers, scattered grasses, a few lone saplings, and piles of rock. "I don't see anything," he said.

"Then you don't see the *true* meaning of this hill." Tana made a sweeping gesture.

"What are you talking about?" Alara was just as confused as Rowan.

"This hill is just one of many sacred areas for the Syvani. It's a place of worship and power for our shamans. Among its many powers, it has the ability to allow people to travel from one part of the land to another."

"Magic," Rowan muttered.

"No magic. Only the power of nature."

"Power of nature?" Alara still wasn't sure what to make of all this.

"Don't worry," said Rowan. "I think I know what she means. The shamans in the Northlands talk about similar things—totems and spirits and such."

"So it's safe?"

"None of the shamans I've heard of can do such a thing," he explained, "but I don't think she'd take us all the way out here just to kill us."

He watched Tana contemplate the mountain peak on the horizon before kicking the ground with her heel. Small tufts of rocky dust fluttered as she did. The longer they remained in the area, the more he noticed a heaviness about the place. It made even the wind seem thick, like syrup, as it passed overhead.

"My mother was a shaman," said Tana. "Before she was captured, she was a rising leader in the land, and wise in the ways of the spirits. After I was born, she told me much of the old ways, including stories about Galba. I learned how to use the mysteries of nature, and its spirits, to work the energies of the land for good and for ill. I was too young to learn more than scraps, but before her death I *did* learn how to use this circle and the others like them."

"*What* circle?" Rowan couldn't see anything of the sort.

Tana kicked a stubby rock jutting no more than six inches from the ground. It was a simple, clean white rock. Rowan noted it had companions with it, who together composed a great circle about twenty feet in diameter on top of the hill.

"How'd we miss that?"

"Because you've helped me," Tana continued, "and want nothing more of me than to be a guide, I'll use this circle to take you to Galba, but I'll not follow you. Galba is a holy being we Syvani revere. I will only send you to her. What comes after that is on your own head."

"Thank you," said Alara. "That's all we ask."

"Stay inside the circle." Rowan and Alara remained where they were, while Tana stepped outside the ring of stones. "Each circle is built on a line of mystical energy like the very veins of the world. The shamans call them Galba's Veins.

"They spread all over the world. Where they cross, a circle will be created to help mark the place and to help the shamans tap into the veins.

"Join hands," Tana instructed.

"So how does it work?" Rowan took Alara's hand in his. Doing so birthed a small flutter in his stomach.

"Very easily, from what my mother told me," said Tana. "With a simple invocation, you can be transported anywhere these lines connect in Arid Land."

"*Anywhere?*" Alara marveled.

"Anywhere. So it isn't as hard to get to Galba as you might think."

"Is there anything else we need to do?" Alara asked.

"No." Tana took another step back. "Just relax and let the invocation lead you to Galba."

Alara surprised Rowan with a small kiss on the lips. "For luck." She grinned as his face turned red. It was so fast he barely even knew what had happened.

"Once the invocation has started, I won't be able to stop it until it's run its course," Tana explained. "Be ready." She put some more distance between them before chanting in her native tongue.

Rowan felt a strong sensation, as if the air was thickening round him, holding him fast, like he was standing in a mug of jelly. The sensation grew more intense as this thickening congealed. The stones around them began to glow a fiery white, like iron pulled fresh from the forge. The world began to blur. Inside the circle, Tana's chant was amplified, seeming to vibrate into his very bones. He concentrated on staying relaxed as the world around him fell into chaos.

Tana's chant grew faster and louder as the stones shot up bolts of white light, arching to form a dome around and above them. The dome grew so brilliant he and Alara had to shield their eyes. Then it collapsed upon them, falling flat to the ground below, leaving nothing behind but the empty circle.

As the stones dimmed, Tana was left alone on the hilltop. She peered over the land at the tall spire of the mountains, imagining her new friends landing safely behind the peaks.

"May Galba be merciful to you," she said in her native tongue, before making her way down the hill, and into her new life.

•●•

Alara and Rowan felt as if they'd been belched from the earth when, with a sudden burst of movement, they felt their stomachs flop back from their throats. This was followed by the sudden realization they weren't on the hilltop anymore. Each took in the grassy glade outlined by the tall pine trees that formed a circle around them.

"Where are we?" asked Rowan.

"We must be near Galba," said Alara as she joined him in getting her bearings.

"But how close?" Rowan turned around, shocked by the amazing beauty of the glade.

"Pretty close," she said, joining Rowan as he stared at a stone circle very different from the one they'd left. These stones appeared like giants in a great ring. Other large stones lay across the posts, forming a solid circle of rock above them. Between the posts and lintels, nothing was visible but grass.

"Hello!" Rowan shouted in Telboros. "Is anyone there?"

There came no reply.

"It's so quiet here," Alara said as a small shiver ran down her spine, "like a tomb or a shrine. Even the trees look afraid to get too close."

"Whatever it is has to be connected to Galba." Rowan rushed for the stones.

"Where are you going?" Alara hurried to follow.

"Someone or something must be around here."

"Just be careful. This place feels odd. It has a certain . . . aura to it. Even *I* can sense it—and I'm not a priest or wizard."

"Woman's intuition again?" Rowan teased. "I'll be fine. Nordicans are—"

His bravado was cut short when he ran straight into some sort of invisible barrier. He hit the grass with a thud.

"Rowan!" Alara ran to his side, helping him as he struggled to sit up.

"I'll be fine." He moved his hand to the back of his head. A quick glance showed both of them it was clean. "No blood, so nothing serious. What did I hit, though? I didn't see anything."

She drew her sword and swung it outward before them. It touched a solid, unseen surface less than a foot away from the stones. "It might not be so easy to get inside after all."

Alara helped Rowan to his feet, then sheathed the falchion.

"So how are we going to get through *that*?"

"Maybe it has some conditions." She tried to make a careful study of the transparent hindrance. "Some magic I've seen and heard about has certain conditions that keep the spell in effect. Maybe this is the same way."

"And what if it isn't?" Rowan asked.

"One thing at a time, remember?"

CHAPTER 25

The quiet before the storm is sometimes the loudest time of all.

—Old Tralodroen proverb

"Maybe it's tied to the sun," Rowan speculated. He and Alara were seated just outside the circle. Hours had passed, and they were no closer to getting inside.

"How would *that* work?" Alara wondered. They were beyond conventional wisdom and were now grasping at straws.

"I don't know. We've tried everything but magic." Rowan echoed Alara's frustration.

"Not everything." A voice speaking Telboros came from behind them. Both turned to see Gilban, a flickering, lavender-tinted image rapidly thickening into his solid form. Beside him was Hadek.

"Gilban?" Alara gleefully rushed to greet the seer. "I thought you returned to Rexatoius." It felt good to see him again. She didn't realize how much she had started to miss him, and Rexatoius, until their embrace.

"I had," said the seer. "But now I have a new task, which is about to come to an end."

"Why are *you* here?" asked Rowan, who was intrigued by Hadek's presence.

"To help Gilban," Hadek said bluntly. "Besides, that temple of his is pretty boring and stuffy."

"Did you have another vision?" Alara inquired, hoping to learn more of this new mission.

"Yes," said Gilban.

"About Cadrissa?" Rowan promptly inquired as he rose.

"No." Gilban's reply slumped Rowan's shoulders. "But she's part of things to come, I'm sure."

"What things?" Alara had almost forgotten how frustrating Gilban's cryptic replies could be when you were looking for quick answers.

"There's another threat coming." Gilban became sage-like and solemn. "And it's fallen to us to deal with it."

"I'm just here for Cadrissa," said Rowan. "Panthora told me I'd find her if I found Galba, but so far all we've seen is this stone circle."

Gilban regarded the knight with his pure-white eyes. "There might be more at work here than you first thought." Alara thought again of Brandon and how this all seemed to be part of a larger trail of bread crumbs. But where was that trail leading?

"I'm beginning to think there is," she said. "More than you're going to share." Gilban's knowing smile confirmed Alara's suspicions.

"All will be made clear soon enough."

"So. What sort of threat?" Alara attempted to glean something from Gilban's face but found it as unreadable as ever.

"All in due time," he replied.

"Do *you* know anything?" Rowan tried Hadek instead.

"Something about a scepter and an orb and Gorallis—"

"*Gorallis?*" Alara half shouted. "Is *that* the threat?" Even on Rexatoius the linnorm's legend was well known . . . and feared.

"In time," Gilban repeated, raising his hand to quell Alara's concern. "All will be made clear, in time."

"Gilban, we really would—" Alara was rebuked once more by the elf's bony hand.

"We have more important matters to attend to at the moment," he said, pointing at the stone circle. "Like getting inside."

"How?" asked Rowan. "We haven't been able to get in since we got here."

Gilban raised his hand in greeting to the stones. "We have come, Galba. We humbly ask for entrance." There was a shimmer of white light that wrapped around the stones, rising to become a dome and then nothing.

"We haven't much time before the barrier returns." Gilban ushered them through the nearest opening.

"How do you know that?" Rowan echoed Alara's thoughts. "Oh wait, let me guess, 'All in good time.' "

Inside the circle, they were greeted by Dugan, Vinder, and two priests of Asorlok. None seemed surprised to see them. In fact, it was as if they'd all been waiting for them.

"Dugan?" Rowan was as puzzled as Alara. "Why are you wearing—"

"Don't ask," came the terse reply.

"How did *you* get here?" Vinder raised an eyebrow.

"A vision from Panthora," Rowan replied, before adding, "and Gilban's help."

"A vision?" Vinder sputtered. "Sure would have been preferable to the way *I* came."

"And how *did* you get here?" asked Rowan as he neared the others.

"*They* brought us." The dwarf hooked his thumb at the two Asorlins.

"Cracius and Tebow," Cracius said by way of introduction.

"You must be Rowan, Alara, Hadek, and Gilban." Tebow bowed his head in greeting. "It's good to finally meet you."

"How do you know us? And why are we all here?" Alara again looked to Gilban, who remained as stoic as ever.

"And where's Galba?" Rowan searched the circle with renewed interest.

"I can answer that." A feminine voice spoke just before a blinding light assaulted the area, causing everyone to shield their eyes. When the flash of light had subsided, all were transfixed by the transcendent person of Galba hovering a foot above the grass. A gray, long-sleeved gown outlined her lithe frame.

Though her attire was unadorned, her face more than made up for that simplicity. Smooth and clear as porcelain, her skin spoke of an eternal youth. Eyes as green as grape leaves hinted at hidden depths and mysteries—secrets no one living had ever seen. Those same eyes were gems of shimmering light, a radiating effervescence, adding richness to her silky, serpentine red locks.

"*You're* Galba?" Rowan blurted out in Nordican.

Ruby lips parted into a smile at once inviting and comforting. "I am," she gently replied in his native tongue while descending to the grass.

"And now that you're all here, we can begin." She shifted back to Telboros.

"I don't like this." Alara saw that everyone else shared the same sentiment. "We've been led here by things outside of our understanding, visions and strange coincidences that just happened to bring us all together to this one spot. I don't like being led around on a leash. What's going on?"

"True, you have all been used for this greater end, and though it might anger you, it's with the best of intentions." Galba neared Alara.

"I don't care *what* the intentions were. You *used* all of us. And I'm sure all of us would like to know why." Alara caught a glimpse of herself in Galba's green orbs as she spoke. She marveled at how small—trivial—her reflection seemed in such a massive expanse of green. In that moment her rage, though it once seemed so important and justified, fluttered away—separating from her like dross from silver.

"She's told us some of the reason already," Cracius offered. "But I don't think she'll mind filling the rest of you in."

"And what about Cadrissa?" Rowan inquired. "I was told you could lead me to her."

"Cadrissa is safe, and en route as we speak."

"Wait. She's coming *here*?" He turned to Alara, clearly confused. "But then why—"

"First," said Galba, "you must listen. *All* of you must listen to what is expected of you. Far from the playthings some of you might think you've been"—Galba gave Alara a nod—"you've been chosen as champions of a great and important cause. All of you have a purpose and a role to play. Some greater than others." For a moment, her gaze lingered upon Hadek, causing the bald goblin to avert his eyes.

"You have been chosen to hold back Cadrith, the one you helped free in the ruins, from claiming his prize," Galba continued. "He's seeking to become a god, but he must not succeed in doing so."

"*Godhood?*" Alara's heart skipped a beat.

"Madness, I know," said Vinder. "I still don't think he can do it, no matter *what* these two say." He jabbed a finger at Cracius and Tebow.

"You really think he could succeed?" Rowan asked Tebow.

"Anything is possible." Tebow's reply was drier than old bones.

"So you brought us all here to stop him from becoming a god?" Alara asked Galba, unsure how such a thing could be possible, let alone how they could even pull such a thing off.

"Yep," said Vinder, nodding.

"I didn't come here for this." Rowan was growing more vexed by the moment. "I've come to help Cadrissa."

"And she's with Cadrith," Galba explained.

"The lich—that skeleton thing," Vinder whispered to Rowan, presumably to clarify.

"All right." Rowan saw Alara watching him as he tried to collect his thoughts. "Then I guess I'll just wait, and when they get here . . . then I guess we can . . . we can . . ."

"Try to stop him from becoming a god?" Vinder smirked. "It's the truth and you know it. Might as well accept it."

Rowan glared at the dwarf. "I came here for Cadrissa, not to defend some circle of rocks from some fool trying to claim godhood."

Alara gripped his arm. "Calm down," she whispered in his ear. "You might want to watch your temper around her. The same power I could feel from the stones before is coming from her too."

"I don't care *who* she is." Rowan shook his arm free. "I'm not going to be someone's puppet in a war that isn't even mine in the first place. I have a duty to Panthora and the knighthood first and to Cadrissa second. Nothing comes between those two priorities."

"On the contrary." Galba raised her hands. The earth beneath them grumbled and shook in a wild tantrum. Each of them did their best to stay upright. "This war is universal. It affects you all." The shaking increased as Galba rose on a mound of dirt jutting from the earth like an overflowing cauldron.

As the mound rose, it shed its soil shroud, revealing a ten-foot-tall marble dais. On top of it rested a majestic throne that looked like it could have seated a giant comfortably. It was carved of solid white marble and decorated with silver and gold scrollwork on the front of the armrests and the tall seatback. Amid the scrollwork were cut gems and precious stones. Even as they watched in amazed silence, the gems shone with a brilliant fire. In contrast to the gems and scrollwork, the shape of the throne was rather simple: a tall-backed chair, rounded at the top, with sturdy, square armrests.

On either side stood two statues, each fifteen feet tall. These were also constructed of white marble, but the images they represented were strange and at the same time vaguely familiar. On the left was a strong human-looking male. He possessed a long mustache, flowing hair, and eyes that pierced the soul of anyone who met their cold gaze. In his right hand he held a great mace with a strong arm while a skirt of leather strips encircled his muscular waist. A cuirass, tall sandals, and a flowing cape that stopped at the back of his knees had been chiseled onto his frame with such skill that they appeared more real than some genuine articles they'd seen.

A statue of a woman stood on the throne's right. She was the same height as the male and also appeared human with longer hair. She carried no weapon and wore no armor. Her frame was draped with a simple gown that fell just below her knees, displaying her sandals. The work was so skilled it seemed as if the gown was actually separate from her figure. Her outstretched hands, along with her face and warm eyes, welcomed them to the dais.

In the middle of these two statues, before the throne, stood Galba. The last of the dirt and debris poured down the white marble steps like water. The quake subsided, and everyone regained solid footing. All remained speechless.

"He comes for Vkar's throne," she said. "Which I've protected since the creation of Tralodren. It has remained here since the beginning, and, though some have tried to claim it, none have succeeded."

"And *we're* supposed to stop him?" Rowan, like Alara, was disbelieving.

"I know," Dugan darkly replied, "it's a suicide mission."

Alara found Dugan's grim statement unnerving. However, the sentiment seemed to be the main current flowing about the circle. They were being asked to do the impossible. Why?

"Not as such." All eyes spun Gilban's way.

"I've secured a means by which Cadrith can be defeated with little effort or bloodshed." The seer lifted a silver scepter for all to see. "This scepter will stop him."

"Where did you get that?" asked Alara.

"Gorallis gave it to him," said Hadek.

"*Gorallis?*" Vinder nearly choked on the name.

"Yeah," Hadek replied softly. "Gorallis."

"Even if that's true," said Dugan, "we're still going to need a plan on how we're going to deal with Cadrith. Unless we want to repeat what happened the last time we faced him."

"Indeed," Gilban concurred. "And we don't have the luxury of being indecisive for too long. He'll be here sooner than we'd like, I'm sure."

Alara rested a hand on Rowan's shoulder, catching his attention. "You can leave at any time you wish. No one would think less of you. You've done more than what you set out to do. If you want to return to Valkoria . . . there's no shame in that."

"I'm here for Cadrissa." His words were resolute, but his face revealed hints of the affection he'd become comfortable sharing with her.

"Who you can rescue as soon as she arrives," she reminded him.

"If you value your commitments"—Vinder's stern glare dug into Rowan's heart—"you'll stay and fight. You had just as much part in setting this lich free as we did. If you ever want to be a good man, as well as a knight, you need to take responsibility for your actions."

Alara carefully watched Rowan. She couldn't know what he might be weighing in his mind, though she could glimpse it in his eyes. Whatever he chose, she'd respect it, no matter how she felt. Neither choice was an easy one, and she wasn't about to try to sway him. And so she waited, reminding herself to breathe after realizing she'd been holding her breath. Finally, he spoke.

"What's the plan?"

Silence.

"No need to be shy now." Vinder's sardonic grumbling was muffled by his beard.

"Perhaps we should assess what each of us knows," offered Cracius.

"A good idea." Alara made her way to the center of the group and they slowly closed ranks around her. Behind them, Galba went unnoticed as she faded from sight.

"Well, I don't know anything," Dugan confessed.

"And don't look at me," Vinder sourly added. "I was done with all of you before these vultures got their claws into me."

"I don't know anything either," Hadek stated meekly.

"I don't think anyone *thought* you would." Vinder fired off his barb just as he caught sight of Alara flinging some darts of her own his way. The rising sneer on his face was quickly aborted.

"So then, what do we do?" asked Rowan.

Dugan shrugged. "I suppose we just wait to kill him."

"We need a plan, though," Tebow offered. "If we run into this haphazardly, we'll be picked off easier than gnats."

Dugan's face had the haunted expression of a man who no longer cared if he lived or died; it made Alara shiver. "There's not much of a plan you *can* have if you're trying to fight someone powerful enough to become a god."

"Then perhaps you should listen to me." All again concentrated on Gilban as he brought the silver scepter up to his chest. "As I was saying, this scepter has been given to me to stop Cadrith."

"So . . . what are you going to do with that?" Dugan studied the scepter with a sneer. "*Pummel* him to death?"

"Not as such." Gilban brought the scepter's head down to his other hand so it rested between both fists at about waist level.

"So what does it do?" asked Rowan.

"It was designed by a wizard king to defeat a god."

"You mean they could *do* that?" Vinder asked, shocked.

Gilban lowered his eyes to the stout warrior. "It was designed to drain a divinity's strength," he continued, "weakening them so the wizard king could face off with them on more equal footing. It also was able to do the same to wizards—making them weaker and unable to call upon their magic."

"Are you all sure you want to save Cadrissa?" Vinder inquired. "I've had my suspicions. I think she wants to be the next wizard king—well, *queen* anyway. And she's been under the influence of this other wizard for a while. She might even be helping him, for all we know."

"*What?*" Rowan turned sharply toward the dwarf. "Cadrissa isn't the threat here. The one who took her is."

"We have to keep on task," Alara advised. "We can't divide over petty issues. Not when we have so much to get done and not that much time in which to do it." Alara made sure Vinder got the message. His frustrated sigh made it clear he had. "Please continue, Gilban."

"The scepter can drain the power of a divinity with the right incantation. However, it can only be used once in the wielder's lifetime. It has such an incredible effect upon these beings that it has to be limited in some way in order to work. Such is the way with magic, I'm told."

"And *who* told you all this?" asked Cracius.

"Gorallis. I've also been told the incantation, as well as what needs to be done once it has been activated. As such, I think it best if I lead the charge, thereby weakening him for the rest of you."

"*You* attack him?" Dugan couldn't hide his disbelief. "Why not just tell *me* the incantation and let me deal with it?"

"No." Gilban's white eyes pierced deep into the gladiator. "Your time to wield it has not yet come."

"So you're going to have us trust a *linnorm* with our lives?" Vinder was beside himself.

"No," Gilban returned flatly, "I'd have you trust *me*."

"Given the terrain and what we're facing, I don't think we'll need a plan to lead an attack." Rowan's words shattered the tension between all gathered.

"No," Cracius added. "If Gilban's to land the blow, then we'll just help clear him a path to strike when the time comes. Galba will take care of the rest."

"Speaking of which." Vinder scanned the area for any sign of her. "Where did she go?"

"She'll be back when the time has come," said Tebow. "For now . . . it'd be best to make some final preparations."

•●•

Gilban heard the others strategizing but only took note of their voices, not what they said. Ever since setting foot inside the circle, the dark enigma plaguing him since his return to Rexatoius had grown, clouding much of his other thoughts. What frustrated him was knowing it was something important—very important—but it didn't want to show itself yet, no matter how hard he tried coaxing it into the light. He'd hoped to be able to dig through some level by now, but even working it over in the back of his mind only stirred more frustration. If this was important—something for the upcoming confrontation—he needed to have it.

He'd been able to get clear on almost everything else so far: the orb, Gorallis, his trip to Galba. But this—this was something else. Everything else had played out already. The orb had gotten him the scepter, and now they were inside Galba. Everything was moving as it should. So what was this nagging sensation entrenched in his mind? What could he be missing?

He didn't think it had anything to do with the scepter. No . . . that he was clear on. He trusted Gorallis. The scepter and the incantation would work. But there were other variables in play. It was something with Hadek, or himself.

He contemplated the goblin carefully. There was his purpose, true. He had a call yet to be defined, but Gilban didn't think it was related to this. It didn't feel the same. The matter with Hadek had remained in the background ever since the two crossed paths. What he was experiencing now was something else entirely. Something that felt like a growing alarm. Something that—

He stopped in his mental tracks as the enigma suddenly revealed its full meaning. The irony wasn't lost on him. He had to decide what to do with the information in the time he had remaining. How could he be of the best use, given the task before him—which he was sure was tied to this new insight?

"You okay with all this?" he heard Alara ask him. The others were still talking. He could hear their voices but understood the topic of conversation had changed, the bulk of the planning apparently finished. "You've been pretty quiet."

He figured she was referring to the plan, which he hadn't heard but could assume involved the others helping him reach Cadrith so he could strike with the scepter. There were only so many variations to be had, and his part remained the same in each.

"I'm ready to do whatever is needed."

"It still seems pretty risky," she continued. "Don't you think it wise to share the incantation with someone else in case something happens?"

"The incantation is firmly in my mind. As is my purpose." Gilban tightened his grip on the scepter.

"I just don't want you to get hurt," Alara confided. "And . . ." Gilban imagined her biting her lip to keep from saying the rest.

"And?" He sought to look into her face.

"And . . . well, you're blind. How are you going to hit him, even if you get close?"

A good question. He'd never really fought anything or anyone after losing his sight. In fact, he did his best to avoid conflicts. Using his staff was one thing but in the midst of combat, things could change very rapidly and unpredictably—even for those with sight.

"Faith and patience." He supposed it was as good an answer as any. He wouldn't be here without either, and they weren't going to be successful without the use of both.

Alara's voice lowered as she asked, "Did you have a vision about it?"

"Something like that." He wasn't lying. He figured what he had been told and now knew via his recent epiphany were tied to the upcoming event.

"So then . . . we'll succeed?" He could feel eagerness and optimism gush from her being.

"I don't know." Gilban could almost see her feathers fall. "But I haven't seen any vision that spoke of our defeat either."

"So we can still fail." All her former optimism fled.

"You should have known that from the beginning."

"I just thought with what you said about the scepter—"

"It will help even the odds," Gilban interrupted. "What comes next has always been up to us."

"Or rather *you*," Alara returned. "That's an awful lot of weight to carry on your shoulders."

"And I'm willing to bear it—for the time being. You've become quite the leader in my absence."

"Only because of you."

"I've just brought out what was already there. You did the rest. You'd do well to remember that when things come to an end."

"I might have missed you, but not your riddles."

"All will be clear soon enough," he assured her.

"He's near." Galba's announcement ended the conversation. "Prepare yourselves."

"Here." Alara took hold of Gilban's hand. "I'll lead you to the dais." Gilban let her guide him as he mentally rehearsed the incantation.

"So did you get a good deal for that horse?" Vinder was staring closely at Dugan, who was crouching alongside him on the step between the male statue and the dais.

"Maybe not as good as you would have liked, but it was something." Dugan was almost as still as the statues. "Not that it did much good anyway. I ran out of coin before I could get my answers." All of them were hiding behind the dais. There was nowhere else *to* hide in the circle, and since the lich was going to be making his way to it anyway, it seemed the most logical place to be.

Vinder paused, letting Dugan's words rest between them before asking, "You really think this will work?"

"You don't want to know what I think," he replied.

"Everything resting on a blind elf." Vinder took a peek over his shoulder and saw Gilban fingering the scepter resting on his lap. He and Alara sat on the last step of the dais, almost directly behind Vinder and Dugan. "At least it'll be over soon."

"Yeah." Dugan was now staring down at Hadek, who was standing between them and Gilban. "You even *have* a weapon?"

"Not really," Hadek admitted sheepishly.

Dugan pulled the last of the daggers the cultists had given him from the belt still slung across his chest. "Here." He handed it to the goblin, hilt first. "I won't be needing it much longer anyway."

"Thank you." Hadek was surprised and pleased by the gesture.

"You see anything?" Vinder asked Rowan, who was crouching behind the female statue across from them, eyeing one of the circle's twelve openings. No one knew where Cadrith would emerge. They'd guessed it would be from the half of the circle facing them, given the layout of the glade beyond it and the placement of the dais, but if they were wrong . . .

"Nothing," said the knight.

"Stay alert," Tebow told the group. He and Cracius were a step below Rowan, hammers in hand and ready to finish what they'd started. "He could arrive at any moment."

"We're finally going to take care of this lich," Cracius told Tebow, a mingling of joy and relief in his voice.

"A winding path," Tebow agreed, "but we've made it in the end."

"I just don't want to fail after all this."

"We won't." Tebow remained calm and collected. "Not if we hold to our faith and do what we've been trained to do. Asorlok hasn't left us, and we still have our hammers. We just need to let Gilban strike first and—"

The sound of something like cracking ice echoed across the circle.

"What's that?" Vinder cautiously inquired.

"There." Rowan pointed at the portal between the standing stones immediately across from them. Everyone stretched for a better view of the scene. They watched the image of the peaceful mountainside between the posts crack and fall away like breaking glass. It was replaced by the scene of the glade behind it.

"He's coming through," said Rowan, his voice low.

"Wait, that's not the same thing we fought in the ruins." Confused, Vinder looked at Cracius and Tebow. "It's just a man."

"He's still a lich," Tebow corrected. "I can sense it."

"But he's got skin and hair now," the dwarf whispered, "and eyes."

"He must have taken a new body," said Cracius.

"It's possible, though risky to try," Tebow concurred. "No matter. One good hit and—"

"I can see Cadrissa." Rowan didn't try to hide his excitement. "She's okay."

"Maybe if we can get—" Alara fell silent when an azure blast of energy struck the wizardess faster than an eyeblink. Cadrissa dropped to the earth with all the grace of a bag of rocks.

"No!" Before anyone knew what was happening, Rowan was charging the lich at full speed.

"Rowan!" Alara cried out, but it was too late.

"So much for sticking to a plan," Vinder grumbled into his beard.

CHAPTER 26

There is magic that is common to many and then there is something else—something greater—for which I have sought and will always continue to seek. For in it lies the greatest of truths: that mortalkind can truly ascend to the divine.

—Morgan Hines, dwarven wizard king
Reigned 263 BV–182 BV

One by one the gods of Tralodren filed into an unfrequented part of Vkar's palace. They'd had their vote and now needed to see what would transpire. Should they be required to act, they'd need to do so quickly.

The large circular room's stone walls rose some one hundred feet into a painted dome. The ancient images showed titans locked in battle, scattering blood. The scenes spoke of an age when the hall was the center of Thangaria, the world that dominated Vkar's planetary empire. Though old and faded with time, the images could still be made out from below in various places, and especially where the images of Vkar and Xora dominated the landscape.

At the dome's center was a large crystal oculus. Clear and pure, it funneled unadulterated light in a fat, continuous beam. This shaft of light fell into the center of the room, where a clean, calm pool rested in a brass basin deeper than a human was tall and four times as wide. A granite lip peeled up around the pool's edge, where silver rails were worked into a display of delicate twisting vines.

This great chamber was the domain of Xora, first goddess, Vkar's wife, and the mother of the pantheon. Xora was fond of divination, a trait passed on to Saredhel. While her husband reigned over his great empire, Xora would aid him, seeing into its far-off corners where rebellion brewed, gathering intelligence, or even seeking events to come.

After she fell by Vkar's side during the bloody ending of his age and empire, the pool remained. Since that distant time the gods used the pool to watch events of grave importance, as they did now. While only Saredhel had the ability to peer into the future, each could use the pool to see Tralodren.

Each of the gods entered through the tall, arched, oak double doors and crossed the black, white, and gray marble checkerboard floor to the pool. They found a spot before the railing, drew their full attention to the pool, and grew still.

"Are you ready?" Dradin asked Saredhel.

"Yes," she said, before waving her hand over the pool, swirling a rainbow of colors until the inside of a stone circle came into view. It housed a white marble stepped dais in its center. On top of this dais rested the throne of Vkar, flanked by statues of Vkar and Xora.

"He's already reached the circle," said Khuthon with shock and irritation, "the *inside* of the circle." They watched the lich force his way through the space between two of the stone posts that encircled the area. "No one's ever done that before."

"He had Nuhl's help," Ganatar said, by way of explanation. "But it won't be able to help him now that he's inside."

"Let's hope not," said Olthon beside him.

"What are *they* doing there?" Rheminas pointed to an odd group trying to hide behind the statues. "I thought this was just supposed to be about Cadrith and Galba."

"So did I," said Aerotripton, his concern and confusion growing. "It looks like they're planning an ambush."

"Which would mean there's something we haven't been told," said Rheminas, quickly locking eyes on Saredhel. "What haven't you been telling us?"

"This isn't really the time," Asorlok informed Rheminas. "We need to—"

"Aren't those two of *your* priests with them?" Drued's question stopped whatever Asorlok was going to say.

"*And* a priest of Saredhel," Aero continued as he stared into the pool. "Not to mention a Knight of Valkoria . . ." The elven god raised his gaze Panthora's way. The goddess of humanity remained still.

"What *is* this?" Rheminas was impatient for answers.

"Maybe it's nothing more than a coincidence," Endarien spoke up. "A final trial for Cadrith."

Rheminas was less than convinced. "Or maybe—"

"It's started," Ganatar interrupted. "Whatever is going on will be made clear soon enough. For now, we need to watch and be ready." The pantheon said nothing further—each focusing their gaze on the pool.

Unlike in her dream, it didn't rain, and Cadrissa was thankful for it. There were overcast moments that caused her heart to flutter, but they proved to be just lazy clouds plodding through the heavens at their own pace. In that way the wizardess envied them. She and Cadrith had made fast work of the morning, pressing with even more determined strides to what she hoped was their final destination. She hated to imagine they were circling back the way they'd come. She didn't know if she could take it, let alone what Cadrith would do.

She'd grown better at ignoring her body's groans and cries, but it didn't change the fact she was still following the rapid lich's lead in the middle of a godsforsaken forest. Then there was the occasional flutter of thoughts, like the butterflies that would sometimes cross their path, about what would happen once Cadrith met his goal. With those thoughts came the memory of this morning's nightmare that would sink its talons into her, but she'd pull away and push on. A tiring effort, but it was what she had to do to keep from being pulled into a worse place mentally than she was physically.

They had taken a short break, allowing her time to consume the last of her commandeered supplies. She figured she needed the strength now rather than later. She wasn't expecting further rest until they finally reached Galba. In a way it gave her something positive to look forward to. It was an incredible place—and being—if what Cadrith said was true, and she'd be lying if she said that didn't intrigue her. In truth, she didn't know *what* to expect, only that they'd be there soon.

Suddenly, Cadrith stopped. "We're here."

Cadrissa's heart pounded as she strained to see a sign of something majestic keeping the throne of the first god secure—a wall or tower or castle. Instead, all she saw were more tall pines. "I don't see anything."

"You're not supposed to." Cadrith's head curled over his shoulder with a mocking grin. "You think it would just be in plain sight?"

She didn't answer—not with the words she wanted to share.

"You've served me well so far." He neared a clump of fat trunks to his right. "I just have one more task for you. Do that, and you'll have served your purpose." The words echoed in her heart. They were the very same ones he'd said in the nightmare. The repetition made her shiver.

"Now come." Cadrith took a bold step into the trees and vanished from sight.

"Some sort of cloaking spell," she muttered to herself. And it was a good one, too, given how well it fooled her even at such close proximity. She was tempted to make a run for it while the lich was distracted but knew that would be utter folly. Taking a deep breath, she made her way into the false pines. The trees became a blur as what was truly behind them swam out of the disjointed imagery: an empty glade dominated by a large stone circle.

Cadrissa gasped. It wasn't an exact replica, but close enough to the one in the dream to cause goosebumps. Her fears were only enhanced by how *everything* had started to seem more like a dream than reality. There was an ethereal presence about the place which made her lightheaded. Just being near the circle gave her the sensation of invisible shafts of power being thrust into her very core. The process filled her with a life—a collection of eldritch energy—the likes of which she'd never known could exist.

The longer she stayed on the outskirts of the stone circle—even at her present distance—the more she felt the need to walk into it. She wanted to possess the energy of the place for her own, and, for a moment, she could understand what Cadrith felt, what he craved. She had to admit, it was intoxicating, tempting, and addicting. It took all her resolve to push the need—the *compulsion*—down.

But she felt something more as well. In the midst of so great an emanation, something else subtly made itself known: the necklace. The heat warming her skin beneath the pockets of her gown was accompanied by a wreath of whispering voices circling her head. As quickly as they came, she shook the thoughts away, banishing the whispers, along with the urge to pull the necklace out of her pocket. Instead, she kept it hidden.

"You feel it too?" Cadrith watched her from his position before the standing stones, visible delight washing his features. "And it's not just Galba. It's what she keeps."

"I don't see anything." From what was visible inside the circle there was nothing but more grass. What was the purpose of the cloaking spell if there was nothing to cloak except an empty glade?

"And you won't until we get inside. It's the last line of defense. The final trial, besides the throne itself." Cadrith raised his hand. The motion caused no immediate effect, though she buckled from the pain of having the lich pull from her to work his magic. The spell was a powerful one, and she was barely able to stand after it. It was some sort of counterspell, meant to undo another protective barrier around the stones.

The doorway created by the two standing stones nearest Cadrith took on a brilliant azure glow, which spread to the stones themselves, leaving the opening clear once more. "Now hurry. I've made it as safe as it can be." His voice was dry and distant. Cadrissa was barely able to keep up behind him. As he got closer, she heard a faint crackle of energy, which grew louder as the lich entered into the circle's heart, passing through the seemingly empty space between the two stone posts. But this wasn't all that caught her eye.

Once again, the horrid black mass of tentacles appeared. It was right beside Cadrith as he made his way into the circle. It simply hovered above the earth, neither venturing any farther into the circle nor straying anywhere from it. She froze at the sight. The dream—the nightmare—was playing itself out in the waking world clearer than ever. And if it was to follow its course . . .

"Hurry." Cadrith beckoned with obvious annoyance. If he saw the same thing he didn't give any indication.

Cadrissa fought to still her heart and listen to reason. It wasn't raining. In the dream it had been raining. So, if things didn't match there then other things might not match in other ways either. She grabbed a tight hold of that logic, keeping it close. But Cadrith was real, as was his growing anger. There was still a chance she could get out of this in one piece, but for that, she needed to follow him into the circle. Fleeing all the memories the dark tentacles evoked, Cadrissa sent her gaze to the ground beneath them. When she did, she discovered something else.

"No shadow." If something didn't cast a shadow, then it wasn't real. Well, not real in the *natural* sense. Maybe it was just an illusion—another defense, like Cadrith had said—a defense tailored to keep her out, since, in a way, she was helping Cadrith reach his goal, even if she was forced to.

"*Now!*" Cadrith shouted.

She took a deep breath before making a dash for the doorway. She kept her focus on it and nothing else, rushing past the gnashing mouths and swaying tentacles without a second glance. She didn't stop until she was well within the circle. She was so focused on making it through she didn't give a second thought to the fact that she'd run through some form of barrier, as if she'd struggled to pass through a gelatinous wall. She suspected the barrier was already re-forming when she entered. If so, then that spoke to the barrier's power, since the spell Cadrith had cast should have destroyed it or, at the very least, stopped the barrier from re-forming for longer than it had.

And then she saw it: the true interior of the circle that had previously been hidden from view. It was breathtaking . . .

•●•

Cadrith made a careful study of the circle's interior and the collection of unrelated images seen in the twelve openings. These landscapes changed at their own rate, shifting from desert to underwater to rolling hills and craggy mountains. As amazing as such sights were to Cadrissa, what really held his gaze was the object at the circle's center. If he'd still been able to draw breath, this was when it would have been held. After years of hard work, and centuries of waiting, he was within sight of the final prize: Vkar's throne. The white marble dais on which it stood made it all the more impressive.

"This is amazing," Cadrissa whispered. "Is that the throne?" She wasn't far from him, and was taken with the sight just like he was. She was getting a taste of *true* power and seeing firsthand the triumph of the path of power over the path of knowledge. Perhaps she was finally starting to see the folly of her beliefs.

"Yes." What came next he needed to do on his own. It was the reason he'd kept his staff all these years. It had helped him in the Abyss, and it would help him here as well.

He'd concluded, through his research, that the ones who weren't seeking the throne wouldn't be hampered when casting spells or making their way to the circle. And he'd proven his conclusion with Cadrissa. At least in part. Galba had been able to alter what Cadrith had cast, much to his frustration. But this, he thought, was because he was using Cadrissa to cast the spells rather than having her cast them on her own. A minor difference, but one that violated Galba's rules enough to allow her access to the spells.

He also had a theory that what was holding him back personally from casting any spells didn't affect his staff since it, in a way, was tapping into another well—namely, the one inherent in the staff itself. While this was true of most enchanted items, it was especially true, he hoped, of the staff, which tapped into the power of the dead infant godspawn whose skull capped its wooden shaft. And there was no better time to test this theory than the present.

Tapping into the staff's well, he was delighted that nothing hindered his interaction with it. That meant he could finally put the last part of his plan into action. The sockets of the infant's skull began to glow with an azure light.

Cadrissa noticeably tensed at the sight. "I thought you said you couldn't cast any magic?"

"The staff isn't me," said Cadrith. "But it will work for what remains . . . now that you've served your purpose." He released the spell, sending Cadrissa toppling to the ground.

A cry rose from the direction of the dais, and he spun around. A lone Nordican was rushing him. Cadrith could clearly see the panther designs worked into the young man's leather armor. Sword raised and shield at the ready, he screamed as he charged.

As the Nordican neared, recollection dawned. This was one of the others Cadrissa had traveled with, before he'd abducted her. His name was Rowan, a Knight of Valkoria. A simple lad he'd used to kill Sargis, sending the demon back to the Abyss. By himself he wasn't really any challenge. But Rowan wasn't alone.

Behind the knight was a large blond Telborian, a blind elven seer led by an elven woman, a one-eyed dwarf, and a goblin. These too had been part of the group Cadrissa had traveled with. With them were two new figures Cadrith hadn't seen before—Asorlins. A motley jumble if ever there was one. Galba was clearly desperate. They wouldn't stand in his way. If this was to be the final trial, he'd make short work of it.

Calling on the staff's well, he gave a dismissive swipe of his hand, slamming them to the earth. "Like lambs to the slaughter," he chuckled.

Taking the staff in both hands, he watched the Telborian named Dugan leap to his feet. He'd changed since last he'd seen him. Dressed in black with smears of greasepaint across his face, he was still the biggest threat among them—though any damage he dealt to Cadrith's already dead body would be minimal. But that didn't mean Cadrith wasn't going to take any chances or allow himself some fun. Since he'd overheard the group's conversations during his earlier surveillance, he knew he had just the thing.

Leveling his staff, he released a violet burst of power. The Telborian flew through the air before suffering a brutal impact with the part of the stone circle to Cadrith's left. But instead of slumping to the grass after the collision, Dugan was stretched between two stone posts, his hands fixed to them by glowing violet bands. It looked as if he were hanging upon a cross.

"Quickly!" The older Asorlin's command returned Cadrith's attention to the others. They'd regrouped between the two priests and were about to charge him. He wasn't surprised Asorlok had sent priests after him, only that they hadn't crossed paths sooner. He *was* supposedly breaking the god's laws by becoming a lich, after all.

"Asorlok, grant me strength," the younger priest said as both priests raised their hammers and charged Cadrith's flanks. The others followed, running up the middle. They thought to overwhelm him. Nothing would really cause him any harm . . . except, perhaps, for the Asorlins' hammers. If they were blessed by Asorlok, as he was sure they were, he'd need to be mindful of where they were swinging.

Cadrith tapped once more into the staff's well, pulling forth a crackling bolt of silver lightning and unleashing it at the five sprinting straight toward him. He planned to take them out quickly, leaving him time to deal with the Asorlins. Instead, the elven female, Alara, pulled Gilban, the blind elf she led, to the ground. The action allowed the bolt to sail harmlessly overhead. The goblin was too short for it to do anything but kiss the top of his bald head.

It was the Nordican who genuinely surprised him. He lifted his shield, deflecting the angry, silvery tendrils. That sort of thing shouldn't have been possible. It should have gone through the shield and at the very least broken his arm, if not killed him outright. The shield must have been enchanted. A closer inspection of the crest revealed a draconic design—stylized and antiquated, but nothing Cadrith immediately recognized.

Any anger he might have had at their evasion of his spell was quelled with the sight of the dwarf getting slammed to the sward. He convulsed in agony as the spell's energy encompassed and riddled his frame. The sole recipient, he took the full brunt of it. Not the preferred option, but workable. Two down. But he had scant time to gloat before the priests were hard upon him.

"Your time has come," said the older one as he swung his hammer with a terrible fury. It would have crushed Cadrith's face had it not been for his staff, which blocked it. The power residing inside helped strengthen the centuries-old wood. Any common staff would have shattered from the impact.

The second priest swung his hammer. Cadrith bent his knees and leaned back. He narrowly avoided another headshot as the hammer swung through empty air. If he were allowed access to his magic, these two would be nothing before him. But with just the staff, and his desire to preserve the most powerful strike for when he'd need it most, he could do little more than dodge and weave.

"You can't prevail against Asorlok's will," the younger priest growled while trying to jab the head of his hammer into the lich's gut. Some quick footwork on Cadrith's part allowed him to sidestep the blow, while also revealing an opening he could exploit.

Cadrith thrust his right palm forward. A burst of charcoal-gray energy erupted through the younger priest's chest, leaving a hole the size of a man's fist in its wake. The Asorlin had no time to react, stammering as he stumbled back a few paces before dropping his hammer and crumbling in a heap beside it.

"Cracius!" the other Asorlin shouted. The distraction allowed Cadrith to lower the staff and release a stream of searing flame directly into his face. The priest was unprepared and dropped to the earth, rolling frantically about in hopes of extinguishing the fire. Cadrith allowed himself a small indulgence and released a few more flaming bursts onto the flailing priest. His brief urge satiated, he searched out those who remained.

He discovered them when Alara sliced into his side with her falchion. Though she intended a deadly attack, the sword did nothing more than cut a line into the lich's robes. With no blood to flow from an already lifeless body, the attack was meaningless. It might have sliced into some of his outer flesh, but his bones and frame held strong. If she'd managed to chop off his hands or even his head, perhaps things would have been different. But she wasn't going to have any more time to try anything else.

He took hold of his staff with both hands and gave Alara a wallop to her gut. She doubled over from the pain. Her new position presented the perfect target, and Cadrith brought the staff hard against her head, toppling the elf easily. He was about to finish her off when a flurry of movement flashed in the corner of his eye.

He avoided the knight's wild swings. He was definitely starting to hate this young pest. He summoned another blast of flames from the staff, but Rowan's shield safely deflected them. There was now no doubt the item was enchanted.

"Why won't you just *die*?" Cadrith snarled, venting his frustration with another surge of flame. From his left, he heard soft muttering. It sounded like words to a spell. Intrigued, he spun his head toward the source and found the blind seer, a silver scepter at the ready. He'd completely forgotten about the elf. From what he'd seen in previous conflicts, the seer wasn't a threat. But the object the elf was holding could be.

"The Scepter of Night." Cadrith was amazed at the sight. He'd only read and heard stories from Raston and others about it, but it was impossible to get confused with anything else. And seeing it firsthand was quite amazing if not surprising. It also spoke to the depths of their desperation if Galba was trying to use it against him. But Cadrith could think of *much* better uses for it.

He made a gesture and Gilban was lifted off the ground, as if gripped by the throat by a much taller opponent. He made a fist, and the elf's neck broke like a twig.

"No!" the knight cried in anguish, charging at full force.

Cadrith had had enough. Tapping into the greater reserves in the staff, he sent a purple bolt straight at the Nordican. The knight tried brandishing his shield again but this time couldn't withstand the force of the impact. He sailed through the air, collided with the dais' marble steps, and fell unconscious.

Cadrith released the dead elf from his hovering and conducted a quick mental tally. Everyone was accounted for . . . except for the goblin. He found him on his right, looking to sneak in when he had the chance. Instead, the goblin froze in place upon being detected. Dagger in hand, he stood open mouthed as Cadrith glared down at him.

"You're welcome to try," he said, mockingly.

Amazingly, the goblin found new courage. He rushed Cadrith with the best war cry he could muster. Cadrith slammed the butt of the staff in the grass, sending a wave of force that kicked the goblin up and over the throne and statues, landing somewhere behind and beyond. He would be either killed or knocked unconscious—both suited him just fine. Everyone was now accounted for. That just left one final opponent.

"Pathetic," Cadrith said while unwinding the counterspells keeping the godspawn's fury bound in the staff. He didn't want to unwind them *all* yet; he had no idea when his assailant would appear. Once unleashed, the fury couldn't be recaptured. "Is that the best you can do?"

"It's not too late to turn back," a woman said, revealing herself at the foot of the dais, opposite where Rowan had fallen. "You have no idea what you're after." Cadrith knew this was Galba. Beneath the white cloak her gray gown wrapped an attractive figure whose breathtaking face was outlined with red curls. In most respects she might have been confused with a common Telborian, but she was far above any human. While her presence commanded others to show her reverence and awe, Cadrith crushed such sentiments under his own sense of greater worth.

"And you have no right to keep it from me," he said, carefully undoing the last of the counterspells. Instantly, he was no longer holding a staff but a shaft of white fire—the spiritual fury of a dying godspawn. It would be more than enough to lay Galba low.

"I won't be denied," he said, lifting the staff overhead like a spear, and aiming it at Galba. With a small wave of her hand the flames were extinguished. Dust and ash rained on the surprised lich like powder. He did well in masking the dread seeping into his bones. Without the staff he felt naked and defenseless. For once, things hadn't gone as they should. Still, he refused to lose while mere yards from the throne.

"You must face the throne on your own," said Galba.

"It seems you've placed much in your favor."

"I won't stand before you. Not for the throne." Galba's words gave Cadrith pause.

"You're lying." It couldn't be true. She was there to oppose all that came for the throne. All he'd read—from the scrolls and the stories—had said as much. She was trying to get him to lower his defenses before making her attack.

"I've only sought to help you see your folly. In the end, it's the throne itself that will be your judge."

Cadrith carefully weighed this new information. She was either lying or telling the truth. There was only one way to find out. "Then step aside," he said with bravado. Galba did as bidden. His way now clear, he inched forward, eyeing Galba as he passed. He reached the first step of the dais and stopped. "You're really not going to stand in my way?"

Galba's silence was all he needed to hear. He fixed his gaze on the throne. He just had to sit to claim his long-overdue prize. But taking that seat would involve some effort, because it was crafted for someone about three times his size. Physically sitting in it called for some creative maneuvering.

With some climbing and pulling, he managed to reach the top of the seat before finally getting into position. He had to stretch his arms in order to touch the armrests with the upper part of his palms. He felt like a child trying to sit in his father's chair, but the effort allowed him a seat in the most powerful spot in the cosmos. This was the very throne from which the first god came to power and ruled a massive empire. And now he'd follow in Vkar's steps.

He didn't have any notes or insight on what came next. No one, outside of Vkar himself and later Gurthghol, had actually sat in the throne. He was now truly on his own.

Flanked by the statues, the throne also felt and looked like an altar. An altar to unadulterated power . . . and Cadrith was its sacrifice. There was no turning back. No surrender.

The throne began vibrating and locked Cadrith in place. It was as if he was made of metal, and the throne was a magnet. He couldn't leave even if he wanted to. The final trial had begun.

He had thought it was painful when he'd cast the spell to become a lich—when he'd felt and even *willed* the last of his biological life to cease in favor of the magic of the spell presently radiating from his bones and spirit. But that had been nothing compared to what now tore his insides.

At first it was like fire. Then it became like ice, only to mix with lightning that made him think his bones would crumble into dust at any moment. He closed his eyes in an effort to stop the pain, but it only brought the image of an ever-expanding cosmos to his mind's eye. It would flow into him, and then he felt himself flow into it. Back and forth, back and forth, like the beating of some massive heart. But there was something else there, too.

He could feel it now so plainly, beyond the pain: the divine power he so craved coursing through him. The pain increased as if a large bucket of acid had been dumped over him.

He screamed. Everything and nothing. Everything and nothing. He could see the cosmic swirling of light and darkness, clashing back and forth like stormy waves against jagged rocks. The origins of Awntodgenee and Nuhl, the cosmic entities credited with the formation of the cosmos. This must have been what Vkar had seen.

But Vkar didn't just witness their creation; he did something about it. And if he was to reap the same rewards, he'd have to do the same. Reaching deep within, he compelled the forces to come to him. Invisible hands took hold of them, pulling them near. As they did, Cadrith resisted losing himself to them. *He* needed to be the master. The swirling masses grew more chaotic as they were pulled into his being. There arose a shudder from his spirit, followed by an explosion that felt as if he were scattered into the cosmos like specks of dust.

Once more he screamed.

Then there was silence. A quiet nothingness that remained thick about him. He was aware of himself but not in the same way he'd been before. His mind was afire with new knowledge and possibilities, as if what he'd known as barriers before—even with his mastery of magic—had melted away.

He wasn't in any pain. In fact, he felt rather good—*better* than good. He could feel life surging through him. Only it wasn't the life he'd known as a mortal: the mere circulation of blood through veins. This was something more—something greater—an augmentation to what he'd known as biological life. At the same time he was part of it but also above it. As the moments passed, he became more acutely aware of himself.

He wasn't the same man who'd sat in the throne a moment earlier. Gone was his former garb. Instead, he wore a deep blue diamond-studded cloak over a robe of fine white silk dotted with rubies and emeralds around the cuffs and hem. These sparkled from the soft illumination coming from the gems embedded in the throne's gold and silver scrollwork outlining the back of the seat and covering the front of its armrests. Around his waist was a leather belt with a golden skull buckle. On his hands were a small assortment of rings.

Upon rising, he noticed he stood slightly taller—reaching, he thought, the upper limits of human height. Taking in a breath, he could feel the new life—the *divine* life—flowing even greater than before. The ever-present cold aura that had been part of him since becoming a lich had also fled. There was warmth. There was a heartbeat. There was breath. Everything of his old life was gone.

"You should have waited, Kendra," he mused as he made a fist. Tan skin covered his bones, with living muscle beneath. The hand of a god.

"And now to claim my throne." He closed his eyes and focused on willing the object to join him as it had Vkar, finishing his elevation and setting himself higher than the rest of the pantheon. But instead of the throne complying to his wishes he felt himself butting up against some sort of powerful barrier.

"The throne remains in the circle." Galba's calm voice had him opening his eyes.

"I've won." He stared down the ancient divinity. Even with his new divine sight, she was a vision to behold.

"The throne stays here. That is part of the pact and cannot be altered."

"Not even by a god?" He tried once more to push through the barrier without success.

"None but one," she replied. "And you're not him."

It was a minor setback, but nothing he couldn't overcome with his new abilities and some time to master them. And there was still another prize waiting for him to claim. As he stood he let his eyes linger over the bodies of his opponents beyond the dais. One in particular held his gaze. He raised a hand, calling for the Scepter of Night to fly into it, but Galba intercepted the object.

"I thought you said you were done with interfering," Cadrith said, peering into Galba's stern but lovely face.

"Concerning your taking the throne, which you've done."

"So you wish to fight?" Cadrith squared his shoulders. He was eager to unleash his new divine might.

"I wish for you to leave. No gods are welcome on Arid Land or in this circle."

"That pact binds the pantheon, not me."

"It binds *all* gods—which now includes you." Galba remained solid. The longer Cadrith stared into her green eyes, the more he could see hints of something beyond her—brief flashes of light escaping from behind a fluttering curtain.

"A convenient excuse."

"The truth."

"Then let me have the scepter, and I'll go." He'd be a fool to let this prize pass him by. With his newfound power *and* the scepter, he could hold back any threat, granting him the time to discover how to claim the throne.

"It's not for you."

"They brought it to stop me, didn't they?" Cadrith was considering the best way to get the better of her. "A good effort but terrible execution." He caught himself trying to grip a staff that no longer existed. "And to the victor go the spoils. You may have denied me the throne but not the scepter." He descended a step. "Now hand it over."

"You're welcome to make me." He caught another glimpse behind her veil. Nothing substantial but enough to know what he'd seen before wasn't a fluke. "Who are you really?"

"I am Galba, and you must leave. There's nothing more for you here."

"You put them up to this, didn't you?" He indicated the bodies with a sweep of his hand. "You pulled their strings and lined them up to try to stop me. Which means you must have been fairly certain I'd survive the throne." He descended another step down the dais. "You must really fear me."

"It's *you* who should fear the one pulling *your* strings," Galba replied.

"What I've done, I've done *by* myself and *for* myself. No *god* or anything else has been able to stop me."

"The day isn't over with yet."

"Whatever you're planning—"

"I will not stand against you," came the familiar refrain.

"No," Cadrith sneered, "you'll find others to do that for you."

"There are certain rules that must be obeyed . . . as you'll soon discover," said Galba, while motioning to one of the twelve openings between the stone posts, which shifted to show the glade beyond the standing stones. "Nor will I be the last to notice a new god in the cosmos."

She was right. His apotheosis wasn't going to sit well with the rest of the pantheon—especially Endarien. It'd be wise to prepare while putting the last parts of his plan into place. Galba wasn't going to be much of a threat to him now; she'd said as much already. And leaving the scepter was only a minor inconvenience. He knew where it was now. It would only be a matter of time until he found a way to finally lay hold of it and the throne.

"We'll meet again." He slowly made his way to the grass. Now closer he could feel the aura of power around Galba. It was amazing—even greater than the swell he felt in himself. That was impossible, he knew, unless . . .

He strode toward the opening created for him, taking special note of Cadrissa as he passed. He still had some options to exploit and took pleasure in the success of his planning. Not even Raston could have done as well. Yet another way he'd triumphed over his former master.

As he marched through the stone posts, he didn't notice a dark shape latch on to his shadow. It flowed to him like spilled ink until his shadow and the image were one and the same. A moment later Cadrith vanished from sight.

•●•

Khuthon was the first of the gods to avert his gaze from the scrying pool. Asora's concerned expression mirrored those of all the others. Finding Endarien, he asked, "You ready?"

"I'm getting into place now," he said. "I'll have to stop using this form, though, if I want to be at full strength."

"Do it," said Ganatar. "We'll see to the rest."

"And don't waste any time either," Khuthon added. "He's still weak."

"Don't worry," said Endarien. "I don't plan on letting him live any longer than necessary." With that he faded from sight.

"Come," Ganatar said, directing the others out of the room. "We don't have much time."

As they departed Rheminas lingered a moment longer at the pool. He carefully took in the aftermath, studying the fallen. He took special interest in the scepter he watched Galba place back beside the dead elven seer. A glance up at the others told him he only had a brief moment—the last of the pantheon was just now reaching the door.

Returning to the pool, he focused on the scepter. It and the area around it rushed forward, allowing him to view it in greater detail. With a wave of his hand the scene changed to Dugan stuck to the posts. Rheminas watched as the former gladiator drew closer to death.

"Rheminas." It was Shiril. "You coming?" She was the last to remain, having stopped halfway out the door to call after him.

"Of course," he said and hurried her way, letting the pool's image fade behind him.

Chad Corrie has enjoyed creating things for as far back as he can remember, but it wasn't until he was twelve that he started writing. Since then he's written comics, graphic novels, prose fiction of varying lengths, and an assortment of other odds and ends. His work has been published in other languages and produced in print, digital, and audio formats.
He also makes podcasts.

chadcorrie.com | @creatorchad

Scan the QR code below to sign up for Chad's email newsletter!